# HAYLEY
# SCRIVENOR

# DIRT
# TOWN

PAN BOOKS

First published 2022 by Pan Macmillan Australia

First published in the UK 2022 by Macmillan

This paperback edition first published 2023 by Pan Books
an imprint of Pan Macmillan
The Smithson, 6 Briset Street, London EC1M 5NR
*EU representative:* Macmillan Publishers Ireland Ltd, 1st Floor,
The Liffey Trust Centre, 117–126 Sheriff Street Upper,
Dublin 1, D01 YC43
Associated companies throughout the world
www.panmacmillan.com

ISBN 978-1-5290-8028-5

Pan Macmillan acknowledges the Traditional Custodians of country throughout Australia
and their connections to lands, waters and communities. We pay our respect to Elders past
and present and extend that respect to all Aboriginal and Torres Strait Islander peoples
today. We honour more than sixty thousand years of storytelling, art and culture.

1 3 5 7 9 8 6 4 2

A CIP catalogue record for this book is available from the British Library.

Printed and bound by CPI Group (UK) Ltd, Croydon, CR0 4YY

Visit **www.panmacmillan.com** to read more about all our books
and to buy them. You will also find features, author interviews and
news of any author events, and you can sign up for e-newsletters
so that you're always first to hear about our new releases.

# DIRT TOWN

Hayley Scrivenor is a former director of Wollongong Writers Festival. Originally from a small country town, Hayley now lives and writes on Dharawal country and has a PhD in Creative Writing from the University of Wollongong on the south coast of New South Wales. *Dirt Town* is her first novel. An earlier version of the book was shortlisted for the Penguin Literary Prize and won the Kill Your Darlings Unpublished Manuscript Award.

*To my mother, Danina. First, and always.*
*And for Daniel, for telling me I should.*

*To all of us, and our disasters.*
*And for those who don't survive.*

# DIRT
# TOWN

# WE

We were waiting for things to converge.

It was still dark. Even if the sun had been up, we would not have needed to look around us. It was the same dirt, lazily punctuated here and there by dry grass, the same rust-ringed cement water trough close to the fence line, the same white cypress pines that dotted our own families' properties. A landscape as familiar to us as the backs of our own eyelids. And we knew we'd found the spot again by the smell. It pushed its way into our nose and throat like a rod of twisted tissue rammed so far it hurt. It was the smell of dead lambs left to rot in the sun.

The stitches in the man's arm tugged as he turned the steering wheel of his ute. From his vantage point in the driver's seat, the main house was just a smudge in the distance. The sun was coming up now. He was checking the fences after his time away from the farm. If he'd driven just a metre closer to the fence line – a metre was nothing on a property like his – he never would have found it. But the ute's cab tipped slightly as he drove over soft ground. The man stood in the space created by the open front door of the vehicle, and the smell hit him the same way it had hit us. He walked around the car and plucked a shovel from the tray. Us kids heard and saw it all.

1

The man's laboured breathing was interrupted only by the occasional *shink* of the shovel in soil. We watched his face as he winced in pain. We took note of the angle of his shoulders as the blade hit something that did not give, something that was not dirt, or a root. We saw him crouch to scoop away earth with one hand, running his fingers along shiny black plastic. It was four days since anyone, including us, had seen Esther Bianchi.

The sun was properly up now. Sweat dripped into his eyes, trickled down his spine. We saw him blink. He stood back, used the shovel to sweep dirt from the edge of the hole. There were only five or six inches of earth on top of the package, which seemed to be much longer than it was wide. The plastic was slippery in his hands.

Later, the police would admonish the man for moving the body. As soon as he suspected what he had found, he should have called someone.

'And what if it was just a calf or somethin', and I called you and you came for nothing?' the man would say, eyebrows pulled high into his forehead.

*Why would a calf be wrapped in black plastic?* the female detective would think but not say.

The man yanked the package with his good arm. The earth gave the parcel up and he fell back, his leg bending awkwardly beneath him. He scrambled away, his stitches pulling, pain unfurling like a flower. He stood and looked towards the distant house before stepping forward. The man unwrapped the plastic, ignoring the pain in his arm, retching at the smell. When the parcel's contents came into view, the man turned away, hand held to his mouth.

What does it all mean? For now, we can only tell you that we were there, that we watched blood seep through the man's sleeve as he walked away from Esther Bianchi's body and looked around him, as if the answer might be found somewhere in the open field.

# RONNIE

Friday, 30 November 2001

Once, Esther tickled me so much that I wet myself. We were at her house, in her backyard.

'Stop, Esther!' I said, laughing through pain.

'No mercy!' she cried.

She was the villain when we played, the person who moved the story forward while I fussed over details. We were eight years old.

I'd fallen to the ground in a patch of dirt. Esther was on top of me. So many years ago now, but I remember the way the laughing-pain swelled as she dug her fingers into the soft dough of my belly. It went on and on, like when you jump in the deep end of the pool and you're waiting, waiting to reach the bottom so you can use it to push up to the surface. I looked down, saw the wetness spreading across my sports shorts before I felt it. Esther saw it too. I shuffled away from her on my bum. I was too big to be weeing my pants.

I'll never forget what she did then. She stood and took a step back. I waited for her to scream or make fun of me. Instead, I saw amber liquid trickle past the hem of her netball skirt and down the inside of her long leg. The white skin was bruised: dusted with little purple and brown marks like the rump of a dappled horse. Her white school socks bloomed with a stain the colour of her kitchen curtains – a buttercup yellow.

She grinned and grabbed the hose, turning the tap on full bore and weaponising the stream with her fingers. We wrestled for it, squealing. My embarrassment washed away, dust swirling on the surface of the spreading pool of water before it soaked into the earth.

Esther's mum, Constance, made us strip at the back door, shaking her head. She gave me one of her shirts to wear home. It was so long it reached past my knees, like a dress, and I wore no underwear beneath it. Constance hadn't thought to lend me some of Esther's, and I hadn't asked. I remember the shuddering thrill as I sat in the back of Esther's dad's ute, nothing between the seat and me but thin white cotton. I always loved being driven home by Steven, as he insisted I call him. When I was alone with him, I could pretend I was his daughter and we were going somewhere. He never talked that much but he seemed to enjoy listening to me. I'd have done almost anything to make him laugh. I could never tell my mum how much I liked him; she always seized up when I asked who my father was. It was something else Esther had pulled off that I couldn't – a father – but I didn't begrudge her. She deserved a dad who was strong, who'd lift her up and spin her around. A dad who loved her like I did.

My best friend wore her name, *Esther*, like a queen wearing her crown at a jaunty angle. She only ever called me Ronnie. I didn't fit the grown-woman name I'd been given. The glamorous syllables of *Ve-ron-i-ca* had nothing to do with me. We were twelve years old when she went missing. I was bossy and solid, shorter than Esther but determined to dictate the terms of our play, the kid who would assign roles when we pretended to be Power Rangers at recess, stomping off in a huff if other kids had their own ideas. But a lot of the time I wasn't getting my own way with Esther so much as saying out loud what she'd already decided she wanted to do. She would hurtle into a room, tongue sticking out, and leap so she landed with her knees bent and legs wide apart. She'd roll her eyes into the back of her head and say, 'Rah!' at peak volume, before streaking out of the room again. I needed things from people, and Esther didn't, not really, and I think that's why I was drawn to her.

It was no surprise Esther's mum thought I was a bad influence. But anything cheeky, and everything funny, started with Esther. Sometimes I only had to look at her – from the corner of my eye at an assembly, in the changing room of the local pool, from across the low tables we had in kindergarten – and I would start laughing. We were always laughing, and I was always running behind, trying to make it look like I was the leader.

That last Friday afternoon in November, the day Esther went missing, I was supposed to be doing my homework at the desk in my bedroom. We finished early on Fridays – at two thirty – and Mum liked me to get all my work done before the weekend. Everyone in the class had to make a poster about a South American country, and I'd managed to nab Peru. It had been a close thing: one of the Addison twins had gone for it, even though everybody *knew* how much I loved llamas. I had pictures of them glued to all my schoolbooks. Now, I couldn't seem to get my pencil drawing of a llama right. He looked cross-eyed and his legs were stumpy-in-a-bad-way, though I'd copied as carefully as I could from the old issues of *National Geographic* Mum had brought home from the newsagency next to her work. Our fat orange cat, Flea, wound himself through the legs of my chair. I slipped the magazine under the poster paper, but it was too thick; I couldn't trace the line of the llama with my pencil. Giving up, I headed to the kitchen for a snack.

Flea darted out from under the chair, bending around the door as I opened it. He surged ahead in the hallway and made it to the kitchen before I did. His full name was Mr Mistoffelees, but 'Flea' had been as close as I could get when I was small, and it had stuck. Mum was standing by the wall-mounted phone in the kitchen, the white handset to her ear, her back turned. I walked towards her in bare feet and Flea pranced ahead, his head tilted back to look up at me.

'Did Esther leave school with you?' Mum asked, covering the phone with her hand.

'Yup.' I walked past her to the sink, took an upturned glass from the drying rack and filled it with water.

'Which way did you walk?'

'To the church.' How was I going to get something out of the cupboard without Mum noticing?

'And then you split up?'

'Yeah.' Apples gleamed in the bowl on the kitchen counter. If I said I was hungry, Mum would tell me to have one. Groceries were expensive. Especially fresh fruit. Some days Mum existed on tea and Mint Slice biscuits, but she wanted me to eat 'properly'.

Mum was impatient, the phone still covered. 'Which way did she go?'

'Left. She always goes left at the church.' I drained the glass.

Mum gave me a long, steady look. 'Veronica Elizabeth Thompson, are you sure?'

I shifted on my feet. When I was smaller, I'd thought *Elizabeth* added after your name meant that you were in trouble. I'd used it on one of my cousins when he'd pinched an Easter egg from my basket at the big hunt we used to do at Pop's farm every year. Everyone had laughed at me.

I rinsed my glass. 'Definitely sure,' I said, reaching for a tea towel. I wiped the glass dry and walked towards the cupboard.

Mum let my words hang for a second, waiting for them to grow into the silence. She tucked a strand of red hair behind her ear. My mum didn't even have a middle name. She was just Evelyn Thompson. For some reason, only the boys got middle names in her family. Her brother Peter's middle name was Reginald, which seemed like a punishment in itself. He was my favourite of Mum's siblings, and I'd been indignant on his behalf when I found out. Flea was rubbing against her leg, but Mum didn't even look down. On any other afternoon she'd have scooped him up, cooing to him that he was her *furry baby* and *four-legged child*. Or she'd have splayed her hand over her heart, pretending to die of shock at seeing me wash up after myself. Instead, she turned her whole body away and said something I couldn't hear into the receiver.

I put the glass away. When I sidled back to my room, there was a mini Bounty bar tucked in the waistband of my underwear.

It's impossible now to unlink my memories of Esther from each other. Like train cars with their couplings soldered together, each memory of her brings with it another one, surging forward, on and on in a long, clattering line. Since we were small, she'd been there, as important and unremarked as the house you grow up in. Esther's dad was born in Durton, like my mum, but had no family in common with my family, the Thompsons – always easy to identify thanks to our red hair. She wasn't related to the Rutherfords, who were wealthy, or the McFarlanes, who were stingy. There were a few Bianchis around – known for being Italian, mainly – but they were older, and their kids had all left Durton already. Esther and I were both only children, which was unusual at our school. Even Lewis was odd because he only had one brother. I enjoyed being an only child much more than Esther did. *Wouldn't you like a little brother or sister?* Mum had asked me once. 'No thank you,' I'd said. *Like you were politely declining a cucumber sandwich*, Mum recalled with a laugh.

Esther would have loved to have had four or five brothers and sisters, or at least a bunch of cousins, like I did. (If she had, they could've walked her home that day.) All I needed, all I ever really wanted, was her.

Mum didn't say much through dinner, didn't even hassle me to eat my corn. Corn made me think of alien teeth. I was waiting to be excused from the table.

'Esther hasn't come home from school yet,' Mum said.

I'd already pushed back my chair. The sun was still up, but it was after six. Esther's mum must've been flipping out.

'Ronnie, are you sure she didn't say she was going to do anything, or go somewhere after school? Could she have decided to go to the pool, or for a walk?'

We'd gone to the pool the day before, but we never went on Fridays. That afternoon had been stinking; only an idiot would've walked anywhere they didn't have to. Besides, Esther's dad always went with us to the pool.

We'd walked out the gate with the flood of other year six girls. What had Esther said to me before she headed off towards her house and I headed to mine? *Bye*, I guessed. Had she turned to wave after we left each other? Had I?

Esther had got out of playing netball that day because she'd forgotten her runners. She wasn't pleased like I would've been. She'd sat with her head resting on her hands, watching hungrily from the sidelines. As we'd gone our separate ways I'd made a mental note to try wearing *my* leather school shoes for the next Sports Day.

'She just went home.' My left foot kicked the wooden bar that ran under the table. 'Like always.' Mum seemed to be waiting for more detail. 'I waved at her, and she gave a little wave back.' As I said it, the detail solidified in my memory. The wave, faint but certain, like the lines of a traced drawing.

The upright lamp in the corner of the dining room came into focus. I knew what I could do with the llama drawing. I could hold the magazine and cardboard over the opening in the lamp. With light behind it, the image would come through the cardboard. It would look so good that people would think my poster was the best. My thoughts raced ahead, playing out possible conversations, finding the obstacles I'd have to manoeuvre around. If someone asked if it'd been traced, I'd have to come clean, but if I just said, 'I drew it by hand,' that wouldn't be lying, would it?

Mum didn't say anything. She nodded to indicate I could leave the table.

Some sort of panic should have taken hold when I was alone in my bedroom. I know it doesn't make sense. How do I explain why I was so unconcerned that no-one knew where my best friend was? That I sat there working on my assignment? All I can say is it felt like someone had said they were having trouble finding the ocean. It was obvious to me that they just weren't looking hard enough, or in the right places.

The phone rang in the kitchen, and after a short while Mum came in. 'We're going to go and see Mack. He wants to talk to you.'

I was writing *PERU* in large bubble letters in the middle of the cardboard. Bubble letters were my specialty.

'About Esther?' I asked.

I didn't want Mum to see me messing around with the lamp. I'd have to fix the llama on an afternoon when she was at work.

Mum smiled weakly. 'Yes, Bup. About Esther.'

Bup was my mum's nickname for me. Sometimes I called her Mucca. At certain times, like at the start of a long road trip – to visit my aunty Kath who lived in Victoria, maybe – she'd say, 'Look at us, Bup and Mucca, off on an adventure.'

Mum's jaw was all tensed up as we drove to the police station. A vein popped in her neck, like a wiry plastic rod had been inserted under her skin, made of the same stuff they made school skipping ropes with, stiff but bendy. I'd never been inside the police station and had only ever seen Officer Macintyre around town or when he came to the school to talk about stranger danger. My mum called him Mack. He lived next door to the station with his wife, Lacey, who jogged across and let us in when we arrived. We walked past the high desk and into a small kitchen. Lacey pulled a bottle of milk from a tiny fridge and poured some into a mug that said COPS ARE TOPS. She added five heaped spoonfuls of Milo and put the cup in the microwave. Someone at school had told me that Officer Macintyre and his wife couldn't have children because something was wrong with her. I looked her up and down as she handed me the cup. She was skinny, but so was my mum, and she had me.

Officer Macintyre walked into the room and sat down. 'Hi, Evelyn,' he said, nodding at my mum. 'Hello, Veronica.'

He smelled of sweat and cologne, and he needed a shave.

'It's just Ronnie,' I said.

'No worries, Ronnie,' he replied, leaning forward on his forearms and smiling at Mum. 'Can you start by telling me what you and Esther did this afternoon?' He said it like when there's only one lamington left, and you want it, but if you reach for it someone will say that you're being greedy, so instead you ask casually: *Does anyone want this?*

He asked the same questions Mum had as I took salty-sweet sips from the Milo. I told him we had netball, that Esther hadn't played. That we'd split up at the church. She'd seemed normal. What I didn't, or couldn't, tell him was that Esther on a normal day still exuded a kind of magic, like she might do anything. She could curl her tongue, she could bend over and place the palm of her hand flat on the ground while keeping her legs straight, she could sing. And she never traced.

'Does Esther like sport?' he asked.

'Yeah,' I said. 'Is she in trouble?'

Officer Macintyre's eyes moved to Mum, her chair pushed all the way back out of my line of sight. 'No, Ronnie, Esther isn't in any trouble. Not at all.'

Out the front of the station afterwards, Mum put her arms around me and just kind of held me until it got boring and I coughed.

'Bup.' She said the word into the top of my head, hairs moving where her breath touched them. 'I want you to go to Uncle Peter's while I help search.'

'But I wanna come with you.'

I always found Esther when we played hide-and-seek, her dark head bobbing behind some tree, too impatient to stay hidden for long.

'The last thing I need is for you to wander off as well,' Mum said, smoothing my hair with her hand.

My uncle Peter met us at the front of his place. He was Mum's older brother and she liked him best; I could tell because he was the only person I knew who really, truly made her laugh, other than me. He smiled his lopsided smile – he'd been slammed into while playing footy in his twenties and the left side of his face drooped a little – and pulled her into a hug. When I was little he'd let me tug at his beard, a goatee that had some white hair in it now. He was wearing a polo shirt emblazoned with the logo of the trucking company he worked for.

He walked side by side with Mum to the front door. The red hair on his arms glowed in the sensor light that clicked on as we approached.

'It's just awful to think about, Pete,' she said.

He nodded. 'Shelly's gone over there.'

Mum had never really hit it off with Esther's mum, but Constance and my aunt Shelly were good friends. Esther spent a lot of time at my aunt and uncle's and she loved the chaos at their place. Esther had the knack of always being herself, unlike me. When I was there, I could tell my aunt Shelly thought I was sly, and when someone thinks that about you it becomes true. I'd feel myself slinking around the backyard, and when I snuck into the kitchen for a snack I always seemed to get caught. Not that Aunt Shelly cared, but I could just tell she thought I was a bit spoiled. It wasn't like that with my uncle. He laughed at my jokes. Once, he made me laugh so hard I farted, which made us both laugh harder, until neither of us could breathe, which was probably lucky because it smelled bad. Another time, he'd brought me back a hat from somewhere on his trucking route that made it look like a sheep was sleeping on your head. I'd worn it every day until Mum said it had got lost in the wash.

My uncle hugged me, tight.

The light was fading as we walked into my uncle's house. I expected any second to see Esther jump out from behind a fence, eyes rolled back in her head, tongue out, laughing.

She'd been missing for six hours.

# SARAH

Friday, 30 November 2001

Detective Sergeant Sarah Michaels pulled the unmarked white sedan to a stop next to a free petrol bowser. Her detective constable, Wayne Smith, was sleeping with his mouth open in the passenger seat. They were around seven hours west of Sydney. They'd been heading back there from another job when a call from their superior had come through. *You're going to be spending some more time in the country, Michaels!* Kinouac had announced. Sarah was just grateful they hadn't made it all the way home before they had to turn around again.

'How ya feeling, boss?' Smithy asked, rubbing his eyes as he stepped out of the passenger's side.

'Hot,' Sarah said, unscrewing the petrol cap.

She'd done the bulk of the driving, the right side of her body in full sun the whole time. Before leaving Sydney she'd taken off the bracelet Amira had given her, leaving it on the glass tray by the bed, and put on her mother's watch instead. That arm stung now, and was already going red.

When Smithy walked inside to pay for the fuel, Sarah took her chance and reached across the driver's seat to grab the vanilla air freshener dangling from the rear-view mirror, pulling on it until the string broke. She threw it in a dark plastic rubbish bin that stood beside a stagnant bucket of water and a well-worn squeegee. The fragrant sliver of foam had been giving her a headache. It made her think of Amira and her endless incense.

Moments later, Smithy stepped back out through the automatic doors of the petrol station, and Sarah walked around to the passenger side. They were only half an hour from their destination; Smithy could drive the rest of the way.

There was a thin woman with dark circles under her eyes pumping fuel at the opposite bowser. She wore a long, pill-ridden cardigan despite the heat. A baby screamed in the back seat. The woman replaced the nozzle and looked over at Sarah. Sarah got the feeling that if she hadn't been there – not in uniform but still obviously a cop – the woman would have left the baby, door ajar, while she went in to pay.

Smithy lowered himself into the driver's seat and shot Sarah a glance. 'Cheer up, Sarge, it might not happen.'

Sarah hadn't realised that she was frowning but refused on principle to rearrange her expression. 'Eyes on the road, Constable.'

Smithy was a gum chewer. His sandy moustache twitched, and the smacking sound of the gum irritated Sarah more as a passenger than when she'd had the road to focus on. Any flavour had to be long gone. It was a relief when they spotted a faded WELCOME TO DURTON! sign and turned off the highway.

Smithy pulled up in front of the smallest cop shop Sarah had ever seen.

'Where'd the air freshener go?' he asked, looking at the rear-view mirror.

'Must've fallen down,' she said.

Smithy craned forward to look under the seat and Sarah got out of the car.

The local sergeant met them at the door and introduced himself as Mack, squinting as he talked. At first, he directed his comments at Smithy. Then Smithy made the formal introductions, including rank, and Sarah caught a flash of a smile stifled by moustache as Mack swivelled forty-five degrees to face her. At least Mack had the decency not to raise his eyebrows. She didn't imagine they had too many female officers out this way. Or maybe they took what they could get.

Mack was a compact, tanned man with a five o'clock shadow who'd followed protocol to the letter. Better than many of the local cops Sarah had worked with in her two years in Missing Persons. He'd gathered the info they'd need to get started. Mack's wife had stayed at the station, making calls. Sarah met her on the way in. Lacey Macintyre was thin but sturdy. With her tan and white-blonde hair she wouldn't have looked out of place in the stands of a polo match, until she opened her mouth and a broad country accent came out.

It was a myth that Missing Persons had to wait twenty-four hours to start searching, particularly for kids. Sometimes, Sarah would arrive just as the child had been found, asleep in a backyard cubby, or lying low at a friend's house. In those cases, she'd smile, shake the hands of the local officers, and file a slim report when she got back. Excluding custody disputes, most children not recovered in the first three hours were already dead. In this case, it had been more than four hours since the child was last seen. Mack handed over the incident log and Sarah tried to ignore the heat in her right arm as she flicked through it. Mack said he'd meet the two officers at the search site later and walked them back to their white Commodore.

The light had faded to a blue haze. Smithy rolled the windows down. The town was flat, brown, the suggestion of hills in the distance.

They drove straight from the cop shop to the small fibro house where Esther Bianchi's parents would be waiting. In the light shining from the porch, Sarah could see they had a novelty letterbox: the outline of a palm tree sprouted from the box, the letters B-I-A-N-C-H-I just visible beneath the tree's silhouette.

There was one woman Sarah thought of whenever she found herself at a front door. Sarah had just moved into Missing Persons from Child Protection. The woman's seventeen-year-old daughter, Carla, had disappeared. A crowded kitchen, a collection of tea cosies. The mother told Sarah, 'When your child is gone, you look around the house, and there'll be things in it that make you sick. If you've wasted time collecting cat figurines, it feels so fucking *stupid*. You'll never be that person again.'

They never found Carla.

A woman watched them walk up the path from her spot on the verandah. Sarah was grateful she'd remembered to shrug her jacket over her sweat-stained collared shirt. It was important to look the part.

Smithy made the introduction and the woman brought them inside.

'Steve's still out looking,' the woman said. 'Esther's father, I mean.'

There was the rumble of a car pulling in outside.

They passed a pair of gumboots with a pattern of daisies on the hallway floor; a man's high-vis jacket hung next to the door. The air conditioner wedged in the dining room window hummed, but the room was warm and close.

'Is she here?' a deep voice called from the front door.

A man in head-to-toe workwear appeared in the doorway. He was a little over six foot, tanned, dark features.

'Perfect timing,' Smithy said, looking at Sarah.

She nodded.

'Would you follow me, Mr Bianchi?' Smithy said.

The girl's father followed Smithy down the hall. Sarah caught the smell of the father's sweat, partly rank, slightly sweet – it reminded her of her own father, returning from a game of squash with one mate or another who was also in the force. She heard what sounded like a back door closing. Sarah would interview the mother, and it was always best if the parents couldn't hear each other. As the woman moved to sit, Sarah glanced down at her folder: *Constance Bianchi*. Sarah joined her at the dining table, which was covered in a green tablecloth that Constance kept bunching in her hand, over and over. The creases in the satiny fabric formed a circle the size of a baby's head.

Sarah asked to check the woman's ID.

The licence confirmed what the mousy roots suggested – the woman was not a natural blonde. There was something sharp about her face that hadn't made it into the photo, even if her cheeks were full and her face was puffy from crying. Smudged mascara ran under her large, dark eyes, which refused to settle on one thing. Her mouth and nose were over-generous. Her lipstick had worn off, but a dark shadow of lipliner remained. On the sideboard to Constance's left stood a large photo of the girl whose school picture was in Sarah's folder: Esther hung from monkey bars, a shiny net of black hair falling around her small face. Her eyes telegraphed her pride at the trick. Sarah didn't see an immediate resemblance to the woman in front of her.

A sound came from the kitchen.

'Who's that?' Sarah asked.

'It's my friend, Shelly Thompson – she's been sitting with me.'

'Okay, we'll want a quick chat with her in a second, too.'

Constance shrugged. 'Sure.'

'Esther is an unusual name,' Sarah observed.

'Yes,' the girl's mother replied. 'I named her for my grandmother, on my dad's side.'

'Are you Jewish?'

'No, and my father wasn't, but my grandmother was. People often ask that. To be honest, I didn't ever really think of it as a Jewish name. That probably sounds silly. I just really liked my grandma a lot.' Constance seemed frustrated with the small talk even as she was making it.

'Do you mind if we take a quick cheek swab? It will be useful to have your DNA on file.'

Constance nodded her assent and Sarah took the sample, always an oddly intimate moment.

There were things Sarah needed to establish. Had Esther wandered before? Had she ever talked about running away? Was there anyone else with a custody claim? Sarah put these questions to Constance, who ran her palm along the edge of the dining table and replied in the negative to each question. Everything matched what she'd already told Mack.

'Have there been any changes in Esther's life recently? Has she made any new friends, started at a new swim school, that sort of thing?' Sarah asked.

'No.'

'Had any work done on the house in the last twelve months?'

'No. I've already been asked all these questions. This isn't like her at all. There's no-one we know who would take her.'

It had always served Sarah to *stay beige*, as her old training sergeant would say. She fought to keep herself on an even keel because it made her a better cop. She tried not to engage with the mother's grief, even as she spoke softly, giving the distraught woman plenty of time to answer. Despite herself, Sarah thought of Amira. The way Amira would pinch Sarah's arm when she tried to talk to her about this stuff, about taking herself out of the equation. *Feels like human flesh to me*, Amira would say, squinting and sniffing until Sarah laughed.

Sarah wished she could take people's brains and just open them up, see all the little details they were too afraid or too forgetful to share and transcribe them directly into her notebook.

'Has anyone been in Esther's room since she left for school this morning?'

'No.'

Sarah could sense Constance's rising impatience.

'You didn't wander in at any point? Put some washing away? Vacuum the carpet?'

'Wait.' Constance put up her hand, like a pedestrian looking to slow an oncoming car. 'I did go in there. When she wasn't home by three, I went into her room in case she – in case she'd come in through the back door or something.'

'What did you do in there?'

'I – I thought about making the bed, but then I didn't because Esther was meant to do it. I picked up some things from the floor.' Her voice went up a register at the end of the sentence, making her words a question, or a plea.

'Okay. We're going to go in there together in a minute and double-check that nothing is missing.'

'Do you have children, Detective Michaels?'

Sarah found that, in general, people were less leery of unmarried, childless female police officers in her line of work than they were of single men. Even if some of them guessed she might be gay, even if that wasn't their cup of tea, they were less suspicious of her than they were of Smithy. She couldn't imagine doing this job and then going home to her own kids. *It's not normal*, her own mother had said. *There's just something not normal about someone who would want to do that kind of work*. She hadn't even known the half of it. Sarah had never spoken with her mother about her time in Child Protection.

Constance was waiting for Sarah's answer. 'No, I don't,' Sarah said.

'You think someone's got my daughter, don't you?' She raised her chin.

'Constance' – Sarah met her gaze – 'I don't think anything this early in the investigation. The only thing I am sure of is that we're partners now. We both want the same thing. We both want Esther home.'

Sarah tried to avoid coming to conclusions too early. What really worried her now was not that Esther might be dead, but that she was alive and being held somewhere. She wasn't going to be the one to expand on the idea with the girl's mother, though.

Constance was silent.

'Do you have another photo?' Sarah asked, holding up the picture Mack had given her. 'Kids don't ever really look like their school photos. Have you noticed that?'


Sarah moved down the hallway, a different photo of Esther Bianchi tucked into her notebook, towards the noise she assumed was coming from the kitchen.

She stopped at the threshold of the vinyl-floored room and was greeted by the broad back of a woman so tall she seemed almost stooped under the kitchen's low ceiling. Sarah coughed and the woman reeled around.

'Shelly Thompson? I was hoping to ask you some questions.' There was a tumbler in the woman's hand. It appeared to be filled with red wine.

'I'm sorry,' the woman said, putting the glass down. She was wearing black leggings and a purple shirt. A grey tiger's head, outlined with small diamantes, stretched across her breasts. Most people became secretive around cops, Sarah had noticed. This woman smiled. 'I'm not a big drinker. I just needed somethink.' The woman ended the word on a hard 'k' sound. 'The bottle was open, but I think it might be old. Tastes bloody awful.' She could have hidden the alcohol easily enough, Sarah reckoned, but hadn't bothered. The woman had short, artificially red hair and was visibly shaking, but Sarah could tell it was not because a police officer was standing in front of her. Something about this woman's world had changed when Esther failed to come home. The woman picked up her glass and put it in the sink. 'But I've got to pull it together, for her.' She nodded towards the hallway.

'Have you known the family long?' Sarah asked.

'Constance is my best friend. We met the day she moved to town,' the woman replied, raising her chin, like it was something to be proud of. 'Her Esther's like one of my own.'

'What kind of kid is Esther?'

'A good one. Some only kids can be stuck up, but Esther gets on with my brood like she was family.' The woman swiped at her eyes with the back of her hand and collected herself. She clearly wanted Sarah to know that the girl was special. 'She's one of those kids who'll have a go at anything. And she trusts people, sees the good in 'em.'

Sarah had seen it before, this urge to impress upon the cops that the missing child was not like any other. Sarah could say it didn't matter, but of course it did. You searched harder for the ones that had people who loved them.

'Do you know anyone who might want to hurt Esther?' Sarah asked gently.

The woman shook her head forcefully, as if repelling the thought.

'And where were you this afternoon?'

'I went to pick up my grandson from my daughter's house a bit after two. I was there for a couple of hours or so. Caleb's just a bub and my daughter Kylie's struggling a bit. I like to give her a break. I brought Caleb home with me – I do that most Fridays. When I got home the kids told me Constance had called.'

'And what time was that?'

'A bit before five.'

'Can you be more specific?'

'I'm not sure. But it wouldn't have been later than five because I had time to get the message and then drive here by seven minutes past five. I remember looking at the clock because I was figuring out how late Esther was.'

Sarah noted this all in shorthand in her notebook. She could maintain eye contact while she did it, a particular skill of hers.

'And where did Constance call you from?'

'Here.'

'Are you sure about that?'

'We've got caller ID on the home phone. I tried to call her back before I left, and I saw her number on the call list.' There was nothing combative about the woman's tone. It looked like she was struggling to keep herself upright.

'Where was Steven when you got here?'

'He was supposed to be at work.' The way the woman said it – *supposed to be* – struck Sarah.

'But he wasn't?'

The woman paused. 'Constance said it took a long time to get him on the phone.' Then, as if guessing what Sarah might be thinking, she added, 'She can never get hold of him when she needs him.'

'What's your opinion of Steven?'

A strange expression crossed the woman's face. 'I try not to poke my nose in.' She reached into the sink and brought the glass, which was still half full of red wine, to her lips. She took a swig then poured the dregs down the sink, grimacing. 'My husband Peter and Steven aren't really friendly, but Esther and Constance are over at my place all the time. My kids love Esther. And she loves them.'

'Where was your husband this afternoon?'

'Peter? He was home with our kids while I went to pick up my grandson.' Sarah sketched a quick triangle next to this information in her notebook.

The woman drew herself up to her full height, like she was preparing for battle. 'Okay. Can I go in and see her? She shouldn't be alone right now.'

'Can I have Kylie's phone number?'

Sarah knew from experience it was the people closest to the missing person whose stories had to be checked most carefully.

'Kylie hasn't got a phone out there. We're working on it. I can give you her address?'

Sarah nodded and Shelly Thompson gave her daughter's address, repeating it to make sure Sarah had caught the whole thing before lumbering past Sarah into the hall.


Steven Bianchi followed Sarah and Smithy in his ute as they drove away from the Bianchi house. Sarah advised against parents joining the search for a number of reasons – the least of which was that they might find a body – but there'd been no stopping Steven.

The sun still hadn't fully set, and Sarah could make out houses hunkered down against the coming night, no lights on, no movement inside. They drove until they reached a wide avenue that split around a long, grassy verge, with established trees spaced out at regular intervals. Old shopfronts were painted in heritage colours, neatly and recently applied, but most of them seemed empty.

'If I saw them walking in the same aisle at the supermarket, I never would've picked them as a couple,' Smithy said. He was always starting conversations, or restarting ones that Sarah thought had been dropped, like he expected her to know what he was talking about. She gathered he meant Steven and his wife. 'He's a good-looking bugger,' Smithy continued. 'Bit thick, though, if you ask me.'

'How do you mean?'

'Well, he's either thick or a bit dodgy.'

Pacing around in his work uniform, Steven Bianchi had kept the furniture between him and the people responsible for finding his daughter. He worked for the council, and he'd told Smithy he was working with a crew all afternoon on a nearby road. Smithy had already phoned and asked Mack to check. Constance Bianchi had left the doctor's office where she worked at 2.30 pm and there was no-one who could confirm her whereabouts between then and three o'clock, when she'd started making phone calls.

Sarah glanced over her shoulder. Steven, in his ute, was so close behind them Sarah thought he might nudge their bumper.

'How'd you go getting a DNA sample from him?'

'No problems,' said Smithy. 'I'm wondering, though, should I organise for forensics on both parents' cars?'

'We can certainly ask, see if they'll consent without a warrant,' Sarah replied. She should have thought of that.

'We probably should have done that first thing, huh?' Smithy's eyes went to the rear-view mirror, made useless by the glare of Steven Bianchi's headlights.

'Hmm.' He was right. Sarah had to focus. The thought buzzed like old electrical wiring under her skin. *You know how to do this, Michaels – so do it.*

She would have liked more officers, but there were two other missing girls – twins – elsewhere in the state. A very high-profile case. Even Sarah, who avoided the media as much as possible – including the coverage of her own cases, when she could – knew that. It was scary to realise that a lot of this stuff was luck. The same way that in a hospital a busy emergency room dictated the level of care you would receive. It was hard maths, a question of limited resources. And people would already be trying to discern a pattern, to work out if the twins' disappearance and Esther Bianchi's were related. Sarah knew it was unlikely but jotted the thought down in her notebook.

While Sarah couldn't call on many experienced officers, she had plenty of people power at her disposal, by the looks of it. Dozens of cars lined the side of the unpaved road near the creek, which – as the way Esther would have walked home – was the locus of their search site. Behind them, Steven peeled off into a tight spot between two other utes. The first thing Sarah did after Smithy had parked was find a uniform and tell him to get the key from Steven – she pointed him out.

'Ask him nicely if we can run some quick checks. Call him *sir*. Tell him you'll run him home when he's ready.'

Sarah knew from experience it would be better to have the question come from someone who looked the way this uniform did – blokey, a bit dumb.

The young man glanced from left to right, like he wasn't sure Sarah had the authority to be telling him what to do. She turned away, making the order final.

'Anyone interesting show up?' Sarah asked Mack in a quiet corner of the Rural Fire Service shed.

The shed had been designated as HQ for the search by virtue of being the closest structure to the part of the creek Sarah wanted to check. Around them, a mix of volunteers and uniforms were getting ready to begin the line search. There were lots of local residents, as well as fireys borrowed from the surrounding areas, State Emergency Service volunteers and cops from Rhodes, the bigger town up the highway. Sarah had been coordinating with the Rhodes team since before they'd arrived, had even worked with some of their officers before, when other cases had brought her out this way.

'One guy I hadn't seen before just said, "I'm Stan," and wouldn't give any other details when he was registering.' Mack's leathery lips barely moved as he spoke. When she didn't reply he continued, 'I told him if he didn't have ID he couldn't search.' When Sarah raised her eyebrows he said, 'Don't worry, I got a picture of him before he left.'

Sarah liked Mack, she decided. She was glad he was their local connection.

'Well, no point waiting any longer,' she said.

Sarah climbed on the tray of a nearby ute and fronted the sizeable crowd; it was always easy gathering a big group for kids. Smithy yelled for people at the back to be quiet.

'I want to thank each and every person here for your patience as we get you registered and set up,' Sarah began. 'If you're uncertain about any of the instructions you've been given, find a marshal.' She gestured to a row of State Emergency Service workers with yellow vests over their bright orange jumpsuits. 'Now, let's get out there.'

The search got underway. As the line of men and women flickered in and out of view through the trees, Sarah allowed herself to enjoy, just for a moment, the flash of purpose. The feeling that they might find the girl and get her home that night. They had over a hundred people searching.

Of course, every local here would have to be checked out in the coming days. If people knew how often the abductor showed up to search, they might not volunteer in the first place.

She'd called in a few favours and diverted a dog team, for twenty-four hours only. She saw them pull up and walked towards their van. On her way, Sarah spotted Steven at the front of the advancing line. There was a pocket of space around him, like people were afraid to get too close. She'd already asked another uniform to go and pick up his wife's car, if she agreed, and take it straight to the motel where she and Smithy could look it over once they were done searching.

After sorting out the dog team and getting them started, Sarah tracked down Mack again. He had prepared a summary of all the properties Esther might have passed on her way home from school. Sarah's mind was doing what it always did in these situations – mentally checking off her actions against a list she'd sketched out in her notebook – even as she nodded along with Mack's words.

'Lacey spoke to everyone who was home and scheduled a time for them to come in tomorrow. The guy on this property' – he gestured towards a dry paddock, a house in the distance just visible in the fading light; behind it, the land continued all the way to the dirt road they'd sent cars down – 'I know him. Name's Ned Harrison. He's away at the moment. A uniform has knocked on the door, just in case.'

'What do you know about Peter Thompson?' Sarah asked. 'He's the husband of Constance Bianchi's best friend, right?'

'The Thompson place is the other side of town. Peter's a good bloke.' Mack's expression said, *Nothing to worry about there.* 'He's a truckie,' he went on. 'Has five kids. A normal guy.'

'He'll be on our alibi list for tomorrow?'

'It's a long list,' Mack said. 'But yeah, 'course he will.'

'Okay, let's add his daughter to that list – Kylie, I think her name was. I'd like you to speak to her, too. We need to check the best friend's alibi.'

'No problems, Detective Sergeant.'

Sarah was sensitive for any hint of pique – some local cops took more breaking in than others – but there was none.

'I wanted to ask you: do you think there could be a connection between this case and the missing twins?' Mack said.

It was amazing how close he could keep his lips together and still be understood.

'It's unlikely, but I'm not ruling it out,' Sarah told him.

Mack rubbed the back of his head. 'It makes me nervous, the thought of some nutjob running around, taking girls.'

Sarah nodded.

It was properly dark when the dogs found Esther Bianchi's scent near the school and started heading for the creek, only to go off in different directions, taking their handlers in circles. No-one found anything in the line search, and nothing came up in the debrief to give them anything to go on. SES workers had taken over the small scout hall near the school, and cot beds were set up for anyone who needed one. They'd search again at first light.

As Smithy and Sarah left the search site, a brunette was extricating herself from an oversized jacket, her microphone already in hand. They were a two-person crew: local news, Sarah guessed. She wondered how long it would take for Sydney reporters to show up. Looking back over her shoulder as she slid into the car, Sarah couldn't hear what the reporter was saying, but saw her illuminated by a circle of bright light. The woman gestured with one hand towards the ground, the fingers extended. The pulsing movement of her hand said, *right here.*

They drove back to the cop shop and stayed there with Mack late into the night, finalising a list of interview subjects for the next day. Uniforms would be patrolling Durton all night. Lacey had organised rooms at the local motel for everyone not on night shift. The dog team would be sharing two to a room, but they'd be leaving after tomorrow, whether they found anything or not. Though Sarah and Smithy both had other cases back in the city, it was looking like they could be in town for a few days at least. The parents' cars had been parked behind the building, out of sight from the road.

It wasn't far from the cop shop to the wide drive of the Horse and Cane Motel. Sarah and Smithy checked in at the bar, the only part of the building still lit up, with a man who said he was the owner. The material of his stained blue singlet forged a clear path through the dark hair on his shoulders like a road running through bush. He reminded Sarah of a character Amira had liked to dress up as for her drag king shows. The daughter of Syrian migrants, Amira had relished dressing as an Aussie boofhead in a stained wifebeater. *What a horrible name for a piece of clothing*, she'd said, her nose crinkling the way it did when she found something absurd. The owner grunted out a few syllables as he gave them their keys and sold Smithy a six-pack of VB. From the blocky concrete reception, a row of rooms stretched out in a straight line.

In the room assigned to her – a musty relic from the early eighties – Sarah kicked off her shoes, lay down on the bed and closed her eyes. Her left hand went to her sunburned arm, landing on her mother's watch. She wore it on her right arm, like her mother did.

Her mother had liked Amira. '*She's* a beautiful woman.' Her mother's emphasis was always on the 'she', as if comparing Amira to Sarah, or maybe even to herself. Sarah looked more like her father had – straight up and down. She suspected it annoyed her mother that Sarah hadn't followed in her genetic footsteps beyond her left-handedness, but Sarah was relieved not to have inherited her mother's chest, her brash, exaggerated way of walking into a room, silently commanding all eyes to her. Of course, wasn't that the kind of woman Sarah always dated? She sighed. It really wasn't the time to think about Amira. And it also wasn't time to sleep. Sarah had arranged forensics for the next day, but they needed to do an initial check of the cars. Sarah stood up from the bed and fossicked through her shoulder bag for a torch.

She walked to the next room in the row and knocked on Smithy's door.

'We need to check the parents' cars.'

Smithy opened the door in his shirt and boxers. There was an open beer on the table behind him.

'Shit, Sarge, you're no fun.'

'I'll see you out there.'

Sarah circled the vehicles, their metal doors dimly reflecting the fluorescent motel sign that rose above the building. She took a deep breath and rolled her shoulders. She wanted to be the one to search Steven's car. She gloved up. Smithy came up behind her and Sarah handed him the key for the mother's Corolla. It felt like a moment from the crime shows Amira always wanted Sarah to watch, even though Sarah found them irritating and plagued with inaccuracies.

'You're my plucky detective,' Amira had said once, running her hands through Sarah's short hair. 'They wouldn't let you be gay, though, in a show.'

'The cops in those shows are always on the verge of a breakdown,' Sarah said. 'I'm nothing like them.'

Amira had just laughed at that.

Sarah crouched to look under the front passenger seat of Steven's ute and her torch lit up the outlines of something resting there. It was almost midnight, but Sarah felt wide awake. Even Amira would have thought it was too easy. It *was* laughable, really, that Steven had made no effort to hide it. Gingerly, Sarah reached in with a gloved hand and tugged. It was a girl's school shoe: black leather, with a buckle on the side. From the detailed description Constance had given them, Sarah knew Esther had been wearing it when she left the house.

Steven was the one who came to the door, like he was expecting them. It was a few minutes past midnight, technically Saturday morning.

Sarah said, 'You'll need to accompany us to the station.'

'Why?' The high tone in Steven's voice sounded both fearful and petulant to Sarah.

Now was a good time for him to be afraid: Mack had confirmed that no-one could place Steven Bianchi where he'd said he was. Mack had also organised an interview room for Sarah at the regional command station in Rhodes. Mack's station didn't have the facilities they'd need for an interview like this one, and doing it in a proper police HQ would make the experience more intimidating. Steven wasn't actually under arrest yet, but Sarah wanted him to feel like he was. He sat silently in the back of the Commodore. Black night streamed past the closed windows. His left leg, the one closest to the gearstick, bounced up and down at double speed. Smithy and Sarah let him stew.

Amira's leg used to bounce up and down like that. 'It is because we *bisexuals*,' she'd gesture elaborately to herself, 'we – how do you say? – just have more *energy*.' Amira would imitate her father's thick Syrian accent to deliver these lines. 'We're not like you lesbians,' Amira would roll her eyes, '*always tired*.' Amira never seemed to imitate her mother's voice, which was breathy and high on the video Amira had shown Sarah of Amira dancing for them at their thirtieth wedding anniversary. Sarah had never met Amira's parents. And now she never would. It had been two weeks since Amira had spoken Sarah's name and promised it would be for the last time. Two weeks since anyone had called Sarah anything other than 'Michaels', or 'boss'.

Sarah closed the door to the interview room and joined Smithy and Steven at the table. She looked at Steven and wondered idly what a jury would make of such a handsome man. His jaw tensed as she sat down. He must have assumed that Smithy would be interviewing him again.

Sarah switched on the digital recording equipment and recited the necessary spiel.

'Alright, Steven. Why don't you walk me through your Friday?' Sarah kept her voice light.

Steven's eyes darted to Smithy, like he was appealing to someone with more sense to save him.

'I've already told you. I was at work. I only got home a bit before five. By the time I got back to the site office and heard my wife had been trying to get in touch with me, it was almost knock-off time anyway.'

'Let's go back a little further. What did you do this morning? Well, yesterday morning, now,' she said, glancing at the clock on the wall.

'Like I told him' – Steven angled his head in Smithy's direction – 'I start late on Fridays, not till ten.'

'That's a nice sleep-in,' Sarah said.

Steven fluttered his eyes closed, like he was blocking Sarah out for a moment.

'Who takes Esther to school?'

His eyes opened again. 'Constance does. You know that.'

He was looking too comfortable. She wanted to shake him up a little. 'Do you and Constance fight much?' Sarah asked.

'A normal amount.'

'How does Esther feel about that? About you two fighting?'

'She felt fucking great about it,' he retorted, looking at Smithy again.

Sarah noted the use of past tense.

'Have you always believed that Esther was your child, Steven?'

'Of course she's mine.'

He seemed to be on firmer ground than before and leaned back in his seat. His hands were flat on the table.

'What were you doing at two thirty, Steven?'

'Like I told your partner, I was out putting new lines on the highway.'

'Is it standard for people in your team to work alone?' Sarah asked.

'No.' Steven bunched his shoulders, like he was reluctant to concede the point. 'Usually someone else is there. But one of the guys was out sick. I was just finishing them off.' Steven looked at her.

'Finishing off what?' Sarah was looking down at her notebook as he spoke. *Sick colleague?* she wrote.

'The lines.' Steven's words were thick with condescension.

'Where were you working, exactly?'

He sighed. 'Near the town limit, on the stretch of road near the sign that tells you you're leaving Durton.'

This matched what Steven's boss had said about where he was supposed to be, but she only had Steven's word for it that he actually had been.

The time had come to show him their evidence.

'Steven,' she said, 'your wife has confirmed that this shoe is one of the pair that your daughter was wearing when she left the house at 8 am on Friday the thirtieth of November.'

Smithy placed the plastic exhibit bag with Esther's shoe on the table.

'For the tape, please note that Detective Constable Smith is showing Mr Bianchi evidence item DN four-six-six,' Sarah said. 'I'm wondering if you could explain how this shoe came to be in your car, Steven?'

Steven's nostrils flared. 'Where did you find this?'

'It was under the front passenger seat of your ute,' Sarah said.

He looked between Sarah and Smithy, and when neither of them answered, he bent to examine the bag with the scrutiny of a man looking for a fifty-dollar note he'd dropped in long grass.

His shoulders slumped. 'It looks like hers. But I don't know how it could've got there.' His tone had changed; it was flatter, less cocky.

'At least two people from the school noticed the shoes she was wearing, Steven.' She looked down to check Mack's notes. 'Your daughter couldn't participate in the netball game because she'd forgotten her trainers. Her PE teacher got a good look at the shoes when she was assessing whether Esther could play in them.'

'You've got it all wrong,' he said, as if only now realising the seriousness of the situation. There was something wooden about him, though. Something fake. The word *bitch* hovered at the end of his sentence, unspoken but palpable.

'You really have no explanation?' Sarah said.

Sarah needed to get him talking, the kind of talking where he would forget to stop. He'd foregone legal counsel when they'd asked, but he could change his mind at any minute.

Silence.

'Steven –'

'Doesn't matter what I say, does it?' he blurted, looking at Smithy, whose head was bent low over the paperwork in front of him. 'Whatever I say, you're just going to twist it.' Steven's mouth hung open as his eyes moved from Smithy to Sarah.

'We're trying to resolve the inconsistencies in your story, Mr Bianchi,' she said. 'That's our job. Surely you can see that finding this shoe in your car complicates your insistence that you were nowhere near Esther at two thirty?'

A memory from a different interview room swam into focus for Sarah. The brown jumper of a man sitting across from her. He'd had his hands clasped together. The ends of his sleeves had a green-and-yellow trim, something like an old school jumper, quite distinctive. The man denied selling films of his five-year-old granddaughter, not realising that Sarah had seen the videos, and that in one of them were shots of a man with no pants on. You didn't see his face, or even really his torso. But as the video technician had pointed out, you could see the edge of a brown jumper, its green-and-yellow trim moving every so often into the frame.

'All I want is for you to bloody find her, but you're too busy wasting time in here.' A high, panicked note came into Steven's voice. It made Sarah think of the way, when a kid falls over, they look around to see if anyone's watching, ready to break into a wail if there's someone who'll come running.

Steven shut his eyes and put his head on the desk. Smithy looked at her. Sarah knew what he was thinking because she was thinking the same thing. This was taking too long. They couldn't arrest Steven with what they had. They'd looked at the shoe under good strong light – no blood on it, and none they could see in the car. A call had already gone in for a mobile forensic team, and someone had agreed to work on it overnight, but she wouldn't have those results until tomorrow at the earliest. They'd drop the shoe off as soon as they were done here, but she'd wanted Steven to see it, to know they had it.

Steven still had his head down on the desk.

Smithy nodded towards Steven as if to say, *Can I have a go?*

Sarah pushed back her chair. *Have at it.*

'What way did you take to the creek?' Smithy asked.

Steven raised his head to look at Smithy. 'I told you: I was at work.' His teeth were gritted.

Smithy leaned in and said something into Steven's ear so quietly that Sarah, and the tape, couldn't hear it.

Steven jumped to his feet. Sarah's heart sank even before he swung out. This would have to be explained at some point, in a courtroom.

Sarah would've said Smithy had pretty good reflexes, above average even, but the wild punch hit him straight on the nose. She sprang from her seat and moved around the table towards Steven, grabbing him around the forearms and jerking him back.

The words came automatically: 'Steven Bianchi, you are under arrest for assaulting a police officer. You do not have to say or do anything unless you wish to do so. Anything you do or say may be recorded and used as evidence in court. Do you understand?'

Steven pitched his head violently back. If she'd been taller – a big, beefy guy – it would have connected with her face. As it was, she ducked it easily.

She looked up at the security camera in the corner of the room, noting the flashing red light. She bustled Steven into the dark hall and found a uniform to pass him to for processing.

Returning to the interview room, she asked, 'You alright?'

'I'm fine,' Smithy said thickly. There was blood streaming down his nose.

'Let's get that seen to,' she said.

'He's not going anywhere now.' Smithy smiled, bloody teeth sprouting from his moustache. Sarah thought of Amira, glistening with sweat on stage, her arms spread wide, her pasted-on moustache drooping as the drunken crowd applauded.

# LEWIS

December 2000

If you had asked Lewis Kennard before that Friday afternoon what his most important memory of Esther was, he would have answered without hesitation. What he remembers most about the afternoon he broke the goldfish bowl is that the classroom was peaceful. Cool and dark. Chairs and tables standing in the gloom like they were waiting for a moment alone to rearrange themselves into more exciting patterns.

This was a year before Esther went missing, when she and Lewis had only recently been made Tortoise Duty partners. All the Tortoise Duty pairs had to be made up of a boy and a girl; it was one of Mrs Rodriguez's many iron-clad directives. Ronnie Thompson would often hang back when it was his and Esther's turn, talking at them through the classroom door. More often than not, Mrs Rodriguez chased Ronnie out, saying she should join the children in detention and pick up rubbish if she had time for hanging around.

'Do you want to put in the lettuce today, Lewie?' Estie had asked as she opened the top of Reggie's tank. When they were alone, they called each other Estie and Lewie. It felt good to use a nickname with someone, even if it was a girl.

Lewis had nodded, pushing his glasses up his nose before reaching over. Of course his elbow connected with the goldfish bowl next to the tortoise tank. In what world would it do anything else? Turning, he looked down in time to see it hit the ground. There was smashed glass and a pool of water and two goldfish who opened and closed their little mouths, bloated eyes looking somewhere behind him, as he stood frozen. Estie grabbed a pencil holder from the low desk next to the tank – it was a tin can, the kind baked beans came in. The label had been removed and the can painted green with poster paint. She lowered it to the ground and slid first one and then the other fish in with her index finger, not even flinching at their slimy bodies. Looking around, she grabbed the old Sprite bottle they used for Reggie's water and sloshed some into the can.

Mrs Rodriguez loomed in the doorway. 'What happened here, Lewis?' she said sharply, looking from the ground back up to the pair.

He didn't seem able to move or speak. It felt as if his guts were about to leak out from under his toenails.

'I knocked the bowl, Miss, but I think we saved the fish.' Estie looked steadily at Mrs Rodriguez as she spoke, the pencil holder in her hand.

A splash of water erupted from inside the tin, a sign of life, backing up Estie's assertion that the fish had survived their ordeal.

He tried to talk to Estie about it after, to thank her, but she just laughed and shrugged, like it was no big deal.

It wasn't long after that – near the end of year five – when all the boys in their class stopped playing with Lewis, as if a stink bomb hidden under his skin had exploded. He first realised something was up on the handball court. The year fives and sixes used the line of concrete slabs between the quadrangle and canteen. The best square was the one closest to the flat-roofed canteen building. As players got out, other players made their way towards that square, like bubbles rising and popping in the neck of a bottle, only to be replaced by more rising bubbles. There was an unspoken rule that boys would get girls out first.

Lewis could remember it was almost exactly a year before Estie disappeared, because they were all waiting for the summer holidays to start. They'd been doing all the things the teachers always had them do in the weeks leading up to Christmas – making log cabins from paddle pop sticks and working on colouring-in sheets that looked suspiciously like the ones they'd done the year before. Mrs Rodriguez let them go to lunch early, and most of the class spread out across the handball court. Lewis was the first player knocked from the competition, off a low shot he wasn't expecting so early in the game. He walked to the bubbler for a drink and sat on the bench to wait for the game to start again. They could fit a few games into a lunchtime. Lewis watched as the last two players battled it out. The squares reset. White polo shirts streaked out from the bench, staking out squares. The higher you went up the ladder, the more people you had gunning for you from the start. He chose a square close to the end. The boys' shots that came his way were low and mean. They laughed as he reached for them. One of his returns was called as 'out' when it hadn't been.

'What the hell, guys?' He could hear the high pitch to his voice.

The boys sniggered. Someone yelled, 'Out you go, old chap,' in an exaggerated imitation of the English tinge to his voice which he got from his mother and couldn't shake. He looked like her too: small and pale, and he had her fine, brown hair.

He turned to walk towards the bench. 'That's right, Louise,' someone else called from behind his back.

It sounded like Alan Cheng. Lewis had always been friendly with him. He'd come over to Lewis's place a few times when Lewis's dad was working late. Once, they'd watched a documentary about natural disasters. Lewis remembered seeing what happened before a tsunami, when the ocean sucks water back into itself and the sand and coral you don't normally see are on display. Lewis's brother Simon loved the sound of David Attenborough's voice and had sat on the floor near the television for the whole program. Alan had never said anything afterwards about the sounds Lewis's brother made, or the way he sat hunched forward, his face almost touching the TV.

Lewis reached the bench and kept walking. He headed for the front playground.

'That's right!' someone called again.

Laughter followed Lewis as he rounded the school building. Estie and Ronnie were sitting under the fig tree at the front of the school. As he walked over to the girls, the laughter from the handball court pulled away behind him, just like that water sucked out by a tsunami. Estie looked up from the face she'd been pulling to make Ronnie laugh, and called out to him to join them.


The rest of the week following the handball game, boys called him 'Louise' and turned away when he walked up to them. They'd always teased him every now and then – especially when Lewis's brother had been seen recently, like when his mum brought Simon to the Australia Day picnic. But now there was a hard edge that hadn't been there before, one that felt like it was about Lewis. He kept sitting with the girls. If he could stay out of sight at the front of the school, he figured, it might just work itself out.

The following Monday, Seamus came up behind Lewis at the bubbler.

'Move, you bloody *poofter*,' he drawled.

Lewis walked away, wiping his mouth with the back of his hand.

He started hearing that word everywhere. Softly at first, then yelled across the playground. Sitting with the girls wasn't so bad.

Ronnie would do nice stuff like give him half of her Nutella sandwich. She did it in a way so you could tell she was impressed with her own generosity. He thought about what his father would say if he knew Lewis sat with girls. There'd been an ugly incident with Estie's father, when Mr Bianchi said that Lewis's father had sold him a dodgy ride-on lawnmower. And Lewis's father wouldn't have been any happier to know that Lewis sat with Ronnie. Whenever he saw Ronnie's mother around town, his father spat the word *junkie* loud enough that you could hear him through the car windows. But Ronnie was okay as long as you didn't listen to everything she had to say. A good rule of thumb was to stop listening after about ten seconds.

There were four concrete slabs near the front office that were the perfect size to play handball. Lewis and the girls started playing there. The girls were both pretty awful, but Estie got better after a few days. The better Estie got, the more frustrated Ronnie became, and her playing would get worse and worse. Her face had the same expression as the tennis players Lewis saw when his dad was changing channels. His father couldn't stand the tennis. *If I wanted to sit here and watch people grunting at each other, then I've got better options than the tennis.*

It would be more accurate to say that all the boys stopped playing with Lewis *at school*. By the last week of that term, Lewis had been sitting with Ronnie and Estie for almost two weeks. Walking home, he saw Campbell Rutherford in front of him. That wasn't unusual. Campbell's house was on the same side of town as Lewis's. Lewis walked so as to keep a distance between them, but Campbell turned and looked at him.

'Enjoying hanging out with your new girlfriends, Lewis?' Campbell yelled.

Campbell Rutherford was muscly, even then, when most of the class still had a baby softness in their faces. He'd been held back a year, so he was older than everyone else. Campbell's hair had been cropped short enough that you could see the smooth line of the back of his skull. He'd slowed down to speak to Lewis, and now he stopped altogether. They were standing quite close to each other now and Campbell's eyelashes were so light Lewis could see them only if he looked carefully. Lewis was afraid that if he answered, his voice would betray him again.

'Oh, that's right,' Campbell whispered, as if responding to something Lewis had said. 'Poofters don't have girlfriends.' A smile on his lips.

Lewis kept his voice as low and deep as he could. 'What do you want, Campbell?'

'Ah, I'm just kidding. Wanna come over to mine and play footy?'

'Fuck you.' Lewis started walking again.

'C'mon. Don't be like that.'

Campbell had all his mates to play footy with. Lewis tried to remember where he'd been during that handball game.

'Seriously, it's going to be boring as shit when I get home. Come around to mine and kick the footy.'

Lewis stayed silent, searching Campbell's face for sarcasm.

A hot wind blew up the road, picking up dust from the broad strips of dirt that ran alongside it. They both lived past the point where the bitumen ran out.

'I have to go home first,' Lewis said. He tensed, waited for Campbell to laugh in his face.

'Alright. You know where my house is?'

Lewis did. Most days he watched Campbell turn at his letterbox and walk across a mowed lawn that was suspiciously green, given the water restrictions. Lewis's dad reckoned they watered it in the dead of night.

Lewis nodded.

They walked in silence until they reached Campbell's driveway.

'See you soon,' Campbell said.

Walking into the hallway at home, Lewis could hear his mum in the kitchen. His brother wouldn't be home for a while yet. Simon's school was in Rhodes, near the hospital. The bus collected kids from all over, and the trip took almost an hour and a half. Lewis's mum was making pastry. Sheets of it were laid out on the countertop. The aircon was set to very cold, to make the pastry easier to work with. His dad was always complaining about the air conditioning. 'That's what I get for marrying an English rose,' he'd say, rolling his eyes. If he was in a bad mood, he'd just turn it off.

Lewis's mother was beautiful, with a long, slim neck and cool hands. Sophie Kennard had lived in Australia for seventeen years. She'd met Lewis's father during a year abroad and never gone home. Lewis tried to imagine what his mother was like before she met his father but could never come up with anything more than a vague picture. One thing he knew for sure was she'd always struggled in the Australian heat.

'Is Dad home?' Lewis asked.

'No, sweetie, he's working until ten tonight.'

'Can I go over to Campbell Rutherford's house?'

His mum searched Lewis's face. 'What will you be doing there?'

'Kicking the footy around.'

It worked in his favour that they'd be playing sport. And his dad got on well with Campbell's. The chances were good, he thought.

'I don't know, dear, it's a bit late notice.'

'Please? I don't have to stay very long.'

His mother looked down at her hands on the kitchen bench for what felt like a long time before rinsing them and turning to the phone at the far end of the kitchen counter.

'I'll need your help giving Simon a bath tonight,' she said. 'You'll have to be home by six.'

He nodded. Anything.

Simon was four years older than Lewis, which meant his parents knew there was something wrong with him when they decided to have Lewis. Lewis was his mother's chance to fix everything, to give his dad the right kind of son. But she hadn't got it quite right, had she? Lewis needed glasses to see. When he watched footy with his father, Lewis sometimes had trouble following the small ball on the screen, which annoyed his father no end. He knew he was not the son his father would have chosen.

Lewis's mum pulled her shoulders back as she punched a number from her address book into the phone. He guessed she was talking to Campbell's mother, because she spoke in the voice she used when she was speaking to women. It was deeper than her usual voice.

'Alright, you can go,' his mum said, returning the phone to its cradle. 'But change out of your uniform first.'

In his room, Lewis pulled on some navy shorts and a t-shirt. He'd kicked off his school shoes at the front door. Picking up his runners, he hesitated. Would it be better to leave the school shoes, which his dad was used to seeing, on the rack in the entryway? That way, if his father came home unexpectedly, he wouldn't think Lewis had worn his school shoes out. But no. Better to put the black school shoes in the closet, and when he came back, he'd take his runners to his room and place the black ones by the door again. That made the most sense.

It wasn't long before Lewis and Campbell were tearing around Campbell's backyard. Lewis's skinny legs whipped through the air as he streaked after the ball. Campbell was stronger, but Lewis could outrun him on an open field. Lewis dodged around Campbell, who held the ball just out of Lewis's reach. He grabbed for it. He'd planned to pop it up and grab it deftly, but he tripped and went sprawling. His glasses flew off his face and he heard the tear of fabric, felt between his legs and found the hole. His shorts were ruined.

Laughing, Campbell walked over to Lewis, bending to scoop up the fallen glasses before extending a hand and pulling Lewis back up to his feet. They stood like that for half a second, their hands still clasped, like blood brothers. Lewis could smell their sweat and the earth beneath their feet, could almost hear the creaking of the streets that stretched out around them, the town suddenly far away. Campbell gave Lewis his glasses and Lewis put them back on his face.

When Lewis went to leave, Campbell walked with him down the driveway. Lewis turned to wave to him and Campbell nodded back: there was something earnest about it that made him look even older. Lewis ran home and hid the shorts at the bottom of his wardrobe drawer to wait for bin night. Luckily, they were an old pair – no-one would miss them.



Lewis stared at the ceiling as his brother splashed in the bath that night. Simon didn't seem aware that Lewis was sitting there, but Lewis still didn't like seeing his brother that way. The soft rolls of white fat, the bubbles on Simon's shoulders, the way Simon hooted and played with his penis until their mum pulled his hand away. Simon liked to lie back slowly and then hurl himself back up, sending water rushing up the sides of the bath. Their mother was busy in the other room, getting a fresh set of pyjamas because Simon had sloshed water on the other set. From the beginning, she was always busy with Simon. He still wasn't walking long after Lewis had started, and was in nappies until he was almost seven. Lewis's mum said Lewis would learn how to do something – pour his own juice, tie his own shoes – and then pretend to forget because Simon couldn't do it. *It was exhausting, Lewis. You kept forgetting on purpose.*

For once, Lewis didn't snarl at Simon when he dug his nails into him as he was pulling Simon out of the bath. The hate that usually sprang up when he was alone with his brother wasn't there. Lewis didn't even think about digging his own nails back into Simon's skin, which was what he would have done if his afternoon with Campbell hadn't been nestled in his chest. It felt good to carry something inside him that his family couldn't see. Something hot and bright.

The next day, the very last day of that school year, Lewis looked up from the bubbler to see Campbell walking across the playground. The first bell hadn't rung yet.

'My mum was mad about those shorts,' Lewis yelled, lying just to have something to say, wanting to see Campbell's smile, or that earnest nod again.

Campbell ducked his head and said something to the boy beside him. They laughed and walked off towards the canteen. Lewis went to sit with Estie and Ronnie. He thought of Campbell pulling him up from the lawn and turned his hand over to look at the palm. Ronnie got annoyed when she realised he wasn't listening and started telling her story again from the beginning.

The school holidays began. Lewis found reasons to walk past Campbell's house until Campbell saw him and called out. If someone else was there, he kept walking. And that was how it went. Campbell would invite Lewis over and they'd play footy or muck about in Campbell's room. A whole summer holiday, a lifetime practically. They spent hours in Campbell's backyard, on his lounge room floor.

When they started year six, Lewis thought things would be different. But Campbell completely ignored Lewis, like before, and Lewis stopped trying to speak to him during school hours.

By the time Estie disappeared, sitting with the girls at lunchtime had become permanent, and all that mattered to Lewis was the time he spent at Campbell's after school. That's how it was between them that Friday afternoon at the end of November when he and Campbell saw Estie in a place where none of them should have been. She was with a man who was not her father, not a man he recognised from around town – a man in a blue-checked shirt. Because of what Lewis did that afternoon, and what he did and didn't say in the days following Estie's disappearance, everything that happened later – especially to Ronnie – was all his fault.

# WE

Friday, 30 November 2001

Ours wasn't the kind of town people visited. There were no roadside stalls selling cherries and our parents didn't run tea parlours where you could buy scones with jam and cream. We were children, and we would have had trouble telling you what the major industry was. We just knew that November was yet another month in yet another year when the price of wheat dictated our parents' happiness. Our town was arranged around the train line, the main street running from one side of the railway crossing to the school. The big old trees that lined the main street had always been there and would always be there, holding the centre of town in place. The shops were on the same side of the tracks as the school and the Horse and Cane Motel. On the other side of the tracks, past the highway that ran alongside it, were the police station and the cemetery. The CountryLink train would stop at the old station, but you had to call ahead and ask.

Summer hadn't even officially begun, and the town already felt like skin reddened and burned by the sun until it peeled. Heat radiated from the concrete of the main street. The paint on the newsagency curled from its walls. Chips of it drifted on the wind, dotting the road with little white specks as far as the school. There was a fish-and-chip shop. Only, one of our fathers said you shouldn't call it a fish-and-chip shop if it was more than three hundred kilometres from the ocean, so we called it the chip shop or sometimes the Chiko shop. We felt the heat and smelled the fryers bubbling as water from our swimmers dripped on the linoleum floor and the owner handed over our ice creams.

Durton had two churches. One of them had a hall attached, and on certain weeknights we gathered around the Girl Guide banner one of the mothers brought in and pledged our allegiance to the Queen, although we'd never met her. Once, Ronnie Thompson scoffed a whole box of the fundraising cookies when no-one was looking and wasn't allowed back. Esther Bianchi quit in protest. On weekends, the other church would host the youth group where we were coaxed into accepting Jesus's love with jam doughnuts and lukewarm lemonade. There was another train track that ran past the outskirts of the showground. It had been built by the wheat company that at one point had owned most of the land around that area. No more trains would ever run there, but everyone still slowed to check nothing was coming before passing over, out of habit.

There was a distinction between our little town and the bigger one up the highway. Our parents made the same word sound different, and we learned from them to say *Town* with a certain capitalising emphasis when we meant the place that involved a twenty-five-minute drive squashed in a car with no aircon. In Town, there was a cinema and a Kmart and a Rivers. There was a racecourse, too, and sometimes we begged our father to take us to see the horses.

'If you want to go to Town, you need to be good, and stop being so mean to your little brother.'

We kids had our own name for Durton: Dirt Town. Nobody knew who had said it first – someone must have thought of the idea, holding the pun aloft like a shiny marble in the playground – but by the time we started school it was just what everybody said. Not with malice or even affection, only in a way that showed we had never thought about the place we lived in terms of good or bad. Our town wasn't a choice, for us. It just was.

Some people muttered that the town was dying.

There was less and less work and more and more drugs. The whole town heard about it when some bloke went berserk – high as anything, high as the fuel prices at the old Brooks service station – and punched out every window of the Wheat Growers Association building, de-gloving his hand of its skin in the process.

But we were children, so all we really thought about that November was the heat that trailed us on our way to school, following us over the train tracks or along dusty side roads. Our classrooms baked in the sun, though at least the ones in the old stone building stayed dark and cool. In the demountables, the heat seeped from the walls and came up from the floor. The teachers sweated as they instructed us on how to do long division or explained what a simile was and had us make up our own. 'He was tall like a lamp that is six feet tall' was the best we could come up with. If we were unlucky enough to have to walk home, rather than take the bus, we would return to our houses pink and breathing heavily, and stand in front of the open freezer. White tendrils of cold air wound past the freezer door and into the room before disappearing. It made us think of that scene from *The NeverEnding Story*, which we watched on VHS every day after school.

That Friday afternoon, it was so hot the edges of the road crumbled. We rode our bikes home from school, grinding chunks of melting tar into the dirt with our wheels. Or we jumped off the small white school bus that doubled as the Returned and Services League shuttle on Friday and Saturday nights. We kicked our younger brother's ankle so hard he tripped and fell, his broad-brimmed school hat flying. When we made it to the end of our long driveway, our mother poured us cool glasses of weak cordial from a jug whose pattern of freewheeling lemons and oranges had long been rubbed away from use.

The last patient of the day hadn't turned up so the doctor at the practice where Constance Bianchi worked on reception said she could head home early. The doctor was old. The practice would probably close when he retired or died, and people would have to drive the twenty-five minutes to Town to have their sprained ankles looked at or their blood pressure checked. Constance would have picked her daughter up, but by the time she got in her car she thought she'd better just go home. They let the kids out at two thirty on Fridays, and Esther wouldn't know that Constance had finished early. If she left now, the chances were she and her daughter wouldn't cross paths, because on hot days Esther liked to cut through the creek. Instead, Constance would go home and get out a packet of biscuits and pour two big glasses of ice-cold milk, ready for Esther's arrival. A nice surprise.

We watched Constance Bianchi as she sat at her kitchen table. She was eager to see her daughter. It had been a hard morning, a flustered afternoon. She'd had a fight with her friend Shelly Thompson. She longed to hug her daughter and lose herself for a while in Esther's excited retelling of her day. After a while, Constance got up. Should she go to the front door, or the back door? She stood there, hovering. Maybe Esther had somehow made it to her room without being seen and Constance should go in there and check? Or maybe it was better to stay where she was, where she would hear Esther coming up the gravel driveway? Every second of not moving was not a single decision, made only once, but a series of oscillating possibilities.

Constance started ringing around at three o'clock, feeling with each call that she might be getting closer to the moment when everything would be revealed. Perhaps she had been distracted that morning and forgotten something her daughter had said about what she would be doing that afternoon. She left messages for Steven at his work, but he rarely got back to her, like he was out there performing surgery instead of standing on some roadside in high-vis, holding a shovel. But it wasn't his fault, she thought, desperate for something gentler, softer, than her own harsh judgement. Perhaps it was just that the other men were not good at getting the messages to him. It didn't matter. Soon one of the mothers from school, from a big farm, wealthy enough to have a mobile phone, would call her back and say, *Don't you remember I said I'd take Esther with us into Rhodes?*

The glasses of milk sweated their way to warmth.

Us? We were underfoot as our older sister tried to get ready to go see a movie in Town. We were jealous because we wanted to see *Center Stage* too. We asked our older brother to let us have a go on his dirt bike and we promised to clean it for him afterwards. The first thing we did when we got home was jump in our above-ground pool, the same blue and white as Colgate toothpaste, not bothering to take off our clothes. And Mum came out and yelled at us that the chlorine would ruin our uniforms, and we remember hoping that they would melt, that the fibres would dissolve, and we wouldn't have to go to school anymore.

When we sat down to dinner, Esther still wasn't home, and it was spaghetti bolognaise with the little mushrooms we hated but it was alright because there was garlic bread and we just ate around the mushrooms, leaving them in piles on the edge of our plate. Or we sat down in the kitchen of our parents' Chinese restaurant and ate sweet and sour pork with a fork because that was our favourite, even though Mum and Dad tried to get us to eat what they ate, the way they ate it, with chopsticks. We put our McCain meal in the microwave – Chicken Parmigiana, the best one – and were happy because our brother got stuck with Shepherd's Pie. Or it was tuna casserole again. Or Mum was on a diet, so we had dry white chicken with salad and thick slices of carrot. We bit down on them and as the carrot cracked, we felt like maybe our heads had split. Like they'd have to scoop up the two halves, our jaw in a pulpy mess on the kitchen floor.

One of our mothers, returning to the dinner table from the telephone, said, 'Someone's taken the Bianchi girl.'

'When? Where?' our father asked – his tone implying that Mum must have been confused.

Most people in Durton didn't have mobiles then. Certainly none of us kids had them. No-one said Esther's name, at least not that we heard. We hadn't seen enough movies or read enough books to know what happened when girls went missing. The word 'taken' didn't mean much to us then. 'Who?' we asked outright, but our parents didn't answer.

'Her poor mother,' said Mum.

She said that about herself sometimes – as in: *Don't you ever think about your poor mother?* – so we assumed that the girl had done something wrong.

Or we understood straightaway what our parents were talking about. We'd seen *Crime Stoppers*. We imagined the scene not as it was, but the way it would look in the re-enactment. A man in a balaclava, a camera-angle change that showed a young girl, a blue school dress. Then a wider angle to show what the scene would look like from afar. A dusty road. Gum trees reaching out of shot.

One of our mothers heard the girl had just wandered off. Or our parents told us her name and left us at home while they went to join the search. Or we lived out of town and neither of our parents said anything, and no-one rang the phone in the hallway, and we wouldn't find out until school on Monday.

# CONSTANCE

Now, when people ask Constance Bianchi if she has children, she tells them she always wanted to be an astronaut. This is not an answer to their question, and most of the time they laugh. In her work now she has to smile, joke, so she adds: *Hard to take a buggy into space, you know*. What she can't tell them is she still wants to be an astronaut. The thought of orbiting the earth – floating somewhere cold and clean, no-one to talk to but mission control – is calming. It makes the days easier. There are no babies in space. Constance had always thought the girls at her all-girl school were stupid for wanting children, for being so desperate to trade one stifled life for another. But then look where Constance had ended up. If she'd still been in touch with any one of her schoolmates in the late nineties, they might well have wondered what the hell she was doing in that town. She was the kind of woman who belonged in a city. When they saw Steve, some of it would have made sense. Constance's handsome Italian husband was explanation enough. Who wouldn't follow that man wherever he wanted to go?

When Constance hung up from that first phone call with Evelyn Thompson on Friday afternoon, asking if Esther had come home with Ronnie, she had a feeling like an animal was chewing its way up from the pit of her stomach. Standing in the kitchen, it hit her: she'd given her daughter one of those names that sounds like the name of a missing girl. Constance said it aloud to the empty room: 'Esther Bianchi.' She'd named her daughter after her father's mother. People often commented it wasn't a name given to young girls anymore. And yet, hearing the name out loud, it had that awful rhythm, one that would sound inevitable when you heard it on the news, like Esther was already gone. She walked through the house again, opening and closing the doors of every room, every cupboard.

Constance had never wanted to hold other women's babies. Other people's children stared at her and she turned away, searching for her wineglass or another adult. But from the moment Esther lay stretched across her chest, strands of urgent love had plaited themselves into rope. There was fear in the love, too. Impossible to tease one strand from the other. The mother-Constance had been born that day. She'd held her daughter and thought, *This one is mine.*

Steve's father passed away when Esther was four. They drove from Melbourne to Durton for the funeral and Steven's mother had looked so frail and alone. Constance could still remember Esther, wearing a grey turtleneck because she didn't have any black shirts. The turtleneck was too warm for the weather and Esther said it itched. After the service, Constance let her take it off. Esther ran between the mourners in her white undershirt. Something had made Constance want to run her hands along her daughter's skin, to touch the hollows underneath her fragile shoulder blades. After the funeral, Steve kept talking about his childhood, how he wanted that for Esther. He wanted her to be able to walk to school and ride her bike everywhere. A small town would be safer, he said. Constance had said yes because she was trying to be the kind of woman who said yes to things.

*

Constance met Shelly Thompson in the summer of 1995, when Esther was six years old. That first summer in Durton, sweating and tired from moving, all the scrubbing and vacuuming and unstacking, Constance had gone to the IGA. She was at the back of the store, which had that corner shop smell – a mix of dusty cans and cheap cleaning products; a smell that went hand in hand with beige lino-leum and soon-to-expire stock. She was crouched by a middle shelf comparing the two kinds of shampoo available – Country Peaches or Clean Apple – when a tall woman walked up to her.

'There's a British woman who runs the salon here, Sophie Kennard. She can get you a great deal on the salon-only stuff. It does wonders.'

Constance's eyes moved of their own accord to the tall woman's choppy haircut. The short hair had been dyed an unnatural, fire engine red and was peppered with auburn and blonde streaks. It was one of those haircuts where, however it turns out, at least you can't be accused of not making an effort. Later, Constance would discover that the 'salon' was just a shed in the British woman's backyard. Women with black plastic capes draped over their shoulders and foil strips folded in their hair would stand around on the lawn and smoke, tossing their butts into the garden beds.

'You're new to town,' the woman said. It wasn't a question, and Constance didn't respond. 'I'm Shelly Thompson. Call me Shel.'

When she stood, Constance barely came up to Shel's shoulders.

'Wanna follow my car and have a cuppa?' Shel asked.

She had a dark green van with chunky silver edges along the exterior, the kind that could seat ten people. It looked vaguely galactic, like it could survive re-entry. Constance had climbed meekly into her silvery blue Toyota Corolla and followed her home.

*

Shel's kitchen was clean but not tidy. Plastic lunchboxes and drink bottles and bowls of fruit crowded the edges of the counter closest to the wall. Shel's youngest, Ricky, was still in nappies then, and her eldest was fourteen. Kylie moved with an exaggerated casualness, wide-hipped and thin-legged. She wore eyeliner and thick, clumpy mascara that upstaged her ginger eyebrows. Like so many girls of fourteen before her, she'd started to go a bit feral. After that first encounter, Constance would see Kylie out walking, the waistband of her school skirt folded three or four times, her thighs glowing white in the sun. Constance had skipped teenage rebellion in the easily recognisable sense. And Steve would never let any daughter of his wear make-up like that. Shel was only six years older than Constance, which meant she'd been young when she'd had Kylie. Within five years, Shel would start nappies all over again when Kylie had Caleb, Shel's first grandson. The baby's father disappeared in the general direction of Victoria before Caleb was born.

'You want some chips, love?' Shel asked as her daughter stalked out of the kitchen, holding a black-and-white packet of knock-off Burger Rings.

Constance nodded and took a pack of Spring Onion.

A tea towel with drawings from *Footrot Flats* hung on the oven.

She pointed to the towel so Shel would know what she was talking about and said, 'That's colourful. I don't have any bright tea towels like that.' As soon as she said it, she worried it sounded condescending.

Shel guffawed. She threw open a drawer, and then another, rifling through bunches of tea towels where the common motif was cartoon drawings of Australian 'blokes' and 'sheilas'. There were a couple that featured the Australian flag.

'You get one Aussie tea towel, and then everyone thinks you're crazy for Aussie tea towels and that's all you get every bloody Christmas and birthday. But I've told 'em all this year that if I so much as smell a tea towel, they're in trouble.' She exhaled shakily in what Constance would come to know as her laugh.

Six years later, almost to the day, Constance had driven to Shel's for a cup of tea after dropping Esther at school, as she did most mornings. Constance dropped Esther off early, at eight, so she could play with her friends before the bell went. Shel had a way of boiling the kettle before Constance got there, of giving her the same cup every time, so that just walking through the door relaxed her. That Friday morning, they sat at a table in the open space next to Shel's kitchen, pine cabinets and square white tiles. Constance could see the new raised garden beds in the middle of the backyard. Shel was so much more resourceful than Constance was; she made everything go further. Shel was a woman who was used to making do. To shops that were only open four days a week and shut at 4 pm. To taking an esky with you to the big shops in Rhodes so things didn't melt on the way home.

Shel dropped four Lipton's Yellow Label tea bags into a white teapot, sloshing in boiling water before putting the lid into place. One hand held something behind her back.

Placing it on the table with a flourish she said, 'Can't let the ratbags see this.' A packet of Tim Tams.

Shel's arms were thick and tanned, but the skin on her face was pale and Constance could see the veins at her temple, snaking up under her short, dyed fringe. She had a broad nose and sparse, weak eyebrows that petered out at the ends. Shel's husband Peter was a truckie who wasn't often home, which made it easier that Steven never came to the Thompsons' house, that Constance never wanted him to come. The more usual thing would have been to organise barbecues between the families, but Constance felt like she could be some other version of herself in Shelly's house, someone less demanding, less shrill and finicky, somehow both less female and more the kind of woman she wanted to be. Shel was the centre of her house. All her kids and all the things in it revolved around her, like she exerted her own gravitational pull, and it made Constance feel safe.

Shel rubbed her hand back and forth against the teapot as they talked, like she was comforting a small animal. She passed Constance a Tim Tam, her warm fingers leaving tiny dents in the chocolate coating.

The two women made it through a refill of the pot before Constance eased into the front seat of her Toyota. The ant hill in the corner of Shel's front yard was getting bigger. Last summer, Shel's boys had run the hose into the hole, and the house had swarmed with the evacuating ants. Shel liked to offer Constance a bargain: *How about my five monsters for your little girl, eh?* she'd say, winking. Shel had always loved Esther, and over the years it had got so that Esther went running to Shel first with a skinned knee or something interesting she'd found in Shel's garden. Constance waved to Shel, sucked Tim Tam chocolate from her knuckle and turned the key in the ignition. The car made a noise, the mechanical equivalent of a horse baulking at a jump, then sputtered and died. When she turned the key again there was only a low, ticking sound.

'Everything alright, love?' Shel called, walking towards the car.

'I'd better call Steve,' Constance yelled back.

'Pete'll be home soon enough. He can have a look at it for you.' Shel was right by her window now.

'I've got to get to work in a bit, and Steve doesn't start till ten today,' Constance said. 'I appreciate the offer, truly, but Steve'll be happy to help. You can guess what Italian men are like about these things.'

A look crossed Shel's face that Constance couldn't identify. 'You'll be needing the phone then.'

Shel turned to go in and Constance opened her car door. Before Constance could catch up, Shel had closed the front door of the house. Constance returned to stand next to her car like that had been the plan all along. Shel brought the phone out, waited as Constance made the call. She'd never once, in the six years they'd known each other, seen Shel go for so long without smiling.

Constance walked closer to the front door to get a better signal on the cordless phone. When she was done, Shel took the phone from her. She still couldn't read Shel's face.

'Well, let me know if you need anything,' Shel said, and went back inside.


When Steve arrived, Shel came out onto her porch, though she didn't wave or walk over, as Constance might have expected. Of course, Steve didn't say hello to her either. Even when they lived in Melbourne, he'd never been interested in talking to Constance's friends.

'I need a smaller wrench than the one I brought with me,' Steven called from behind the bonnet. 'I'll have to go back home and get one.'

'Just ask Shel,' Constance replied through the open window. 'I'm sure Peter will have one somewhere.'

As Steven approached the porch, Shel seemed to . . . prepare herself, that was the only word for it. She pushed her shoulders back. Steven said something that Constance couldn't hear. Then there was Shel's pinched face saying something through clenched teeth. What were they talking about?

Constance got out of the car, her natural instinct to get between the two of them. Shel turned away and said loudly – Constance couldn't help thinking it was for her benefit – 'I'll go get that wrench.'

Steven didn't turn as his wife approached. Constance stood there, unsure of how best to break the silence.

When Shel came back she smiled.

'Here you go,' she said casually, handing Steve the tool. The strange moment Constance had seen from the car wavered. What had she just seen?

Steve did whatever it was he thought Constance's car needed and drove it home to hear it run. She took his ute. It had a double cab, and she wasn't used to driving a manual anymore. She hoped he couldn't hear the grinding of its gears as he drove behind her. Some of their best conversations had happened while she and Steve were driving together. Something about being physically close to someone without having to look them in the face made it easier to talk about things that mattered. As the world moved past the window, things felt temporary, words could be tried out. In his old ute – he'd bought a bigger ute when Esther was born, one with a back seat – they'd talked for the first time about getting married. She'd let him know that it wasn't important to her, but if he wanted to, it would be alright with her. He'd listened, nodding thoughtfully at the white lines that stretched down the middle of the road. He'd proposed on St Kilda Beach, on a winter's day about six months later. *Do you think you could marry me?* he'd said. It was the same question he'd asked in the ute, but this time he was holding a ring.

Constance thought of Shel waving them off, a strained smile on her face.

'I didn't know you and Shelly McFarlane were so friendly,' Steve said, as Constance followed him into the kitchen. He hung her car keys on the hook above the phone.

'I go over there a lot,' she said. Without knowing why, she'd never really let on to Steve that she and Shel were good friends. For years she'd let him think she was running errands. No, it wasn't quite right to say she didn't know why; his mother had kept herself so busy with the affairs of the house Constance had felt the pressure to do the same. Early on, she'd had the impression Shel and Steve hadn't got along in high school. Shel had never once come to Constance's place. 'And it's Shelly Thompson now.'

'I wouldn't bother with her,' he said, brushing past her to open the fridge.

She turned and watched him as he evaluated the contents. 'What do you mean?'

Steve swung the door shut without taking anything out. 'She only cares about herself, that one. Got a real chip on her shoulder.'

'She was in a bit of a funny mood this morning,' Constance said, already angry at her own spinelessness for agreeing with Steven about her friend. Why did who she was in a given moment depend so much on the other person? She disgusted herself. 'You can't dislike my only friend in town, Steve.' She tried to keep her tone light and airy.

It had always been the Bianchis against the world. Steve would take his family's side in any argument, she knew. Maybe that was it. Steve's mother Maria had died a couple of years earlier – a heart attack. Steve had been the one to find her. Constance had thought that might mean they would leave. They could resume their life in Melbourne and put Durton behind them. But Steve wanted to stay. Even with his mother gone, he still had an aunt and some cousins who lived in the town. Constance was out of place at those loud Italian gatherings. At first, they'd thought she was shy. Then they thought she was cold. Now, she was pretty sure they thought she was a bitch.

She handed Steve his keys, letting her fingers brush his. 'Will my car get me to work, do you think?'

Six years was a long time. Had she really never seen Shel and Steve talk to each other before now? It was just another way her marriage wasn't normal. It wasn't normal not to have friends outside your family. Why had they never been over to the Thompsons' for a barbecue? Constance didn't know Peter very well, but he was always nice enough. She didn't get the sense that he was annoyed to have her or Esther there. Suddenly, it struck Constance as strange that Shelly, with her easy hospitality, had never asked the whole family over, only ever Constance and her daughter alone. And Shel never wanted to come to her house.

'I've sorted it,' he said coldly, and left the room.

She started on the dishes from the previous night's dinner, letting the cutlery drawer bang and the pots and pans smash against each other. Not too loudly, not so loudly that Steve would come in, but enough to give vent to her anger at herself.

From the window over the kitchen sink, she watched as Steve pulled himself into the driver's seat of his ute. He'd gone out the back door to avoid walking past her again. The shock of seeing how handsome he was never wore off. The facts of his face were unavoidable, his dark brown eyes and strong jaw. It was a curse in its own way, having the kind of husband that other women saw photos of and said, 'Well, aren't *you* a lucky lady?' That was another of the things she liked about Shel – she never implied Constance had won some kind of jackpot. Shel listened when she complained about how Steve wanted everything just so, the way his mother would have done it, which had only intensified after Maria's death. Constance couldn't compete with Shel – her husband was away all the time and she had five kids – but Shel never tried to make Constance's problems smaller by saying hers were bigger. She'd never had much success making or keeping female friends, but Shel was easy, smoothing everything over with that laugh of hers, a sound like an iron lung being switched off.

Constance had contemplated calling Shel, but she knew from experience it was better to let her concerns sit. The promise that she would chat to Shel and it would all be fine was all the more tantalising by being put off. At ten, Constance had finished dressing for work – she started at eleven on a Friday – and was tackling the pile of laundry on the couch when there was a knock at the front door. Her first thought was that it was Steve. He'd be popping in to make it up with her. She wasn't in the mood to make up the way he preferred to, though she knew that she would end up being talked into it, if it was what he really wanted. She opened the door.

'Shel! Did I forget something?' It had been less than an hour since she'd left Shel's driveway.

'Constance.'

The sound of her own name made her pause. Shel always called her 'love'. She called everyone that, but it didn't make Constance enjoy it any less.

'Everything alright?'

'Do you have time for another cuppa?' Shel asked.

'Of course. Come in!' Constance said, waving her inside.

Shel followed her down the hall to the kitchen and Constance checked the clock on the wall. She put the kettle on and prepared a mug for Shel and a rounder, more delicate cup for herself.

Silence.

'Thanks again for this morning – sorry it was such a to-do.' A pause where Constance waited for Shel to contradict her, but nothing came. 'Actually, I'm glad you're here. I wanted to apologise for Steve. I know he's not the most social person.'

Shel still wasn't saying anything.

The kettle clicked – it had already been hot – and Constance poured water into the cups. She carried Shel's cup to the table, bottle of milk in her other hand.

'Was he rude to you this morning? He gets into these moods. I'm sorry you had to see it,' she said.

'No, it's not that. And I'm sorry, too. I know I was acting strange.'

Constance's body was flooded with relief. She took a deep breath.

'What did he say to you?' she asked, eager to resolve the issue. 'He can be such a grump.' She smiled.

'Constance,' Shel said.

Without knowing exactly what Shel was about to say, Constance sensed it was something she might not want to hear.

'There's something I need to tell you,' Shel said. 'I should've told you earlier. I just never knew how to start.'

'What is it?' She tried to adopt an open expression, wanting to be the kind of friend who made space for hard things.

Shel took a seat at the kitchen table. 'I have to ask: have you ever heard anything about me?'

Constance sat too. Shel was looking at her intently.

'No,' Constance said.

Shel took a deep breath. 'One night, when I was eighteen, there was a party out on Toni Bianchi's property,' she said.

Toni was one of Steve's uncles, Constance knew. She'd never met him. He'd passed away not long after she and Steve met. Steve had gone home for the funeral, hadn't asked her to go with him, and she hadn't pushed.

'We were in a corner of Toni's property, out near the woolsheds. Toni'd already turned in. There was a bonfire. Someone had brought a few bottles of Southern Comfort. Most of the other girls from school were on an excursion to the Royal Easter Show in Sydney. My parents couldn't afford for me to go, and I didn't care. I'd rather be drinking with the boys. I was the only girl. I didn't notice the bottle was only going halfway around the circle before being sent back to me. It got to the point where the boys were just passing it to me without drinking themselves. I'd sip from one bottle only to be handed another. They were laughing at me and I was laughing right along because I thought it was funny too. I was cutting loose, because for once my big brother wasn't there, scaring everyone off. My Peter wasn't there that night either. He was a year older than me. He'd finished school, and he'd gone to work on a farm up north for a while.' Shel smiled, looked at her hands on the green tablecloth. 'He wasn't my Peter then, of course. Just Peter Thompson, another boy from school. We'd been talking a bit, smiling at each other. I thought he fancied me, but I couldn't for the life of me figure out why. I was the tall girl nobody looked twice at. He wrote me a letter from up north, said he wanted to meet up when he got back. Told me he'd been thinking about me. I don't think Peter ever wrote another letter in his life, but I still have that one.'

Constance resisted the urge to stand and fetch her cup of tea from the kitchen bench. She found she couldn't look Shel in the eye, so she watched her mouth instead. She'd read in some magazine that looking at someone's mouth while they were talking made them feel like they were being listened to. Whatever Shel was saying seemed important to her.

'Please, go on, Shel,' Constance said.

Shel hadn't poured any milk in her tea. She held the steaming cup between her hands.

'So I was happy, because I was thinking about that. Maybe that's why I drank so much. Because I was so looking forward to seeing Peter and it was like people could tell I was happy, and they wanted to be around me. Anyway, it got late. It must have been four in the morning. I still remember, I said, "Looks like this little lady should be getting home, folks," and I laughed at my own joke, because I towered over quite a few of them. And then I tried to stand and fell over. We were laughing and some boys picked me up and we were walking, we got in someone's ute. All the boys had utes. I've tried – I've tried to remember whose car it was. Boys piled in the tray, I don't know how many. I fell asleep in the cab, and when I woke up I assumed we'd stopped because we were at my place. The door opened and I fell out. We were near the creek, I could smell the water. I was lying facedown on the dirt. It was cold.'

Constance was hyperaware of the expression on her own face, the position of her hands on the table.

'Someone touched the back of my leg. They lifted my skirt up and pulled my underwear down and I scrambled to pull myself away. I was all covered in mud. Hands went around my face and covered my mouth because I was yelling, real loud.' She paused. 'It stung. I was a virgin, y'know. And it hurt. All four of them hurt. It might have been only two and they had a couple of goes each. I'll never be sure.'

Constance longed to stand and put the kettle on, like her brain was offering her another path, something else to think about instead of the words, but Shel was still talking.

'And then at the end they put me back in the ute. I lay in the tray and when they stopped at the end of my street, I pulled myself out. It must've been five in the morning. I was covered in mud, all down my front, on my face and hands. No-one got out with me, but I remember Steve looking at me through the passenger window as they drove away. He was one of them. He was only fifteen, but he done it with the rest of them. He raped me.'

The last sentence was the one Constance had begun to fear was the natural conclusion to the conversation. The feeling surging through her stole the breath from her body.

'What did Steven say to you this morning?' Constance asked.

'He told me to stay the fuck away from you, actually,' Shel replied. Her voice was flat. The telling of the story seemed to have deflated her; she was hunched over the tea. She still hadn't brought it to her lips. 'I hid it from my parents. I went around the back when I got home. I showered. I threw away the clothes. I didn't want anyone to know. I wasn't even sure who else was there, other than Steven.'

Directly behind Shel, on the wall, was a portrait from a photo shoot Steve had given Constance as a gift on Mother's Day. The three of them, Constance, Steven and Esther, all wearing white shirts and jeans, posed together against a studio backdrop.

'What do you want me to do with this?' Constance's voice sounded like she'd just run up a long flight of steps.

Shel contracted, like when you poke a slug and it contorts away from the stick, the initial reaction fast, the edges of it still moving seconds after the stick has been pulled away.

Constance stood. It felt like she'd drunk a glass of soda water too quickly. The anger fizzed in the back of her throat. 'What the actual fuck am I meant to do with this information?'

Shel's face was blank. 'I thought you should know.'

'Know. More like believe. You expect me to *believe* that?'

Shel stood. The line of her mouth was hard, reaching into the depths of her cheeks. Though she was a foot taller than Constance's mother, the way she stood with her weight on one leg, like she was ready to take off, reminded Constance of her, and it pissed her off.

'Get the fuck out of our house.' It was like Steve was standing behind her, his arms crossed. She'd never been surer of their love than in that moment. The bad things melted away and all she could think was, *I love this man.*

Shel walked a few steps backwards without turning – keeping Constance in her line of sight, like you might do when confronted with an insane person.

Constance caught up with Shel just as Shel made it outside. Constance slammed the front door hard, heard the lock click. She breathed heavily, seemed to be having trouble getting enough oxygen. There was the sound of Shel's car driving away.

She thought about the tender skin along her husband's ribs, the way she'd poked him there when they had the teasing fights of their

71

early marriage. Steve had been so loving then, so playful. She had no idea what to do now except pick up her tea from the kitchen bench. Then she was standing in the bedroom, a cup of tea in her left hand, looking at the light coming in the bedroom window and thinking so hard that she let go of the cup. It dropped on her foot before landing on the thin grey carpet – which had been laid directly on the house's concrete slab – and breaking into three pieces. The broken ceramic looked like the husk of an orange that had been peeled, like if it tried hard enough it could pull itself back together to make an orange-shape again. The hot liquid surged between her toes like a tide. Pain glittered across her foot. It took a moment of concentrated stillness to overcome an urge to walk on the pieces, to grind them into the floor with her bare feet.

Stepping around the shards, Constance staggered down the hall towards the bathroom. She didn't bother to close the door. Shelly Thompson wasn't coming back. The elastic in Constance's underpants was going. The sagging material looked like discarded skin in the fluorescent light that bore down in the small room. She wiped herself, flushed, then washed and dried her face. She went back to the bedroom and sponged the tea from the carpet, put the broken cup in the bin. She would be late for work if she didn't leave soon.

Constance spent the rest of the morning moving through fog. She kept making stupid mistakes. During her lunch break, when there were no patients or paperwork to distract her, she resolved that she would have to talk to Shelly. Make sure she wasn't going to repeat the accusation to anyone else. She almost felt sorry for the other woman, but the image of a fifteen-year-old Steve brought her up short every time. Shelly had been drunk. She'd been confused. She'd said herself she wasn't sure how many boys it had been. Constance would not indulge this. And then it was two thirty, and Dr Spalding said she could leave work early, and Esther didn't come home when she was supposed to. Ten minutes late. Twenty minutes late. Thirty. She called everyone she could think of but hadn't been able to speak to two of the people she really wanted to. No-one at Steve's work had been quite sure where he was, and Constance had dialled Shelly's number without even thinking about their argument. Shelly's kids had told her on the phone that Esther wasn't there and that their mum had gone out to pick up Caleb. Constance called Mack, who said he wanted to bring in people who were experts at looking for missing kids, and he wanted to do it straightaway.

'But isn't it too soon?'

'Put it this way, I'd rather be a bit embarrassed for overreacting and know we left nothing to chance. Wouldn't you?'

When she'd finally got hold of Steve, a bit before five, he was home within minutes and went straight back out to search, coming home periodically to see if Esther had returned before heading out again. Constance was aware of every minute passing.

And then Shel arrived, pulling Constance into her broad arms in the hallway. Constance cried and cried.

'Sorry I took so long – Kylie still doesn't have a phone out there,' Shel said. 'The kids told me soon as I got home.' She paused, as if listening for noises elsewhere in the house. 'Is Steve here?'

'He's out searching,' Constance said.

In that moment, it was silently agreed that they wouldn't talk about what had happened that morning. Not yet. All that mattered was Esther.

Constance's hands felt translucent; she could feel her heart beating in them.

'I can't believe it,' Shel said. 'She should be in her room. She should be here.'

Constance sobbed into her friend's shoulder.

'It's going to be okay, Constance. It will.' The women clung to each other. Constance's hot tears and snot poured onto Shel's shirt. 'It's going to be okay, love,' Shel said again.

Constance couldn't fathom the idea of leaving the house when Esther could return at any second. In between laps of the front and back yards, she watched the news, as if she might see her daughter in the background of a local news story about the delay in the cinema renovations in Rhodes. She thought about where Esther might be, and what might be happening to her, about the socks Esther had been wearing, about the clean socks in her daughter's drawer. No-one said the word *rape*, but everyone was thinking it: the city detective who interviewed her, hours after Esther was supposed to be home; the woman from the welfare unit who spoke nonstop until Constance was able to get her off the phone.

Shel made herself scarce, slipping into the bathroom or one of the bedrooms when a car pulled into the driveway, and Constance was grateful. Steve had borrowed someone's car, because the police had taken his. He only ever ducked his head in to check for Esther before going out again. At eight thirty, some of Steve's family, the ones who weren't out searching, came to sit with her. The sound of someone at the door was painful because her body kept thinking it was Esther. She could feel herself waiting, wanting so hard that she seemed to vibrate with need.

Time kept passing, not having the decency to stay frozen, minute after minute after minute. Shel chased away Steve's relatives. She answered the phone and told a journalist the family wouldn't be making any statement. And then there were pictures of Esther on the late news. These were shocking in themselves, Constance's brain firing for a moment: *That's it! Here she is! I've found her!*

She felt an uncontrollable urge to be in motion. She walked into Esther's room to replay her conversation with Detective Michaels, to catch the thing she had overlooked, to find the clue. As if she still might find Esther hiding in her own room. What she saw instead was Steve, sitting in the dark, his back against the white built-in closet. The driveway was empty and she hadn't heard him come in. He was sobbing. Dry sobs that shook his whole body but did not make any sound. He didn't see her, because he had his hand over his eyes, squeezing them closed. He looked so pathetic, so much like someone trying to keep quiet as he gulped down sobs, that she backed out of the room, all sense of purpose cruelly taken away. She walked out into the kitchen and told Shel, without meeting her eye, that Steve was back from searching and Shel should go home to her kids. The clock on the kitchen wall said it was 11 pm.

'I don't wanna leave you here, love.'

'Just go, Shel.' It came out rudely, but Shel didn't look offended.

''Course, you'll want to be with Steve. But I'm just a phone call away, alright?' Everything that was still unsaid hung in the air. 'Everything is going to be okay,' Shel said. 'I know it will.'

Her friend had come, that was what mattered.

Constance hugged her tightly. 'Shel, this morning –'

'Don't think about it, love. Let's just focus on getting through this.'

It made Constance sick to see her go. As soon as Shel got in her car, Constance wanted to ring her back.


It was just after midnight when the detectives returned. Shel had been gone for about an hour, and it was just Constance and Steve in the house. They heard the knock on the door just as he was getting ready to head out again. When Steve realised what was happening, he asked calmly if he could give the torch in his hand back to his wife. Constance took it, unable to speak as he was bundled out the door. When Constance was shown her daughter's black school shoe – sealed in a plastic evidence bag, numbers written on a white label – she had no idea what it meant. The female detective told Constance that Esther's shoe had been found in Steve's car. The other detective had already taken Steve out the front.

'But he was at work this afternoon.'

'Listen, Mrs Bianchi, I'm sorry. The best thing to do now is just let us get this sorted. Some uniformed officers are going to search the house. Is there anything you want to tell us before they get started?'

Constance thought of what Shel had said about Steve. The words rang in her ears, but she couldn't make them come out. She shook her head.

The detective asked if there was anyone she could call, and Constance recited Shel's number. Detective Michaels told Constance that if it came out later that she'd kept any information from them, it could result in a conviction against her. For a moment she thought about telling the detective what Shel had told her, but no: she couldn't speak against him while he was being taken away in a police car. She didn't know, yet, what to think.

The detectives left. Constance sat at the kitchen table as the uniformed officers searched. It was ridiculous, but even as she sat there, she still felt like they might find Esther in the house – the way certain things won't turn up until a second person looks for them.

Later, Constance would think she'd already made her decision. In the moment when she gave the detective Shel's number, she'd subconsciously chosen a side. Something had already shifted, had gone away when she saw the shoe inside the sealed bag, and it wouldn't be coming back again.

When Shel arrived, Constance let her in, checking that the door didn't lock behind her. It seemed very important not to lock the front or back door, like Esther might simply turn away and disappear back into the night if she tried the door and couldn't open it. Shel bustled around, washing dishes, making tea, and Constance stared at Steve's roster on the fridge. He'd been at work that afternoon, of course he had. This was only a misunderstanding. His house keys were still on the bench.

Shel didn't ask what had happened. Constance sat at the kitchen table, the same chair she'd been sitting in, on and off, since three o'clock, hoping that each time she stood up it would be to see that Esther had come home. Hard to believe that had been nine hours ago. The green tablecloth had rings where Steve's family, uncomfortable to be sitting around with nothing to do, had slopped their tea in their haste to drink it and be free. It was so late, but it still felt like at any minute Esther might run through the door with some story about how she'd lost her shoe and hadn't come home because she thought her mother would be mad at her. Steve would come back and it would be revealed that the detectives were frauds, running a pretend investigation. They were tricksters from out of town, but they were gone now, and everything could go back to the way it had been. Constance's conversation with Shel this morning had been a dream that had infected her waking life, the same way Constance sometimes woke up cranky with Steve for something he hadn't actually done.

Shel was in the kitchen. It was one in the morning. Constance stood to go into the bedroom and call her mother. They normally got by on a single phone call a year, on Esther's birthday. Constance called her mother then because despite everything – despite the fact that she'd never played that role for Constance – she was waiting for her mother to solve all her problems. Waiting for a get-out-of-jail-free card, a note she could carry with her that said, *That's enough now. That's all Constance can take.*

When her mother picked up the phone, sleep and steel in her voice, Constance burst into tears. She sobbed so loudly that Shel ran into the room. Shel took the phone and spoke in a low voice as she explained the situation.

'Tell her not to come, Shel.' Constance was frantic. She had to make Shel understand.

Shel looked at her, a confused expression on her face, but relayed the message.

After a few more moments, Shel nodded and hung up the phone. 'She says she won't,' Shel said, as if she couldn't believe the message even as she was saying the words. 'She says to ring her as soon as you hear something.'

Constance could already imagine what her mother being there would do; it would suck all the remaining oxygen out of the room.

It was her curse, to be so consumed by the people around her.

She returned to her chair.

Constance wanted to ask what Shel thought she should do about Steve, about what it meant, but her face felt soggy, and she didn't know how to put the request into words. There were tears on Shel's face, too, she noticed, and Constance had the sudden, urgent need to talk about something, anything except what was happening. Her foot still hurt from where she'd dropped the cup that morning. It felt like a thousand years ago.

'Did I ever tell you why my mother and I don't speak?' Constance said. She knew she hadn't, but it seemed the simplest way to begin.

Shel shook her head, wiping her face with the back of her hand.

'My father died when I was young – but not so young that I don't remember him. He was everything my mother wasn't. Warm, loving. When he paid attention to you, it was like you were the only two people in the world.'

The kettle clicked and Shel stood to make the tea.

Constance didn't twist her head to watch; she just kept talking to the tablecloth.

'My mum stayed single for a long time after my father died. But then she started dating one of his friends. It was all above board. He was checking up on her and they started to get close. But they kept it secret. I didn't know about it until he moved in.'

Constance remembered being a teenager. On the surface she'd been a good child. It was impossible to be anything else in the icy chill that emanated from her mother. Sometimes, in a secret place deep within herself, she'd allowed herself to feel the anger, to wallow in the injustice that it was her mother who had lived.

'Frank was like my father in a lot of ways,' Constance continued. 'He was kind.'

'I've never heard you speak about him,' said Shel, placing two cups of black tea on the table. They'd run out of milk.

Constance had felt terror around her mother, but then when her stepfather had placed his hand on her back, it had been like they were in a bubble. It had been soft and warm, tinges of red, streaks of purple: one of those giant nebulas you saw in photos.

Shel shifted her chair so that she was sitting next to Constance, her body pressed against Constance's side.

'You can tell me,' Shel said.

'She found us together. I was fifteen. It was only a hug. I think he figured I could use some affection. But Mum imagined it was a lot more and screamed the house down, wouldn't listen to us. She never forgave him, or me.'

The only thing she couldn't have handled was Shel's pity. Instead, Shel said, 'Well, there goes your Christmas card, I guess.'

Constance laughed. A strange, high sound in the dark room. A wave of gratitude washed over her. It flowed over what had happened afterwards. Her mother had sent her away to boarding school. She'd been alone in the world until she'd met Steve. He was the first person in a long time who'd made her feel like she might belong to someone.

'I'm sorry,' Shel said. 'That sounds tough. You were only a kid.'

It occurred to Constance that when she'd last thought about the distance she'd maintained between Esther and her grandmother it had been sad, but not in a way that registered in her body. Now, it felt like the thick insulation that had existed between her and the fact was gone. She felt like a freshly shaved head exposed to wind. Constance imagined Esther cold and naked somewhere. She started sobbing.

Shel waited until Constance could speak again.

'And I never told Steve. He just accepted that my mother and I don't talk. Which makes you think, you know? How could I not share something like that with my husband? How could I not tell him? What else weren't we talking about?'

Constance was sure Shel knew what she was really asking.

Shel moved her arm and ran her palm back and forth on Constance's right shoulder blade. It was hard to tell if she did it because Constance had started crying again, or if Constance had started crying because she did it.

'He hasn't rung yet. But I don't even know if I want to speak to him,' she said. 'They found her shoe in his car, Shel. I can't think how it got there.'

Shel's eyebrows shot up, but she didn't say anything.

Constance continued, 'He says he hasn't seen her since I took her to school. I don't know what to believe. I just keep thinking, *If he could hurt Shel, he could hurt her.*'

Shel held her gaze.

'What should I do?' Constance looked down at her hands. She wanted Shel to decide for her.

'You don't have to think about it now, love,' Shel said, pulling her into a hug.

Just after 2.30 am, the phone rang. Constance snatched it from the kitchen wall.

'Constance?' It was Steve.

'Steve. Are you alright?'

'I'm okay. Sorry it took so long to call.'

'What happened?'

'They showed me her shoe, Con, and for a second I got excited, you know? I thought they'd found her. But then one of the cops, well, he said something awful. I couldn't take it. I punched the bastard. I reckon that was his plan, too.'

'What? Where are you?' Steve had *punched a cop*?

'I'm about to be processed. Listen, I need you to get in touch with our lawyer.'

'And who is that?' The only lawyer Constance knew about was the man who'd given them documents to sign when they bought their house.

'His number's in my bedside table.'

She would realise later that Steve hadn't said anything about the shoe, about what it was doing in his car.

'I have to go. I love you. Tell them they've got to keep looking. And don't forget the lawyer.' There were other voices in the background.

'Okay. I love you too.' Her words and the dial tone ran into each other.

She hoped that Shel hadn't heard what she said. She hung up the phone.

*

'I'll call Pete. I can stay here tonight.'

Constance looked up at Shel towering over her and realised she was sitting on the floor in the kitchen. 'I'll be fine.'

'That's okay,' Shel said, placing her hand on Constance's shoulder. 'I'll just be here while you're being fine.'

'I need to call the lawyer for Steve.'

Shel nodded.

Constance stood and moved past Shel and into the bedroom. Shel didn't follow. Constance rifled through Steve's drawer and found the piece of paper. She'd intended to pick up the phone in the bedroom, but instead walked down the hallway and into Esther's room. There was a large window. Steve had bought it second-hand and installed it himself, knocking out the wooden frame of the old window, cutting into the wall to make it bigger. The windowsill was crammed with things Esther had found and liked the look of: small plastic toys from Kinder Surprises, interesting sticks, and a couple of Smelly Bellys collectables. In her life before that moment, Constance had read books about missing children. In them, the child's room was always kept as a shrine. But Esther's bed had been stripped and the sheets bagged and taken away by the police. As Constance had told the detective, the bed had been left unmade. Shel's children made their own beds every morning, but it had been a struggle to get Esther to do the same. *I'm just going to sleep in it again tonight, Mum*, she'd say.

Standing in her daughter's room, her bare feet were held by the thickness of the shaggy white rug, and the urge to vomit came so suddenly that she took a step back.

She ran to the toilet, tried to throw up, couldn't.

It was the moment in hide-and-seek when you say, 'Okay, you can come out,' but nobody moves, and you are still alone.

It had been hours now.

Shel came in to find Constance still kneeling in front of the toilet. She helped her up and said Constance should try to lie down with her eyes closed for a little bit.

'I've got some painkillers, love. They could help.'

Constance didn't respond.

'I'll be here when Esther comes in,' Shel assured her. 'She'll see me in the lounge room.' There was something sad in Shel's voice that made Constance want to comply.

Constance followed Shel to her room. The fear of not knowing where Esther was spiked in erratic waves, like the read-out from a heart monitor. The urge to slip into not-thinking and not-feeling was strong. The edges blurred a little when the painkillers kicked in, but sleep was unthinkable. What was Steve doing now? It was strange to lie in their bed and not be able to picture the place where he was, but less urgent than it was with Esther. Someone had him. He was safe. The shoe flashed in her mind. How was it possible they'd found it in his car?

Constance grabbed the cordless phone from its cradle and yelled for Shel to bring sheets and a blanket from the linen cupboard. Constance stood in Esther's room while Shel remade her daughter's bed. Shel tucked her in, pulling the edges of the blanket taut over her shoulders. Shel's face glowed white in the moonlight that came through the window and her lips were a dark stain. The smell of Esther was everywhere in the small room. In the smaller bed it didn't feel strange that Steve wasn't there beside her. Constance curled herself around the phone, willing it to ring.

She must have fallen into some kind of sleep, because she had a dream in which she was looking for something. Esther was in the dream, calling instructions that Constance couldn't quite hear from a place that Constance couldn't see. She woke and, for a few moments, consciousness was just a thick, featureless cloud. Gloriously blank and formless. And then Constance sensed the wall at her back and remembered with a sharp tug where she was and what had happened. It was four in the morning. She got up and went outside and walked around the house, circle after circle, holding the big Eveready torch Steve kept on top of the fridge in case of power outages, calling her daughter's name. Shel had parked close to the hedge on the lane that ran alongside the house instead of in the driveway, to keep the driveway free. The thoughtfulness of the action, especially given the way Constance had acted that morning, made her clutch at her own clothes.

As the sun came up on Saturday morning, a whole dark night since her daughter had last been seen, Constance walked to the front door and turned the handle to check it was unlocked. She'd already called and left a message for the lawyer. Esther was gone. The thought eclipsed everything.

Shel emerged from the lounge room. She'd slept there, even though Constance and Steve's bed was free. *Of course she didn't want to sleep there*, Constance thought.

Esther had got lost, but she'd been found and looked after by good people, people who hadn't been able to call or make contact for some reason that would make perfect sense in hindsight. Like someone running their hand along the individual palings of a fence, feeling the familiar boundaries of each one with her fingers before moving on, Constance reached for hope. With that sickening lurch you get when someone moves a chair after you've begun to lower yourself into it, she found it wasn't there. The police thought Steve had done something to their daughter. That he'd seen her after school and lied about it. Her body flooded with an acidic liquid that was her shame, her anger, her fear, the undissipated energy from her argument with

Shel. She raged against the fact that they'd ever come here – this was Steve's town. She screamed. She screamed until she was finally able to throw up, just making it to the garden bed by the front steps in time. All she could think of, as she emptied her stomach, was her daughter's shoe.

Constance stumbled back to the kitchen. She realised she was holding the card Detective Michaels had given her in her right hand. How was she supposed to start that conversation? *Hello, there's something you should know about my husband.*

Constance found she couldn't do it. Despite everything. Not now. She would ring a bit later. Then she might be able to find the words.

She heard Shel behind her.

The two women looked at each other.

'Shel, I'm sorry,' Constance said. 'I'm so sorry that happened to you.'

She was sobbing into Shel's chest before she could get any other words out. Shel enfolded Constance in her large frame, her long arms reaching across Constance's back. Constance felt Shel's own tears trickling down her neck.

Later, in a magazine article on the story – it will become quite famous; Constance will be asked to go on *60 Minutes*, but will say no – there'll be a photo of her from some time that week. She'll recognise the front of their house but have no memory of the photo being taken. The caption will read: *Constance Bianchi, mother of missing girl Esther Bianchi, and what she never saw coming.* Constance looks fat and exhausted in the photo, like there's more gravity where she's standing.

'I'm not going to stick by him,' Constance said, as Shel held her.

Birds called outside, announcing the morning.

# RONNIE

When my mum came back from searching, I was in bed. It was my cousin Ricky's bed, and it had one of those plasticky bottom sheets that stop you staining the mattress if you wet yourself. I'm not sure what time it was exactly – the glow-in-the-dark clock in Ricky's room had stopped – but at that point Esther must have been missing for about eight hours. Fear for my friend had grown in the small, strange room. I wriggled and shifted, unable to get comfortable, sweating and listening to the crinkling sound my movements made. On an old cot mattress on the floor, Ricky kicked and mewled in his sleep. The room smelled faintly of wee.

The door opened. A wedge of light. Mum.

My voice came out cracked. 'Why don't we go home, Mum? We can sleep there.'

She closed the door, stepping out of her jeans and into the bed, arranging her body around mine. 'I'm tired, Bup,' she whispered back. 'We'll go home in the morning.' She pulled me close to her.

'Did you find Esther?'

'Mmmmm.'

Later, Mum would swear that she did not say yes. But she did not say no, because in that moment I was convinced they'd found Esther.

The world had shifted, only to click surely back into place. My friend would be in trouble, wouldn't be allowed to go out for a while, probably couldn't come over on Sunday like I'd hoped she would, but she'd be at school on Monday.

I wanted to ask where they'd found Esther, but Mum was already breathing heavily. The room was hot and airless. I hugged Mum, pressing my head against her chest, listening to her heartbeat. Sleep seemed impossible with another body so close. Pulling up my shirt, I pressed my back against the plaster wall, which radiated coolness. The regular rhythm of Mum's breath in my face made it hard to fully relax. When she sucked air in, I held my own breath, waiting for her to breathe out. As hard as I tried, I couldn't get our breathing to sync. I tried inhaling when she exhaled, but it made my lungs hurt. Turning to face the wall, I stretched along it, reaching my fingers into a fresh cool spot at the top of the mattress.

When I woke, the top sheet was wrapped around my legs. Light seeped through the thin curtains of Ricky's room.

'Mum,' I said.

Her eyes shot open and she hurled herself into a sitting position. 'What is it?'

'Did you know that llamas sleep standing up?'

The digital watch on Mum's wrist beeped. She was out of bed and pulling on her jeans.

'C'mon, kiddo, we'd better get going.'

'Did you know that the scientific species name for llamas is *Lama glama*?' I said, scooting off the end of the bed. Ricky wasn't on his mattress on the floor.

'Is that so?' Mum's tone said she wasn't listening.

I'd told Esther that same fact the day before. She'd said that my species name would be *Ronnie gronnie*. I said if I was *Ronnie gronnie* then she was *Esther gesther*.

Mum left the room. I pulled on my pants and hurried to catch up.


Everyone else in the house was up. Uncle Peter had left for work already, but all my cousins were either in the lounge room or the kitchen.

'Where's Aunty Shelly?' I asked Ricky, who was sitting at the kitchen table.

'She stayed at Esther's place last night,' he said. He lisped, so it sounded like *Ethter*.

The house relaxed around me.

Mum was on the phone near the kettle. She spoke in a low voice, and I tried to listen. There were Homebrand Coco Pops *and* Froot Loops out on the bench. Knowing my aunt wasn't around opened up the possibilities.

Ricky raised a freckled hand to get my mum's attention. 'Aunty Evelyn, Ronnie is having both kinds of cereal.'

'Veronica.' There was a warning tone in her voice.

Mum turned away, listening to whoever was on the other end of the phone. She leaned against the kitchen counter. Her cup of tea, with its picture of a fat koala wearing an Australian flag vest, sat next to her on the counter.

The milk left in the bowl after I'd eaten the cereal was a browny purply green.

'Aren't you going to drink that?' asked Paul, one of the older boys.

'I never drink the milk,' I said.

He leaned over and grabbed my bowl, lifted it to his mouth and tipped his head back. A thin trickle of green milk ran from the side of his mouth and into his shoulder-length red hair.

'Ah.' He smacked his lips.

'Gross,' I said.

Mum hung up the phone.

'We're going to the school this morning,' Mum said, looking at me.

'But it's Saturday,' I said.

Paul leaned forward in his seat, like he would have loved nothing more than to repeat my words back to me.

'The detectives looking for Esther will be there; they want to talk to you about what you told Mack,' Mum said.

'But you said they found her.' I could hear the panic in my own voice.

Mum's face scrunched up, like she'd banged her knee. 'No, sweetheart. We didn't.'

The presence of other people in the room was the only thing that stopped me from screaming and stomping my feet. I was angry at myself, at her, at my dumb cousins who were all just sitting there with their stupid sleepy expressions. Something spread in my gut, like red cordial spilled onto a library book, steadily soaking through the white pages. Nobody knew where my friend was.

The drive home wasn't long enough for the air conditioning in Mum's car to start blowing cool air. I kept trying to catch Mum's eye. I wanted her to acknowledge what she'd done, to say sorry, but we drove in silence.

When we got home, there wasn't time to discuss what I had or hadn't heard.

'Can't Officer Macintyre tell them what I said yesterday?' I asked as Mum hurried me into my bedroom to change out of yesterday's clothes.

She fussed around picking out something for me to wear. 'They need to hear it directly from you,' she said in her *and that's enough of that* voice, throwing a shirt onto the bed. Flea, curled in a ball in the scrunched-up duvet, raised his head to give Mum a disgruntled look, then jumped from the bed and stalked out my bedroom door.

The shirt was short-sleeved with buttons down the front. Little metallic threads were woven through a pink and lime green plaid.

'I don't want to wear that,' I said.

'The last thing I need is them thinking I don't look after you properly.' Mum sat behind me, pulling my hair into a high, tight ponytail.

The bristles of the hairbrush scraped against my scalp. Yelping would only make it worse, so I held myself still until she was finished.

When we walked out to the car, Mum was still wearing what she'd had on the day before: jeans and a t-shirt, a man's long-sleeved shirt thrown over the top. I opened the passenger door and Mum said my name.

She ducked to look at me through the open car doors. 'You've got to tell them the truth, Ronnie. The only way you'll get in trouble is if you don't tell the truth.'

The interview was in Mrs Worsell's office. I'd only been in there once before, when I'd dared Esther to write a rude word on the blackboard one recess. She'd flicked an eyebrow and said if it was such a good idea, why didn't I go first. Mrs Rodriguez had guessed it was me because of the chalk on my sports shorts.

A woman sat in the principal's chair. She had short hair that made her look like a boy and peered at her paperwork through glasses with rectangular black frames. I would have liked glasses, but Mum said I didn't need them. The woman smiled at me and said the day and time into a tape recorder on the table. She had a flat chest, like Mum. She nodded at my mum as she said my name and Mum's name and that she was present for the interview. There was a man in the corner, in similar clothes to the woman – dark pants, a white shirt with a collar. The only difference was he was wearing a tie. He didn't speak or look at me.

'Hello, Veronica,' the woman said.

'Hello.'

It didn't feel like I could tell this woman to call me Ronnie. I looked at Mum and she smiled at me.

'I'm Detective Sergeant Sarah Michaels, but you can call me Sarah. I was hoping I could ask you some questions. Before I do that, though, I just need to check: do you know what a lie is?'

I nodded. It was a stupid question.

'You and your mum drove here today, is that correct?'

I nodded.

'So if I said you walked here today, that would be a lie, wouldn't it?'

'Yes.'

'And if I asked you tomorrow how you got here, what would you say?'

'That I came by car?'

'What about if you couldn't remember?'

'What?'

'If you couldn't remember how you got here, what would you do?'

'I'd ask Mum.' Was this woman simple?

'I'm just saying, you don't have to give an answer if you don't remember. You can just say, *I don't remember.*'

'Oh, okay.'

'So, I hear Esther is your best friend.' When I didn't reply she continued, 'What's she like?'

'She's really funny.' I looked the woman straight in the eye. She needed to know this important thing about Esther.

'Why is she funny?'

'She can do voices and she jumps around and squirms at you until you laugh.'

'She sounds great,' the detective said.

I nodded. 'She is.'

'Did Esther ever talk about her mum and dad?' she asked.

'Yeah.'

'What did she say about them?'

'Um, just normal stuff. Her mum worries about her a lot.'

'What does Esther's mum worry about?'

'Everything,' I said.

'What about her dad?'

'He doesn't worry as much, but he yells a lot more than her mum.'

'What does he yell about?'

'Esther forgets stuff, or she doesn't hear you the first time. That makes him angry sometimes.' I paused. I looked at my mum, who was looking at the detective. 'Esther's dad comes into the changing room at the pool and yells at us when we're taking too long,' I said.

'He comes into the girls' change room?' she asked.

'Uh-huh. Last time, one of the mothers told him to leave and he was cranky about it.'

The woman was writing something down in her notebook.

'Did you know that when llamas fight, they spit at each other?' I said. 'That's how they sort out their problems. Except I can't figure out how you *win* a spitting fight.'

'No,' she said. 'I didn't know that.'

I'd wanted to tell the detective more about Esther. That her parents worried too much about her, not seeing that she could, in fact, do anything. Of course, I couldn't have said I sometimes pretended that Esther's dad was *my* father when he drove us to and from swimming.

The way he called me 'llama girl' and was always delighted when I had a new llama fact to tell him. Even his occasional silences and his anger – that strange, male phenomenon – weren't scary so much as intriguing.

One car ride home, when Esther's dad was annoyed that she'd taken so long to come out of the changing rooms, I'd enjoyed playing the role of the obedient daughter, sent in to speed Esther along. I hadn't got across to the police how exciting it had been when he'd come in after me. He'd stood there, in the pool changing room, his big hairy toes spilling out of his thongs, the white skin of an ankle that was usually hidden inside a work boot. The man-ness of him was strange. I didn't quite know what to make of that.

It was another thing that made Esther a little bit magical – that she could be the source of all this fuss.

After the interview, Mum made me wait outside. It wasn't long before the detective walked Mum back out onto the verandah. When she'd gone back into the office, Mum produced a packet of Twisties from her bag.

'I know this must all be pretty scary, Bup,' she said.

We walked to the car and I settled into the passenger seat. The car took a few goes to start.

'Bloody thing,' Mum said, smiling at me. 'Lucky we've already got that Lamborghini on order.'

Mum'd been saying she had a Lamborghini on order since I was young enough to believe it.

As the engine spluttered into life, all I could think about was all the things Esther and I were supposed to do together. We wanted to be able to swim the whole length of the pool on one breath by the end of the summer. We wanted to find out where Mrs Rodriguez's husband had gone. We had a plan to free the motel dog which you could always see from the highway, looking skinny and sad, and then we would somehow convince Esther's parents to let her keep it. Because it would be happier with them. Because she'd always wanted a pet of her own. Every time we passed the motel Esther would say, *That poor dog*. And, *We're going to fix that man*. The motel owner seemed to know what we were thinking and always kept a beady eye on us, so we didn't know when we would get our next opportunity. But we were biding our time. We were going to go to high school together the next year – which was a little less exciting than it could have been because we would still be going to the same place, although some of our classmates would be getting the bus to go to the big high school in Rhodes – but we would get to use the science labs and have free periods, and at least Esther and I would have each other. And maybe Lewis, too; we hadn't been able to find out yet which high school Lewis's parents were sending him to. The main thing was that Esther and I would be together, and we *would* cross the pool in one go and we *were* going to free that dog and together we would be unstoppable, always.

As Mum drove, I took my time biting each Twistie in half, feeling the craggy surface with my tongue. I picked up a big one, shaped like a caveman's club, covered in fine orange dust that came off on my fingers. I bit it in two and the dust pushed its way into my gums. In that moment, I forgave Mum for what she had or hadn't said in the darkness of Ricky's bedroom. I ate the Twisties one by one, and certainty filled my belly. Esther would turn up any minute. They didn't know her like I did.

Mum took me with her to her shift at the IGA. She wanted, in her words, *a constant visual*. This meant I had to sit on the bench just outside the supermarket, so Mum could see the back of my head from the counter.

Her boss muttered darkly to himself when he saw me.

I didn't like the way men treated my mum. They smiled at her too much, or they talked to her like she was a little kid.

I had an animal facts book with me. Mum had bought it after I showed her the Book Club catalogue and pestered her for weeks. It turned out that there was only one page of llama facts and I already knew all but one of them. The back of my legs sweated and stuck to the bench.

I got up and wandered into the IGA.

'Llamas are pregnant for three hundred and fifty days,' I said.

Mum looked over from the shelf she was stacking. 'Ugh,' she said. 'Seems unfair.'

When my mum was pregnant with me, we lived with my aunty Kath in Victoria – *because she had air conditioning*, Mum always said. She made it sound like that was the only reason she left Durton, but I suspected it was more complicated than that. Sometimes, I thought that my dad must be from Melbourne. There were so many people there that the chances seemed good. We came back to Durton when I was just a year old.

Mum's boss walked past me. He was a big man whose belly sagged over his belt buckle. When he reached for something on an upper shelf you could see a bronze eagle. I wondered if the tips of its wings ever stabbed his fat stomach. If he were my dad, I'd have to leave town.

'You better wait outside. I'll be on my break soon,' Mum said.

I went back to the bench.

'Mum, this is boring,' I said when she came out a while later.

'I know, Bup. I'd take you to your cousins', but your uncle has his hands full. Aunty Shelly is helping out Esther's mum.'

If Pop were still alive, Mum would have taken me there, but his funeral had been in September. His golden retriever Lola had died two days after he did. They were very alike, Pop and Lola. They both smelled like tomato sauce.

'I don't want to stay here,' I said. 'It's too hot.'

She handed me a Bubble O'Bill and I pounced on it, tearing off the silky plastic wrapper to reveal the bubblegum nose beneath. They'd poured the ice cream badly, and the pink and brown lines of the cowboy's face were warped. The bullet hole in his hat was in the right place, at least.

'Listen, I'm going to run you home, okay? But you have to promise me you'll stay home and keep the door locked. You can turn the fan on.'

I nodded eagerly, sucking on the blue gumball from my ice cream. I was sick of the bench.

When we got home Mum kissed me goodbye and I let myself into the house. I walked into the main room. There were still apples in the bowl, the placemats still sat in a pile at the end of the dining table. Flea was curled up on one of the chairs. I called to him, making small *tsk tsk tsk* sounds. He jumped off the chair and stalked past me, his orange tail feathering the air. I wanted it too badly.

I hurled myself onto our overstuffed couch.

Esther's house was better than ours. Her parents owned the house they lived in. Our place was *subsidised housing* I found out when snooping through a stack of papers on the kitchen counter; I'd had to look up what that meant. The clock on the wall showed it was just after twelve thirty. The fan whirled overhead. It was slightly off balance, so it swung a little. All it did was move the hot air around. I was still cranky with Mum for telling me they'd found Esther. But I also knew if something had happened to my friend, I would feel it. My fingers would tingle, my nose would itch.

My mind cycled through all the places she might be.

And then I sat up abruptly. I couldn't believe I hadn't thought to check before.

Hadn't we left each other notes there all last summer? There would be a note and it would say where Esther was. I needed to go. Right now. I grabbed my schoolbag and threw in my water bottle and a mini Bounty bar.

I walked for so long, I worried I'd missed the spot. The long grass near the creek scratched my legs. But then the familiar stump appeared, perched on a high sandy bank in the middle of the water. I tried to jump the shallow channel of slow-moving creek water, but didn't clear it. One of my runners was soaked through. The ice-cream container was there, under the leaves we'd put over it, covered in the crumbled insides of the tree. Inside were things that only Esther and I knew about. It was very clear to me, then, what would happen. There'd be a note from her – she'd be waiting nearby somewhere – and we'd head home together, and her parents would buy us fish and chips and we'd be allowed a can of Sunkist each and everything would be okay. My mum would come over with Neapolitan ice cream and I'd eat only the chocolate and strawberry.

But there was no note. There were two halves of a pendant designed to be worn on two different necklaces. We had called them our 'Befri Stends' pendants – because that's what the left and right ones spelled when apart, the rainbow letters stacked on top of each other. I had BEFRI and Esther had STENDS. For a long time, we had taken to saying things like, *You know you're my Befri Stend, right?*, writing *Befri Stends for life* in elaborate handwriting on our notes to each other. Under the pendant halves was a drawing of a pirate I'd done for Esther. She didn't say anything, but I knew she could tell I'd traced. In the container there were also two Pokémon cards: a Jigglypuff and a Ponyta. I didn't say it out loud, but I asked the contents, *Where are you, Esther?*

I felt in my pocket for something, anything, to leave so Esther would know to write a note. She'd guess I wanted to know where she was, that I missed her. There was nothing in my pocket, but right at the bottom of my bag there was a packet of Tiny Teddies. The white packaging stood out against the blue plastic of the container, which I sealed tight and put back in the stump – she couldn't miss it. I walked away to a spot where I could sit comfortably. Sitting and watching was like staring at the toaster after you've pushed the bread down. Esther was sure to pop up.

The creek was silent except for the rustle of leaves. It sounded like someone crinkling and smoothing a Roll-Up packet over and over. I could hear the heat, a low humming sound that filled my whole body the way hot Milo fills a mug. I took the Bounty out of my bag and ate it. Once, Mum had taken a picture of Esther and me standing in our swimmers in our backyard. Esther was looking away, at something behind Mum. I was giving the camera my best grin, so wide it looked painful. Our bodies were turned in towards each other, hair wet and stuck to our heads. Esther's long skinny arms and legs and my chubby ones. Thinking of the photo, I could almost feel her beside me. Then the image of Esther's ear swam into focus, the ridge of skin inside of it that formed the outline of another, smaller, paler ear. The way she would laugh if I blew in it when her head was turned to the side, perhaps lying on the floor, our legs in the air.

I was suddenly aware that I'd been sitting there for a while. What time was it? I ran towards the creek bank. It'd be faster if I jogged back along the side of the creek. My back felt damp under my schoolbag. I looked behind me to the stump, part of me still waiting to see if Esther would step out from behind it. There was nothing and I scrabbled up the bank. A bird flew up to my right with a flap of wings that sounded like someone throwing a fat stack of papers on the ground. Sweat poured down my back as I jogged through the trees. I was late.

As soon as I walked in our side gate, I knew I was in trouble. Mum was sitting on the back step, smoking a cigarette. She quit smoking when I started primary school. She was staring at our trampoline which stood, drooping and rusting, in a dusty patch in the middle of our yard. Flea sat on the step to the outdoor laundry, tail twitching. My uncle Peter appeared behind Mum, screen door slamming shut behind him, the cordless phone held to his ear. Mum looked up and saw me. She sprang to her feet, throwing her cigarette down on the concrete. Uncle Peter said something into the receiver then hung up.

Mum ran down the path, Uncle Peter following her.

'Veronica Elizabeth, where the *hell* have you been?'

'She's alright, Ev,' Uncle Peter said.

He put a hand on Mum's shoulder, to slow her maybe, but Mum lurched forward, hugging me so hard we fell over, tipping into the dead grass on one side of the path.

'I just went for a walk,' I said.

'Don't you *ever* do that to me again!' Mum barked. 'We agreed you would *stay at home*.' We were on our knees and she had me by the shoulders.

She pressed her face into my t-shirt.

'She's alright, Ev,' Uncle Peter said again. 'She's alright.'

Uncle Peter kneeled down and put a hand on my head and the other hand back on Mum's shoulder.

'Everything's fine, Ev. She's fine.' My uncle raised his ginger eyebrows and smiled at me over Mum's shoulder. I knew he wouldn't let her go too hard on me.

'Morning, love.' Mum ruffled my hair as she put the milk down in front of me. Sunday morning, in our kitchen.

My Mini Wheats tinkled as they hit the bowl. I poured in milk and watched as the pale parcels floated above the milk line, tapping them with the back of my spoon so they would absorb some of the liquid and sink to the bottom. Flea threaded through the legs of the chair, a furry shark. The ginger rail of his back arched away from me when I bent to pat him, so I brushed fuzzy air.

'You know I love you more than biscuits, right?' Mum was looking at me sloppily across the table.

'I'm sorry about yesterday,' I said.

The paste from the inside of one of the wheat parcels was stuck on a back molar. It was supposed to be blackberry flavour, though I'd never eaten a blackberry, so I couldn't tell if it tasted like one.

'I know, Bup,' Mum said, pouring milk into her cup of tea.

'Will I come to work with you today?' I was not looking forward to another day on the bench, but I figured I deserved it.

'No. Uncle Peter called this morning. He's taken a few days off and asked if you'd like to go to the pool with the cousins today.'

'Cool. Will Aunty Shelly be there?'

'No, she's still at Esther's place. Not that it should matter if she was there; she's family, Bup. And I need you to behave today.'

'Promise.' I shovelled the cereal into my mouth before the parcels got too soft.

Mum smiled at me. It had been a while since I tried my luck, and I decided to go for it. 'Mum, will you tell me who my dad is?'

It was a risk, asking hot on the heels of being in so much trouble, but maybe her defences would be down.

She sighed. 'I've told you, Bup, he's no-one. No-one you need to worry about.' She stood up and walked into the kitchen, and the conversation was over.


Mum dropped me off at Uncle Peter's, saying she'd pick me up from the pool after work so he didn't have to go out of his way. I sat on the brown corduroy couch in the living room. It took a long time to get everyone ready. Mum had already been at work for a couple of hours by the time we left for the pool.

Uncle Peter let me sit in the front seat of their big, green van. I could hear my older cousins complaining in the back as I buckled my seatbelt.

Uncle Peter winked at me and said, 'The boss don't like it when I take time off like this, but stuff 'im!'

When I didn't say anything, he said, 'You gave your mum quite a scare yesterday.'

I nodded.

'Quiet today, huh?' he said. 'That's not like you!'

He started to tickle me. I tried to stare him down, but he knew about the tickly bit on my left side and I dissolved into laughter despite myself.

He smiled. 'That's better.'


I trailed behind the older boys as we entered the squat brick building that housed the pool canteen. The wife of the old man who did the swimming lessons took my two-dollar coin and waved me through the turnstile. I tried to remember a time when I'd come to the pool without Esther, and I couldn't. Uncle Peter set up camp on the far side, under the trees. He flapped his towel out, following it with his eye as it sailed to the ground. The cousins flicked their towels out around him, squawking at each other. I slipped into the water and swam to the middle of the pool, which was too deep for the younger cousins and out of range of the older ones, who preferred the deep end.

I practised moving through the water like a dolphin, clenching my legs together and thrusting them up and down. Esther had always been better at it than me. After a while I let my legs splay out and just dived for the bottom and corked back up again, feeling the air in my lungs come out my nose in a great *whoosh*. Lewis and I never went to the pool with each other. Once, he'd come over and played UNO with Esther and me. It'd been less exciting to have Lewis in my room than I'd imagined. I thought the fact we hadn't become closer had something to do with the intensity of our feelings for each other, the way it's uncomfortable to stand too close to a bonfire. But it was difficult, when I was *with* him, to be sure of the unique and unshakeable connection that I was otherwise a hundred per cent certain we shared. That afternoon he'd told us that we played the wrong rules for UNO and accused me of cheating. It'd taken an entire recess the following day for me to forgive him. Not that he'd apologised; he wasn't like that. Instead, he'd noticed my silence and asked me questions, so I knew he was sorry.

I moved up and down in the water, bursting through the surface, wishing Esther or Lewis were there to see me. I thought about the way, in a llama herd, a llama's spot in the group can change at any time. They have little fights that move them up or down in the social order. Sometimes, I worried because Lewis could make Esther double over with laughter. He liked to make jokes at my expense, which I took as a sign of intimacy, proof of our bond. Sometimes it hurt when Esther would laugh, but I could afford to be generous because it was Lewis who was the addition, the extra. I was pretty sure I loved him.

He made me feel tingly – they both did, Lewis and Esther, but Lewis was a *boy*. I reasoned I could be the bigger person, let him make fun of me and get away with it.

I heard Uncle Peter calling me over for lunch. He wore baggy swimming shorts, his thighs milk-white above the knee. Dripping on the picnic rug, I nibbled my Vegemite and cheese sandwich. As soon as I was done, I rushed back into the water.

I loved the way all the noises of the pool – the shrieking children, the announcements over the loudspeaker about not running near the edge – were gobbled up when you put your head under. And you couldn't smell the chlorine when you were *in* the water. I knew crocodiles had two sets of eyelids – they kept one set closed to stop water going in their eyes when they went under. Maybe my nostrils had a lid? A thin bit that stopped all the water rushing in? I kicked off the tiles to float on my back, my eyes closed against the sun, my ears in the water.

Uncle Peter waved at me from the side of the pool.

'Your mum'll be here, Ronnie,' he said, one hand on his hips, the other rubbing his goatee.

Still dripping, I emerged through the turnstile and spotted Mum's red car parked on the other side of the street.

'Hop in, Bup.' Her mouth was set in a line as I opened the passenger door.

The second my seatbelt was clipped into place she pulled away from the kerb. 'There's something we need to talk about.'

As ridiculous as it sounds, my first thought was of my traced llama drawing. The familiar pang of bad conscience hit me; I wasn't a good person like other people were. I had tried to be special when I was not, and my mum knew.

'Esther's great-uncle came into the store today. He told me that they've arrested Esther's father.' Both of Mum's hands gripped the wheel as she turned onto the main street.

My belly felt like when you try to slide one thing out of the pots and pans cupboard and everything tumbles out at once.

'Why?' I pictured Detective Sergeant Michaels and her partner in their business shirts.

'Because of Esther. Because they haven't found Esther and they think he knows what happened to her.'

'They think he knows where she is?'

Mum paused before answering. 'Yes.' She said the word like it deserved special attention.

Part of being a child is not thinking about how the adults in your life get their information. If she'd told me then *why* Steven Bianchi had been arrested, maybe things would have been different.

I remember feeling very calm. I knew, of course, that they were wrong about Steven. He loved Esther as much as I did. It made sense to me that Mum would believe whatever false thing had been said about him. She was always jumping to conclusions about men. There was that time she'd yelled at the lollipop man, who was just helping me tie my shoelace. The whole school had seen.

We drove the rest of the way home in silence. Mum was wearing a faded black t-shirt from Kmart. The shoulders had a haze of orange over them from drying in the sun for too long. She smelled like Mum, the peculiar mix of her deodorant and milky tea and Mint Slices. She parked in the driveway and we sat in the car. The heat seeped in even though the engine was running and the air conditioning was on. I didn't want to get out. It felt as if something would be over when my feet touched the ground.

Mum turned in her seat. She looked me in the eye so I would know it was important. 'I know you love her, Bup. I know she's your best friend. I know this shouldn't be happening. But I'm your mother and it's my job to keep you safe. Some people will think that you're too young for me to be telling you this, but I think you're old enough to know. They've arrested Steven because . . . because they think he may have done something bad to Esther.'

An image of Esther that time when we went ten-pin bowling and she threw the ball so hard it jumped over the bumper bars and knocked down pins in the wrong lane. She'd got this look on her face, like she'd done something naughty, but she was also kind of proud. She'd covered her mouth with her hands and laughed.

'I have to ask, Ronnie . . .' Mum was staring at me intently. 'Has Esther's dad ever done something that made you feel . . . uncomfortable? Something you didn't like?'

'Mum! No!' I shook my head vigorously.

'Okay, Bup. I had to ask.'

'Do they . . .' I couldn't finish the question. Mum waited for me to try again. 'Do they know where she is?'

'No. That's what they're trying to find out.'

I started to cry. They were tears of relief. They didn't know where she was and that meant she was still alive. Mum was wrong about Steven; they all were.

Mum held me while I cried. She smoothed my hair and let me drip snot all over her shirt and at one point we were rocking from side to side. Mum must have used a free hand to turn the key in the ignition, because the engine shuddered off. We stayed there, still rocking, until the heat in the car became unbearable.

The police were looking for Esther and they hadn't found her. And now Steven was in trouble. It struck me that I had to speak to Lewis on Monday. He could help me come up with a better plan. My trip to the creek had been an unfortunate blip, but no-one knew Esther better than I did. In that hot car I understood, with my whole body, that I'd have to be the one to bring her home.

# SARAH

Saturday, 1 December 2001

The owner of the Horse and Cane Motel kept his dog chained up behind the rooms – a kelpie the colour of an old car left to rust. Detective Sergeant Sarah Michaels had brought the animal some of the dry petrol-station muffin she hadn't managed to choke down for breakfast. The dog had a narrow, sand-coloured face and a roiling, restless energy. The chain around its neck was thick and showed black where the plating had worn off. It wolfed the muffin down but took several steps back when it was done eating. It had the low-eyed wariness of an animal used to a swift kick for no reason. Its eyes followed Sarah as she sat going over the day's interview schedule. The air was dry. The yellow scrub and pastel orange dirt stretched out from the motel verandah, thrown into relief by a completely blue sky. No sound but the clinking of the dog's chain.

Her mobile rang.

'Plenty of your girl's skin and hair,' said the forensics person on the other end of the phone, a woman Sarah hadn't worked with before.

'Well, it is her father's car. Any blood?'

'Nothing like that. We've been here overnight and there's no blood in either car.'

'What about the shoe?' Sarah asked.

'No blood there either. Of course, her DNA was all over it. We did find a significant amount of DNA from someone else, though.'

'A relative?'

'No, that's the one thing we can be sure of. Whoever it is, they aren't a blood relative of Esther Bianchi. But that's all I can tell you, at this stage.'

'And have you cross-checked Esther Bianchi's sample with Steven Bianchi's? Are we sure he's actually her father?'

The woman sighed. 'That wasn't one of the tests I was asked to do. I was only asked to search for a blood-relation match on the shoe.'

'But you have Mr Bianchi's sample, yes? When can it be processed? I'd like that report as soon as possible.'

The woman exhaled loudly and asked Sarah to hold the line. Sarah heard the tapping of computer keys. The pathologists and technicians on the crime shows Amira liked were always much more proactive than they were in real life.

'I've logged it,' the woman said, and hung up.

The dog wandered towards her. It stood at the end of its chain and growled. Something in its lowered head told her they were in for a stinking hot day.

Sarah leaned against the side of the white Commodore, waiting for Smithy to emerge from his motel room; they were heading to the school to do their interviews. She'd been up for hours already, making calls, working through her list. She'd never trusted the hunches and superstitions of the older male cops she worked with. She liked to get her thoughts down on paper: seeing the next steps laid out in a notebook soothed her. She jotted a reminder to make a follow-up phone call about Steven Bianchi's DNA sample.

The look of hope on Constance Bianchi's face from the night before kept pushing its way to the front of Sarah's thoughts. 'It's hers,' Constance had said, when Sarah showed her the shoe, once Steven was safely in the back of the car. Constance had cradled it through the plastic as if her daughter might materialise: a genie from an odd-shaped bottle.

Sarah rocked her feet on the bitumen. Her arm had reached the itchy stage of sunburn. It would start to peel soon. She buttoned the sleeve closed and resisted the urge to scratch. She had no idea what was taking Smithy so long.

Sarah's training sergeant used to say, *You can untuck something when it's tucked, but you can't unfuck something when it's fucked.* It meant you should be ready to untuck an idea, not keep it folded in because it's neat and convenient, but there are certain things you only get to do once. Untucked minds, unfucked events – that's what he'd told them to shoot for. Sarah thought of Amira. *You're so afraid all the time*, Amira had said. *It's doing things to you, this job.* But Amira was the one who wouldn't tell her parents about Sarah. How was that for fear? *They won't get it. There's no point. Don't push.* In the end that was all they fought about, work and parents.

Smithy appeared, raising a hand to Sarah in apology before easing himself into the driver's seat. His nose was swollen from the night before, though he'd taken the bandage off already. Steven's outburst had bought them some time – they could hold him now. Not for the first time, Sarah thought about asking Smithy what he'd said to Steven. And not for the first time, she figured it would be better if she didn't know.

As Sarah got into the car, Smithy was buckling his seatbelt. She followed suit. Some police had a laissez-faire attitude to seatbelts, but both of them had spent time on road patrol: Sarah on her first assignment out of the academy, and Smithy before he'd left Western Australia. They'd both seen lots of people who were wearing them but had died anyway – a seatbelt wasn't going to help you if you slammed into a tree at a hundred kilometres an hour, Sarah knew that better than most – but it was the ones without a seatbelt who ended up strewn along the roadside. If she had to die, she wanted it to be in one piece. A nice bit of blunt trauma to the head, so you went out before you knew what was happening.

Lukewarm air puffed through the black plastic vents in the dash.

Sarah turned her head to check the road was clear as Smithy pulled onto the highway. 'We'll never get a conviction with just the shoe,' she said, eager to air the thoughts that had been bouncing around her head since she'd woken at four that morning. 'No jury is going to charge him without the body.'

'Kinouac'll be under a lot of pressure with this case,' Smithy replied. 'The newspaper articles will be out today.'

As if to punctuate his point, Sarah spied a television crew outside the school. A blonde woman was speaking into a microphone, the front gate of the school in shot. Sydney reporters had arrived. You could never win, with the media. Police were punished when things went badly and rewarded with silence when they went well.

She imagined her superior sitting in his office, newspapers laid out in front of him. 'You'd think people would get sick of this stuff,' she said.

'It's catching, don't you think?' Smithy said, his eyes fixed on the road.

'What?'

'Little girls that go missing. Their picture ends up in the lap of some sick fuck in his lounge room who gets the idea that a girl is something you can pick up. If the newspapers let us bloody get on with it, shit like this wouldn't happen.'

Sarah knew Smithy kept up with the papers and the news reports. It was one of the reasons she didn't have to.

'You think so?' she asked.

'Nah, maybe not. There'll always be sick fucks. I mean, *he's* her dad. But they don't help, these reporters. It just fuels the fascination.'

'We still can't be sure Steven did it.'

Smithy blew air through his nose, the same way Amira did when Sarah picked a boring movie.

When Smithy and Sarah arrived at the school, the principal was waiting for them. She was their first interview of the day. They covered the same ground they had the day before on the phone, this time for the record.

'What can you tell me about Veronica Thompson?' Sarah asked, once they'd discussed Esther, who was *a good kid, if a little wild.*

'Well, she's a good kid too. Bit of a know-it-all. Esther's best friend. She lives with her mother, Evelyn Thompson.'

'Who's Veronica's father?' That part of Veronica's school file had been left blank.

'Nobody knows. Evelyn left town without saying anything, and when she came back, Ronnie was a year old. Everyone's always called her Ronnie. Even I call her that, I confess.'

She paused and Sarah could see her thinking of the word 'confess' and why she'd used it. Talking to a cop was a bit like talking on a phone line that repeats back to you what you've just said: everything amplified and strange.

'Is Evelyn seeing anyone now?' Sarah asked.

'No. If she were, we'd know.' Noticing Sarah's raised eyebrow, the principal continued, 'I mean, it's a small town.'

'Anything else we should know?' Sarah asked.

The principal shook her head.

Veronica Thompson was a chubby kid with aggressively red hair that wisped free despite an obvious attempt to wrangle it into a neat ponytail. Her mother was slim, in jeans and a thin white t-shirt, an unbuttoned man's flannel shirt thrown over the top. Sarah couldn't help but notice that she wasn't wearing a bra. Her hair was like her daughter's, only with the saturation turned down. Small and strong-looking, there was something delicate about her, like an ice skater. She kept her chin tucked in and her gaze roved over the room, scanning for threats. Sarah could tell her eyes would be different colours in different light. The first woman Sarah had loved had eyes like that. She winced inwardly. This was not the time to be perving on the mother of an interviewee. She brought her mind back to the task at hand. They were conducting the interviews in Mrs Worsell's office, one of the few rooms in the school with air conditioning. It smelled like those hard lollies that you bought in round tins at the chemist. Sarah worked through the day's sequence of events with the girl. Sarah pretended to be confused about what had happened, and Veronica corrected her in the right places. What Veronica said matched with everything she'd already told Mack, and with what the principal had said.

During their interview, Sarah thought of other children she'd spoken to, in other schools. In her days in Child Protection, Sarah often did the initial interview in a classroom. No way for a possible offender to know that the child had been spoken to. *You don't have to tell anyone but your mum that you spoke to the police today. You're not in trouble. You were such a good boy/girl. You're very brave.* She'd been particularly struck by one little boy's grave nod, a child made old before his time, silently assuming another secret. The boy's mother had been white with tension, sitting in a twisted imitation of casualness in the corner of the room, tears streaming silently down her face. There was something about the way Veronica Thompson's mother watched her daughter that brought to mind those other school interviews for Sarah. Evelyn Thompson held herself like

112

someone listening to evidence being read against them in a court-room. She was also clearly a good mum. Veronica's ease when talking to adults was proof enough of that.

At the end of the interview, Evelyn said, 'Bup, why don't you wait outside for a second? I'll be right out.'

Sarah could see Veronica wanted to complain, but Evelyn silenced her with a look. It wasn't angry or aggressive, but the girl hung her head and went outside.

Evelyn turned to Sarah. Evelyn's eyes had settled on hazel, with flecks of gold. Her face was flushed and free of make-up, and freckles dusted her nose and cheeks. She was a full head shorter than Sarah.

'I just hope you're doing everything you can to find Esther. She's Ronnie's world.'

'I can promise we are,' Sarah said. There was the faint smell of talcum powder in the air.

Evelyn held her gaze. 'I hope so.'

Sarah looked over at Smithy, ignored in the corner, trying to hide a tight smile beneath his moustache.

'What do you make of what she said about Steven Bianchi, about him coming into the changing rooms?' Sarah asked.

'Ronnie loves Esther's dad. Poor kid's desperate for a father figure, I guess.' As if she felt like she'd given too much away, Evelyn added, 'I don't think she understood what it sounded like.'

'Have you ever had any concerns about Steven Bianchi?' Sarah asked.

'Look, I have concerns about most people, when it comes to my kid. But I let him drive Ronnie to the pool because she likes him, and I trust him. That's the truth.'

Of course, Evelyn didn't know yet that Steven Bianchi had been arrested. Sarah was trying to keep that quiet as long as they could.

When Sarah and Evelyn emerged from the air-conditioned room, the heat squeezed, ropy and muscular, like a snake winding around its victim. Sunlight bore down on the verandah, and Sarah was grateful that the long sleeves of her shirt covered her sunburn.

'Thanks for coming in,' Sarah said, nodding to Evelyn, who was trying to smooth her daughter's hair.

The chalky note of talcum powder lingered in the room. Sarah wrote up what Veronica Thompson had said about Steven Bianchi in her notebook and drew a triangle next to it. Sarah's training sergeant always said it was important to have conversations with yourself in writing. *That's what separates us from the animals, our ability to make notes for ourselves, to store information outside our bodies. That's the difference between us and the friggin' apes.* Sarah used triangles because they were easy to see when flicking through pages of notes and because they made her think of conspiracies, of complicated things, hidden from view.

Without a conscious thought, Sarah took her phone from her pocket and stared at the small green screen. She felt the weight of it in her hand and thought again about deleting Amira's number. Even though it would be a largely symbolic act – she had the number memorised – maybe it would shake something loose, set free the part of her mind that kept going back to Amira and brooding over how it had ended.


Once they'd talked to the children Sarah had most wanted to speak to – the girls and teachers who'd been with Esther in the final minutes before she left the school, a boy they'd been told sat with Esther at lunchtime – she checked her notes. *Call Constance Bianchi, provide update.* It had seemed unnecessary to write it down, but now she was glad she had. Sarah prided herself on keeping the family up to date. This was an even higher priority given that Constance's husband was now in custody. Sarah was reminded that she needed to externalise everything. When it was so important that she didn't think she needed to write it down was when things tended to go pear-shaped. In the car, she keyed in the Bianchis' number. The phone was answered instantly.

'Hello, Mrs Bianchi. This is Detective Sergeant Sarah Michaels.'

'Any news?'

Sarah could hear the desperation in the woman's voice.

'Nothing to report, I'm afraid. I'm just calling to check in. Is everything alright?'

'Yes. But . . .'

Sarah braced herself for what was coming. Constance would want to know more about what Steven had said in the interview, and Sarah wasn't allowed to tell her. She was also keen to avoid discussing the moments leading up to the punch.

'I'm sure you've got some questions, Constance,' she began, 'but I would warn you there are certain things I can't discuss with you. The most important thing to say is that we have not yet charged your husband with anything related to your daughter's disappearance –'

'Can you come here?' Constance interrupted. 'To my place? There's something I need to tell you.'

'Of course. We're on our way,' said Sarah, raising her eyebrows at Smithy, who was already adjusting his route.

Constance Bianchi's Toyota had been checked and returned to her. It was standing in the driveway when Sarah and Smithy pulled in.

'Thanks for coming,' said Constance as Sarah and Smithy took a seat in her lounge room.

'It's no problem, Mrs Bianchi.'

'Please, it's just Constance.'

'You said you had something to tell us,' Sarah prompted.

'Yes.' The woman paused, as if searching for the right words. 'You need to speak to Shelly Thompson about my husband. About something he did.'

Sarah and Smithy exchanged glances.

'Can you give us an idea of why we should do that?' Sarah asked the question as gently as possible.

'She's only just left.' Constance looked at Sarah. 'But I think it's something you should know.'

'Was it something that happened on Friday?'

'No. Just speak to her, please.'

'You want us to go there?' Smithy asked.

'I know it sounds silly, but I just couldn't find a way to ask her if it would be okay. It's her story to tell.'

Then why had Constance asked them to come to her? 'Constance, it would really save us some time if you could tell us in your own words,' Sarah said. She was sympathetic, but they had a big to-do list to get through as it was.

It only took Constance a beat to decide.

'When they were kids, Steven was part of a group of boys who . . . who raped Shelly. It was at a party on Steve's uncle's farm. Shelly was in her last year of high school.'

As Sarah gently guided Constance through as many particulars as she could get, she tried to ensure her body language didn't change. She felt it, however: the ripple of excitement that meant they were closer to getting their man.


Sarah used the map Mack had thoughtfully provided to navigate to Shelly Thompson's house.

The house was long and low, made of cheap materials. There was a broad, dry front yard, and a shoe rack by the front door was crowded with shoes of all different sizes. Smithy knocked on the door.

The tall, broad-set woman Sarah recognised from the Bianchi kitchen opened it. She raised a hand to her mouth.

'Is everything okay?'

'There's no news, Mrs Thompson. We were just hoping we could speak to you again.'

'Call me Shelly,' the woman responded, opening the door wider and gesturing for Sarah and Smithy to follow her inside.

The house was dark and, mercifully, cooler than outside.

'Can I offer you a cup of tea?' Shelly asked.

'No, thank you,' said Sarah, answering for both herself and Smithy, who she felt sure would have said yes.

Sarah saw a photo of Shelly and a man who must be her husband, Peter. Going through files she'd realised he and Evelyn were brother and sister, but the resemblance in the photo was striking and immediate, though his hair was a more determined ginger, flaming orange in the photo.

'Where was your husband on the afternoon Esther went missing?'

'I told you: he was home with the bigger kids while I went to go and get Caleb.'

'Is he home at the moment?' Sarah had no way of knowing if a historic rape allegation would be news to Peter Thompson. A thought nagged – she'd meant to check in with Mack about how his interview with Peter had gone.

'No, he's at work. He's doing the Melbourne run. How can I help?'

No sense in beating around the bush. 'Constance Bianchi seemed to think you might have some information that would help in our investigation.'

The woman's entire body stiffened.

When she said nothing, Sarah continued, 'About Steven Bianchi?'

'That's my business,' Shelly said. Sarah was surprised by the vehemence of the words, the end of the sentence almost a hiss. Shelly turned away, as if composing herself. 'I can understand why Constance told you, but it's not good for me. I don't want to go back there. It's not relevant.'

Sarah thought it was relevant. When it came to trial, any instances of sexual violence on Steven Bianchi's record would be kept from the jury, something she found very frustrating. It was like prosecuting someone for shoplifting and not mentioning they'd stolen from the same store a dozen times before. But it mattered when it came to sentencing. It was her job to get the case to that point. And to do that she needed to know as much as she could about Steven.

'Did something happen between you and Steven Bianchi?'

Shelly stood up. 'I'd like you both to leave, please. I just came home to shower and change, and then I'm going back over there to be with Constance.'

Sarah didn't say anything, just held Shelly's gaze.

'Look, I'd do anything if it would help Esther. But it's not good for me to go back there. I've learned that the bloody hard way. And there were never any charges laid. I can't prove anything, alright?'


'I wonder how long ago we're talking?' said Smithy, when they were back inside the car.

Sarah checked her notes. 'Constance said it happened when they were in high school. Steven's younger than Shelly by a few years.'

'We've got to get back to the school for the next batch of interviews,' Smithy said. 'But we're hardly going to leave it at that, are we?'

'We'll push harder if we have to, later.' For Sarah it was enough, for now, that they knew.

\*

After hours of interviews that felt like a waste of time, Sarah and Smithy repaired to the motel for a burger – nowhere else seemed to be open for lunch that late on a Saturday. They speculated as they ate on what to do about Shelly Thompson. 'We'll have to speak to Mrs Bianchi again,' Sarah said. It was expected, as a female officer, that Sarah would be better at talking to kids and women, but she always had to work at it, and she was tired. At least with kids, their lies were usually obvious.

'This is disgusting,' said Smithy, pushing his plate away. The patty was grey, the bun stale. 'We need to solve this thing and get the hell out of here.'

Sarah couldn't have agreed more.

'I forgot to tell you,' Smithy said. 'Remember that colleague of Steven Bianchi's who was off sick? I looked into it, like you asked me. Turns out he really was sick. He checked into hospital at 1 pm that day – a nasty case of food poisoning apparently.'

'Wonder where he picked that up?' Sarah said, throwing down what was left of her burger.

Saturday afternoon, and Esther Bianchi had been missing for twenty-four hours. The Commodore was parked under a line of trees that were the only shade near a dam on the outskirts of town. Sarah had wanted to speak to Steven again straightaway, but Smithy had made the point that it might be good to check in with the diving team, let Esther's father stew a bit longer.

'Any evidence out there is deteriorating by the minute, and they won't transfer Bianchi until tonight,' he'd said, and Sarah had to admit he was right.

Smithy was leaning against a tree now, running his hand over his nose. It was so hot that if she wanted to end her own life, all Sarah would need to do was sit in the car with the windows closed. She'd sat in court, once, while the Government Medical Officer had explained what would have happened to the body of a two-year-old who'd been left in a hot car. It didn't sound like a good way to go. She remembered the GMO had made a joke with the guard on her way out, and the urge to hit her had washed over Sarah.

As hot as it was, Sarah still didn't envy the police divers moving through the dark, murky waters of the dam. The diving team had been at it since the early morning – they'd been to three different properties. With Steven Bianchi on remand, and no confession, Sarah needed them to find something else, anything, that they could add to the shoe. Though what they were most likely to find in this kind of search, Sarah admitted to herself, was a body.

The divers had been in a long time. At least they still had plenty of daylight.

'Visibility must be crap down there,' she said to Smithy.

Smithy turned to look at her.

For a moment, Sarah imagined the press of brown water and focused on the sound of her breathing.

Smithy warmed to her theme. 'And as a bonus, you get to bring up *bits* of people.'

Sarah sometimes thought about what she might have been if she wasn't a cop. She'd met a girl at a job centre she'd been attending while waiting for the next intake into the academy. Sarah's father had just died. She stayed with this girl on her parents' farm on the edge of Canberra. They drank a lot. They stayed up late. Sarah would wake early to the smell of sheep shit and the taste of her own furry mouth. Then she'd sit, hungover, on the verandah and watch her breath in the cold morning air. The girl's parents had a dam on their property, and Sarah would stare at its surface, much like she was doing now. Maybe Sarah could have stayed there, become a farmer. *I'm not interested in dating a cop*, the girl said when they broke up. How many women had said that to Sarah now? She'd lost count.

Ripples formed a ridge in the water, coasting along the surface of the dam before dissipating into its muddy edges. The divers were coming up. Sarah and Smithy moved out of the shade and closer to the shore. The pair – a man and a woman – emerged from the dam, the former sliding his mask from his face. He shook his head when he saw Sarah looking. She noticed he was holding something the size of a thick hardback, wrapped tightly in duct tape.

'We found something interesting,' said the man, holding up the wet package.

He handed it to Sarah. Slivers of shiny black plastic showed through gaps in the tape.

'From the weight, it's definitely drugs,' Sarah said.

'I'd say you're right,' the diver replied.

'It was attached to this.' The female diver held up what looked like a small buoy. Some fishing line was tangled around a rock held in her left hand. 'So someone clearly planned on retrieving it.'

The pair walked past Sarah and rinsed down from a tank and hose in their van. There was a faded tattoo of a trident on the woman's right shoulder blade, bisected by the strap of her swimsuit. Her skin glistened with dam water. Sarah made herself look away.

After Sarah had waved the pair off, Smithy giving them strict instructions to avoid the food at the Horse and Cane and eat somewhere along the highway instead, Sarah assessed the location. The dam couldn't be seen from the road, but wasn't that far from it. This was clearly some kind of drop-off point. A way of moving the drugs between two people without anyone seeing them together.

With nothing more to be learned at the dam, Sarah and Smithy headed back to Mack's station. They were no closer to a resolution than they'd been before the search of the town's dams. All they had was the shoe they'd found in Steven's car. What Shelly Thompson had refused to speak to them about pointed to Steven Bianchi having a violent past, but Sarah wouldn't push for now. Better to keep everyone cooperative for as long as possible. At this stage it was a very real possibility that they'd find nothing else. But the drugs were a development. Could Esther have seen something she wasn't supposed to? She struck Sarah as an inquisitive kid. A scenario played in Sarah's head. Esther walking home alone from school. What would happen if she stumbled across a scene she wasn't meant to see? Would someone kill her to stop her talking? Sarah needed to speak to Mack. Figure out the best way to pursue the drugs angle. Her fear was still not that Esther was dead, but that she was very much alive. Being held somewhere. It was the worst thing Sarah could imagine. And it was always happening in those damn crime shows.

'What are you thinking, boss?' Smithy asked once they were both inside the car.

Sarah turned the engine on so the aircon would start. The sun was starting to set.

'Drugs would be one sure way of making money out here.'

She'd made a small slit in the package with her pocketknife to find the telltale white powder. She was confident that it was speed, and a decent amount of it too. The dam was on a vacant property, so there was no owner to speak to.

'Do you think her father could be involved?' Smithy asked.

'We've got nothing to tie it to him, unless his name and address are somewhere in there.' Sarah tipped her head back to indicate the package, swaddled inside a large plastic evidence bag on the back seat.

'We could make a lot of money with that, on the street,' said Smithy in a low voice.

When she turned to look at him straight on, he laughed.

'I'm just kidding, boss.' He leaned back, a grin pasted on his face. 'God, it's almost too easy with you.'

Sarah's sergeant's words echoed in her head. *You can untuck something when it's tucked, but you can't unfuck something when it's fucked.* She thought of Amira, doing cocaine in front of Sarah at a party at a friend's house, teasing Sarah when she wouldn't try it. Fairy lights in a dark room and the anger roiling inside Sarah, even when all she wanted was for Amira to pull her into a hug, to tell Sarah she loved her. That's all Sarah had wanted by the end: to have Amira hold her.

'Anyway,' Smithy said, 'at least we can grab a decent feed in Rhodes when we drop this off.'

Sarah nodded. As soon as Smithy had done up his seatbelt, they set off. Images of Esther, bound and gagged, whirred in Sarah's mind as she drove. When they reached the main highway and the green and white road sign, Smithy waggled his eyebrows and said, 'All roads lead to Rhodes, eh?' Sarah refused to give him the satisfaction of groaning.

In daylight, Rhodes was surprisingly green, with big open streets. It seemed half-empty to Sarah, diffused with a country slowness, although its size and all the full parking spots suggested it was a bustling centre. Smithy said he'd go on the hunt for some decent takeaway.

'Fine, I can do this solo,' Sarah said.

'It's a pity our team is out west on that twin case,' said the young female officer at the reception desk of the Rhodes command building. 'It's bad luck for your girl.'

She held Sarah's gaze. Female solidarity in a male-dominated workplace, or something more? The woman's eyes were dark and searching.

Sarah straightened her shirt and didn't say anything in reply. The woman wasn't wrong. After logging the drugs into evidence and seeing it transported to the evidence room at the back of the station, she had the young woman double-check Steven Bianchi's record. Not only were there no narcotics convictions, he had no convictions of any kind. Of course, any file from before he was eighteen would be sealed.

'We'd like to speak with Steven Bianchi again before he's transferred,' Sarah said.

'Not a problem.' The young woman was already on her feet, slim calves clad in dark blue cotton drill, tapering into standard-issue black boots.

The second conversation with Steven Bianchi was no more fruitful than the first. Sarah spoke to him alone. The knuckles on his right hand were discoloured, bruised from punching Smithy. He was totally mute for several minutes, speaking only to demand his lawyer be called.

When she'd returned to the car, to find Smithy hunched over a greasy burger wrapper, beetroot-coloured juice running down his wrists, Sarah wrote, *Link to drugs?* next to a page in her notebook that asked, *Connection with the missing twins case?* She wrote the same question at the bottom of each page: *What is the connection with Steven Bianchi?*

'We're looking for a missing girl, not drugs,' Smithy said, making his side of the argument clear in Mack's kitchen that evening, after Sarah had explained to Mack that their new priority would be finding out how the drugs came to be in the dam.

'In a town as small as this, someone must know what's going on,' she said. 'And there's more than a decent chance the two are connected.'

Smithy's arms were crossed and he looked less than impressed to be concentrating their efforts in that area, but it was her investigation.

'You could ask Evelyn Thompson,' Lacey said. Sarah hadn't seen her in the kitchen doorway. Lacey leaned against the frame, one long, tanned arm dangling. 'She's long clean, as far as I know. But there was a time when she wasn't . . .'

Sarah found it hard to picture lithe, self-composed Evelyn Thompson doing drugs. She thought of the oversized flannel Evelyn had worn despite the heat. It would have covered any track marks.

'Any other ideas?' Sarah looked at Smithy and Mack.

Both men shrugged.


Sarah called Evelyn Thompson. It was after 11 pm on a Saturday night, so Sarah was expecting to leave a message on an answering machine, but Evelyn picked up. She said she had to work the next day, but she was home now and her daughter was in bed – if Sarah could come to her, she was happy to answer any questions. Smithy was doing paperwork and it had already been a big day for Mack, who'd been working through a long list of interviews – every bloke in the town who had a car, and you needed one out here – so Sarah went alone. She hoped she wasn't wasting her time.

Evelyn and her daughter lived in a small, dilapidated house. Long, dry grass was just visible in the orange glow of a streetlamp, tickling the edges of a cracked concrete verandah and a huge tree in the front yard. It was so big Sarah wouldn't have guessed it was a fruit tree if she hadn't seen the dropped apricots on the ground, split and stinking sweetly, even though the sun had long set.

'Sorry, it's been a big couple of days,' Evelyn said, clearing the table in the lounge room after she'd let Sarah in. Evelyn dumped the things she'd cleared onto a side table. 'Though, I guess it's only really been a day and a bit since Esther . . .' She trailed off.

Sarah noticed a purple plastic school lunchbox and a tarot deck in the pile of items swept from the table. There was a tapestry hanging in the hallway, visible through the open door. An image of a sun with a nose and mouth, the eyes heavily lidded, small stars twinkling in the woven heavens.

'How's Veronica holding up?' Sarah asked.

'Gave me a bloody heart attack this afternoon,' Evelyn said.

'What happened?'

'Oh, she went looking for Esther. I got home from work and she wasn't here. My brother and I drove around but we must have just missed her. She came home and I could have throttled her.' She looked at Sarah, realising what she'd said.

Sarah smiled. She could smell talcum powder again.

'How's Constance?' Evelyn asked, rubbing her arms as if there were a chill in the small room.

'About as well as can be expected,' Sarah said. 'Have you been to see her?'

'You know, we're forced together all the time, since Ronnie was in kindergarten, but we've never really had a proper conversation. Constance has always been a bit too good for this place. I don't hold it against her, but it would be weird to go over there when we're not really friends.' Evelyn smiled; it brightened her whole face. 'S'pose that's how everyone feels when something like this happens. Like they don't want to intrude. Not really the time to worry about being polite, though, is it?'

'It must be tough, just you and Ronnie,' Sarah said.

'Oh, not as hard as being a copper, I'm sure. People must get really jumpy around you.'

She was deflecting.

'People do act differently,' Sarah conceded.

'And I'm lucky, really. I've got family here.' Evelyn wrapped an arm around herself and shrugged.

'Can I ask who Veronica's father is?' Sarah hadn't wanted to ask the question in front of Veronica.

'No-one she'd want to get to know,' Evelyn said with an air of finality.

'I wouldn't ask if it wasn't helpful for the investigation. A girl is missing.'

'This has nothing to do with that.'

Sarah was a cop. She was used to pissing people off, to asking them questions that made them uncomfortable, but she had to push herself to ask the question of Evelyn. 'Okay. I don't want to be indelicate, Evelyn, but I'm looking into some drugs we found. I was given your name as someone to speak to. We found a commercial quantity of speed.'

Evelyn stood up.

'Do I have to talk to you? Legally, I mean?'

'No,' Sarah said.

'Right,' Evelyn said. 'Then I'd like you to leave.' She walked over to the door; Sarah saw the determination in her face.

Sarah rose from her seat and followed. 'Please, I know this must be difficult. I'm not saying you're involved, I'm just looking for a name, somewhere to start looking.'

'I haven't done drugs since I knew I was pregnant with Ronnie,' Evelyn spat. 'Not once.'

'I'm so sorry if I've upset you.' Sarah placed a hand on her arm.

The air between them crackled. Sarah fought the urge to place her hand on Evelyn's chin, wrap her arm around the smaller woman's waist. It wasn't Evelyn, not specifically. It was the desire to hold, to be held, to feel heat from another person's skin.

Sarah pulled her hand back abruptly.

'Do you have any idea what it takes to get yourself away from that shit?' Evelyn was trembling as she spoke.

'I can imagine.' Sarah really hadn't wanted to upset her. 'You seem like a great mum.'

The anger drained from Evelyn's face.

'I'm sorry.' Sarah couldn't bring herself to feed Evelyn the usual copper speak. 'I wouldn't ask if we didn't really need something to go on.'

'Clint Kennard was the one who got me into drugs, when I was still in high school. Take a look at him.'

The name was familiar. 'He's the father of a boy we interviewed. His son is in Veronica's year, right?'

'Not much gets past you.' Evelyn was being sarcastic, and it didn't suit her. 'He never did the drugs – he likes to be in control too much for that – but I'd be surprised if he's not involved.' Evelyn paused. 'Although, you should know, my drug of choice was always heroin, so I'm not sure about speed.'

Evelyn led the way to the front door.

'I appreciate your frankness,' Sarah said.

'Good night, Detective Sergeant,' Evelyn said, crossing her arms against her chest.

It was unusual for a civilian to remember Sarah's exact title.

Sarah stepped outside and Evelyn closed the door behind her. Sarah heard the lock click. She scrawled the words, *Veronica Thompson – father?* in her notebook. A sweet smell followed her down the overgrown path to the gate.

# WE

Whenever one of our fathers heard something he thought wasn't right, he would say, *That doesn't quite fit through the fence.* Even as children, we started to understand there were great stretches of lifeless, marshy country between what people said and what they thought and did. The best liars were the people who could believe their own bullshit. We became adept at thinking ourselves into particular points of view. We would tell ourselves we hadn't understood what someone meant, that they had been unclear, and we were blameless. We would tell ourselves so hard we believed it. Another of our fathers said, *If you're waiting for somethin' not to have happened, you'll be waiting a long time.*

On Friday night, we'd seen Steven escorted away from his home by the two police officers from somewhere else. The town reacted as you might expect. So many lips flapped it was a wonder the whole of Dirt Town didn't lift into the air, dragonfly-like, and float away. Perhaps we would all be blown so far that we'd touch down near the sea and a new, infinitely more coastal existence could begin for us all. A future where our fathers went fishing and our mothers spent their days with their toes in the cool water of a vast ocean that rushed forward in its eagerness to embrace us.

News of what the cops had found on the abandoned property near the highway wouldn't percolate in the same way, though there would be few people who would have been genuinely surprised if they had heard.

Our fathers drank, or smoked, or abstained, and later we would copy them or swear never to do what they had done. We knew what it meant when the words of our father and his friends began to run together – a whine that chilled us to our bellies – and we stayed out of sight. Our father hated drugs, but drank something savage. On the nights he took it too far, when he got really stuck in, we'd find him in the bathroom, head slung over the edge of the bath, gently singing to himself. The vomit coming in waves. *An awful business, drugs.*

# LEWIS

Saturday, 1 December 2001

No-one thought to tell Lewis Kennard that Esther was missing until Saturday morning, and by then she'd already been missing for hours. Lewis's mother Sophie came into his room after his dad had left for work.

'Darling, Esther Bianchi didn't come home from school yesterday.'

The idea that Estie had not slept in her own bed seemed ridiculous, like coming to school in your pyjamas or wearing face paint in church. Lewis's next thought was of what he and Campbell had seen. The man in the blue-checked shirt. *Estie*. He nearly blurted it all out to his mother, but the thought of Campbell made him stop. Lewis's mother said the police were interviewing kids at the school and they had to go down there. Cold terror gripped him. He needed to talk to Campbell. Normally there was always something firing in his body, but the feeling that coursed through him now was a kind of numbness. He felt like a heavy bell held in a meaty fist, fingers clasped around the ringer so it wouldn't make a sound.

'Lewis, darling, you need to get up. We have to leave right this minute.'

His mother was calling from Simon's bedroom now. Simon had turned fifteen a couple of months earlier but spent his Saturday mornings playing with Duplo. Lewis could hear him banging it against the wall.

The Addison twins were walking out of Mrs Worsell's office with their mother when Lewis and his mother arrived at the school. He'd worried Ronnie might be there. He didn't want to see her, didn't want her to ask him how he was. He worried he might blurt everything out the moment he saw a friendly face. But there was no sign of her. There were two police officers – a man and a woman – in the room when Mrs Worsell waved them in. Lewis had always liked the principal. Sometimes when you walked past her after assembly, she'd fix your hair, winking at you if you looked up at her. Both of the officers wore formal, long-sleeved shirts. He tried to imagine either of them as the parent of one of the kids at school, and couldn't. The man sat in the corner, taking notes. Something about him – the way he looked Lewis's mother up and down, the way he seemed to buzz with energy – reminded Lewis of his father. The woman smiled at his mother and introduced herself as Detective Sergeant Sarah Michaels. She confirmed some details with his mother about his name, address and date of birth.

'Lewis is eleven – he's the youngest child in his year,' his mother said.

He kept his head down as the detective looked over to gauge his reaction to this. He wouldn't be twelve until March the following year. He'd started early because of his brother. Someone must have thought their mother needed all the extra time she could get.

'Do you understand why I need to speak to you today?' the detective asked.

Her voice was kind, and you could tell that she'd use the same one with all the kids she interviewed, like she cared about you.

This made Lewis angry because he knew she didn't care about him; how could she?

'Yes,' he said.

'No-one has seen Esther since she left school. We believe she walked home along Durton Creek.'

He nodded. He'd felt his body tighten at the mention of the creek.

'What did you do yesterday afternoon?' the detective asked, when he didn't say anything.

Friday was Sports Day. It always ended with the boys on the oval playing footy with Mr Rank, and the girls on the netball courts with Ms Davidson.

'We had footy. I was supposed to go to another boy's house for a bit after school, but I changed my mind and came home instead.' He told the lie, speaking as slowly as he could, and resisted the urge to glance at his mother.

'What's the boy's name?' the detective asked.

'Campbell Rutherford.' Lewis didn't feel like a bell anymore. Instead, something in his chest felt like it had been placed in a freezer. A run of ice crystals started in his heart and bloomed outwards.

'Have we spoken to Campbell?' the woman asked, looking at the notebook that lay open in front of her on the table. She was speaking to the man who reminded Lewis of his father.

Her partner looked at a list of names in front of him. 'Not yet,' the man replied. 'He's scheduled for after lunch.'

'And Campbell's your mate, is he?' The woman's focus was back on Lewis now.

'No,' he said. The detective tilted her head to the side, like Campbell's dog when you held a ball above its head. 'We just muck around at his house sometimes,' he added.

'Did you see anything unusual while you were walking home?' the detective asked, frowning.

Lewis forced himself to look up from her hands. Her fingernails were neat and short. Her right hand was sunburned, but not her left. 'No,' he said, looking into her eyes.

'What time did you get home?'

No-one had asked him, yet, what time he'd left school.

'About ten past three,' Lewis's mother answered for him. 'That's when he usually gets home on a Friday, if he doesn't go to the Rutherford boy's house.'

His mother couldn't have known how helpful she was being by not making him say the words himself. She had no way of knowing that what she'd just said wasn't the whole truth. She just wanted to get out of there as quickly as possible. Mrs Cafree from across the road didn't mind being called on to sit in their lounge room on the rare occasions when Lewis's mother had to duck out, but she must have been worried about what would happen if Simon emerged from his room. Lewis knew Simon would sit in there happily until he got hungry, because that's what Simon did every Saturday.

The detective's eyes flicked to Lewis's mother before returning to Lewis. 'Why didn't you go to Campbell's house?' she asked.

'It was hot,' he said. 'And Campbell doesn't have aircon.'

He told himself that they must already know about the man. They wouldn't tell a kid everything they knew. They didn't need to hear it from him.

There was a moment when he thought the detective was going to ask another question, but she just wrote something he couldn't see in her notebook and stood. Thanking Lewis's mother, she walked them towards the office door, holding it open for them as they left the room.

Driving home from the interview, his mother talked breathlessly about what she was going to make for lunch. His lie had worked, and the ice crystals in his chest melted, flooding his stomach with a sloshing, heavy feeling. He looked out the window, his face perfectly still in case she looked over.

When they got home, his mother had a list of chores for Lewis to do, and even when they were finished, she wouldn't let him go over to Campbell's place.

'I don't think it's a good time to be wandering around, darling. Besides, you heard the officers – he's got to go to the school as well.'

It was just Lewis, Simon and their mother at home that day. When she went into Simon's bedroom to do his enrichment activities with him, Lewis seized his chance.

'I'm just going to play out the back, Mum,' he yelled.

'Okay, dear,' his mum called back. 'Lunch soon.'

The backyard glared. Lewis's father's shed squatted in the far back corner. He always kept it locked, carried the key on him. 'I don't ever want you mucking around in there,' he'd said, making a show of slipping the key into his wallet. His mother had used to cut hair in that shed, Lewis remembered, but his father hadn't liked having women from the town in and out of the backyard, and one day he'd simply up and sold Lewis's mother's equipment. 'It's not like it brings in real money,' he'd said.

The cinderblock fence that ran along one side of the backyard had been painted with thick, cream paint. Lewis kept an old tennis ball tucked inside one of the openings, behind a lavender bush. When his father wasn't home, Lewis could play handball against the brick wall that ran parallel to the shed. The clothesline was empty, all of the pegs packed away and taken into the laundry. The soapy smell of lavender mixed with the sharp, acrid smell of the fertiliser stacked in the shed. Everything in order.

Lewis skirted the back verandah and made for the gate. His dad wasn't supposed to be home for a couple of hours, but his movements were never totally predictable – there was every chance he could see Lewis if he went out onto the road. Lewis manipulated the childproof gate lock, applying pressure to the metal frame so it wouldn't squeal as it opened.

Lewis ran to Campbell's house, following the unpaved road. The channel between the trees and the road made a tunnel of shade. Upturned gum leaves stood to attention, tumbling in his wake as he ran. He neared the house and an ocean surged in his ears. Campbell's bike lay on the front lawn. Campbell was kneeling over it, peering at the chain. Lewis could hear Campbell's sisters laughing in the backyard.

'Campbell,' Lewis called.

Campbell saw him and his hand cut down hard into the air, indicating Lewis should come to him, quickly. His body tingled with the understanding that Campbell was angry. He'd told him not to come here anymore.

Before Lewis had a chance to speak, Campbell hissed, 'What did you tell the police?'

'I told them I went straight home.'

'Good,' Campbell said. 'That's what I'm going to say too.'

Lewis tried to hold Campbell's gaze, to make him see that they needed to talk, but it was like his eyes slid right off Lewis.

'And that's what we're going to keep saying. Right?'

Lewis nodded mechanically.

'Now, bugger off, Lewis.'

Campbell turned his back, and Lewis had no choice but to leave.

There was a yellowed newspaper on the road outside Campbell's house. The ends fanned out from a thin rubber band tied around its middle. The newsprint had the puckered quality of paper that had got wet and then dried again.

When Lewis was little, his father had clenched his hand tight around a rolled-up newspaper.

'Take the newspaper, Lewis.'

Lewis had waited, unsure.

'Try and take it off me.'

Lewis had grabbed both ends of the newspaper, wrenching it up and to either side, like a dog shaking a bone. His father's firm, closed fist followed the flight pattern of the twisting object, his wrist moving to the right and left, never losing his grip.

'Go on, try and do it,' Lewis's father had said.

Anger bubbled up. Lewis put all his energy into it, until the paper had gone damp from the sweat on his hands.

'I can't do it,' Lewis said, breathing heavily.

His father had shown Lewis how to pull at the fingers, starting with the pinkie and working his way along the hand, weakening the grip, until Lewis could pluck the newspaper from his father with ease.

That moment was all Lewis could think about as he ran back the way he had come. The feeling that there was some trick he was missing, a better way than what he was trying, surged through him. Campbell often made him feel that way.

He slipped into their yard just as his mother came out the back door.

'I've been calling you, Lewis,' she said.

'Sorry, Mum.' He was standing beside the lavender bush.

'Listen, your dad won't be home until later. We'll have to pick him up from the RSL.'

'Okay, Mum.' His heart sank.

A soapy smell washed over him. He looked down to see that he'd crushed some lavender. The flower fell in segments from his palm when he opened his hand.

Streetlights illuminated the long white poles at the end of the open barriers of the railway crossing. Lewis kept his eye on them as the car sailed through. They looked like broomsticks painted white, and were bolted onto the solid metal frame of the raised gates on either side. Like every other time they crossed this way, he couldn't shake off the image of their car pinned by the poles and stuck on the tracks. It wasn't really the poles he was afraid of. It was the idea of being trapped and not knowing how long you had before the train came screaming through. At least then they wouldn't have to go to the RSL.

They arrived and sat for a moment in Lewis's mother's Volvo. His father was inside, at the bar. His mum's car was a fluorescent orange that wouldn't have looked out of place on a footy player's mouth-guard. The orange had a shade of purple under it, if you looked at it for too long in the light. The car had belonged to a mate of Lewis's father and he'd bought it *for next to nothing*. Simon was strapped into the front seat. Lewis's father always sat in the back when they picked him up. While they waited, Simon liked to throw his head back against the headrest, squealing. He would stop when their dad got in.

They waited in the car until his mum shifted in her seat and said, 'You'd better go and grab him.'

He walked into the building, past the untended sign-in book, past the packable plywood dance floor and up to the bar. There was a sign that said, NO UNACCOMPANIED CHILDREN, golden letters embossed along with the dress code. It was better when Lewis went inside to get his father from the club. If his mother went, it was more likely his father would come quickly, smiling and winking at his mates, but he'd be in a foul mood by the time he made it to the car.

Lewis's father pretended not to see him at first. Lewis thought about what Mrs Rodriguez had said in class once: that the planet and everyone on it was moving through space. *It feels like we're standing still but we're all actually moving very fast.* Ronnie had refused to believe it.

'But look, Miss,' she'd said, holding her hand out in front of her so the whole class could see. 'My hand isn't moving at all.'

Standing there at the bar, Lewis could almost feel the earth spinning on its axis, could imagine that they were whooshing past other planets. The men talked to each other and no-one looked at Lewis. The wooden bar gleamed in the downlights and the yeasty smell of beer lingered in the dankness of the air conditioning. The Chinese restaurant inside the RSL club was open, and diners crowded that end of the building. The wall that ran along one side of the small club had big windows and Lewis could see out to the bowling green. The lights were off.

As Lewis's father neared the end of his drink, he flicked his eyes in his son's direction. His father shaved every day and the pink rash that was always on his jawline looked particularly raw and angry that evening.

One of the men, as if seeing Lewis for the first time, remarked that Clint's old lady was looking younger every week. Lewis recognised Roland Mathers, the owner of the local motel. He was red-faced, wearing Stubbies so short that Lewis could see his thighs resting flat and fat against the bar stool. Lewis's father laughed louder than anyone else at the joke.

As his father took his final sip, white suds sucked down between pursed lips, another friend cried out that it was his shout. Without looking at Lewis, the barman poured more cold beer into fresh glasses. Lewis stood there, knowing better than to say anything as his father started on the full glass.

Once, Lewis's mum had tentatively suggested that, instead of rushing his father out of there, why didn't she just come when he was ready? But his father wasn't interested in calling Lewis's mother when he wanted to leave. 'I'm not a fucking teenage girl needing to get picked up from the fucking dance. What would you be doing anyway?'

Finally, his dad stood, emptying the last of the beer in his glass in one long swig. He shook the hands of his protesting friends before turning and walking out the way Lewis had come in. Lewis trailed behind at a respectful distance. His father would wait until they were all inside the car before he revealed his true mood.

He walked steadily through the front doors. Lewis jogged ahead to reach the car first to open the back door for his father. As soon as his father was within sight of the car, he became more unsteady on his feet. He lowered himself behind Lewis's mum with a loud exhalation of breath. Lewis shut the door and ran around the other side, slipping into the seat behind Simon. Once they were all entombed behind the car's orange doors, his dad might start singing. Or he'd be swearing and threatening as soon as the door closed, the town far away. Sometimes he fell asleep before they got home. Those were the good nights.

'Look at this cat bum my wife has where her mouth should be,' Lewis's dad said, poking his head between the two front seats, like a kid trying to get his parents' attention on a long road trip, before throwing himself back into the seat with a thud.

Compared to other nights Lewis had seen him like this, he seemed harmless. Still laughing at his own joke, his father scooted sideways so he was sitting directly behind Lewis's mother. She hadn't started the car yet. Lewis's dad reached both hands around the driver's headrest, his elbows splaying out like a woman doing washing on an old-fashioned washing board, like the one Lewis had seen when he went on the school trip to Ballarat. His father put his hands around his mother's neck and wrenched it back against the headrest. Lewis watched in the rear-view mirror as her eyes bulged. Her hands flew up and scrabbled with his wrists, trying to grab between his fingers. Some of her brown hair had been trapped between her neck and his dad's hands. There was no-one around. The lights of the RSL glowed.

Lewis wondered if his father had ever shown his mother the trick with the newspaper that he'd shown Lewis. She looked at Lewis in the rear-view mirror. The moment hung there. Lewis thought of the goldfish on the classroom floor, of Estie stepping in at just the right moment. His father let go, and Lewis heard his mum take a deep breath that caught on something between her lungs and her mouth.

His dad laughed, flinging himself back into the seat. 'Can't anyone in this family take a fucking *joke*?'

His mum coaxed the car into life, letting it idle for a moment under the streetlight, her breathing ragged. She didn't say anything.

Lewis thought about the men in the club. Did they like his father? Did they know what he was like after he walked out those front doors?

When they got home, Lewis's father went into the house ahead of them. As Lewis entered, his father was coming out of the kitchen with a large glass of water in his hand. Lewis heard his mum bringing Simon in behind him. She whispered something to Simon.

Lewis's dad looked at Lewis like something had just occurred to him. 'What state is your room in? Have you been keeping it clean for your mother?'

'Yes, Dad,' Lewis replied. He kept his voice even.

His father looked as if he might hit Lewis there and then. Instead, his dad strode down the hall towards Lewis's bedroom. 'We'll see about that. Follow me.'

The floor was clear and Lewis's bed was made. His dad pulled open a couple of drawers. Seeing nothing but neatly folded clothes, he pushed them back in with a slam. He was breathing heavily. He walked towards the closet in the corner. Lewis still hadn't thrown out the shorts he'd torn when playing with Campbell. It had been almost a full year since that afternoon. At first, it had just been because it would have been unthinkable to put them in the kitchen rubbish, which his dad sometimes went through. The plan had been to drop them directly into the outside bin, or a bin at school. But then, Lewis had found he didn't want to get rid of them. They were physical proof he wasn't making up his friendship with Campbell. A watery sensation swept through his lower body at the thought that his dad might find them.

His dad must have seen Lewis look towards his closet, because he bridged the distance to it in one mighty stride and wrenched it open. He pushed aside the clothes on hangers before kneeling to yank open the drawer at the bottom. Lewis had wedged the shorts in at one end, underneath his cricket knee pads. Like he knew exactly what he was looking for, Lewis's father reached his hand in. His eyes narrowed and he pulled out the navy shorts, the bedroom light shining through the hole Lewis had torn.

'What the fuck is this?'

Lewis tried to speak but couldn't.

'You fucking answer me when I speak to you.' His father had him by the arm now. 'You think this is why I work myself to the bone? So that you can rip up your stuff?'

Lewis wanted to spit in his face. He could feel that he was about to start crying. The skin where his father held his arm was burning. He was pulling so hard Lewis was almost lifted off the floor.

'Clint!' Lewis's mum was standing in the doorway, the shadow of a mark on her neck.

Lewis's dad strode towards her. Lewis wiped his face with the back of his hand and his dad slammed the door shut. Raised voices. Simon's high-pitched whine coming from his room. Lewis sat with his back to the wardrobe. There was the sound of something breaking, and then it was quiet.


The next day was Sunday. Lewis's father didn't work on Sundays, so the whole house held its breath. Lewis was never really sure what his dad did. *A bit of this and a bit of that*, his father always said. He worked for himself but spent a lot of time on people's farms. And since he'd got it at the start of the year, he was always on his mobile, laughing loudly at some joke he'd made.

Lewis was wearing the t-shirt with the cut-off sleeves that he wore when his dad asked him to help mow the lawn. His arm still hurt from where his dad had grabbed it. He wanted his mum to see the bruise, to say something about it. Simon had noticed it that morning, had wrapped his sticky fingers around it and squeezed. Lewis had jabbed Simon in the soft flesh of his belly with an index finger and he'd gone into full meltdown mode. 'I don't know what gets into him sometimes,' their mum had said brightly.

His dad had sent Lewis inside because he kept *getting in the bloody way*. So he was in the dining room, vacuuming, keeping his eyes fixed on the hallway so he'd see if his dad came in. Lewis was tired. He'd dreamed of Esther the night before. Hundreds of identical white poles had clattered down from the sky, beating him and Esther and Campbell – Campbell had been there too – into the ground like a golf tee pushed into the green.

There was a knock on the front door. Lewis switched off the vacuum cleaner. Seconds passed without the sound of his dad's footsteps or his mum calling to the person knocking to wait *just a minute!* so Lewis padded on bare feet to the front of the house. The person knocked again. Undoing the child safety lock involved angling a firm piece of rubber just so, sliding it off the hard plastic peg. His brother Simon was strong but not adept enough with his hands to open it.

When Lewis finally got the door open, he saw Peter Thompson on the front step. When men visited his father, they usually went straight around to the shed without coming into the house. Peter was wearing Town clothes – slacks and a collared shirt – and when he smiled the left side of his mouth drooped a little in a way Lewis found sinister, like Peter was laughing at him before Lewis had even said anything. Peter held a hat in his hands and his receding red hair was mussed. Lewis couldn't think of a time that Peter had come to their house before. His dad generally didn't like 'jolly' men, which was how Peter had always seemed to Lewis. He was Ronnie's uncle, and she adored him. She was always going on about something funny he'd said or done.

'G'day, mate.' Peter's eyes travelled to the bruise on Lewis's left arm, but the moment when Peter could have asked, *What have you done there?* came and went. Instead, he looked at Lewis's face and spoke louder and a bit faster, the way you do when you've done a fart that smells bad and you're trying to distract the person standing near you.

'Is your dad here? I need a word.'

'I'll go and get him.' Lewis turned and ran towards the back of the house.

'Thanks, mate!' The words followed him up the hallway.

As Lewis neared the back door, he slowed so his dad wouldn't see him running. It occurred to him that he should've invited Peter Thompson in, instead of leaving him standing at the front door. But what if he'd decided to come in without taking his shoes off? His dad would never let on he was angry with Peter, but he hated shoes in the house and it was Lewis who would pay.

Lewis's dad was leaning over the lawnmower, squinting in the sun. He disliked people who wore sunglasses (not only indoors but at all). He thought they looked *shifty*, and no-one in the family was allowed to own a pair.

'Have you finished the vacuuming?' he barked as Lewis trotted across the half-mown lawn.

'Peter Thompson is here to see you, Dad.'

Lewis's dad picked the bucket hat off his head, wiping his forehead with it.

'Bring him into the dining room.'

Lewis's mum was weeding around a rosebush. Simon must've been in his bedroom because he wasn't in the sandpit. Lewis walked back towards the house.

'Make sure the boy stays in his room,' his dad called after him. That's what he always called Simon, just *the boy*.

Peter Thompson had come inside, but he was still standing on the small square of tiles at the entryway. Peter rubbed at his red goatee and winked at Lewis. Lewis was struck again by the feeling that he wasn't in on the joke. He looked down to check Peter's boots hadn't trespassed onto the cream carpet before ducking behind him to secure the Simon-proof lock.

'Sorry,' Lewis said, 'but do you mind taking your shoes off?'

Lewis's dad came through the back door as Peter leaned down to slide off the boots.

'Mate!' Lewis's dad exclaimed as Peter added his R.M. Williams to the neat row by the door. 'Don't worry about your shoes, mate – Lewis can be a bit uptight.' He shrugged, as if to say, *What can you do?* 'Can we get you something to drink?'

'Glass of cold water wouldn't go astray,' Peter said.

Lewis's mum appeared behind his dad, like a balloon on a string tied to his father's belt. She was wearing a cotton scarf that she hadn't had on when Lewis saw her in the garden. 'I'm on it,' she said, smiling.

Lewis's dad showed Peter through to the dining room. He loved nothing more than company for short periods. He liked to show off his clean house, for people to see how his family ran around after him, but soon enough he'd get tired of being affable, of pretending not to care if people put their drink next to the coaster instead of on it.

Lewis thought about slipping into Simon's room, where he'd

145

be invisible to his father. He ducked into the lounge room instead, shutting the door behind him, sinking into the couch.

Lewis could just hear his mum. It sounded like she was setting a jug and glasses on the table in the dining room.

'I'll leave you boys to it.' Moments later, the back door opened and closed.

Lewis pushed his glasses up on his nose, which was slippery with sweat.

The men waited a few moments before speaking.

The muffled sound of Peter Thompson's voice carried a tinge of anxiety. Lewis didn't think he'd ever seen Peter Thompson anything but happy.

'Look, I told you not to worry about it, right?' Lewis's dad said sharply.

As if realising they were speaking too loudly, the two men dropped their volume.

Lewis couldn't catch anything but the rise and fall of their conversation until Lewis heard his father's voice again: 'Haven't you heard? The coppers've taken Steven Bianchi in. We need to lie low for now, but no-one is looking at us.'

Lewis knew, without really knowing how, that his dad had been in some trouble with the police when he was younger. His dad didn't trust them, and thought they were stupid. *Maybe the boy should sign up for the academy*, he'd say sometimes, jerking his head towards Simon. *They'd take him.*

'Steven Bianchi?' came Peter Thompson's clear response.

'They've gone and arrested him. Roland told me.'

Lewis thought of his father's drinking buddy with the fat thighs from the night before.

Lewis turned his head so his right ear was angled towards their conversation.

'Apparently, Steve Bianchi stabbed a cop when they brought him in. Funny – he doesn't seem the type.' There was a tinge of what could have been respect in his father's voice.

The police had arrested Estie's dad? A hot, greasy feeling frothed in Lewis's guts, like a half-empty deep-fryer turned on full. He didn't believe Steven Bianchi had stabbed someone. It was ridiculous. It was just the kind of detail his father would add to embellish a story.

'You know what's perfect?' Lewis's father was so loud now, Lewis was sure even his mother could hear him from outside. 'One of my mates on the road crew said no-one saw Steve the whole afternoon, that he was off working alone until the end of his shift. And I know they were looking near the creek on Friday night.'

Lewis's lungs crumpled in on themselves.

'How good is it? Personally, I wouldn't piss on that bloke if he was on fire.' This was followed by some muffled words Lewis couldn't make out, then: 'Now, I just need to make sure you're ready.' The rustling of paper. Some more discussion Lewis couldn't catch. 'Roland'll be right. We can trust him.'

There was the sound of chairs being pushed back.

Lewis sat bolt upright on the lounge.

'Anyway,' said his dad, speaking loudly again, 'don't lose faith now, alright? The cops don't know anything. Fucking nothing, right?' The sound of his barking laughter and a hand slapping the table, as if emphasising a point.

Lewis stood up from the couch but there was nowhere to go. He sat back down again, hoping that he'd draw less attention to himself that way than if he were standing in the middle of the room. Lewis's dad followed Peter to the front door, still talking. The men weren't looking in his direction, and Lewis took the opportunity to slip back into the dining room.

He hadn't understood most of what they were talking about, but one thing was crystal clear: Estie's father had been arrested.

The front door shut and heavy steps moved towards the dining room. Lewis sat up straight, but the footsteps passed and continued towards the rear of the house. Lewis heard the sound of the back door slamming shut. Then he heard a thump. It sounded like it had come from Simon's room, and Lewis went to investigate.

The entire contents of the Duplo box were strewn around the floor in the corner of Simon's room. His brother didn't look at Lewis when he came in; he just kept playing.

'But her dad wasn't there,' Lewis said to himself softly.

The back door opened.

'Have you finished the vacuuming, Lewis?' his mum called.

Simon covered his eyes with his hands.

Lewis had to speak to Campbell – properly this time. Estie's father had been arrested. He couldn't let the enormity of it touch him. Maybe together he and Campbell could figure out a way to tell someone what they'd seen without telling the rest.


It had been sweltering that Friday, the day Estie had gone missing. It was so hot that Mr Rank let the boys abandon their footy game early. He told them to head back to the classroom, grab some water and wait for the two-thirty bell. Campbell had dumped his bag behind the chicken shed at the back of the school, near the bike racks, anticipating a quick exit after PE. Lewis had followed suit, making sure he didn't drop his bag too close to Campbell's, even though no-one was around to see. Lewis's dad wouldn't be home till late and his mum had said he could go straight to Campbell's place after school.

Campbell and Lewis were right at the back of the pack of boys.

'Let's sneak out,' Campbell whispered. Mr Rank was far ahead of them, stooping to pick up a stray ball from the dry grass. 'It's only ten minutes till the bell goes anyway. We'll slip around behind the canteen.' Campbell smiled. 'No-one will miss us.'

The group passed the low canteen building and Campbell ducked behind it. Lewis followed a second later. They ran, holding in laughter as they used the building for cover.

'My dad says that in his day people rode horses to school and tied them up here,' Campbell whispered, nodding to a spot in the shade of the big Peruvian pepper tree that grew behind the chicken shed.

Scooping up their bags, they waited for a sign that they'd been seen – a yell from the cluster of school buildings – but nothing came. Lewis felt strong and light. He could've jumped right across the oval in a single leap if he'd wanted.

The roots of the tree snaked under rusted chicken wire. The shed had been empty for years. Most kids in their year had snuck inside on a dare at some point, brushing through old cobwebs that stuck to hair and clothes. Lewis had run inside with Alan Cheng once, before turning and running right back out again. It smelled like dirt and something else that caught in the back of your throat. It was hard to imagine that Campbell's parents and Lewis's dad had gone to this school. That they'd snuck into the same chicken shed, ordered finger buns from the same canteen, run on the same oval.

Campbell slowed once they reached the big silver van that belonged to the PE teacher. They hid behind it and Campbell took a packet of salt and vinegar chips out of his bag.

'Seems a bit mean for the horse, tied up all day,' Lewis said.

'Yeah.' Campbell rubbed his nose with the back of his hand and looked over his shoulder as he munched his chips.

The boys crossed through the back gate and the bell hadn't rung yet. The town was theirs. Lewis felt a satisfying pity for everyone stuck back in school and tried not to think of what his dad would do if he knew what Lewis was up to. Campbell was taking a risk too. If the boys were found, they'd be found together. That made Lewis happy.

Campbell slowed. 'Wanna go down there?' he asked, nodding across the oval in the direction of a dirt track Lewis knew ended at the creek. In the distance, trees clotted around it, two or three deep, the way kids surround a fight on the playground.

'Sure.'

The afternoon – the extra minutes they'd stolen from the day, the heat, their rhythm as they walked, the stillness of the school oval without people on it – all of it meant Lewis had to say yes. He followed Campbell. They stuck near the trees, trying not to be seen.

'Won't your mum be expecting us at your place?' Lewis said after a while.

'She's in Rhodes this arvo. Besides, school isn't even over yet.'

They reached a place where the ground fell away, rocks and twisting tree roots forming the creek's border. The two boys walked close to each other, their shoulders brushing, sending electromagnetic tingles up and down Lewis's spine. He heard the school bell ringing in the distance.

Entering the shade of the trees that surrounded the creek that afternoon, the last afternoon that Estie would be seen alive, it felt like Lewis and Campbell were leaving the town behind altogether. It was cooler and smelled of earth. Campbell walked in front. Lewis followed him as he shuffled down, clinging to roots to slow their descent to the creek bed.

Crashing footsteps moved through the leaves on the other side of the creek, near the tree line at the top of the bank. In unison the boys eased themselves behind a large boulder, putting it between them and the sound. Through a gap in the rock, Lewis could see a man in profile. There was a girl walking alongside him. Lewis couldn't see her face at first because it was blocked by the man's body, but there was the thick black hair Lewis knew well, blowing in the hot, dry wind. What was Estie doing here? They were far away but walking closer. Lewis thought the man with her must be Estie's father, but then he saw that it wasn't the man who'd come around that time to yell at Lewis's father, not the man who had scooped Estie out of the pool when she'd won her heat at the swimming carnival. This man wore a blue-and-white-checked shirt that reminded Lewis of a crisp new tablecloth and the sun gleamed on his bald head. Campbell nudged Lewis's head aside from the gap with his cheek. He wanted to see too. An electric shock as Campbell's close-cropped hair touched Lewis's ear. The man and Estie were far enough away that Lewis was sure if he and Campbell stayed where they were, they wouldn't be found out.

Lewis heard Estie's voice. She and the man were both calling out, 'Blacky!'

The man was not yelling as loudly as a man who genuinely wanted to find his dog would yell. He had the air of a presenter on *Play School*, playacting for a story.

Campbell's face was very close to his. Lewis could smell a mixture of sweat and something tangy he couldn't name. *Go away*, he urged the man and Estie silently, even as he wondered what the hell Estie was doing there.

Lewis stared at the rock they were crouched behind. He heard the sound of Estie and the man, and his own heartbeat. The stone had at least a dozen colours in it. Lines of dirt recording how high the creek had once been. Campbell moved his head, no doubt following the man and Estie, and then the two boys' mouths were side by side. Lewis took a breath and Campbell kissed him. There was a jolt as tooth hit tooth, before they found a balance. While they kissed, Lewis didn't think about his parents, or the heat. He forgot about the man and Estie moving along the other side of the creek. Campbell's mouth tasted of salt and vinegar. His hand raised and clasped the front of Lewis's shirt. Lewis had spent hours thinking of Campbell. His conscious thoughts had been innocent enough. He wanted to be near Campbell. To be next to him, Campbell's legs kicked casually over Lewis's while they watched the wrestling at Campbell's house when his parents weren't home. Campbell hadn't seemed to mind when this happened, hadn't moved away.

The two boys pulled apart, and Lewis shifted to see the back of Estie's head through the gap as she walked out of sight, hand in hand with a tall, bald man who was not her father. Campbell and Lewis, still crouched behind the boulder, looked at each other. It was a look that said, *I won't give us away if you don't.* Estie was speaking to the man. The words didn't have the strength to reach the boys where they sat, so close to each other, their hands not touching, now.

After Estie and the man were gone, the two boys sat behind the boulder for a little longer, not looking each other in the eye.

'You'd better go home, Lewis,' Campbell said, but not in an angry way. He looked like someone who'd lost a footy game but had still had a good time. 'And I don't think you should come over anymore.'

There was only the shade and the sound of Campbell's breathing. Lewis's whole body felt cold.

# CONSTANCE

Saturday, 1 December 2001

Constance hadn't seen her daughter since Friday. The thought made something inside her squeeze and release. Acid, anger. Anger at Steven, who was on remand in custody. Constance had asked the prison to take the house phone off Steve's list of approved numbers. She knew if she heard his voice she would lose all her resolve. But nothing he'd say could explain the shoe. He'd lied about seeing Esther, and if he was lying about that then she'd be stupid to think he wasn't lying about everything else. She couldn't be sucked back into his bubble. She wouldn't let it happen. Her husband and her daughter were gone and everything was broken and Constance wandered between her backyard and the kitchen.

Constance had worried that Shel would be hurt or angry that Constance had told the police about what had happened. It was lunchtime on Saturday when Shel returned.

'Oh, Shel, I'm sorry,' Constance said, wiping away tears – she seemed to have sprung a slow leak, the tears always just on the surface.

'It doesn't matter, love. Really. I just wish I'd never said anything. I don't know why I brought it all up again. It was behind me.'

If she was honest with herself, Constance had known Shelly wouldn't really mind. It was a bad habit, imagining that Shel's mental landscape was smaller and smoother than her own. But Shel was so unflappable, the bass note to Constance's high-strung personality, Constance couldn't help it. And who could stay angry at the mother of a girl who was missing?

'I understand now, why you never came here,' Constance said to Shel, gesturing to the kitchen, meaning the house as a whole. 'It must have been hard for you.'

'I didn't know, when I first met you. I swear, I had no idea. By the time I figured it out it was too late.'

'What happened after? I mean, it must have been horrible.'

'I tried to talk to Steven, to get him to tell me who else was there. He exploded. Denied it. He must've talked to my older brother. I hadn't wanted him to know, because I thought he'd tear the blokes what done it limb from limb. But he just took me aside one night and said what did I expect? He didn't want a slut for a sister, and I should just shut up about it. And the hardest part was I never actually said anythink, you know?'

'Sounds awful.'

'In the end, the town was split between people who said I'd made it up, and people who said I'd gone with them willingly. So after a while I just told myself it didn't happen.'

Detective Michaels called and updated Constance regularly, but none of the phone calls were the one she was waiting for. It felt like birth. It felt like you wanted the thing that you knew would hurt so at least it would be over. And then she would bite her fist and howl at her wicked thoughts. Because it was the opposite of birth; because she was waiting to hear that her daughter was dead.

When the detective asked Constance if Steven was Esther's biological father, or if there was any chance he wasn't, Constance just felt numb. 'Yes, of course,' she said, somehow unable to muster even a sliver of outrage at the question.

Constance thought often of the fact that Steven hadn't said anything about Esther's shoe. He thought she was so firmly under his thumb that she wouldn't even question him. Steve had always been passionate in his declarations of love for Constance. He'd say, 'You're it for me, love,' as if no further action was required by anybody. Well, now she had nothing but time to review their marriage, to hold all their moments up to the light and watch as it flooded through the cracks. Detective Michaels had sounded surprised that Constance wasn't talking to Steven. What did other women do in this situation? she wondered. What did you do when you discovered the person you had chosen to share your life with had lied to you, to the police, had refused to explain how something their daughter had been wearing was in his car?

Reporters had cornered Constance when she was going to the bin. 'Mrs Bianchi, how are you feeling?' 'What is your understanding of your daughter's case?' 'Do you think your husband did it?' Shel ran out and told the reporters to fuck off. And there were those missing twins on the front page of the newspaper, rather than her daughter, and that made her angry.

On Sunday, the detective asked Constance if she would be willing to do a press conference, saying it would be better than being confronted with questions at home, that she would get to speak without anyone else talking. And she assured Constance that she didn't think Esther's case was related to the twins' disappearance, but how could she know? How could anyone know anything? Constance agreed to the conference. What choice did she have?

The most important thing was that Shel never asked Constance what she was going to do. They met each minute like you do incoming waves, riding some, ducking under others. And the waves kept coming. Sometimes the pressure was so great that Constance longed to die. The scary thing was that she could already see how time might continue on in this way. What would it be like if there was still nothing after another two days? Two weeks? A year? It was unimaginable. Almost as unimaginable as waiting, as unthinkable as her daughter's empty bed.

# SARAH

Sunday, 2 December 2001

Sarah was up before the sun on Sunday morning and checked her notebook for loose tasks she could follow up. She saw the scrawled address for Kylie Thompson and decided to drive out and see Shelly Thompson's daughter herself, as Mack hadn't got around to it. Smithy wasn't up yet. She took a gamble that a young mother would be up early and was vindicated when she pulled up and saw lights through the kitchen windows.

It was a small fibro building on the edge of the showgrounds. Mack had explained that Kylie Thompson and her son lived there for very little rent in exchange for Kylie cleaning the showground toilets. 'Her mother does it for her a lot, though, particularly since the bub was born,' Mack had said.

Sarah parked the Commodore in a spot marked with a log that had been painted white. Someone had cared about the garden here, once, but that person was not Kylie Thompson.

The door opened a good three minutes after Sarah's knock. The smell that wafted from the house carried with it tomato sauce and sour milk. A television blared in the background.

'Hello, Ms Thompson,' said Sarah.

'Whaddya want?' The young woman had a nasal voice and the

same low-saturation red hair as her aunt, Evelyn Thompson. It was dirty and piled high on her head with a scrunchie.

'You're Kylie Thompson?' Sarah didn't take the woman's tone personally. She looked like she hadn't slept in a week.

'That's me,' she said.

'I'm here to ask you some questions in light of Esther Bianchi's disappearance on Friday afternoon. Can you walk me through your afternoon on the thirtieth of November?'

'Any idea what bloody time it is?'

Sarah smiled winningly. 'It seemed to me you'd be up.'

Kylie's frank stare lingered a few seconds before she spoke. 'I was home on Friday arvo. I'm always fucking home, at the moment. If I'm not at the doctor's.' The woman's face softened. 'Poor little bugger.' She threw her head back, presumably to indicate the little boy Sarah had been told about, sleeping somewhere at the back of the house. 'He hasn't been well.'

'Did your mother come here on Friday afternoon?'

'Yup. She did what she always does: made me a cup of tea, packed a bag for Caleb. She potters around and tidies up a bit.'

'What time did she arrive and leave?'

'She gets here a bit before two thirty, leaves a bit before five.'

'You mean usually? What about that day in particular?'

'Same as always,' Kylie said, looked bored. Sarah noticed the sodden stars around the young woman's nipples – breast milk leaking – and adjusted her gaze up.

Sarah checked her notes. 'What about your father?' He hadn't said anything, but Sarah had a feeling Mack still hadn't cross-checked Peter Thompson's alibi. She circled his name in her notebook.

'I dunno. I assume he was home with the other kids. He doesn't work on Fridays.'

'What do you know about Steven Bianchi?'

'He's a bit of a prick. The Bianchis have always been up themselves.'

'Constance Bianchi is a good friend of your mother's.'

'Loves a lost cause, my mum.'

Sarah's eyes flicked to the messy room behind the young woman. Kylie Thompson evidently did not see the irony in her statement.

While it was hardly the most useful conversation, the drive back from seeing Kylie Thompson did spark an idea. As Sarah glanced idly at the farmhouses she passed, it occurred to her that, though they weren't set close to the road, many of them could be seen clearly from the car in the morning light. That meant they could see her in return. Someone might have spotted a car, or someone they didn't recognise or who didn't belong. Like Steven Bianchi far from his worksite. Sarah decided to do a public callout for information to see if anyone recalled seeing anything there, or around the rest of the route that Esther would have followed home.

'Okay,' Constance Bianchi said, when Sarah broached the idea over the phone. 'Does this mean you want me to ask if people saw Steve?' she added flatly.

'We'll be asking for anything out of the ordinary people might have seen. We won't mention your husband specifically,' Sarah said.

Constance Bianchi's appeal for information was broadcast on local and national news. Sarah stood back until Constance had left the podium, then gave a final statement, providing the number for people to call. Sarah resisted the urge to smooth her hair or touch her face. She disliked speaking for the cameras. It occurred to her that if the Sydney news picked up the conference, Amira might see her.

From the corner of her eye, Sarah saw Shelly Thompson help Constance as she climbed down from the low stage. The lights from the television cameras illuminated the two women. Constance looked down at her feet, her dark roots a thick line on top of her head. Shelly was a bulky presence, her hair a bright red, glowing orange at the edges like a halo. Sarah supposed it was her one vanity, the one thing she did for herself in that house of five children and a husband who was away for work most of the time. The taller woman almost had to physically lift Constance from the stage. The cameras kept snapping and Sarah felt a wave of pity for the woman whose daughter was missing and whose husband they had in custody.

But they were far from sure of convicting Steven, and Sarah wanted to do her due diligence on the drugs they'd found. After her chat with Evelyn Thompson on Saturday evening, she'd been keen to speak to Clint Kennard, who'd agreed to come in after the press conference. Mack had already spoken to Clint on Saturday – one of the dozens of men whose alibi Mack had to check, she reminded herself. According to Mack's notes, Clint had been at the pub, meeting with a man named Roland Mathers on the afternoon Esther went missing. She didn't recognise the name, but when she pulled up the image on Mack's computer, she saw it was the owner of the motel where she and Smithy were staying. According to the file, Mack had already interviewed Roland, who corroborated Clint's story, although perhaps a little neatly for Sarah's liking. As had been the case with quite a few people in the town, it looked like Roland and Clint were each other's only real alibi. The publican dimly remembered seeing them on Friday afternoon, but wouldn't be drawn on when they'd left and arrived. Sarah thought again about the shoe in Steven Bianchi's car. Not impossible that Roland Mathers and Clint Kennard could be involved, that both men knew something. Now, she wanted to speak to Clint herself.

*

The first thing Sarah noticed about Clint Kennard was the angry red rash across his neck. He must have been handsome once, and the smug smile on his face seemed to be a holdover from that time. He was still muscled but had started to go to fat around the middle. When he sat down, she saw that his hair was thinning, the glint of his scalp visible in the fluorescent light.

Clint seemed to fill the station's small kitchen space.

'Thank you for coming in again, Mr Kennard,' Sarah said.

'Always happy to assist the police,' he said. The words were chased by a shit-eating grin.

'Anything unusual you remember about Friday afternoon?'

'No. I finished up for the day and met Roland Mathers for a beer. But I already told Officer Macintyre all this.'

'Any idea why the publican would be fuzzy on what time you left? He remembers you there at two but isn't sure after that.'

'That old codger. He's a fuckin' idiot. Couldn't find his arse if you handed it to him on a breakfast tray.'

Another Australian male worthy of one of Amira's drag king performances, Sarah thought to herself.

'Any special reason that you and Mr Mathers met at the pub?'

'Just after a cold beer on a hot day. If there's a better reason, I don't know about it.'

'Bit early for beer, wasn't it?'

'One of the advantages of working for yourself, officer.'

'What do you do, Clint?' Sarah asked.

He sucked his gut in. 'I'm in agricultural sales,' he replied.

'Come again?' said Sarah.

'You know, large farm equipment, tractors, threshers, things like that. I do okay.'

'Would you permit us to search your car or property?'

'Nup.' Clint smiled. 'Not bloody likely.'

'It would help us rule you out as a suspect.'

'If it's really necessary, you can get a warrant. I know my rights.' Clint looked Sarah up and down and gave a leering smile that made her skin crawl.

'What about DNA? We could take a quick sample now?'

Clint looked at her as if she were simple-minded and said nothing.

'What's your relationship with Steven Bianchi?' she asked.

'Relationship's a bit of a stretch, officer. He's pretty, but he's not that pretty.'

'Do you see much of him?'

'We've barely exchanged two words. Actually pretty hard to do in a place like this. Probably doesn't help he's a bit of a cunt.'

'Why do you say that?'

'I'm not trying to offend anybody's delicate sensibilities.' His eyes were on Sarah's tits now – clearly the implied location of said sensibilities. 'That's just the best word for him. Ask anyone. A pretty-boy cunt.'

'What do you know about a package of speed we found in a dam on the outskirts of town?'

She watched his face carefully. Something flickered across his expression before he rearranged his features into a careful blank, she noted.

He shrugged his shoulders and said nothing, still smiling.

Sarah asked him about his previous convictions – all more than fifteen years old now.

'Listen, love, you're barking up the wrong tree. That's all behind me. Now I only get high on life.'

He winked at Sarah, his gaze travelling down her body, stopping to refill his canteen somewhere near her hips, and she had to refrain from rolling her eyes. *Now who's barking up the wrong tree*, she thought.

*

'How'd it go?' Smithy asked her, once Kennard had left.

'I'd really love to get some physical evidence on Clint Kennard and his connection to the drugs,' Sarah said.

'Do you think he's got anything to do with the Bianchi girl?' Smithy asked. The fact that Steven was being held thanks to Smithy's little stunt in Rhodes passed, unspoken, between them.

She put her elbows on the kitchen table, rested her forehead on the back of her hands. 'No point speculating until we have evidence,' she said into the table, eyes closed.

'Isn't it fun, though?'

Sarah laughed. Smithy made her think of her dad. An irrepressible font of energy.

'Tomorrow's another day, boss. We'll get there.'

She hoped Smithy was right. That was another thing that reminded her of her father: he had always insisted that time was on his side. There would always be tomorrow, always some new angle to work. Sarah felt keenly that time was running out for them in Durton.

# WE

One of our fathers liked to read the paper at dinnertime, folding it flat and tucking it under the plate of meat and three veg as he read, lifting it to turn the pages at long intervals. (Breakfast, we knew from the movies we saw and the books we read, would have been a more usual time to read the paper.) Over dinner that Friday night, our father told us about a man a couple of towns over who had fallen into a silo, thanks to some problem with his harness. The details in the article were unclear; the wording made it sound like he had drowned in the grain, great waves of it crashing down on his head. Our father explained that the grain would have sucked the man down into itself, and no-one had been around to help get him out. The man was not a local, not the father of anyone we knew.

'The pressure from all that grain must've been immense,' our father said, eyes still on the paper.

Reading about an accident in the morning, there was the feeling that something could and should be done. By the evening, though, everything seemed fated. There was nothing to be done but have dessert – natural yoghurt and banana or, if Mum had been shopping, a crème caramel cup, the kind you peel the foil off – and be grateful that the world and its disasters had overlooked us and ours for the day.

And then there was the thrill of seeing our town mentioned in the paper on Sunday. Someone had spoken to one of us, and learned that we called it Dirt Town. One headline read: THE DIRT TOWN DISAPPEARANCE. We were famous.

But back then we still thought Esther would come home. It had only been a couple of days. She might still be found, hungry, thirsty and sunburned, walking on one of the endless long and dusty roads out of town.

Monday was the first day back at school since Esther had gone missing. Our broad-brimmed hats blew off our heads as we ran, the adjustable straps pulling against our necks, our backpacks bouncing. We moved about the school, sometimes in groups, sometimes alone. We ate our lunches and scrawled notes to each other in our exercise books and giggled at nothing. We talked about Esther, because it had been spoken of in the assembly and because it was all that our parents could talk about. We did not understand, yet, that she would not be coming back.

# RONNIE

Monday, 3 December 2001

On Monday morning Mum walked me all the way to the school gate. This hadn't happened since my first week of kindergarten. Durton had a central school, which meant it was both a primary school and a high school. All the kids in town came to the same place every day, except for the ones who went to school in Rhodes because they were too stupid or too naughty or too smart.

Before I could walk through the gate, Mum wiped at my face with her thumb, making a tutting noise. There must have been traces of that morning's strawberry jam on my chin. She ran the hand without jam on it through my hair. 'I love you, Ronnie.' She hugged me goodbye before turning to leave.

'Mum!' I yelled.

She turned around, concern in her face. I wanted to ask her where she thought Esther was, but I knew that would only make her upset again.

'Did you know llamas have an attached tongue that can't go more than thirteen millimetres out of their mouth? So they can't do this.' I stuck my tongue out as far as it could go.

'Be good, Ronnie,' was all she said in response.

As I roamed the playground, I kept seeing Esther out of the

corner of my eye. I'd brace for the running hug, only to realise it was someone else. It would be just me and Lewis that day, and I felt a jolt of excitement. I looked around – handball court, bubblers, the oval – but couldn't find him. He was always, *always* early; all three of us were.

I looped back to our usual spot. Lewis still hadn't arrived, and I decided to stay put. Uniformed children appeared at the gate and scattered, like marbles spilling across a table. I shifted into a cross-legged position, my runners pushing into the skin of my legs, and rested my chin on my hand. I thought that people would probably want to talk to me about Esther. I was her best friend, after all. That had to mean something. I waited, but none of the marbles rolled towards me.

Fishing my lunch bag out of my backpack, I pulled out the Dunkaroos Mum had packed for recess. She bought Black & Gold groceries for everything else, but she knew how much I loved Dunkaroos.

In my schoolbag was a book that Esther had lent to me a couple of weeks earlier. It was about horses and I'd brought it to show Lewis because I thought, together, we might be able to decipher the clue it contained. The cover said *Free and Wild* in bold purple letters above a picture of a glossy black horse. It was a library book, and if I didn't return it no-one would guess that I had it. When Esther got back, she'd be in trouble and wouldn't be allowed to borrow any more books. Esther always returned her library books. The fact that I was sitting there holding this one meant that she had to be alright.

As I sucked the last of the thick hazelnut-chocolate dip from my fingers, the bell rang. An announcement rustled through the spider-webbed speakers dotted around the playground: there would be an assembly. All I had to do was wait where I was for Mrs Rodriguez to show up with our class.

This was the last year my class would have to sit on the ground. From years seven to ten, we'd get to bring the chairs from our classroom. The year elevens and twelves stood right at the back, barely upright as they slouched and balanced against each other. They were practically adults in their white polo shirts and navy pants. I was in the junior dress, a tartan of dark blue and white on a light blue background. It was crumpled. Mum hadn't had time to iron it. She hadn't even noticed my scuffed sports shoes when she dropped me off, when she was usually on top of any uniform code infringement. I'd felt the strength in her grip when she hugged me and felt a tug of guilt for what I'd put her through on Saturday.

Despite her exotic name, Mrs Rodriguez had a doughy, pale face, which always looked like she'd just heard something vaguely surprising. She directed kids from our class to the left of the massive fig tree as usual, her flushed cheeks shining with sweat. The smaller kids sat in front. Some had their fingers in their mouths, their faces slack. Others held their shoes by the toes and tapped them in the dirt. Everyone had filed in. Lewis was still nowhere to be seen.

Mrs Worsell was taking her place at the front of the assembly, getting ready to speak. We were standing for the national anthem when Lewis arrived. He ran to where our class was sitting, but sat down two rows ahead of me, too far for me to whisper to him. Maybe he hadn't seen me.

A ripple of excitement swept through the seated rows. Low murmurs came from the seniors at the back. Two people were standing to the side while Mrs Worsell spoke into the microphone. They both wore suit jackets, despite the heat. I recognised them from Saturday in Mrs Worsell's office.

The kid next to me turned and whispered, 'What's going on?'

Half the school seemed to be whispering. Principal Worsell raised her hand for silence.

'These detectives are going to speak to all of you now.' Her look implied that if we were not silent our lives would no longer be worth living.

Everyone was hushed now. No tapping, no squirming: the whole assembly waited to see what would happen. The man walked up to the microphone. He didn't look at us as he addressed us, but stared off to the side, as if standing up at the front of our assembly was boring, or embarrassing. He hadn't spoken the entire time I was being interviewed on Saturday. Now, he explained in a loud, clear voice that they were still looking for Esther. That they'd spoken to many of us already, but if anyone had any information they should tell a teacher. They needed our help to find Esther, he said.

Once, Esther had wanted to play Chinese whispers. We were lying on my bed, seeing how far upside down we could hang before we fell off. Esther had already hit the ground twice. The first thud had sent Flea running from the room.

'I'll whisper something into your ear and you have to tell me what I said. It'll be harder because we're upside down,' Esther said.

'You can't play Chinese whispers with only two people,' I said. 'I've got a better game. Why don't we tell each other a secret?'

'But I already tell you everything,' Esther said, kicking her legs up so she inched over the edge of the bed.

Esther wasn't like me. If she thought something, she said it. You knew where you stood with her. *That hat makes your head look weird, your mum looked bored during the school play, I won't lend you money because you didn't pay me back last time.* It could have been cruel but she was too matter-of-fact. I had so many secrets from her. It's not that I was lying. I would never lie to Esther, not a big lie. Mostly, I just couldn't figure out what I actually wanted to say. For every sentence that came out there was another, realer sentence floating somewhere else.

'Alright, let's play Chinese whispers then,' I said.

At that moment, Esther reached the point of no return and crashed off the bed. I wriggled off to join her and we laughed in a tangle of arms and legs.

The man was coming to the end of his speech. I could see the backs of all the kids in front of me. Some of the white shirts were yellowed, some looked brand-new. The crowd around me moved like a dog twitching with fleas. Arms swung listlessly, weight shifted from a right to a left leg, kids scratched and sighed and yawned. Some looked up into the roof of leaves that waved overhead, a rippling shield from the hot sun. I could see the back of Lewis's head. He hunched forward as the man spoke. He was trying to whisper something to Campbell Rutherford, who was sitting in the row in front of him. Campbell rubbed the back of his shorn head, like he was rubbing off Lewis's words. This was an interesting development: Lewis never talked to Campbell.

The assembly ended. There was no musical item. Esther had been practising with Mrs Worsell's choir for weeks. She had a solo. I wanted badly, now, to speak to Lewis. But he stood up with the rest of the class and walked off, hands shoved in his pockets. I ran to catch up, but when I rounded the main school building, he'd vanished. Ducked into the boys' toilets, probably. When he came into the classroom, everyone else was in their seats and Mrs Rodriguez told him to sit down straightaway.

Mrs Rodriguez did roll call, and it felt wrong when she skipped Esther. There was the pause as she got to the name but didn't say it. She moved to the next name on the roll – Emily Brooks – and everyone carried on as normal.

I wanted to see Esther so bad. It felt like a scab I wasn't supposed to pick at.

*

Lewis stayed in to talk to Mrs Rodriguez over recess. I hovered in the doorway, but he didn't look at me. He was talking about an assignment that wasn't due for ages. Esther was the glue that held us together, and he was never really chatty, but he hadn't even said hello.

'Hey, Ronnie,' he said, nodding at me as he walked away from the teacher's desk. As if to punctuate his words, the bell rang.

Everything I'd planned to say melted away.

After recess, I gave Mrs Rodriguez my poster on Peru. She made an odd face when I handed it to her. Almost no-one else had done the homework, and I hoped that meant it would be displayed on the classroom wall. Mum had been home on Sunday afternoon, so I hadn't been able to use the lamp in the end. Instead, I'd traced the llama from the magazine onto a separate, thin piece of paper and then stuck it onto my poster.

When the bell rang for lunch, Lewis came up to my desk. 'I've got Bible group,' he said, already walking away, like he'd guessed that I wanted to talk to him but he didn't want to talk back.

He'd never gone to Bible group before. My mum had signed the note excusing me from Friday Scripture, but I hadn't passed it on to the teachers. More often than not, Mrs Cafree had mini chocolates that she doled out for correct answers to questions like *Who will love you forever?* She was an easy mark: *Jesus* was the answer to almost all her questions. But it was Monday and the Bible group didn't even have snacks; you had to bring your own lunch. I sat alone under the fig tree and ate the sandwich Mum had packed for me.

When the bell rang for the end of the day, I stood up and walked straight to Lewis's desk.

'I need to talk to you,' I said. 'I feel like you're avoiding me.' I enjoyed the drama of the statement. It was something my Barbies might say to each other. 'I'll see you out at the bags.'

Lewis took ages. I waited as everyone else in the class drifted towards the buses or the hot walk home. The verandah of our classroom was empty by the time Lewis reached his hook.

'I have to find Esther,' I said.

Lewis unzipped his dark blue backpack without looking at me. I had to get his attention.

'And you're going to help me,' I added.

'You know where she is?' Lewis's face was a small, pale moon.

Mrs Rodriguez hadn't come out of the classroom yet. She always took ages packing up.

'Will you come and look with me?'

'Where?' Lewis folded his arms across his chest and looked back towards the classroom.

Maybe if he thought I knew where she was, he would come. 'The creek.'

His eyes widened.

'People are looking for her. Adults, who know what they are doing.' Lewis's arms were still crossed. He looked like he was giving himself a hug.

'But they haven't found her, have they?' I stepped closer to Lewis. 'Maybe she's scared of something? Maybe something is stopping her from coming home? Maybe she thinks she'll be in heaps of trouble? I dunno.'

From where we stood, I could see the top of the fig tree at the front of the school.

'Ronnie, I can't. My dad will be home.'

'Tell him you're coming over to my place, and then meet me at the creek.' This conversation was important. Lewis and I meant something to each other.

'That won't work. I've never asked to go to your place before. He'll be suspicious.'

'But you came over to my house that one time to play UNO.'

'That was Mum. Dad didn't know about it. It was the school holidays and she had to go somewhere.'

Once my mum hardened down on something, that was it. But I'd heard about how other children played their parents off against each other. 'Can't you get your mum to tell your dad that it's fine?'

'No,' replied Lewis. 'I can't – my dad'll lose it.'

I hardly ever saw Lewis's dad, a big, loud man named Clint. On the rare occasions he did come to a barbecue with Lewis and his mum, he'd be in the middle of a group of laughing men. Mum never made me go up to offer him a cocktail frankfurt, although she was usually vigilant about these things.

'Listen, I've already got in trouble once for going out looking on Saturday. I need your help.'

'I've got to go, Ronnie,' he said.

Lewis rifled through his bag for a moment, not looking at me. He swung his bag onto his back, a gesture that said, *Do what you want.*

'What's that?' I pointed to his left arm.

A spattered yellow bruise peeked out from his white short-sleeved school shirt. Its purply brown shadows made me think of the milk in my cereal bowl the morning at Uncle Peter's.

'I hurt myself mucking about in the backyard,' he said, ducking his head.

'How'd you hurt your arm all the way around like that?' I asked. It was like the tattoo Pocahontas had in the Disney movie I'd watched with my cousins.

'I dunno. I just did.'

'Did you tie a rope around your arm or something? Have you seen *Pocahontas*?'

'What do you want, Ronnie?' Lewis's face was twisted into an expression I'd never seen before.

The words spilled out. 'It's not right. She should be here.' I wanted to show him the library book, I wanted him to tell me we would find her.

I waited for him to say I was wrong. That they'd found Esther that morning. Everyone had forgotten she was being picked up by her grandma to go away for the week, to the beach maybe, somewhere without a phone. She was with her mother's mother who lived somewhere far away and who I'd never met. It didn't matter that Esther didn't like that grandma.

'The cops arrested her dad,' Lewis said quietly.

'Esther's dad wouldn't hurt her. If they've arrested him, that's just one more reason why we have to find out where she is.'

'Listen . . .' Lewis looked towards the front of the school; the line of kids streaming towards the front gate had thinned. 'You're right about her dad. He wasn't there.' He stopped speaking and looked around again. I thought he was going to say something else, but he looked at me instead, like he was begging me not to ask what I was going to say next.

'He wasn't where, Lewis?'

'I saw Esther that afternoon.' His whole face was pulled tight, his brow low, scrunched below the line of his glasses. It looked like it was physically hurting him to tell me. 'I saw her after school.'

I asked the first question that came into my head. 'Where?'

'At Dirt Creek.'

My heart, tied to the end of a kite, lurched up and down inside my body. That was where Esther's and my box was hidden.

'I saw a man there too,' Lewis continued. 'It definitely wasn't her dad.'

'Are you sure you know what her dad looks like?' I asked.

'Of course I do,' he replied. 'I've seen him a bunch of times.'

'What were you doing at the creek?'

'Nothing,' he said. 'I was mucking about.'

'After school?'

'Yeah.'

'Well, what time was it?'

I took a step towards Lewis and he braced like I was going to hit him. And I wanted to. I had to make him see I was right. This was far more serious than any conversation between Barbies.

'Have you told anyone about this?' When Lewis didn't say anything, I continued, 'Didn't the police ask you? Don't you realise this is really important?' I wanted to scream in frustration. 'Esther is your *friend*.'

It was like all the panic I should have been feeling since Friday afternoon hit me at once. The tips of my fingers tingled, and there was a taste in my mouth like the time Esther had dared me to lick a metal fence.

Lewis's face was impassive. It was a familiar look: it came over his features on the playground all the time – his snub nose flaring as he tucked into himself and backed away from the other boys, eyes narrowing behind his glasses. I doubt he knew he was doing it. Seeing it made me angry: angry like you get at something small and weak that can't help itself.

'It doesn't matter, Ronnie. My dad said Mr Bianchi stabbed a police officer, so he must've done something.'

'Your dad told you that?' I asked, looking at him hard. Steven wouldn't do that, *couldn't* do that.

'Yeah,' said Lewis, returning my gaze.

'It doesn't matter,' I said. 'We should –'

'I've got to go.'

'You need to talk to the police,' I said, out of breath all of a sudden. He had to tell them they were wrong about Steven.

The word *police* made him look like he'd just swallowed an Extreme Sour Warhead whole.

'It doesn't matter now,' said Lewis. 'Can't you see that?'

'They still don't know where she is! As long as they think it was her dad, they're not going to look for her.' I stared at him, still not saying anything, not moving. 'I'm not kidding,' I said. 'You need to go see them *now*.'

Lewis's eyes scanned the playground.

'You're a coward,' I said, as it dawned on me that he really didn't intend to go anywhere.

'And you're a know-it-all,' he retorted. 'You think you can just tell everyone else what to do. You're just acting like this because Estie's the only person who can stand you for more than five minutes. You're always stuffing your face and telling everyone what *you* think. Well, maybe I' – I took a step away from him – 'maybe I don't give a shit what you think,' he spat. I could see tears in his eyes behind his glasses. 'Why don't you piss off?'

Lewis turned on his heel and ran.

There was a sound behind me.

Mrs Rodriguez called out from the door of the classroom, 'Oh good! I caught you. Wait a moment, will you, Ronnie?' Her cheery tone implied she'd heard none of what Lewis and I had just said to each other.

I stood, my feet stuck to the smooth boards of the old verandah, reeling. All I wanted to do was run after Lewis. Bring him back. Make him see. Make him take back what he'd said.

'I thought you'd like to keep this,' she said, a rolled-up piece of cardboard in her hand. I knew without unrolling it that it was my Peru poster. 'I really liked the llama.'

'Thanks, Mrs Rodriguez,' I said, grabbing one end of it. Why wasn't she going to put it up?

'You got an A,' she said brightly, still holding on to the other end.

I looked over my shoulder. Lewis had legged it and would be far in front of me by now. He was a lot faster than I was.

'Listen, I'm here if you ever need to talk to someone,' she said, finally letting go of her end.

For half a second, I considered it. But she never believed me. Once I told her I'd seen a mouse in the classroom and she'd said in front of everyone that I had an overactive imagination.

'Thanks, Miss,' I said, edging away.

Mrs Rodriguez turned to go back in. My bag was the last one left on its hook. I crammed the poster inside. I could feel the weight of Esther's library book. If I ran, I might still be able to catch Lewis.

But then something struck me. I didn't need to convince Lewis. I could go straight to the police and tell them. They might not believe me at first, but I would stay until they did. I didn't care if I got in trouble from Mum. The police needed to know. I would go and tell them, and everything would be alright. They would find Esther and bring her back to me.

# LEWIS

Monday, 3 December 2001

When Lewis made it home, he ran inside and slammed the front door shut. He waited for a knock from the other side, for Ronnie to run into his dad, who might have just pulled up in the driveway. For his mum to call out, asking why Ronnie was here, and what was that about the creek?

There was nothing except the thudding in his ears. Lewis had asked Campbell once if he also got that sometimes – the sound of his own heartbeat in his ears. Campbell had said yes. He liked to listen to it until he fell asleep.

Lewis slipped the child lock back on and walked away from the door. In his bedroom, he sat with his back against the edge of the bed.

Everything he'd been holding in since the kiss, since his mother had told him Estie was missing, everything he'd been afraid of – it felt like it was all happening at once. And Ronnie had asked the question he'd been dreading: *What were you doing at the creek?* The ice crystals bloomed in his chest, slick and solid and impossible to break. This was so like Ronnie. Why should he listen to her? Why would anyone care what she said? A new thought clanged in his brain. If Estie's dad went to prison, it would be his fault.

Lewis had enjoyed being able to dismiss Ronnie, acting like he didn't care what she thought, but that was because deep down he knew she would excuse anything he said. She was the one person who always saw the good in what he did, who called, 'Nice shot, Lewis,' from the sidelines when they played handball. But this was different. Ronnie was out there cursing him. And, of course, there was Esther. Where was she? He hadn't let himself think about it, not really. Was something bad happening to her, something that he could prevent? A wave of shame washed over him. He wasn't brave enough to talk to the police. Ronnie hadn't even been able to fathom that level of cowardice. She'd expected better of him, like she always did. But he was nothing. No wonder his dad thought he was weak.

The urge to come clean snapped through him. To run after Ronnie and say he'd go, he'd go right now. He could tell the police he'd gone to the creek alone, that he'd snuck out of school early, which was why he hadn't wanted to tell anyone, but that he'd seen a man with Estie and that man wasn't her dad. But why had he gone to the creek in the first place? Because it was hot, and he wanted to put his feet in the water after footy?

That would have to do. It would have to.

Lewis's mum was moving down the hallway. His heartbeat thudded out of step with the breaths he was taking. She'd been watching him like a hawk since Saturday. He hadn't been able to run to Campbell's again or even use the phone.

'Mum?' he said, hoping for a moment that she might not have heard him.

His mum stuck her head in the door, leaning over the washing basket she carried in her arms. 'What's wrong?'

'I have to tell you something.'

She walked into the room and put the basket down. 'What's up, darling?' She smiled.

She looked achingly beautiful.

'There's something I didn't tell the police the other day.'

He gave her the version of the story he'd prepared while sitting there, the one without any mention of Campbell. As Lewis was speaking, he thought about how low the water had been. 'I saw a man with Estie. I'd never seen him before.'

'Are you sure?' his mum asked, giving him a searching look.

He nodded.

'Lewis, if what you're saying is true, then this is very important information. Why on earth didn't you tell them this on Saturday?'

The fear on her face was not fear at what the police would say, he knew. The spectre of his father hung between them. And he knew she knew the answer. Just the thought that Lewis had spoken to the police would be enough to send his father into a rage.

Lewis's mother had told him before how she and his father had met. His father had been working in Rhodes, at the racetrack. *He was just this charming cowboy, and I was a girl from Surrey on a gap year, and I fell for him hook, line and sinker.* What they never talked about was what came after that. When it was that his father had changed. At some point it seemed like Lewis's mother had given up so much that what she wanted didn't matter anymore.

'I know,' he said, trying to imbue each word with the weight of what they both understood.

'Okay. We're going to have to bring Simon this time.' His mum said it under her breath, thinking aloud. 'Here, put this on.' She passed Lewis a red polo shirt from the washing basket. It had longer sleeves than his school shirt. 'You're all sweaty,' she said.

Within minutes they were on their way to the police station.

'I just hope this all wraps up before your father gets home,' Lewis's mum said as they stepped out of the bright orange car. 'Then there'll be no need to tell him.'

Lewis nodded.

It was the same small police station that had always been there, but now his throat constricted when he looked at it. It was a normal cottage except for the blue-and-white-checked sign out the front that lit up from the inside. The word POLICE cast a light that shone on the small gate when you drove past it at night. 'Why do they need it bloody lit up?' Lewis's dad said whenever he saw it. 'Everyone around here knows how to bloody find the bastard.'

Lewis had prepared himself to see Officer Macintyre, but when they walked into the reception area, he could hear several voices coming through the open door that led to a small kitchen.

'Hello,' his mother called.

Officer Macintyre came out, shifting his gun belt on his hips.

'My son Lewis has something he needs to tell you.'

He was regretting having said anything at all. Damn Ronnie.

Behind him, Simon stood moving from foot to foot. He had a red ring around his mouth from the icy pole their mum had used to get him in the car. He was starting to grow wispy hair on his chin. Their mum would have to start shaving him soon, on top of everything else.

Officer Macintyre looked down at Lewis from over the counter. Behind it, on the wall, there was a calendar that hadn't been changed in months. The weekend squares lined up with each other, the words *Saturday* and *Sunday* printed in bright red ink.

'It's about Esther Bianchi,' said Lewis's mother.

Officer Macintyre looked at her, and then at Lewis. 'You'd better come through.'

Lewis walked past the counter and through the open door to the kitchen.

'This young man says he has information about Esther Bianchi,' Officer Macintyre said.

The two officers he'd spoken to at the school looked up at him from their seats at the table. The woman took her glasses off and placed them beside her.

'Please, sit down,' she said.

Lewis's mum ushered Simon over to a chair by the wall.

'Do you want to speak with Lewis in private?' Lewis's mum asked, eyeing Simon.

'No, ma'am, we need you to stay here because of your son's age.' The detective shifted her seat so she was directly opposite Lewis. 'Alright, Lewis. We'd love to hear what you've got to say. Now, we've spoken to you before, haven't we? Is there something you forgot to tell us last time?'

'I said I just went home after school that day, but that wasn't true. I left a bit before the bell rang,' he blurted out.

'But you were in PE – all the boys were,' Officer Macintyre interjected.

The male detective gave him a look and Officer Macintyre fell silent.

'I didn't walk back to the classroom.' Lewis had almost said 'we'. *We didn't walk back to the classroom.*

'Why not?' asked the woman.

'It was – hot. It was really hot. I decided to go home early. I'd left my bag near the chicken shed, so I didn't need to walk all the way back to class.'

'Did anyone see you leave?'

'I don't think so,' Lewis said. All he could see was Campbell's face. *My dad says that in his day people rode horses to school and tied them up here.* The curve of his cheek, the way the shade from the tree had fallen on his face.

'So, you left before the bell rang. Did you walk straight home?'

'No,' Lewis said.

Her eyes moved to her partner before returning to Lewis. 'Where'd you go?'

'I went past the creek.'

'Is that on your way home?'

'Sort of.'

The male detective who reminded Lewis of his dad shifted in his chair. Lewis could feel the ice blooming in his chest.

'Why'd you go there?' asked the woman.

Officer Macintyre stood in the corner of the room, hand on his gun belt, as if he were holding himself back from saying something.

'I dunno, I just wanted to go there. It was hot. I wanted to put my feet in the water, I guess.' It sounded like a lie.

'And what did you do when you got there?'

'I saw Esther.' Her name was like electricity in the air. Lewis had said it. Put Estie and himself together in the same place.

The female detective's voice stayed steady. 'What was she doing?'

'She was with a man.' Everyone at the table seemed to lean towards Lewis at once.

'And what did that man look like, Lewis?'

There was a tea towel on the table. A cluster of mugs were bunched together next to the sink, ready to be washed.

Simon laughed. A flat, dead sound, like a bird imitating laughter. Lewis looked over at him, but no-one else did. They were all looking at Lewis.

'He was bald. Like, maybe some of it was just shaved, but he was bald on top. It wasn't Esther's dad.' Lewis wanted to tell her there had been something about the man that seemed off. Lewis needed to make her understand.

'And what were Esther and this man doing?'

'They were calling for a dog.'

'Does Esther have a dog, Lewis?' Everyone in the room was still looking at him.

'No.' Lewis wanted to say, *That's the point. She doesn't*, but the words still weren't there.

The female detective turned to his mum. 'What time did Lewis get home, Mrs Kennard?'

'A bit after three,' said his mum. 'He sometimes goes to Campbell Rutherford's house, but he was home earlier than I expected. I mean, when he told you that he came straight home, he was home at the right time for that to be true. He's never left school early before.'

Lewis kept his head low, focusing on keeping his expression the same as before his mum had said Campbell's name.

'Now, you know how important it is to tell the truth to police officers, don't you, Lewis?' said the male detective.

Officer Macintyre looked at the female detective, like someone waiting for the umpire to respond to a bowler's appeal.

'Yes.' Lewis tried to tell them with his voice that he knew.

The male officer spoke again. 'And why didn't you mention that you saw Esther when we spoke to you the first time?'

Lewis couldn't speak.

'What were you doing at the creek, Lewis?' the female detective asked, her voice gentle.

'I told you, it was hot.'

'Not really enough water to make it worth your while, is there, mate?' said Officer Macintyre.

'I wanted to put my feet in,' Lewis said.

A door swung open. It sounded like it was at the back of the station.

'Soph,' yelled a voice. The frozen ice in Lewis's chest melted, flooding his lungs.

Lewis's mum looked at the female detective before answering. 'We're in here, Clint,' she said softly.

'What's he done?' Lewis's dad was standing in the doorway at the rear of the kitchen.

Simon turned away and stared at the floor.

'Nothing, Clint. Lewis thinks he saw Esther Bianchi the day she went missing,' said Lewis's mum. She was speaking so quickly, Lewis snuck a look at the officers to see their reaction.

'Of course he saw 'er. They go to school together, don't they?' Lewis's dad raised his eyebrows as he moved to stand next to Lewis's mum, like this flight of fancy was the kind of thing he had to deal with all the time from his wife and son. The angry pink rash on his jawline glowed in the station's fluorescent lighting.

Lewis's mother kept her head down, her face arranged in a neutral expression.

'We'll be going now, officers,' his dad said, moving towards Lewis and dropping a hand onto his shoulder. 'As you can see, my eldest boy has special needs.'

'Please, Mr Kennard, we'd really like to finish asking Lewis some questions.' The female detective had risen from her seat.

'Sorry, we've got places to be. And this is the fourth time you've spoken to me or my family in three days.'

'Mr Kennard,' the male detective said, also standing.

'This is verging on harassment now. You can't talk to my son without his parents' permission, right? And as of now, you don't have that.' Lewis's dad looked at his mum.

'Mr Kennard,' said the male detective again.

'Look' – Lewis's dad's voice was calm – 'we're going. You've already spoken to my son and I am not letting him speak anymore. He gets ideas in his head, likes to make stuff up. I'm sure you've all got better things to do with your time.' Lewis's dad smiled.

How could this be happening? How could a room full of adults be listening to his father?

Lewis stood. His dad put his arm around him in a protective motion. He squeezed the spot where Lewis's bruise was healing beneath the sleeve of the red polo shirt.

Officer Macintyre looked at Lewis's mum, who was fiddling with something in her purse and did not return his gaze.

Lewis's dad had moved Lewis in front of him, and his mum trailed behind as they walked out of the kitchen and down a short hall to the door his father had come in through. Lewis could hear his mum struggling to get Simon to go that way. He wanted to go out the way they'd come in. There were concrete cells on Lewis's left. Perspex covered the metal bars, which were thinner than he'd imagined they would be.

Lewis's dad's hand closed over the back of his neck, guiding him out through the flyscreen and into the blinding light.

# SARAH

Monday, 3 December 2001

That morning, Sarah had woken early to the sound of a dog barking. The noise slid out from the folds of her dream and into the real world as she rolled over. She blinked against the light that shone through a gap in vertical blinds that wouldn't sit flush and was grateful that she'd managed to drift off at all. Her first conscious thought was to wonder if Smithy was sleeping through the noise. He probably was, the bastard.

She wasn't sure how long she lay there before pulling herself into a sitting position: a climber hauling herself up and over a cliff edge. She'd been dreaming about Amira. Replaying their last fight. No matter what she did, it ended the same way. For a moment, Sarah contemplated staying in the room, making a crappy instant coffee, but something in the insistent bark – a warning – sent her to the door.

Sarah walked around the side of the building. It was early enough that the earth beneath her feet was still cool, the sky an insincere blue. The dog was on its feet, straining against its chain. She'd kept hoping to see the motel owner since her interview with Clint Kennard, but he'd made himself scarce. She would have to call him in for a formal interview if she wanted to speak with him.

'Hey,' Sarah said to the dog. Her voice rasped, the sound like a key inserted in the wrong lock.

The animal stopped for a second before looking away dismissively and barking again, its whole body one flexed muscle. Sarah looked around the yard for the owner. In the end, she went back to her room. She was tired. It was only a dog barking.


Smithy surfaced – no, he hadn't heard the dog – and at around 7 am they climbed into the Commodore. It was three days since Esther Bianchi had last been seen. They didn't have enough for a warrant to search for the drugs, and while Clint Kennard was a prick whose alibi was far from rock solid, Sarah could tie nothing concrete about Esther to him, and wasn't convinced that Evelyn didn't have some grudge of her own because Clint had got her mixed up in drugs when she was still a teenager. Shelly Thompson's claim about what had happened between her and Steven was relevant, but as Shelly was not yet prepared to make the allegation herself, they could only go off what they'd got second-hand from Constance. For lack of any other leads, they were driving to take another look at the area around the creek before they went to the school to speak at an assembly.

Smithy, sitting in the passenger seat, broke into Sarah's thoughts.

'More men are killed by men than women are killed by men,' he said. 'But you wouldn't know that, to watch television. It's like men hurting each other isn't interesting anymore. Unless it's bikie violence or something, nobody cares when they do it.'

Sarah made a noncommittal 'hmm' sound. Where was this coming from?

'When we stopped having world wars, that's when I reckon this idea of man as woman's natural predator took hold.' He leaned back into his seat, one hand tucked behind his head.

She'd been a police officer long enough to see women be violent in ways she'd never imagined. And Sarah knew what it was to give in to that impulse, like letting go of a heavy rope, the simplest thing in the world, in the moment, until whatever it had been holding came smashing into you. But she knew why some women thought of men as predators, and she was sure Smithy did too. Certainly, in her time at Child Protection, she'd never apprehended a female perp. She looked at Smithy to gauge if he was being serious and couldn't tell. The swelling in his nose was going down. It was more than forty-eight hours since Smithy's scuffle with Steven Bianchi in the interview room. They were holding Steven for assaulting an officer but had nothing except the shoe to tie him to Esther.

'Don't you think we'd have found anything worth finding at the creek by now?' Smithy said, when Sarah said nothing.

He'd not been convinced by her idea of going to the creek again. What he really meant was it was too hot for busy work.

But it was a basic principle of policing to start with the known facts – the last place seen, whatever physical evidence there was. It wouldn't be the first time that going over what Sarah already knew would reveal new ways forward. Technically, the last place Esther had been seen was the church, where she and her friend Veronica Thompson had parted ways. But Veronica had seen Esther head in the direction of the creek. And they needed something else on Steven. She still couldn't shake the idea that Esther was being kept somewhere. And the drugs. The drugs could be connected.

They turned off the highway to cross the train line. A road crew flashed past on the passenger side.

Smithy slipped some gum from a pack in his pocket and chewed on it thoughtfully before saying, 'Can I ask you something, boss?'

'Go ahead.'

'How many men were working back there?'

'What?'

'How many men did you see working on that site?'

Sarah slowed at a railway crossing sign. She peered down the track, checking for an oncoming train, not trusting the signal light. 'Three,' she said.

'Nup. There were eight. Not including the ones inside machinery.'

'Is that so?' Sarah said.

'My point is that nothing makes you invisible like fluoro. Unless you were in a short skirt and had to walk past a line of them, when was the last time you noticed a guy in fluoro on the side of the road?'

'I'd buy that in a city, maybe,' Sarah replied.

Smithy's comment about the short skirt was supposed to be funny, she was sure. He'd only ever seen her in suit pants. But there had been that skirt of Amira's, the short, leopard print one Sarah had worn for a party. *You should keep it*, Amira had said. *It suits you*. But then she'd dropped it in the box with her other things and left. Sarah shook her head, trying to shake off the memory.

'But Steven grew up here,' she went on. 'All the people we interviewed were sure they hadn't seen him, and most of those people have known him since he was a little kid.'

Her eyes were on the road, but she could sense that Smithy was looking at her. He leaned back, pressing his shoulders against the window as if trying to take her all in.

'You're looking a little rumpled there, boss.'

She plucked at the collar of her shirt and registered the wetness in the underarms. Her sleeves were rolled up as high as they would go.

'Personally, I don't sweat,' Smithy said matter-of-factly.

She looked at him out of the corner of her eye, unsure if he was taking the piss.

'Seriously!' he said, as if sensing her scepticism. 'It's a curse. I look fine and then bam, I pass out. That's why I left WA. Too bloody hot.

But then, here we are.' Smithy held his hands up, gesturing to the landscape they were driving through.

They lapsed into silence again.

'Whatever happened to that bloke who thought he was Cher?'

'What?' Sarah said. Smithy and his bloody non sequiturs.

'The first night, at the search, there was a bloke who wouldn't give Mack his last name. Do you remember?'

'Oh, him,' she said. 'His name's Stanley Gollasch. Parking ranger from Rhodes. Surveillance footage shows him at early knock-off drinks with his colleagues from around two thirty. I think he's just a bit of a conspiracy nut, which was what the ID issue was all about.'

'Right,' Smithy said. 'So, do you like anyone for the drugs?'

'Could be half the town – almost anyone here could use a little cash.'

'You seemed pretty taken with your girlfriend's theory,' Smithy said.

For a moment Sarah thought he was talking about Amira and her eyes cut to him.

Smithy laughed. 'Oh, toochie!'

'Are you trying to say touché?'

'Sorry, I never did make it to those Spanish lessons at the academy.'

'I'm going to pretend you said French.'

'That's what I like about you, boss. You've got a healthy imagination.' A smile glinted under Smithy's moustache. 'And don't worry, I think Evelyn Thompson could be persuaded.'

When Sarah had first met Smithy, he'd been in a rush to tell her his sister was gay. 'Congratulations,' Sarah had said dryly. Not talking about her private life was a hard habit to break.

'Yeah, right up until I accused her of being a junkie,' Sarah said.

They could joke about it, she reasoned, because Smithy knew there'd be no way she'd endanger their case. He was just passing the time.

Sarah's phone rang.

193

'Detective Sergeant Sarah Michaels,' she said.

'I'm calling with the DNA comparison you were after for Steven and Esther Bianchi?' It was a different woman from the one she had first spoken to on the phone.

'Yes?'

'Sorry for the delay. It's been crazy here. I'm just calling to let you know there's a paternal match. In real terms it's incredibly unlikely we're looking at anything but a father–daughter relationship.'

'Okay. Thank you.'

Sarah hung up and slapped the steering wheel.

'Bugger,' said Smithy.

So, the other DNA on the shoe was still unaccounted for. They desperately needed a development now. They were trying to build the evidence against Steven Bianchi, but they'd hit a wall. A body, a sighting of Steven that afternoon, something concrete that said the drugs were tied to Esther's disappearance, more info on the drugs themselves, even if that led them away from Steven and towards Clint Kennard. Sarah would take any of it. Clint had refused to give a DNA sample or submit to having his home or car searched, she remembered. She had no way of forcing him to do anything with what she had. And soon, she knew, they'd have to let Steven go. Even with the friendliest of remand rulings, they couldn't hold him on the assaulting-an-officer charge forever. If Steven hadn't been Esther's real father, and if he'd found out about it, it might have been the beginning of an angle she could use to persuade a judge. It helped that it had been a weekend, that the regional courts moved more slowly. But now it was Monday.

They pulled up on the side of the road at the beginning of the path to Durton Creek. It was crowded with trees, including some willows, which seemed too English for dirt the colour of sun-bleached terracotta. The muddy brown water was only centimetres deep, for the most part. But anyone could fall and hit their head and that would be all it took. Sarah was reminded of that feeling you get when you've lost something and you start to think of ever more improbable places where you might've left it. She imagined rounding a creek bed, a small, white-socked foot poking out of some brush, dark hair fanning out from a head facedown in a small puddle, Esther's blood on the tree branch above. It was a scene in a movie where the camera angle lets you see some vital thing left behind as a character shuts a door, their serene face at odds with how badly the audience knows they've messed up.

Before Amira and Sarah had the fight that would end their relationship, Sarah's mother had invited them over for lunch. The two women had met before, but Sarah was still nervous. Sarah's mother had played the part of a gracious hostess, bringing out the good plates, pouring soda water into gold-rimmed glasses and asking questions about Amira's 'Persian roots'. She'd even showed Amira the family tartan. Sarah kept catching her looking at Amira when she thought Sarah wasn't looking.

After lunch, while Amira was using the loo before they got in the car to drive home, Sarah said, 'Thanks for having us, Mum.'

'Of course,' her mother said, rubbing her hands on the shiny material of her pantsuit.

'You know, it means a lot to me that I can bring Amira here,' Sarah said.

Quickly, like she'd been holding it in the whole time, her mother replied, 'Well, it's hard for me. No woman will ever make you happy. You must know that. I'm doing my best, but just because I let you come here together doesn't change the fact.'

The earth shifted under Sarah's feet. 'Why are you saying this?'

'It's a hard world out there, Sarah. I can't always pretend to be happy about this. You're my daughter, and I love you, even if I wish things were different –'

'Yeah, well, it's a hard world in here,' Sarah hissed, and stormed down the hallway to the bathroom. 'I'll see you in the car, babe.' She said it extra loud, so her mother would hear.

The horrible, empty feeling of being *tolerated*.

Later that night, in bed. 'It's a hard world, isn't it?' Amira said. She was teasing Sarah. Trying to get her to smile. They'd just had sex, something Amira instigated whenever she felt Sarah had become unmanageable. Sarah could feel herself blurring into the mattress, the skin on her fingers pruney. Sated and calm for the first time since the argument with her mother.

An episode of *Law & Order* played on the small television in the corner of the bedroom. Sarah would never understand why Amira wanted to watch those kinds of shows before bed.

'I'm sorry I stormed us out of there,' Sarah said. 'It's just been a massive week, you know? It felt like the last straw.'

'So it's really about work,' Amira said, propping herself up on her elbow to look Sarah in the face.

On the television, two detectives were speaking to a sullen witness through a door held only slightly open. Sarah didn't even need to listen to the words; just the beats of their American-inflected speech were enough to know what was happening.

'I'm allowed to be tired.' Sarah heard the defensive note in her own voice.

So much for the sex smoothing things between them.

'Maybe the real problem was it was your first proper day off in a month and you took me to see your mother.'

'Yeah, well, in hindsight it was a bad use of my time.'

Amira's eyes narrowed. 'What about my time?'

They'd been dating for a year. This was already an old argument they were rehashing.

'You act like your job is your life,' Amira said when Sarah didn't reply.

'Is that so wrong?' Sarah should have said, *You're my life*. That's what she knew Amira wanted to hear. But she was angry, tired, sick of having to translate herself for Amira. Had it never occurred to her that Sarah could use a little understanding? Sarah wasn't just a cop, but it *was* part of her. An important part. The truth was Amira had been uneasy about that part since day one.

'Just because you piss your jobs off every ten minutes doesn't mean you need to make me feel like shit because I care about mine.' Sarah knew this was not the way to handle Amira, but couldn't stop herself. 'The only job you've managed to keep is the one where you dress up like a man and dance around on stage.'

'You know, you sound just like your mother,' Amira said, her tone flat.

It was the worst thing she could have said.

'And what would you know?' Sarah felt suddenly protective of her mother. 'Your life looks pretty easy from where I'm standing,' Sarah said. 'You don't know what my mother's been through.'

'You think it's easy to be me?' Amira got out of bed, leaning over Sarah with her hand on her hip.

Sarah shuffled out of bed. She didn't like Amira standing over her like that.

'I am not going to sit around and be the fun thing in *your* life,' Amira continued. 'I'm not just here to reflect your moods. You think that it's my job to be the happy one, the energetic one, and you and your job are what really matter. It's exhausting. I don't *want* to love you anymore.'

Anger boiled up. Couldn't she see Sarah was trying? Sarah couldn't bear it, Amira so close, that look on her face, her hands on her hips. Sarah pushed her. She'd just meant it to be a little shove, but Amira staggered back and lost her balance. Her head hit the bedside table, sending Sarah's mother's watch, and the glass tray it sat on, flying. There was the thud of the tray hitting the carpet. A few terrible seconds before Amira stood up, blood at her temple.

'Amira,' Sarah gasped. 'I'm so sorry.'

'That's it,' Amira said. She sounded completely calm as she pulled herself to her feet. Unharmed enough to look royally pissed off.

Sarah had got lucky. She knew in her gut the injury could've been much worse. Amira pressed her hand against her head then examined the blood on her fingers.

'Mira, please.' Sarah reached for her. If she was honest, the first thing she'd thought about, once she knew Amira wasn't too badly hurt, was her job.

Amira held up her hand. 'I don't ever want you to touch me again.'

Sarah was so shocked at what she'd done that she didn't follow Amira when she left the room. There was a sense of queasy unreality about the scene, like Sarah was looking at everything through the curved bottom of a thick glass tumbler. On the television, the two detectives were walking on a bridge at night, arguing about something. Sarah walked over and turned the television off. She heard the front door of her apartment slam shut.

Sarah had only seen Amira once since then, when they'd met to swap boxes of belongings a couple of weeks before Sarah had come to Durton. Amira had refused to look Sarah in the eye. She couldn't fix it. She'd been waiting for a phone call saying she'd been suspended. And she'd kept calling Amira, leaving voicemails, when she knew she shouldn't. The thought ached and mingled with a wave of nausea from the heat.

It was so hot, and the creek moved so slowly. Sarah felt like someone making a stupid mistake. Smithy was right: it was too fucking hot for busy work.

\*

The planned participation in the school assembly wouldn't take long and was something else to be crossed off the to-do list in Sarah's notebook. Standing in the shade, Sarah looked across the rows of children while Smithy addressed them. Durton had never struck her as the kind of place where murder happened: road deaths, farming accidents – sure. The kids had probably seen their fair share of that. Then she remembered something Amira had said to her. 'Baby, something bad is happening everywhere. This is *Australia*. Think about whose land you're standing on. The catastrophe is ongoing.' Yet more proof that Sarah couldn't see what was in front of her, that it had always fallen to Amira to point out the bleedingly obvious. All those little white faces, getting burned even in the dappled shade of the tree. Nothing peaceful or idyllic about it. Nothing at all.

It was a relief to be back at Mack's station. It was a small space, but it had air conditioning and wasn't the motel, and she could work at the kitchen table.

She asked Mack for an update on his interviews.

'I finally managed to speak with Peter Thompson,' Mack said, rubbing his brow with his left hand. 'He came in with his eldest son, their story checks out, so that's done.'

'So what were they –' Sarah's words were interrupted by movement at the front of the station. Lewis Kennard's small face appeared, then his mother and a tall boy Sarah took to be his older brother.

Sarah hastily gathered up documentation from the case, slipping it out of sight. Lewis's face, with its upturned nose, reminded Sarah that something had bugged her about him. She'd drawn a triangle on his interview notes, but without anything concrete to go on, she hadn't followed up, putting it down to him being a nervous kid.

His mother spoke with an English accent. She had elegant, long-fingered hands and a grace in the way she held herself. Sarah wondered how she'd ended up in Durton.

Other children they'd interviewed had mentioned that Lewis and Esther sat together at lunchtime. *He* hadn't actually mentioned that, now she thought about it, but based on the interviews they'd done, Sarah was confident that he and Esther had left school in different directions. She'd thought that perhaps he just didn't want his mother to know he sat with girls, and she hadn't pushed.

During the second interview, Sarah could tell from the way Smithy sat and the questions he asked that he thought Lewis was a timewaster. But then the boy said he'd seen Esther with a man he didn't recognise. Why would the kid lie?

Then Clint Kennard had showed up. Every fibre of her body told her that Clint Kennard was violent towards his family. She recognised instantly the control he needed to exert over his wife and children. He was more than just your garden-variety sleazebag. Sarah knew that Lewis Kennard was his son, but it was still a shock to see the big man in the station again so soon, the shaving rash on his neck, his thinning hair. Lewis hadn't told them everything before being dragged away, Sarah was sure of that. With what she'd already heard from Evelyn Thompson, it was starting to look like Clint had something to hide. If it weren't for what happened next, that would have been her focus, maybe just the development she was looking for. Sarah would have called Kinouac and explained that they needed to stay. That they had a solid lead for the first time since they'd arrived, that they may have been mistaken about Steven Bianchi. She would have found a way to speak to Lewis at school the next day and made it her mission to find out just what Clint was up to. As it was, she would see Clint sooner than she could have expected.

# WE

We should say that what happened to Esther and what is about to happen to Ronnie were not the only bad things to happen to children in our town. People's parents died. Older brothers killed themselves or were maimed in motorcycle accidents. Once, Missy Henderson was hit by a glowing coal thrown by one of the boys at a bonfire night. It struck just above a frilly sock that an aunt had given her as a First Communion present. The synthetic lace caught fire and left her with a taut, pink burn that went all the way up her leg for the rest of her life. In the confusion it was never entirely clear who had thrown the coal. We really did convince ourselves it could have been any of us. When she was older, Missy would take to wearing long peasant skirts. She revealed the burn when she felt like it, by crossing her legs a certain way and flicking the material aside.

It all matters to us – we remember it with the same part of ourselves. The same part that liked to drink from long, cool glasses of weak cordial. Only we didn't know they were weak because back then we had only ever had the cordial that our mother made for us. We are not sure if it was our childhood or just childhood in general that has made us the way we are. For every girl child there seemed to lurk a dead-eyed man, hair receding prematurely, with a car and the offer of a lift and a plan and a knife and a shovel. Did we create the man by imagining him or was he idling there in his car regardless? Hard not to imagine him, when the smiling faces of the missing blonde twins were splashed across all the newspapers and we were all speculating about what had happened to Esther Bianchi.

We understood, even then, that bad things happened. And we understood that sometimes people *made* them happen. Sometimes those people were people close to us, or even ourselves. We had all squished small, hapless insects to see what it felt like. One of us had even hit a kitten with a large stick. It was not our kitten, but one that we found. After we had struck the kitten, sending its little body into the air, it made a noise as it lay, motionless, on the ground. Those of us who saw it happen felt physically sick. We ran away. We ran for two streets before it occurred to us to drop the stick. The pathetic sound that a kitten makes sounds like a lot of other things. It sounds like the squeal of brakes in the distance or the scrape of chair feet across a tiled floor, even years later.

# RONNIE

Monday, 3 December 2001

I walked out of the school gate and then broke into a jog. Then I was running, my schoolbag rising and thudding into the small of my back. Lewis's words rang in my ears. He'd seemed so angry with me. For a moment I wanted to cry, but I stopped myself. Mum would be expecting me home soon. I thought of Esther's face at the bowling alley when she'd knocked down the wrong pins and what I'd say to the police.

I ran alongside the huge eucalyptus trees that grew back from the road. Past the church; the red-brick building looked tiny on its big block. Lewis had seen Esther with a man who wasn't her father on Friday afternoon. He'd told me but refused to go and tell the police. I thought about how I would explain it to them. It was vital that they listened to me. That I convinced them to speak to Lewis. His words still stung, and the person I most wanted to tell in the world was Esther.

My feet rubbed in my runners.

How fast could llamas run? I wondered. I thought of a photograph I'd seen once of llamas at the Royal Easter Show. It's hotter in Australia than in the mountains of Peru, I guess, because they were standing with large metal fans blowing onto them, and one of them had its eyes closed, like Mum does when she takes a sip of a really good cup of tea and wants to enjoy it. The police station was on the other side of the train tracks from the school. Rather than turning for the main road, I headed northwest. I couldn't remember if Mum was working that day, or if she'd already be at home, but this path meant it was unlikely she'd see me.

I worried about someone spotting me from the houses that lined the road. I slowed to a walk in front of some places, paranoid that I saw a curtain twitch, or heard a voice calling out to me.

I reached the motel, which meant I was halfway there. I could take a shortcut by running behind the row of rooms, but I had to be careful not to let the owner see me. He'd spotted me and Esther near the dog once and yelled at us, told us never to come back. It had already taken me so long to come that far that I decided to risk it.

I saw the dog that Esther and I planned to free chained at the centre of a dusty circle next to the verandah that ran in front of the rooms. I remembered the fear and shame that had pulsed through my body when the owner had told us off. It had felt like someone was pouring me out, so that what was left sloshed around in a dark, empty space.

Something orange and fuzzy on the ground caught my eye.

'Flea!' I cried in a half-whisper. 'What are you doing here?'

He squinted his yellow eyes. He was sunning himself in the dirt, his fluffy ginger tail spread out behind him. He looked totally calm, despite the nearness of the barking dog.

I walked towards him. 'What are you doing here, buddy?'

He rolled over to expose his belly, and the dog ran to the end of its chain at full speed. Its collar grabbed and the motion whipped its head back. In a flash, Flea darted under a big white van parked between me and the motel's main building.

'Don't go that way, kitty!'

I heard a thud coming from the van. It was too loud to be Flea. It sounded like someone banging against the inside of the van.

There was the squeal of a heavy door opening. I ran for the verandah and crouched by a small table and chairs in front of the closest room, sneaking a quick glance down the line of rooms to make sure no-one else was around. I heard another thud. It was coming from inside the van. I thought of Esther. What if she'd come here after school on Friday to free the dog and the owner had caught her at it? What if he'd been keeping her in there since then? The van would be like a room that he could move around whenever he needed to.

My heart smashed against my chest. I didn't know why Esther wouldn't have asked me to come with her. But maybe it was because she'd guessed how scared I was.

I saw the shadow of feet moving on the other side of the van. The motel owner came into view. He was carrying something; a black plastic bag was slung over his shoulder. He supported the base with one hand while keeping the end of the bag closed with the other. It looked heavy. I poked my head out just far enough so that I could see him. He wasn't looking in my direction. What was he doing? I thought of the police at the assembly, about what they'd said. Anyone could help them find Esther. They needed our help.

My legs hurt from crouching but I stayed as still as I possibly could, listening to the sound of my own breathing, straining for a better look. What if she was in the van and I just stood there and did nothing because I was afraid? Esther would never do that. Esther would come looking for me.

'Fucking SHUT UP!'

I froze, sure for a moment I'd been seen, before I realised the owner was yelling at the dog, which was still barking furiously.

I couldn't see into the van from where I was. A huge bag of cat litter leaned against the building; it was the same cheap brand that my mum bought for Flea.

Flea. I hoped he would be safe under there.

The owner grunted as he lowered the bag through the open back doors of the van. There was a dull smack as it slipped out of his hands and hit the floor. He turned away from the van and I readied myself to run. I had to look inside. I had to do it for Esther. Every nerve in my body was telling me to stay hidden, to turn back, to go home. I heard his steps moving away and I knew this was my opportunity. I had to look inside the van before he came back again. I launched myself from the verandah. I was running, flying, faster than I ever had.

There was a sound, which I figured out later must have been the chain snapping. I didn't see the dog before it was upon me. There wasn't time to be frightened, but I do remember kicking out. Then I was on the ground. Jaws closed around the right side of my face. Screaming. I saw a man's legs and even in my pain I was afraid of the motel owner. The sound is what I remember, shuddering in my jaw: a sound like the ending of the world.

# SARAH

Monday, 3 December 2001

There was an uncharacteristic quiet in the small police station after the Kennard family left by the back door.

Smithy, who was pacing the kitchen, was the first to break it. 'Well, I don't like this Clint Kennard bastard one little bit.' The words seemed forced out, like his moustache was a thick curtain they had to push through.

'We haven't talked to the family four times, have we?' Sarah asked.

'Well,' Mack said, 'I spoke to Clint on Saturday, and you two spoke to Lewis on Saturday at the school, and then we brought Clint back in on Sunday after your conversation with Evelyn Thompson. So, yeah, I suppose today was the fourth conversation.'

Smithy snorted derisively. 'Seems to me the prick has a reason to be keeping count.'

'We'll find a way to speak to the boy.' Sarah held Smithy's gaze. 'He knows something, I'm sure he does. At least, Clint is worried he does.'

Smithy said something Sarah couldn't hear over the sound of the phone ringing. Mack picked up the kitchen extension. It was hard to make out what was happening from his replies alone.

When he hung up, Sarah asked, 'Who was that?'

Mack glanced at the clock on the wall. 'At the motel. A kid's been bitten by a dog. Evelyn Thompson's little girl.'

'Shit,' said Smithy. 'Is it bad?'

'The ambulance is already there, apparently. The dog's under control.' Mack looked at Sarah. 'Listen, are you two right to go? I've got one last follow-up interview from the batch you wanted me to do. I'd brief one of you on it, but it would take longer than it's worth.' He checked the clock again. 'I could cancel it, but it's been bloody impossible to get this guy in.'

'We can handle it.' Sarah snatched up her notebook and nodded at Smithy, who was already heading for the door.


When Sarah and Smithy pulled up at the motel, there was no sign of the ambulance, but an older man in a red flannelette shirt was waiting for them in front of a hastily parked ute.

'I was just driving past when it happened,' he said. There was a smudge of blood under the man's eye. 'I saw the whole thing.'

The dog was tied to a brick post. Its eyes cut wildly from side to side, its rust-coloured rump moving in and out of the shadow of the main building.

'What happened?'

The man in the flannelette shirt wiped his face with the tips of his fingers. 'She was out the front running away from the rooms and the dog just went for her. I've never seen anything like it. Knocked her clean over and went for the face. She didn't see it coming.'

'Are you injured?' Sarah said, looking at the blood on the man's shirt.

His flannelette shirt was open over a singlet and stubby shorts. When he shrugged the shirt off, Sarah saw a gash on his arm.

'Mate, why didn't the ambos take you as well?' Smithy said.

'She was screaming, and then she stopped. I think she passed out or something.'

'But why didn't you go with the ambos? You'll need a shot for the bite, at the very least,' Sarah said.

He looked at his arm. 'They wanted to examine me, but I told them I was fine. It didn't hurt, at first. I thought it was just a graze. I thought it was her blood on me shirt. They only let me be when I promised I'd ring the cops.' The old man looked sheepish.

'And you are?' Sarah asked.

'Ned Harrison.'

'Right, Ned,' Sarah said. His arm looked pretty bad to her. 'Any idea how the dog got loose?'

'The chain must've snapped. It's over there.' The man gestured with his good arm.

Sarah turned to Smithy. 'You can take Ned to the hospital in our car,' she told him. 'Use the siren when you get to the highway.' She turned back to Ned. 'Where's the owner of the dog?'

'The bloke who runs the motel was here. He cleared off as soon as we got the dog tied up. He didn't say anything, but when I said I was calling you he just left. He should have stayed, shouldn't he?' The man looked to Smithy for affirmation.

'Did you see which way he went?' Sarah asked, turning and checking the road behind her.

'He fanged it towards the main street, so he could have been headed for the highway, but I couldn't be sure.'

'What's his name?' Clint had mentioned it in the interview on Sunday but she couldn't recall. Had it been Ronald Matthews? She knew that wasn't quite right.

Strange that the man Clint had been drinking with on Friday afternoon had cleared off as soon as he'd heard the cops were coming.

There had to be a connection with the pissed-off Clint Kennard who'd practically dragged Lewis Kennard out of Mack's station.

'It's Roland Mathers,' Ned said, glancing back towards the driveway leading up to the motel reception. Maybe Roland Mathers was someone he didn't want to get on the wrong side of. 'I should tell you, too, that I've already called the girl's mother. She said she'd go straight to the hospital.'

Smithy placed a hand on Ned's shoulder. 'That's good – one less thing for us to do.'

Sarah nodded her agreement. She asked Ned, 'What kind of vehicle was he in?'

'It was a white van. I'm pretty confident it was a Toyota HiAce.'

Sarah knew the van; she'd seen it parked at the motel before.

Smithy stepped between the man and Sarah. 'So, I'm taking Ned here in the Commodore?' he asked.

'Yup. Ned, is it alright if I take your car back to the station?' Sarah asked, nodding at the ute. 'I can pick up Mack's car from there. I want to find out where Mr Mathers has got to.'

'Yeah, no worries.' Ned's arm was held to his chest now, his shirt tucked around it, his big tummy shifting on skinny legs.

Sarah opened the back door of the Commodore and retrieved her shoulder bag from behind the passenger seat.

'What about the dog?' said Smithy, motioning towards the animal.

'The dog'll be right,' said Ned. 'I had a choker chain in the car. It won't be getting out of that anytime soon.' He fished the car keys out of his pocket. 'You've got to pull the ring around the gearstick up before you can put it in reverse.'

Sarah walked around the front of Ned's ute to the driver's side door, giving the dog a wide berth. Its eyes followed her. She lowered herself into the driver's seat and was struck by the smell of dust and engine oil. It reminded her of her father's workshop, of long afternoons spent watching him work. He was the reason she understood anything about cars. No daughter of his would be stuck on the side of the road waiting for someone to come and save her.

Ned called out and Sarah looked over at the Commodore.

'When she came to, the little girl was asking for the police. She said she had to tell you something. Said it was urgent. She was pretty delirious, in and out of it, but she was determined.'

Sarah raised a hand to confirm she'd heard him, then she turned the key and the engine roared into life. So Veronica Thompson had wanted to talk to them. Lewis Kennard and Veronica Thompson were both Esther's friends, weren't they? Now Sarah wished she'd taken the job of driving Ned, but Smithy was sure to follow up with the girl at the hospital.

Smithy waited for her to back out before he started his car. Sarah gunned the engine; she didn't want to give the motel owner time to get far.

She'd driven less than a kilometre down the road when she saw two boys running across the road out the front of the IGA. At first glance, they appeared to be playing, but then Sarah realised they were being chased. A man ran in front of the car – was that Clint Kennard? – and she swerved hard, only narrowly avoiding the concrete kerb, and braked. The contents of the tray thumped against the back of the cab as she came to an abrupt halt. She stopped just in time to hear the shriek of brakes and a low thud coming from the other side of the long nature strip that divided the main street.

Sarah's heart pounded in her ears as she sprang out of the car and jogged across the road.

Clint Kennard, waxen-faced, was still on his feet, but he looked to be on the verge of toppling over sideways. Sarah moved closer, ready to catch him. The door of the other car opened and the driver got out. Sarah gaped at her. What was Constance Bianchi doing here?

Constance's face was a picture of anguish, her hands held in front of her, like she was begging forgiveness.

The bright, blue sky pinned the town to the ground, making it feel low and small. Sarah could see the two boys out of the corner of her eye, standing on the pavement and watching, open-mouthed. Sarah recognised Lewis Kennard. Next to him was the boy named Campbell. She'd been in the room while Smithy interviewed him at the school.

Clint was angry. Something about the way he began yelling at Constance made him look like an Australian character actor from the shows Amira loved: the truckie who knew more than he was telling, or a man who'd pissed off the wrong people and gone on the run – someone with nothing left to lose.

'Is everything alright?' Sarah called, moving towards Clint and Constance, determined to place herself between them.

If her training sergeant could have seen her, he'd have shaken his head. *Your first priority in any situation is self-preservation, Michaels. Self-preservation is your responsibility to our force, your community. The people we deal with don't need an assaulting-an-officer charge.*

Sarah went to put a hand on Clint's shoulder. 'Steady on.'

He turned and grabbed her by the neck. He pulled her towards him. She smelled beer on his breath. A familiar panic took hold of her. Almost as quickly, her conditioning kicked in. All the hours. All her training. She knew how to do this. Every muscle in Sarah's body contracted. Clint's hands were around her neck, choking her, but her body remembered what to do. She brought her arms up and between his, forcing them outwards and breaking his grip. He grabbed her shirt and she pulled in closer to him, twisting her body and placing her leg under his left knee. She used her body weight to bring him down. Sarah's only thought as they fell was that now she'd have something else she needed to explain to Kinouac.

Pain exploded in the side of her head as they hit the ground. So, this was what it felt like.

She lay on the ground, face up, dazed.

Smithy was on Clint before Sarah could right herself, and there was the glitter of sun on silver handcuffs. From her horizontal position, she marvelled that Smithy had thought to snatch them from the glove box as he exited the car. He must have been just behind her and seen it all.

Constance Bianchi crouched beside Sarah. 'Are you okay, Detective Michaels?'

Sarah's head hurt and her ears were ringing, but she could see clearly. She sat upright.

'Take it easy,' said Constance, putting a hand on Sarah's shoulder.

'I'm fine,' Sarah said. And she was.

Smithy had handcuffed Clint and was walking him towards the Commodore. Ned stepped out of the passenger seat. Sarah noticed Lewis's mother standing by her car in front of the IGA, looking over at them. The woman kept her head down.

The boys were gone.

'Did you catch the dog?' asked Constance, nodding in the direction Sarah had come from.

'It's tied up at the motel,' Sarah said, getting to her feet.

'Ronnie's mum called me,' Constance explained.

It had seemed natural that Constance knew what had happened, like the town was a living, breathing entity. Information would be carried on the wings of small, dull-coloured birds and the backs of open-mouthed lizards, drawn through the dry dirt by the whispering of gnarled roots, swept overland on hot breezes.

Smithy walked towards them. 'Are you okay, boss?'

'Yup,' Sarah said, brushing the dirt from her shirt.

'I've got to go,' Constance said. 'I've got to get Ronnie's mum to the hospital.'

Sarah turned to look at Constance's car. The front seats were empty.

'I was just driving to her place to get her,' Constance said, following Sarah's gaze. 'I have to go?' It sounded like a question, but she was already moving.

'Someone will need to take Ned to the hospital.' Smithy motioned towards the Commodore with his head; Clint Kennard was in the back. 'I shouldn't be long at the station with this loser, but it would be better for Ned to see someone sooner rather than later.'

'You've got the secure rig' – Sarah glanced over at the Commodore – 'so you take Kennard to Rhodes. Radio Mack on the way and get him out looking for Roland Mathers. Ned can ride with me to the hospital.'

If Smithy was confused by the change of plan, he didn't show it. 'Got it, boss.'

'Great,' Sarah said. Going to the hospital with Ned would give her a chance to speak with Veronica Thompson. The second kid in one day who'd taken it upon themselves to try to talk to the police.

'Get Rhodes to help you find out the licence plate number of the van. And it would be good if we could find those boys, ask why Kennard was chasing them.'

There was a connection between Clint Kennard and Roland Mathers. With Clint in custody she'd be able to take her time working out how deep it went, and what it might have to do with Esther Bianchi.

'On it,' replied Smithy.

Ned must have heard Smithy and Sarah discussing the change in plan, because he walked over to them. His arm was tucked up against his chest. The flannelette shirt holding it in place was dark with blood.

Sarah eased into the driver's seat of the ute, her pulse thudding in her temples.

Ned climbed into the passenger seat. 'Clint Kennard's always been a prick,' he said as Sarah started the engine.

Sarah put the car into gear, a little clumsily, with Ned's eyes on her.

'Where do you think Roland Mathers has cleared off to?' she asked. Might as well use her time with Ned productively.

'Oh, he'll try and go to ground in the bush somewhere, I reckon,' said Ned. 'He did that a lot as a teenager. His father was a nasty piece of work. Roland would take off for weeks at a time.'

'Have you ever seen Steven Bianchi and Roland Mathers together?'

'Steve isn't the most social bloke; he's like his father in that respect. But I do see Roland with Clint Kennard quite a bit. Lately I've seen Peter Thompson drinking with them sometimes, too.' Ned wiped sweat from his brow. 'I wonder why Clint was chasing those boys?'

Sarah gripped the steering wheel. 'Yes, that would be good to know.'

She hoped Smithy was getting to the bottom of it as they spoke. She'd already confirmed that Steven Bianchi didn't have any close mates. She couldn't imagine Steven and Clint Kennard, or the motel owner, together. And Peter Thompson. There was that name again. She'd been about to ask Mack about his alibi back at the station when they were interrupted by Lewis Kennard's arrival.

'It's your job to look for missing people,' said Ned.

'Yes,' Sarah replied. 'Kids mainly.'

'Do you think the Thompson girl is going to be okay?'

'She's probably at the hospital by now.'

It wasn't an answer to his question.

'Has Steven Bianchi got something to do with his daughter going missing? I heard he was arrested.'

'I'm sorry. I can't talk about the case.'

'Fair enough,' said Ned amiably, turning to look out his window.

A Tooheys New bottle opener swung from the rear-view mirror as they rode over imperfections in the road. They drove past brown paddocks, faded road signs, white lines on the bitumen.

Sarah had entered the police academy because she needed to feel like what she did mattered, that the world was different because she'd come to work. Coming up as a recruit, she'd been faced with the reality of the job: that very few people she interacted with thought of police as 'the good guys'. Keeping women and children safe had always been at the centre of her father's approach. Not that he'd done much to help herself and her mother. Maybe she needed an excuse for her own inadequacies, too. In police work, they became a strength. Sarah felt the same quickening feeling she'd got countless times over the years, like she was on the verge of pulling off a familiar party trick. She needed to figure out the connection between what she had just seen and Esther Bianchi's disappearance. She knew that if she could sketch it all out in her notebook, she would find a thread that would lead her to the answer.

Out of nowhere, the old man spoke in a small voice. 'Can you pull over?'

'Is everything okay?' Sarah stole a glance at him as she eased the ute onto the shoulder.

The old man opened the door and vomited extravagantly onto the roadside. When the wave had passed, he rubbed a hand over his mouth and shut the door.

'You alright?'

'Yeah. Often happens when I lose a bit of blood. It runs in the family.'

'How's your arm?' she asked.

'Fine,' Ned grunted, lifting his chin to the road to indicate Sarah should resume driving.

Sarah patted her pocket and felt the comforting bulk of her notebook. She was sure Smithy would have already radioed Mack and got him out looking for Roland Mathers. Clint Kennard would be locked up for at least the next couple of days. She accelerated off the shoulder, possible next steps swirling in her mind.

# LEWIS

It was Dick Summers who'd seen Lewis Kennard and his mother and brother going into the police station. He was the one who'd blabbed to Lewis's dad at the pub.

After his father had interrupted the interview, they all had to leave the station together in Lewis's mum's car.

'It's lucky Dick could drive me, or you lot would still be in there,' Lewis's dad said.

Not even his dad thought it was a good idea to drink and drive to the police station.

It didn't occur to Lewis to wonder why his father had come. He was always where you least wanted him to be.

Simon whined when he couldn't sit in the front seat. Lewis's father was silent as Lewis's mother drove over the dry field behind the police station, shaking his head theatrically as she worked her way up the gears. Lewis could smell booze.

Lewis's dad bounced in his seat, as if unable to contain himself for a second longer. 'What is fucking *wrong* with this family?'

Simon laughed his empty laugh again. Lewis's mum said nothing. They turned onto the main street.

As they approached the long string of trees that divided the two

217

sides of the road, Lewis's dad said, 'Pull into the IGA. I need to speak to the owner.' He sounded drunker than he had in the station.

Lewis's mum pulled a little too quickly into one of the angled parking spots that thrust out from the kerb. It was Monday afternoon and the street was empty.

She had to brake hard to stop. Lewis could tell without even looking that she hadn't parked flush inside the white lines. His dad swung his door out and stepped onto the road, shutting the door with a fat, metallic slam. The car was sitting in full sun.

'Wait here,' he said. He looked first at Lewis's mum and then at Lewis. 'We're going to be having a chat about this, believe me.'

What business could his father have in the store at this time of day? Lewis wondered. His mother always did the shopping.

When Lewis's dad reached the threshold of the shop, Lewis's mum wound her window down and looked longingly at a shady area five or six spaces away before closing her eyes. Lewis hated her in that moment: for not saying anything, for not throwing the car into reverse with them in it and driving away from his father, for not even daring to move to a spot in the shade. He sweated. His mum breathed in and out, the only sound in the car. The only sound in the whole bloody town. Images of what would happen next whirred through his mind. Perhaps his dad would want to stretch it out. Let them tiptoe around until he exploded about something else. No. His dad was pissed off. It would happen as soon as they got home. A wave of contempt and revulsion and fear swept through him. It was hard to tell how much time passed in the car. He didn't have a watch. The small analogue clock in the dash was long broken.

He rolled down his window and hung out of it. There was no breeze, nothing to combat the rising temperature. Nothing moved. How could she let Simon sit in here?

'Can I go stand in the shade over there, Mum?'

She didn't respond.

'Please. I'll keep an eye out for Dad.' How could it possibly get any worse? Lewis thought.

'He won't be much longer.' Her voice sounded strong, decided. The voice of a woman who would never let a man hit her.

'Hot,' said Simon.

'That's right, Simon!' Lewis's mum said, turning in her seat to look. She was so pleased when Simon spoke.

Lewis saw Campbell Rutherford walking on the same side of the road as the IGA. Lewis's body crackled with electricity. Lewis's father was still inside, but he didn't care. He'd been trying to talk to Campbell since Saturday. Lewis threw open his door. His mum turned in her seat. She looked through the car window, checking for Lewis's father or for any witnesses. They were always so afraid someone would *see* them.

'Lewis,' his mum said in her firmest voice.

He swung the door shut behind him and took a step away from the car. A breeze caught the sweat on his upper lip.

'Lewis,' said his mum, slightly louder now.

He took another step.

'You come back here.'

There was something in her voice that reminded him of morning cartoons – of Yosemite Sam or Porky Pig: characters who didn't know how ridiculous they were. He resented the pink flush in her cheeks, her soft English voice, hated everything about her.

Lewis jogged towards Campbell. There was no-one else on the street. Campbell was looking down, his shaved head nodding in rhythm with his steps.

'Campbell!' he yelled.

Campbell looked up. Spotting Lewis, he cast a glance behind him. He was still in his school uniform.

Lewis jogged the rest of the distance.

219

'I need to talk to you,' Lewis said.

'What about?' Campbell was still scanning the street.

'Campbell, I've just come from the police.'

'What?' Campbell's eyebrows shot up. He was paying attention now.

'I told them about what happened at the creek.'

'What?' Campbell grabbed Lewis's polo shirt and dragged him towards the IGA.

Lewis pulled away, not wanting to go inside the shop where his dad was, but Campbell pulled him into the shade between the fence and the side of the building. In the alleyway they were largely hidden from the street, and there were no windows in the wall of the IGA. Campbell still had Lewis by the shirtfront. What would Lewis's mum be thinking?

'Why did you talk to the police?' Campbell hissed.

'Because they needed to know,' Lewis replied.

'Why do they need to know?' Campbell said, almost pleadingly.

'They need to know we saw her.'

'Saw who?'

'Estie. Esther. I had to tell them what we saw. Well, what *I* saw. I didn't tell them you were there.' Lewis added the last part in a rush, realising he should have opened with that. 'I just told them about the man. I told them it wasn't Estie's dad.'

'Right.' Campbell's face creased with confusion.

'But I don't think they believed me. I think they need to hear it from you as well.'

'Hear what from me?'

'What we saw at the creek.'

'Sorry, mate' – Campbell turned his head to look past the ice machine and towards the road – 'but what exactly did we see at the creek?'

'We saw Estie and the bald man.'

'What are you talking about, Lewis?'

'ESTHER!' Lewis yelled.

'That girl wasn't Esther, Lewis.'

'What?'

'Listen, that was a different girl. She had dark hair, sure, but she was older. She wasn't wearing a school uniform. It wasn't Esther Bianchi.'

'She must have got changed,' Lewis said.

'Didn't you see her face? And the bell had just rung,' said Campbell. 'We heard it, remember? When we started walking down into the creek? We were the only kids out of school.'

Alone in his room, Lewis had replayed that thirty seconds so many times since Saturday morning. The man's shirt; the back of Estie's head; her voice, lost to the wind. Estie had a strong voice. She'd looked small next to the man, but how tall was the man? He'd been distracted by what had happened, by the kiss shared – yes, shared, they'd both wanted it, no matter how Campbell acted afterwards. But why had it never occurred to him that the girl he saw wasn't wearing a school uniform?

Lewis stepped back, bringing his right hand up to his head.

'I was really scared there for a second.' Campbell smiled.

The alley was tipping. 'There's still a chance that man had something to do with it, right? I mean, maybe no-one but us knows he was in town.'

'My dad said they're sure her dad did it. That's why they arrested him.' Campbell suddenly looked much older than he was.

'My dad said they only arrested him because he stabbed a cop,' Lewis said, recalling that he'd told Ronnie what he'd overheard in his lounge room like it was true, even though he'd never really believed it.

'That's what my dad heard too, that he stabbed someone. But that was just a dumb rumour. He only *punched* a cop. Lacey Macintyre told my mum.' Campbell said it quietly, moving closer. 'Still, isn't the kind of guy who'd go around punching cops the guy they're looking for?' He released the front of Lewis's shirt. 'Not everything's your fault, Lewis.'

It could only have been half a second. Campbell's hand grabbed Lewis's, maybe to make his point, to make sure Lewis wasn't going to tell. Maybe he was going to start beating the shit out of Lewis. Maybe they would've kissed again. Lewis wanted to. Whatever it was, in that same moment there was movement at the end of the alleyway. Lewis's dad was standing there, his shoulders blocking the light.

'What the fuck are you doing?'

Campbell dropped Lewis's hand.

'What are you fucking doing?' Lewis's dad took a step towards them.

His dad had seen the wanting, had seen right through Lewis down to the watery bits of his guts. He knew. Lewis knew he knew.

'Run!' Lewis yelled at Campbell.

Lewis turned and ran down the alleyway, away from his father.

Campbell hesitated for a second before sprinting after him.

'What are you fucking *doing*?' Lewis's dad yelled after them.

Something inside Lewis ripped in two, like when you wrench a Fizzer apart with your bare hands – sticky pink strings tearing and breaking and falling away into brittle strands that can't hold themselves up and sink, dipping towards the floor.

Lewis's dad bolted after them down the alleyway, and just as they were about to reach the end, emerging into the sunlight, Campbell jerked abruptly. Lewis's dad had clamped a hand on Campbell's shoulder. Lewis skidded to a stop. Maybe his dad would've turned on his jokey voice, maybe he would've tried to charm Campbell like he charmed everyone else, but Lewis would never know because he turned and, without thinking, kicked out. He got his dad in the balls. His father made an *oof* sound and bent forward, releasing Campbell.

'Run!' Lewis yelled again.

They needed to get out into the open where other adults could see them. They ran around the back of the building and down the alley on the other side, emerging into the street.

Lewis's mum was standing next to the orange car, leaning with her hips and back resting against it, her hand shielding her face from the sun. Simon was in the back seat, his face in the open window. There weren't any other people on the street. Lewis ran across the road directly in front of the IGA, losing precious seconds as he looked both ways. Campbell joined stride with him, not bothering to check for cars. They arrived at the strip between the two sides of the main road, a sloping grassy hillock, studded with trees. Lewis stumbled, caught himself. There was a presence behind his left shoulder. How had his dad caught up so quickly? Campbell was to Lewis's right. They were running down the other side of the verge now, picking up speed on the incline. Whatever might be coming on the road would hit Lewis first, knocking him into Campbell. The thought of contact, of skin on skin, was thrilling. And then they were on the road and there was something coming on their left, too late to stop. Lewis grabbed Campbell by the arm and then they were clear and Lewis's dad was behind them and there was a squeal of brakes.

Lewis turned to look, nearly tripping over his own feet. Lewis saw his father in the moment he leaped away from the car. He stumbled and fell to the road just behind the driver's door of the now-motionless car. His father sprang up right away, like a cat righting itself. Lewis wanted to keep running but found he was frozen to the spot. Campbell, too, was staring, mouth open, his gaze flicking between the driver of the car and Lewis's dad, who now stood, arms and legs akimbo, in the road.

'Where the fuck did you learn to drive?' Lewis's father roared.

He covered the few steps between him and the car in what seemed like one movement and slammed his hands down on the roof.

The driver opened the door and stepped out. It was Estie's mum.

'Are you okay?' she asked.

'It's a fucking main street. You could have killed those kids.'

'I'm sorry, I didn't see them until the last possible moment. It's not – it's not a pedestrian crossing.'

'*It's not a pedestrian crossing,*' Lewis's dad repeated, mocking her.

Estie's mum squared her shoulders. 'Why were you running across the road in the first place?' Her tone had hardened.

Lewis heard a voice coming from his left. 'Is everything alright?' It was the female detective.

Her remark seemed to be addressed to all of them, and she took in the whole scene, looking at Lewis and Campbell before looking across at Lewis's dad and Estie's mum.

His mum was watching from her spot by the car but couldn't leave Simon.

The female cop had come from a beaten-up farm ute which she'd parked facing the wrong way. The male detective emerged from a white car parked across two spots on the IGA side of the road.

Lewis had a bad feeling.

The female officer was almost next to his dad now. 'Steady on,' she said.

'Let's go, Campbell,' Lewis whispered.

Campbell's eyes moved to the cop and the stopped car and Lewis's father and Estie's mother, all arranged on the road. No-one was looking at them. Campbell nodded and they walked away, breaking into a run as soon as they hit a side street.

Lewis focused on the rectangle created by the back panel of Campbell's school shirt. He thought that at any moment his mother was going to pull up alongside them, but when he turned to look, no-one was following.

Campbell plunged into a shortcut through scrub that ran along behind the butcher's shop and past the park, taking them away from the main road.

They only slowed to a walk when they reached Campbell's lawn. Running, sucking in hot air, the sweat that made Campbell's shirt cling to his back, all these things had kept the image of Lewis's father's face at bay. Now, all Lewis could picture was his heavy-lidded eyes, his mouth twisted in disgust. Campbell's house was across from the town's oval, where men played cricket in the summer. Lewis could see Campbell's mother through the kitchen window, which faced the street. Lewis had heard her say before that sometimes when she was doing the dishes, she'd look up and see the mob of kangaroos that liked to gather there at dusk. *It's like they've headed home for tea.*

Campbell opened the front door and Lewis ducked in behind him. They both slipped off their shoes.

Campbell's mum appeared at the entrance to the kitchen. 'No-one told me you were coming over, Lewis,' she said, taking in their sweat-soaked shirts.

Campbell's mum's smile came too late to soften what she'd said. At the back door, Campbell's dog whined.

'We're just going to watch some TV,' said Campbell, still catching his breath.

What Lewis wanted, more than anything, was a glass of water.

'Does your mother know you're here?' Campbell's mum looked right at Lewis. There were dark smudges under her eyes.

'We just left her at the shop. I saw Campbell on the street and then we came here.' That was basically true, Lewis thought.

Campbell turned to look at Lewis, eyebrows raised at his smooth lie.

'She usually calls me before you come over.'

Lewis tried to make his face as blank as possible.

'I'm sorry, Lewis,' she said. 'Campbell's got chores to do. It would be better if you went home.'

Campbell looked at him and shrugged.

Lewis bent down to put his shoes back on. They could have no idea what would be waiting for him at home. Surely his mother and father would have driven there by now. Even though the police officers had seen Lewis's dad yell at Estie's mum, he knew his father would've made some joke and smoothed everything over. Clint Kennard could talk his way out of anything. Lewis felt the thrill of using his dad's name: *Clint Kennard is a prick*, he said to himself. *Clint Kennard is going to kill me.* Clint could still be driving around looking for him right now. Or Campbell's phone might ring at any moment. Lewis was floating above what was happening instead of being inside of it. He'd never done anything like this before.

'Besides, Lewis, I think your mum will want to keep you home after what happened to Veronica Thompson,' Campbell's mum said.

'What happened to her?' Campbell asked, before Lewis could.

'Lacey Macintyre just called. Veronica Thompson was attacked by a dog near the Horse and Cane. They've taken her to the hospital, apparently. Lacey said she was in a bad way.'

The Horse and Cane was past Ronnie's place. Why would she go there? Hadn't she said she was already in trouble for going out on Saturday? Something in Lewis knew instantly why she'd been at the motel – she'd been on her way to speak to the police. It was the only reason he could think of.

'I better go,' Lewis said, already heading for the door.

'Yes, you should go straight home to your mum.' Campbell's mother's mouth was a firm line. 'In fact, I'd be much more comfortable driving you.'

'That's okay, Mrs Rutherford.' He was out the door before she could reply, shutting it behind him. His shoelaces were still undone. *Ronnie was hurt.*

At the end of the lawn, he turned left. He needed to speak to Ronnie. Who was in hospital. There was only one hospital she could be at. Lewis needed to know she was okay, and he had to explain that he'd gone to speak to the police, that he wasn't a total coward. He considered his options. His mum shimmered in his mind, but only for a second. There was no way she would take him anywhere, not after what had happened, and to get to her he would have to go through Clint. Lewis wasn't sure where they were, but he ran until he hit a cross street his parents would have no reason to drive down. He ran past pepper trees, towards the highway. He'd emerge near the sign marking the edge of Durton. From there, he'd have to rely on a car picking him up.

The sun drilled into him; sweat was streaming down his face and back. Lewis tried to ignore his thirst, pushed it down. It helped to have something else to focus on, something to beat the image of Clint's face out of his mind (still that small thrill from saying *Clint*, even just to himself). Lewis ran past empty lots, the occasional house. The pavement ended in front of the roller doors of a khaki-coloured shed. He continued along the shoulder of the road. At the railway crossing, he glanced up out of habit, but this crossing didn't have boom gates, just an old sign that said: LOOK FOR TRAINS.

Standing on the edge of the highway, Lewis didn't know exactly when he saw it – it was like looking at the dark bark of a tree for a moment before noticing a shimmering screen of small, whirling insects in the air. The car seemed familiar; it had to be someone he knew. Should he step forward? Run away? It slowed, the left front wheel leaving the bitumen, so that the left side of the car was lower than the right when it pulled alongside. Someone he couldn't quite make out through the heavily tinted windscreen leaned over and rolled down the passenger window.

It was Peter Thompson. Ronnie's uncle wasn't in his Town gear today, but a grubby singlet, his red hair under a baseball cap.

'You looking to get run over there, mate? It's not that bloody hot is it?' He looked over his shoulder back at the road behind him, laughing at his own joke.

'Ronnie's in hospital,' Lewis said. 'A dog bit her. It's really bad. I need to see her.'

Peter's face fell. 'Shit, mate. Did this just happen?'

'Yeah, I think so. At the motel. She's hurt real bad.'

'Was her mum with her?' Peter asked.

Lewis shook his head. 'I don't know.'

'Where's your dad?' Peter ducked his head and peered out the passenger window, as though Clint might be behind Lewis.

'Please, both my parents are busy. We need to go now.' He bent down so Peter could see his face through the open window. 'Please?' Sweat ran down his forehead and he was on the verge of tears.

Peter looked him over. Lewis thought of the moment, in the doorway at his house, when Peter had seen his bruise and said nothing.

'Alright,' Peter said. 'I'll call them when we get there.'


Peter Thompson had something in the back of his throat. He kept trying to clear it as they drove, the only sound in the car except for the hiss of bitumen rolling underneath them. Something about the sound added to the distance between them and their destination. Peter's freckled hands gripped the wheel, ginger hairs on his knuckles. Maybe he was thinking that he should've taken Lewis home instead. He could still turn around, throw a hard right and take Lewis back to Clint.

'Do you think Ronnie will be okay?' Lewis asked.

'I'm sure she'll be fine, mate,' Peter said, rubbing his red goatee with the back of his left hand. He kept his eyes on the road.

Peter hadn't even known that she was in hospital.

Lewis looked out the window. What was happening in his gut didn't feel like normal fear. It was like opening a drawer and realising that something had been moved or taken away. The contents didn't roll into each other in their usual way. This new feeling was higher up. Like one of those metal rings – the kind his mum used to fry Clint's eggs into perfect circles – had been pushed down his throat. He couldn't swallow, couldn't sit comfortably. Air rushed in through the window, like someone pushing their way to the front of a line.

'What was Ronnie doing at the motel?' Peter asked.

'What?'

'What was she doing there? It's out of her way.' Peter turned to look at Lewis through narrowed eyes.

Lewis remembered the conversation he'd overheard between Peter and his father. His guts contracted. Hadn't Peter and his father mentioned Roland Mathers, who ran the motel? Lewis moved his hand so it rested in the groove near the handle of the car door.

'I know you two are friends,' Peter said, and Lewis avoided the look he could feel Peter was giving him from the driver's seat.

Lewis kept his eyes on the road ahead. It hadn't been a question and he didn't know what to say in reply.

Peter cleared his throat again.

Trees started to appear in steady rows. They were getting closer to Rhodes, to the hospital. The speed limit changed and there were more buildings. They were pulling into the car park. Peter hadn't come to a complete stop before Lewis opened the door.

'Hold on, mate,' Peter yelled as Lewis ran towards the main hospital entrance.

Ronnie's mum was standing just outside the big glass doors with a lit cigarette in her hand.

'Is Ronnie alright?'

He'd startled her. She threw the cigarette on the ground and stamped on it.

The words MAIN ENTRANCE were plastered across the sliding front doors of the hospital, split in half when the doors opened. Estie's mum emerged. Her eyes found Ronnie's mum's before landing on Lewis.

'What are you doing here?' Estie's mum looked out into the car park, her eyes scanning the rows of cars. 'Is your dad here?'

'No. I came with Ronnie's uncle,' Lewis said.

'Peter,' Ronnie's mum said, lurching forward.

She was so short she only came up to Peter's chest, and he wrapped his arms around her.

Lewis was struck by the idea that these adults had been kids once; Peter Thompson was the big brother of Ronnie's mum Evelyn.

Estie's mum walked towards Lewis. 'What are you doing here?' she repeated.

'Is Ronnie okay?' he asked again.

'No.' Evelyn was looking away from him as she spoke. 'She's not okay.'

'Honey, you shouldn't be here,' Estie's mum said, putting her arm around Ronnie's mum. She looked at Lewis, as if to say, *Look what you've done*. Her eye make-up was smudged.

'Please, I want to see Ronnie.'

'The poor bugger stopped me on the road, he was so keen to see her,' Peter said.

'You can't see her right now, sweetheart,' Estie's mum said, shooting a look at Peter. Ronnie's mum turned to her brother, pushing a sob into his chest.

'But I need to see her!' Lewis said. He could hear the frantic note in his own voice.

'Why don't you come with me?' Estie's mum took a step towards Lewis.

'Now,' she said more firmly, ushering him through the sliding doors. 'Let's get you a drink.'

She sat him down beside a vending machine.

It was all his stupid fault that Ronnie was here, that her mum was crying. He was the reason Ronnie had been anywhere near the Horse and Cane, because she thought he didn't have the guts to tell the police what he'd seen. He wanted to tell Estie's mum that. She was treating him like a kid throwing a tantrum.

Estie's mum bought a Sprite from the machine and handed it to him.

'Does your mother know you're here?' she asked.

'No,' he replied, eyes down to the floor.

'It's going to be alright,' she said. 'Ronnie's going to be fine.'

He held the cold can without opening it.

She told him to wait where he was and went away. He cracked the can and took a swig of the Sprite. It fizzed and burned, gloriously cool as it surged down his throat. The smell of the hospital was overpowering: oddly sweet, but also familiar. The smell of the disinfectant his mum used in their bathroom.

He waited for Estie's mum to come back but she didn't. After a while, he stood. If he'd had any idea where Ronnie was he could have gone to her, but he couldn't figure out the map on the wall. He sat back down and rubbed his hand against his shorts over and over again. The Sprite bubbled in his stomach and he felt sick. He had to see Ronnie.

The main doors of the hospital parted. Lewis's mother walked in, her eyes scanning the lobby. Esther's mother must have called her.

She had Simon with her, was almost dragging him behind her. Her eyes were red and the skin around them was puffy.

Lewis rose from the seat, his body already preparing to run, although that wouldn't be a smart way to play it.

'Where's Clint?' he asked as his mum got closer. The name had just slipped out.

'Your father's been arrested,' she said. 'Things got out of hand with one of the officers.'

He didn't respond. Couldn't conceive of a single possible thing to say.

'Now, let's go. Don't you ever do anything like this again, you hear me? Do you have any idea what could have happened to you? I was sick with worry.'

'Can I see Ronnie before we leave, Mum? Please?'

She looked away and sighed. Her mouth was a thin line in her face. 'You've done enough for one day, Lewis.'


Lewis's mum spent a long time speaking to Estie's and Ronnie's mums at the opposite end of the hallway from where Lewis sat with his brother, holding his hand. Simon started making more and more noise. It echoed down the long corridor. Finally, his mum hugged each woman then returned to her sons.

Lewis, Simon and their mother walked together out to her car, the orange body almost glowing in the glare of the hospital car park.

'Fuck!'

He'd never heard his mum swear before.

'I got a *fucking* parking ticket.'

His mum opened the car door with her key and sat down, covering her face and emitting the high breathy cries he'd only heard once before, when her mother died over in England. Simon, who was standing by the car, hit out at her, a dull smack to her side. She didn't react. People were walking past. They looked everywhere but at the orange car. Lewis watched Simon, ready to catch him if he decided to run off into the car park. There was the wail of an approaching ambulance and, somewhere, a car door slammed.

# WE

Monday, 3 December 2001

In a place like Dirt Town, we had to make our own fun.

Near the station, not far up from the railway crossing that divided the town in two, the railway track passed through a high, steel galley structure housing the signal lights that told the trains when to stop and go. At our station these lights glowed green day and night. The entire signalling structure was made of slim steel bars, evenly spaced like the links in an aluminium school fence. Trains thundered underneath it without slowing, on their way to the coast or returning. If we were nearby, a tingle in our feet, an itch in our nose, announced the arrival of the train before we could see it.

One of us already had our feet on the first rung of the steel ladder by the time the train came into view.

It was not the noise or even the feeling of suction we noticed most as we hung at the top of the ladder, but the changed quality of the light as the train streamed past. The small, roaring bubble that we occupied underwent changes in atmosphere, punctuated by bursts of light that passed through the openings between freight carriages. As we clung to the metal frame – our hands clammy, our fingers weakening – we understood, for the first time, what it might be to die. With the train plunging past, our hands slippery with sweat, this lifeless vision calmed us. The train clacked past.

We held on.

Then came the last of it and we were engulfed in silence. The train had propelled itself out of sight before we could make ourselves climb down on shaky legs.


We tell this story to point out that we all do stupid things as children, and most of us live through them.

# CONSTANCE

Monday, 3 December 2001

Esther had been gone for three days. It was Monday afternoon, and in any normal week Constance would have expected her daughter home from school. But Constance was waiting, of course. Still.

The phone rang.

She took the same deep breath she always took now before answering any phone call.

'Constance,' said a voice.

She noticed, for the hundredth time, a piece of paper stuck to the base of the phone. It had Steve's work number written on it in his large handwriting. Next to it was the detective's business card.

'Who is this?' Constance asked.

'It's Evelyn Thompson.'

The last time Constance had spoken to Evelyn had been the afternoon Esther first went missing, three impossible days ago.

Ronnie's mother didn't strike her as the kind of person who would call for information, as so many busybodies had done in the last few days. Waving their sympathy like a ragged flag and pressing Constance for details. They said they would pray for her, but they really just wanted answers. Why was Steve still being held? Had official charges been laid yet? Steve was still being held for attacking an officer and they were working on him, she believed, to get the location of their daughter's body. She also knew that she didn't want to see him, or speak to him, until he told them.

'Yes?' she said.

'Constance, they've taken Ronnie to hospital. Ned Harrison just called me. It's bad, he said. Can you come? My car won't start, and I've called everyone I can think of. No-one's picking up.'

Evelyn sounded calm, but the fact she felt no embarrassment in revealing that Constance was not the first person she'd called revealed the state the woman was in. There was no preamble, no apology for calling to ask for a favour. Constance recognised the tone. When things got so bad that you couldn't even allow yourself the luxury of panic, of extra words.

'I'm coming right now,' Constance said.

'I'll wait out the front.' Evelyn hung up.

Constance reached for the keys on their hook above the bench. For a moment, the shift in emotional pitch felt like a cool change in the weather. And wasn't that just like her? Something always digging into her skin, something always shining into her eyes, something always *off*. Trust her to feel better *now*, in the midst of someone else's pain.

Shel had not long left. The spot near the hedge where her van had been parked for the last three days had a groove in it. Shel had come as often as she could. There'd been uniformed officers, too, over the last three days. But now there was no-one and if Constance left, the house would be empty. She called Shel and left a voicemail message, asked her to come back as soon as she could.

She scrawled a note to Esther and left it on the green tablecloth.

*When you get home, I want you to SIT AT THIS TABLE and DON'T GO ANYWHERE.*

She was out the door, which she left unlocked, and in her car before she thought to examine the emotion that fizzled in her gut. If she were being generous, she might have called it purpose, but she knew it was elation. Elation at getting into her car knowing that she was driving towards someone else's suffering. In that moment she wasn't *Poor Constance Bianchi whose daughter didn't come home and whose husband was in prison.* Steve was only on remand, for the time being, but it didn't matter: that's what people would say. That and, *What's wrong with Constance Bianchi?*

A swarm of pink galahs flew low to the road as Constance drove away from her house. They dipped sharply to the left and right in front of her. Their wings were like boards of wood balanced on their tin-can bodies. They overcorrected and changed direction, flew lower to the ground, before darting back up and away, leaving Constance alone on the road that led to the main street.

The nasty business with Clint Kennard on the street outside the IGA threw Constance. The brutal speed of events was such that she wasn't entirely sure it had really happened. It had been good to see the detective take him down, though. Watch Clint Kennard hit the concrete and be taken away in handcuffs. It'd felt right.

Evelyn was standing in her driveway when Constance arrived. She wanted to tell Evelyn what had just happened in front of the IGA – Constance could still feel the reverberations of the sudden stop in her body – but the small woman hunched forward in the front seat of the little Corolla like it might get them to the hospital faster and Constance kept silent.

It used to be that when Constance talked to Evelyn – which

happened often, their girls were such good friends – it always felt like Constance was hearing herself through strange ears, and it made their conversations stilted. Steve was often late back from the pool when he took Esther and Ronnie to their swimming lessons. Evelyn was younger than Steve, but they had a shared history – they'd gone to the same school, the same rodeos and whatever else passed for fun in this town. Constance had sometimes poked at the thought of Steve and Evelyn together the way you explore a bruise – to see how much it could hurt. Now, she found she felt nothing. Refreshing.

She drove faster than she ever would have dared with her daughter in the car. As they sped along the highway, Esther's absence made itself felt in the things Constance didn't have to do. The lack of an enquiring voice in the back seat, the total silence.


Evelyn ran wordlessly for the main doors of the hospital as soon as Constance stopped the car. Constance paid for a parking ticket, placed it on the dashboard and locked the doors. She found Evelyn inside, speaking loudly at the woman behind the desk. The woman stayed in her chair, rolling it sideways to connect with a second screen. She rolled back before telling them that the patient had been taken straight up. She gave them directions to a waiting room. Evelyn set off in the wrong direction and Constance took her by the arm. In the waiting room, they sat side by side in chairs made from hard beige plastic.

'Do you know what happened?' Constance asked.

'It's her face. The dog attacked her face.'

'Whose dog? Where did it happen?'

Why did people ask for details when bad things happened? The same way people had asked Constance, *Who's the investigating officer? Where have they searched? How many people?*

'Ned Harrison said it happened at the motel. He's the one who rang. He's the one who waited with Ronnie until the ambulance came.'

Constance nodded.

'He found Ronnie after the dog had already got her on the ground . . .' Evelyn seemed unable to continue.

Constance looked up and down the hospital corridor, searching for someone who could tell them what was going on. Evelyn perched on the seat and stared at the floor.

'They should let me be with her. She's only a kid.'

'I nearly hit Clint Kennard with my car on the way to your place,' Constance said. Evelyn looked up at her. 'He's fine. He just ran out in front of my car. But he lost it. I think he was about to hit me but then those detectives appeared out of nowhere. The female one tried to stop him and he attacked her.'

Evelyn leaned back in her chair. 'Nice to see he's branching out. I thought he only hit his wife.'

'I didn't know that.'

'Yeah,' Evelyn said. She was kind enough not to say, *Why would you know anything?*

Steve, Esther and Constance had been living in the town for six years, but Constance was only friends with Shel.

The sounds of the hospital bubbled around them. In the distance, Constance could hear an announcement over the PA, but she couldn't quite make out the words.

She shifted in her seat. The chairs were so uncomfortable.

'Do you think he did it?' Evelyn asked. Seeing Constance's confusion, she continued, 'Steven, I mean. I just heard about it yesterday. Do you think he had something to do with Esther going missing?'

'I don't know what else to think,' Constance replied, the seat beneath her somehow no longer level.

'Why do they think it was him?' Evelyn asked. Emboldened by what had happened to Ronnie, Constance supposed.

She didn't mind. For once, she found she wanted to talk about it.

'He had her shoe?' Constance didn't know why she'd made it sound like a question. It was a bad habit of hers. 'It was the shoe she was wearing when she left school, so he had to have seen her on Friday afternoon.'

'I'm sorry, Constance,' Evelyn said, bursting into tears. 'I'm sorry I haven't called. I'm sorry I even asked you that.'

Constance waved away the apology.

She thought of Steve, the way he'd been on Friday morning. He'd raised himself into the cab of his ute, unaware she was observing him after their fight about Shel. The image came to her so clearly it almost took her breath away. There was the dislocation of the memory catching up with her emotions. Constance thought about his smell, his handsome face, before she thought about what he'd done. That morning, her biggest problem had been her fight with Shel. Even in the depths of it, she'd known it would be okay. Her family would be okay. Constance felt unreal. Hazily undefined in the hospital hallway. The smell of disinfectant undercut by the cloying scents of apple sauce and cheap gravy. The whole scene had that quality you sometimes get in dreams, where you're planning something and are brought up short by the realisation that the person you are planning with has been dead for years. Or you find yourself making lasagne using only pumpkin skins and a container of Milo.

A nurse strode by, purpose in her every movement.

Evelyn leaped up to intercept her. 'When can I see my daughter? She was just admitted with a dog bite. Her name is Veronica Thompson.'

The nurse promised she would come and get Evelyn as soon as she was allowed in.

When they were alone again, Constance found she also wanted to tell Evelyn about what Shel had told her, but couldn't formulate the words. Maybe Evelyn already knew.

'I should call Shel,' Constance said, hearing the abruptness of it in her own voice. 'I want to make sure she made it back to my place.'

She stood and another inscrutable announcement surged and receded.

'Wait!' said Evelyn.

Constance turned and Evelyn looked up at her from the seat.

'Her shoe. You said Steven had Esther's shoe? Are they certain?'

Constance wasn't sure why Evelyn was asking her. Did she feel the need to rub it in?

'I saw it,' Constance said. 'It was her shoe.'

Evelyn blanched. 'And that's why they arrested him? The only reason?'

'Well, the actual charge was because he hit one of the cops when he was being interviewed.'

It sounded so pathetic when it was said out loud. Her life some ridiculous soap opera.

'Oh god.' Evelyn brought her hand to her mouth.

'What?'

'I think . . . I think it might have been Ronnie's shoe. Her school shoe in Steven's car.'

Constance's gut folded in on itself like a faulty deckchair. 'What?'

'I'm so sorry, Constance – I didn't notice because her room is such a bombsite. But this afternoon I started cleaning up and I found one black school shoe in her swim bag. I looked around for the second shoe but I couldn't find it. I'd already torn the whole house apart by the time Ned Harrison called me. And you know Ronnie and Esther have the same shoes.'

Evelyn's words clattered around in Constance's mind. She and Evelyn had probably bought the girls' shoes at the same fucking

243

Country Target in Rhodes. Constance lowered herself back onto the plastic hospital chair.

'They told me that the shoe had Esther's DNA in it,' was all Constance could say.

'I know when it happened,' said Evelyn. 'Steve dropped Ronnie off after swimming the day before Esther went missing. Ronnie always changes into her thongs at the pool. She and Esther have accidentally swapped shoes before, you know. One of her school shoes must have dropped out of her bag into the car on the way home. And Ronnie prefers her damn runners. She knows she's not supposed to wear them to school on Mondays, but I was distracted. Oh, Constance. I don't know what kind of mother I am that I didn't ask her about them.'

The thought was like a physical slap. No-one had made the connection that the two girls had the same shoes? They were best friends. No-one, not a single one of their teachers, had noticed?

And then it struck Constance. The only person who had known about the shoe – outside of Steve and the cops – had been her. Of course, the police had warned Constance against discussing the case, and she hadn't wanted to tell people. But Constance was the one who should've noticed. How often had she driven Ronnie home? Ronnie always liked to sit behind the front passenger seat so she could see the driver, cross-legged, leaning forward to ask long, annoying questions, or to tell Constance yet another fact about llamas. The police had decided not to release the information about the shoe to the general public. Still, the thought struck her: if Evelyn had picked up after her daughter . . . The image of Steve in a cell flashed in her mind.

'I'm so sorry, Constance.'

Didn't Evelyn know that by saying sorry she was pointing out that it was Constance who should have known? And now Constance was expected to forgive *her*?

'You couldn't have known.'

'I'm so sorry, Constance,' Evelyn repeated.

'Are you sure? I mean, it could still be somewhere in the house, right?'

'I had a really good look,' Evelyn said gravely.

'I have to tell the police,' Constance said, standing.

Constance felt none of the warm, comforting pity she'd felt when she'd been driving to pick up Evelyn. She stalked down the corridor and found a reluctant nurse, who showed her to a phone.

She needed to know if Shel had made it to her place yet. She dialled her own number. Shel answered on the third ring.

Constance told her what Evelyn had said.

'But that's good news, isn't it, love?' Shel asked. 'It could mean Steven was telling the truth.'

Constance felt anger flare in her gut but held her tongue. Shel had never encouraged her one way or the other, had never told her what to do. Constance had been the one who made the decision not to take Steve's calls.

'Listen, Shel. I've got to go. I haven't even told the police yet.'

'Alright, love. You know where I'll be.'

# SARAH

Monday, 3 December 2001

When Sarah pulled up to drop Ned off, the main driveway to the hospital was blocked by two ambulances facing each other.

They'd had to stop a few more times for the old man to be sick.

'I can walk from here,' Ned said, a little shakily, as he stepped down from the cab.

'I'll take your ute to the police station in Durton, alright? I'll leave the key there for you,' Sarah said.

Ned nodded. He'd gone grey about the face.

'You can give them a ring and someone will come and pick you up.'

'I'll just get a cab,' he said.

Sarah wondered how many taxis there were in a town like this.

'The nurses' station will have the number. I'm sure someone can pick you up.'

She could tell he wasn't going to do it, but he nodded and raised a hand.

Sarah turned out of the hospital car park and into a spot on the side of the road that someone was leaving. As the engine powered down, the smell of dust and oil made Sarah think of things that were repaired, made whole.

Her mobile started ringing.

'Michaels.'

'It's Smithy. Where are you?'

'I've just dropped Ned at the hospital. What's up?' She reached for her notebook and cracked it open on the steering wheel.

'You'll never guess what I found on Clint Kennard.'

'What?'

'Some lovely little packets of speed.'

A thrill ran through her. 'Excellent! That means we can check his property. We may even be able to compel him to give DNA.'

'I'm five steps ahead of you, as ever, boss. I dropped him with Mack to babysit while I went and had a quick look at his house.'

'Did you find anything?' Sarah tried to picture the Kennard house. What would the place where Clint lived look like?

'Well, I parked in the driveway, blocking in a white Toyota HiAce – and who emerged from the shed at the back but a very startled-looking Roland Mathers.'

'Shit. That's great!' she said, grinning. 'I assume you've got him in custody?'

'He's in the back of the car as we speak. Gave me a run for my money, though.'

'Fantastic.' Sarah felt a stab of guilt at her own elation. A young girl had been seriously injured and Esther was still missing. But the sense of movement was invigorating. 'What was in the van?' Sarah knew if there was any obvious link with Esther, Smithy would have opened with it, but she was still curious.

'He'd tried to drag as much of it into the shed as possible. Mostly bags of over-the-counter flu meds, kitty litter, the usual ingredients. No sign of our girl, in case that's what you're thinking.'

'Roland Mathers was Clint's alibi on the Friday afternoon. And Ned Harrison says the men are mates. If they're lying for each other about that, then I'm fairly confident there's a good reason.' She still needed to figure out if any of it connected with Steven Bianchi.

'Mack spoke to Sophie Kennard, the mum who came in with her son this afternoon,' Smithy said. 'She admitted Clint Kennard has a history of physical violence against her.'

'Right.' *No surprises there*, Sarah thought. The chances of this woman following through on charges were slim to none, and Sarah was irrationally angry at her for a moment. 'Did you find the boys he was chasing?' Sarah asked.

'Not yet. Sophie Kennard's getting pretty worked up,' said Smithy.

'Okay. I'm sure they won't have gone far. See if Mack can do a drive around.'

'Will do, boss.' Smithy paused. 'It's strange, you know. I've never heard of a kelpie attacking a kid.' Smithy's voice wavered for a second before he caught himself. 'Still, it's a working dog. The way it was kept locked up like that. Maybe it was inevitable it'd snap.'

Unease washed over Sarah. She'd seen the chained dog. Done precisely nothing about it.

'I'd better go,' Smithy said when she didn't respond. 'I'll see you back here at Mack's.'

'Okay.' Then, as a thought struck her: 'Make sure you keep Clint and Roland separated. Get Mack to bring Clint to Rhodes, as per the original plan, but you can keep Roland there, in Durton. I don't want them to speak to each other before I get a chance to interview them. I'm going to try to speak with Veronica Thompson now if I can. See if I can get a better idea of what the hell happened at the motel. Then I want to speak to Roland.'

'Alrighty. Take care of yourself, boss.'

Smithy rang off and she sat with the phone to her ear for a few seconds.

Her phone rang again almost straightaway. It wasn't a number Sarah recognised.

'Detective Sergeant Michaels speaking.'

'Detective, this is Constance Bianchi. I think there's a chance the shoe you found in Steve's car isn't Esther's. Evelyn Thompson just told me that she thinks it might belong to Veronica, her daughter.'

Sarah's eyes flicked towards the hospital building.

'But you said yourself the shoe was hers.'

'I know I did. But I didn't realise that the girls had the same shoes. And Steve took them both to the pool on Thursday. On Fridays they wear sports uniform, so Ronnie was in her runners. Evelyn thinks the shoe could have been there, under the seat, since Thursday afternoon.'

Sarah had an image of the shallow creek. She'd missed something important.

'But you identified the shoe as belonging to Esther. We found her DNA on it.'

'I know. But it never even occurred to me that they had the same shoes. And Evelyn says the girls have come home in each other's shoes by accident before.' There were tears in the woman's voice.

Sarah reminded herself that Constance had more at stake than physical evidence in a case. It was her husband they'd been holding.

'Where are you calling from?'

'I'm at the nurses' station, at the hospital.'

'It's really good you rang. I'll definitely look into this, Constance. In fact, it's perfect timing. I was just coming to see Veronica and her mother.'

Sarah checked the bag she'd thrown in the back and was relieved to find there were a couple of DNA kits inside. If they could rule out the second set of DNA they'd found on the shoe as Veronica's, then they'd know for sure. Sarah was itching to jump straight into interviews with Roland and Clint, but she needed to see the girl first.

*

'Visiting hours haven't started yet,' said a tight-lipped nurse when Sarah asked for Veronica's room.

The woman's eyebrows were overplucked thin lines that didn't follow the path suggested by her bone structure.

Sarah flashed her ID. 'I won't be long,' she said.

'Up two levels, and it's the last door on the left,' the woman said.

The doors of the lift dinged open at Veronica's floor, and Sarah hesitated for a moment before turning down the corridor and finding the room. The door seemed to spring open when she touched its chrome handle, like the hospital was alive underneath the whir of air conditioning and the smell of disinfectant.

Evelyn Thompson was standing in the doorway. She'd clearly been about to step out. 'Detective Sergeant Michaels,' she said. 'Can I speak to you in the corridor?'

Evelyn looked thinner than the last time Sarah had seen her. Sarah thought of their conversation at Evelyn's house; the urge to reach out and touch her was strong but lasted just a second or two.

'How's Veronica?'

'She's alright, thank god. The doctor says it could have been a lot worse.' Evelyn took a step closer to her. 'Listen, Ronnie keeps saying that Lewis Kennard told her something, which is why she was going to talk to the police. She keeps talking about Esther, she thinks she could have been there, at the motel. She's convinced. She should have come straight home. I've told her a thousand times to come straight home.'

Sarah nodded to show she'd heard Evelyn's concerns and stepped into the room. One bed was empty; Veronica was propped up in the other. There were bandages on the girl's face. A streak of phantom pain shot from the base of Sarah's spine up her lower back.

Veronica's eyes followed her as she approached.

'Hi, Veronica. How are you feeling?'

The girl scrunched up her nose like it was a stupid question.

'Can you tell me what happened at the motel?'

The girl swallowed, wincing, before she spoke. The words came out in a rush.

'I was coming to see you, and I thought I'd cut through the yard. That was all. Then I saw my cat, Flea. He ran and hid under a van. I was hiding in front of the rooms.'

'Why were you hiding?' Sarah asked.

'I heard the man who owns the motel. I didn't want him to see me.'

'What was the motel owner doing?'

'He was carrying something in a black plastic bag, something that looked heavy.' Veronica looked at her mother. 'He was loading it into the van. Then I heard a sound and I *knew* Esther was in there. We've been to the motel before. I thought maybe she went there alone and got caught and he put her in a van and kept her there. It's like a room you can move around in. I thought, *That's why no-one's been able to find her.*'

Sarah looked at the girl's mother. 'Can you describe the van?' she asked.

'It was white.'

Sarah wrote *Van* in her notebook and underlined it.

'Did you actually see Esther? Hear her voice?'

'No, I just heard a thud.' The girl seemed to slump in on herself.

'What else did you see? Could you see inside the van?'

'No, the van doors were on the other side and I couldn't see in. There was a big bag of cat litter on the wall near the van. But I know the owner doesn't have a cat.'

'So, all you saw were the things the motel owner was loading into his van. Isn't there a good chance the thud was just something he lifted in?'

The girl screwed up her face.

'You're sure you didn't hear any other sound? Nothing that sounded like Esther?'

'No.' The girl sounded almost petulant.

'Well, I can tell you that we found the van, Veronica, and there was no-one in it. The stuff in the van was bad, you were absolutely right about that. The motel owner was definitely doing things he wasn't supposed to. Even the kitty litter you saw was being used for something bad.' Sarah's eyes flicked to Evelyn. No need to talk Veronica through the intricacies of speed manufacture. 'But there was no sign of Esther there, okay?'

'Are you sure?'

'I'm sure,' said Sarah. 'Now, the question I have to ask is why you were in the motel yard at all. Your mum says you were supposed to come straight home. But you said there was something you wanted to tell us?'

As if only just remembering, the girl's eyes opened wide. 'Yes: something important. Lewis Kennard said he saw Esther the afternoon she went missing. At the creek.' The girl said the words deliberately, like she'd thought about how she would say them. 'He said there was a man there with her.'

Some gentle questioning revealed that Lewis had told Veronica even less than he'd managed to tell the police before his father took him away. Sarah really needed to speak with the boy again.

Sarah asked for Evelyn's approval to take a DNA swab from her daughter and did it as quickly as she could. She could tell Evelyn was losing patience.

'Listen, we're doing everything we can, Veronica,' Sarah assured the girl as she prepared to leave. 'I promise you, we're following every lead.'

*

253

Sarah called Smithy as she was returning to Ned Harrison's ute.

'I need to speak to Lewis Kennard again,' she said. 'Tonight if I can. Have you found him?'

'Yeah.' Sarah could picture Smithy in the small station, phone held to his ear by his shoulder. 'He's at the hospital, apparently.'

'What? How the hell did he get here?'

'Not sure, but his mother just left to go and get him.'

Sarah turned and looked back towards the large brick building. 'Maybe I should go back in and wait for her.'

'I've already made her promise to call as soon as she's home. I guessed you'd want to talk to him again.'

'Okay, thanks.'

The next person she wanted to speak to was Roland Mathers, which she could do while she waited for Lewis to make it back to Durton. She'd need to get what she could from Roland before she talked to Clint Kennard again anyway.


Back at the station, the small room was filled with the smell of sweat and something sharper, more chemical. Roland Mathers was in the same stained blue singlet he'd been wearing the day Sarah first arrived in town. In another world, one without Esther, she would have been giving him a hard time about his dog. But there were more important things to talk about.

'Why did you drive to Clint Kennard's house after leaving the scene at the motel?'

'I didn't leave the scene. I made sure there was a bloody ambulance coming.'

'You left with the supplies you had in your van and headed straight for the lab on Clint Kennard's property.'

'No comment.'

'Why did you leave? It was very unlikely we would have searched your van if you'd just stayed put. Instead, you ended up leading us straight to the heart of the whole operation. Was there something else you didn't want us to see?'

Roland crossed his arms.

'Where is Esther Bianchi?' Sarah asked.

'How should I fuckin' know?'

'You've never had cause to have Esther Bianchi in that van of yours? You'll want to go on the record about that now, you know. We're checking the van as we speak, so telling me now just saves us a little time. Could make things better for you when this comes to trial.'

'Tell you a secret?' Roland said.

Sarah leaned in.

'I'm not as fuckin' stupid as I look,' said Roland.

'So, how long have you and Clint been working together?' Sarah said conversationally.

Roland held her gaze. 'No fucking comment.'

'What if I told you that I'm speaking to Clint Kennard next?'

'I said, no fucking comment.'


It was dark outside by the time Sarah was finished with Roland Mathers. He knew she had him for the drugs, but she'd need more evidence that Esther's disappearance was connected in some way before she would get anything out of him. The idea that Esther had seen something she wasn't supposed to and it had got her killed was hardening in Sarah's mind. But she needed more ammunition before she went into another interview with Clint Kennard.

In the lounge room of his home, with his father in custody, Lewis was less forthcoming than Sarah had hoped.

His mother sat next to the boy on the three-seater couch, while Sarah perched on the edge of an armchair. You could tell it was the kind of house that was kept clean – it hadn't been hastily tidied up just for Sarah. Bleach and air freshener and snow-white tiles.

The first thing Lewis Kennard said was that he'd been wrong about what he'd said earlier that day, that it hadn't been Esther after all.

Sarah had never really believed there was a man. She had assumed that Lewis was trying to tell them something, something about his father that he couldn't just come right out and say. But Sophie Kennard looked at her son, eyebrows raised.

'How can that be, Lewis?' Sophie said. Her face was drawn.

'Mrs Kennard,' Sarah said, 'I want to hear from Lewis, if that's okay.'

Sophie crossed her arms and settled back into the couch.

'I think you can understand why your mum is a little shocked, Lewis. Why are you so sure?' Sarah asked.

'I just am,' he said, leaning forward. His hands were outstretched, like he was imploring her to believe him. 'I thought about it, and I realised it wasn't her. It was another girl who looked like her.'

Sarah paused, letting the boy's words dangle in the air. She didn't want to call him a liar. She needed to gently guide him to the reason his story had changed and hope she could make him feel safe enough. She also sensed that it was not a time for euphemism.

'Does your father hit you, Lewis?'

The boy trained his eyes on the floor and nodded.

'You have to say the words, Lewis. For the tape.'

'Yes.' The boy's voice was flat.

'I just want you to know that your father's behaviour is wrong, very wrong, and he is in custody, okay? He's in a lot of trouble. And we're going to keep you safe. I want to help you. But I need you to tell me the truth.'

Lewis nodded again.

'Can you tell me why your father was chasing you and Campbell Rutherford? Does it have something to do with what you told me about what you saw?'

'I don't know why Dad lost it,' he said.

A sound came from the bedroom. 'That's Simon,' Sophie said, jumping up. 'I better check that he's okay.'

Sarah clicked the tape recorder off.

Lewis glanced towards the corridor. He turned back to Sarah, like he'd been waiting for this moment.

'There was someone else there that afternoon at the creek,' Lewis said quickly. 'It was Campbell Rutherford. I spoke to him today and he was sure it wasn't her. And he was right. The girl I saw wasn't in a school dress. They had the same hair, and I just thought it was her. I got it wrong.' The boy's eyes were wide behind his glasses. 'But please, you can't tell Campbell I told you. Please?'

It would never hold up in court. Sarah shouldn't even be speaking to him without his mother being present. But it was enough to satisfy her. It had cost the boy something to tell her, she could see that. She nodded, put a hand on his shoulder. She thought she had a pretty good understanding of just why Lewis had hidden this boy from his parents.

There was movement in the hallway and the two of them fell silent. The door opened and Sarah waited for Sophie Kennard to sit back down before turning the tape recorder back on.

'Have you ever seen your husband with a man named Roland Mathers?' Sarah asked. This was the other reason she'd come to speak to the Kennards. That the boy had been wrong about the girl was important information, if not verifiable right at that moment. She would have to speak to Campbell, but she could do it discreetly, later.

'They're friends,' Sophie Kennard said.

Sarah nodded, then refocused on Lewis. 'What about you?' she asked.

'I know they drink together,' said Lewis cautiously. 'I've seen Mr Mathers at the RSL. When he comes here they go into the shed.'

Sarah thought about what Ned Harrison had said about Roland and Clint, that he'd seen the two men with a third man a lot lately. 'What about Peter Thompson? Have you ever seen your dad with him?'

'He was here on Sunday,' Lewis said. 'He came by to speak to Dad.'

Sarah was silent. Sometimes, that was all it took.

Lewis looked at his mother then said, 'Peter and Dad stayed in the house. I could hear them in the dining room. They were talking about Esther's dad being arrested.'

'They were talking about Esther?' Sarah asked.

'It sounded like Mr Bianchi getting arrested was a good thing, according to my dad.'

'What did your father say specifically?'

'Just that it was good that the police thought it was Mr Bianchi. He said that would make it easier.'

Sophie's shoulders sagged as Sarah made a note in her notebook. 'And what did Peter Thompson say to that?'

'I couldn't really hear what he was saying. I'm not sure.'

Sarah asked more questions but couldn't get anything more from Lewis, and Sophie had fallen completely mute. Sarah wrapped up the recording and asked the woman to follow her into the hallway. Sarah took Sophie through the next steps, but couldn't be sure if what she was saying was going in. Sophie wouldn't return Sarah's look as she shut the door.

Clint Kennard had been pleased to hear that Steven Bianchi had been arrested. That was important information. Sarah sank into the driver's seat. Her ears popped as she opened her mouth wide to release the tension in her jaw.

As she drove away from the Kennard house, Sarah felt a sticky weariness descend when more than anything she wanted to feel sharp. Her father had died on a night like this, late, coming back from a job he should have saved for the next day. Her mother had been so angry at him for so long.

It was dark, and to speak to Clint Kennard she would have to drive back to Rhodes, where he was being held overnight at the police station. What harm would it do to interview Clint the following day, when she had her wits about her? Sarah would be able to ask Kinouac for more time, now they'd found the speed on Clint and arrested him and Roland Mathers. They were close to a breakthrough, she was sure of it. Resting her forehead on the steering wheel, Sarah rubbed the back of her neck and yawned wide.

# RONNIE

Monday, 3 December 2001

After the detective left, there was pain and bright light and woozy moments that passed without me being able to grab at them. Brisk nurses who got me to confirm my name before they did things to me.

Then, Mum and me, alone.

It was easier to lie flat in the hospital bed than sit up.

Something moved down in the hospital car park, creating a reflection on the ceiling, a splash of light that disappeared and reappeared.

I asked again and again if Flea was okay. Mum promised she'd have someone go to our place and look for him.

The detective had said that Lewis had gone to the police.

A wave of pain rippled through me.

'Are you okay?' asked Mum, appearing beside my bed.

'Can you get the nurse?' I asked, teeth gritted. It felt like someone was yanking on a dozen fishhooks buried between my skull and my right temple.

Mum ran out into the corridor and I slumped back into my pillow.

I thought about the walk home from school the last day I'd seen Esther, her half-wave when we'd split up. I was overcome by the physical memory of her standing over me in her yard when we were small – laughter and the sound of running water – and missed her so badly it felt like my body would give way.

# SARAH

Tuesday, 4 December 2001

Kinouac called just as Sarah was falling asleep in the early hours of Tuesday morning.

She tried to keep the resentment out of her voice. 'Michaels.'

'Those missing twins have been found, alive and unharmed,' he said.

'Coxley must be over the moon,' she said, smudging her eyes with the heel of a hand.

'Thought you should know. Means I can give you another week.'

Before she could get out an intelligible reply, she heard the click that told her that her boss had already hung up.

Sarah woke to find that Smithy was up before her, for once. He'd been for the newspapers already and said he'd never seen so many four-page spreads.

'Turns out those girls were squatting in a house,' Smithy said as they left the motel.

They were going to Rhodes to interview Clint, and afterwards they'd see Steven Bianchi, who was still on remand. Steven didn't know it yet, but they would have to release him that day. A judge had told them as much, and Sarah hadn't fought it. Her gut told her the answer lay in the direction of Clint and Roland.

Sarah was driving. 'Now the father's up on charges,' Smithy continued as she turned onto the main street. 'The papers didn't say what they were, but they weren't for kidnapping. Must have been something bad enough to make the girls run away.'

They both knew what that meant.

As they neared the Durton police station, they heard a honking up ahead, loud and insistent. She recognised Ned Harrison's ute before she saw the man himself. He'd driven right up onto the lawn of the police station.

'What's he doing here?' Smithy asked.

She pulled the Commodore over and she and Smithy got out, just as Ned Harrison emerged from the cab.

'I've got her,' Ned called to them. He placed a hand in front of his face, like he couldn't bear to look at them.

Leaning over the tray of the ute, Sarah pulled back the plastic and saw Esther Bianchi. Not being held alive in a shed somewhere but *here*, still dressed in her school uniform. She was wearing both her school shoes – covered in dirt but a perfect pair.

Glancing up at the sky, Sarah covered the girl with plastic again. She didn't want the girl's skin to burn. There was something horrific about the thought, something unnatural. She'd seen bodies before, but somehow when she remembered being physically close to them, it was always cold and overcast. And Esther's body was too small, the smell overpowering. A strange sense of unreality washed over Sarah, like everything had gone 2D, like they were all cardboard cut-outs being moved around.

*

'I didn't do it,' was the first thing Ned said inside the station.

Sarah had to resist the urge to reply, *I know*.

'I couldn't leave her there.'

'What were you doing when you found her?'

'Just checking the fence. I probably shouldn't've been' – he gestured towards his bandaged arm – 'but it drives me crazy, sitting around the house.'

Sarah had decided it would be best for Smithy to drive Esther straight to the hospital in Ned's ute, to avoid any more movement of the body. It was the second time in two days that car had been driven to the hospital by someone who wasn't Ned. She knew they did post-mortems there, and she just had to hope someone would be available to take a look at Esther's body soon.

'Where were you last Friday?'

'Visiting my sister up north,' said Ned.

She already knew Ned's alibi. Ned had been in the first round of men interviewed by Mack. Smithy had requested the CCTV footage from a petrol station in Lismore. A receipt Ned had in his glove box placed him there at 2 pm on the day Esther went missing. She would have been at school, sitting on the edge of the netball court in the shade, and he was hours away. Smithy had since arranged for Ned's sister to go into her local station and make a statement.

'Who had access to your property while you were away?'

'I didn't have anything to do with it, and neither did Clay,' Ned said.

'And who's Clay?' Sarah asked. She wished he'd stop repeating he had nothing to do with it; it made him sound guilty.

'Clay Rutherford. Well, it's Clarence Rutherford, I guess. He's never gone by Clarence. Why would you?' He kept talking, his words falling over each other. 'He lives over past the grain silos. He was feeding my animals for me while I went to see my sister. Anyone could've got in – I don't have padlocks on every gate. I'm more worried about animals getting out than people getting in, you know.'

Clarence Rutherford would turn out to be the father of the boy Sarah had seen with Lewis Kennard before Clint Kennard was arrested, the same boy Lewis was with the afternoon Esther Bianchi disappeared. The knowledge would make her feel the crushing weight of what it was to live in such a small town. Everything and everyone touching everything else. Clarence had been visiting his mother in a nursing home in Rhodes on the afternoon of the thirtieth of November. A room full of witnesses, including staff of the home, had seen him.

Sarah left Ned sitting at the kitchen table. Mack followed her into the reception area of the station, closing the door behind them.

'The reality is, anyone could have got onto Ned's place,' Mack confirmed. 'We've established he wasn't there, but someone else could have seen something.'

'Only locals would know Ned was away,' said Sarah. 'Unless someone chose his property through sheer dumb luck.'

Sarah knew what she had to do next. She called to check Constance was home and then drove to the Bianchi house to give Esther's mother the news. Cops in TV shows were always saying it was the hardest part of the job, but Sarah disagreed. It was a rite of passage and it made Sarah feel, weirdly, like she'd done something real, something tangible. She'd been the person to deliver the news that someone would never be coming home. It was a horrible thing to do, yes, but honourable in a way so many parts of the job weren't. She knew it was a waystation a loved one had to pass through. There was something almost religious about it. Something hummed within her, like standing too close to power cables. The thought of a living, breathing Esther flashed through her mind, a girl watching from the sidelines of a netball court.

Sarah had offered Constance the option of having someone else identify Esther, but Constance wanted to be the one to come to the hospital and see her daughter's body. Sarah stood by as a member of the hospital staff described the condition of the body to Constance, warning her that she couldn't touch Esther, because there were tests they still had to do. She said she was sorry about this, but that Constance could spend as much time with the body as she wished.

Sarah waited outside.

Constance avoided Sarah's eye when she came back out. 'There's dirt in her ears,' she said, so softly Sarah almost didn't hear it.

'I'm very sorry, Mrs Bianchi.' Sarah's words sounded hollow. 'We'll do everything we can to find the person responsible.'

Nothing Sarah could say was going to make it any better. Now, the only meaningful help Sarah could offer would be to catch whoever had done this.

Sarah offered Constance a lift home, but the woman said she had someone coming for her. Sarah was pleased not to have to drive back to Durton. It turned out that someone from the regional pathology team was available to do the autopsy and already on their way. It seemed that an upshot of the twins being found was that now resources could begin to flow to Sarah's investigation.


Unwrapped from the black plastic, Esther Bianchi looked different from what Sarah had expected. It wasn't just what her time under-ground had done to her – she was slighter than she'd sounded in her mother's words and the photos Sarah had seen. Sarah had known her height as a number in centimetres. Laid out on a metal table, Esther looked smaller. The body had been cooled, which helped with the smell. The plastic, Sarah noted, looked like the same kind they'd found wrapped around the brick of speed. The initial forensics found no semen, no sign that Esther had been raped or sexually assaulted. She had some badly broken bones. These indicated extreme blunt trauma, or even, the pathologist speculated, a fall from a serious height.

The pathologist, a man with greying hair, pulled off a glove and adjusted his glasses.

'What's most likely, though, is impact from a car. It'd be large and fast enough to explain this kind of injury. I'll know more when we x-ray her.'

Sarah noted his conclusion that traumatic brain injury was the most likely cause of death. Most interestingly, for Sarah, were the four short hairs the pathologist had found on Esther's clothing and in the plastic. Sarah watched as they were transferred into evidence bags. They glowed orange in the light.

Sarah scribbled a description of the hairs.

'How long till you can test those?' she asked.

'Not so long to analyse the sample, but if we don't have a match on file, it won't be much use to you.'

The pathologist threw his glove into a bin and walked Sarah to the door.

'Did anyone touch her?' was the first thing Steven asked when Smithy told him his daughter's body had been found. They were in an interview room at the prison an hour from Durton where he was being held on remand. They'd already informed him that he was being released that day.

'There's nothing to indicate any sexual activity, no,' said Smithy.

Steven lowered his head, ran fingers through his dark hair.

Smithy absent-mindedly ran a finger over the bump on his nose. There was yelling outside the room, the sound of running feet.

It was unfortunate that Steven had been their main suspect, but Sarah shrugged it off. She wouldn't apologise for doing her job. She tried not to think about what she'd done to Constance Bianchi, a woman who'd seemed ready and willing to believe the worst. And Steven still had the assaulting-an-officer charge to answer, which was all he'd been arrested for. The facts were that Esther was dead and her body had been found in Durton. It was still most likely that Esther had been killed by someone she knew. And with the girl's father ruled out, Sarah still couldn't shake the feeling that the drugs were too much of a coincidence not to be related. Sarah wanted the pathology results, and she wanted them as soon as possible.

# LEWIS

Tuesday, 4 December 2001

On Tuesday morning, after his heart-pounding interview with the female detective on Monday night, Lewis and his mother drove to the hospital in silence. She wore no make-up and looked tired. The windows were down because the air conditioning had stopped working; all they could get was an asthmatic *puh* sound followed by a *click click click* when you tried to turn it on. It hadn't worked since his mother's trip to Rhodes to pick him up after he'd hitchhiked to see Ronnie. It felt like the car was taking its instructions from Clint, had stopped working to spite them.

When they arrived at the hospital, Lewis's mum marched through the main doors and into the lift, Lewis trailing behind her. They walked down a corridor to a large blue door, almost double the normal width. It had a small glass panel set just above his head height. Lewis's mum tapped on it and a few seconds later the door was opened by Ronnie's mum.

There were two beds in the room, but one of them was empty. Ronnie was lying in the bed closest to the window with her eyes closed. The whole right side of her face was covered in bandages.

He'd wanted to see Ronnie, to talk to her and explain: explain how he'd changed his mind, how *she* had changed his mind. But what if she wouldn't talk to him? What if she yelled at him or asked him again what he was doing at the creek? There was a feeling in his stomach like the expanding foam he'd seen Clint use on the shed once. He'd sprayed it into a crack, and Lewis had watched it get bigger and bigger until it outgrew the edges. Lewis had thought it might never stop.

'You look like you could use a coffee, Evelyn.' Lewis's mum placed a hand on Ronnie's mum's shoulder. 'Why don't we go get one together? Lewis can stay here.'

Ronnie's mum shrugged off the hand, but turned to look at Ronnie before saying, 'Okay.'

She scooped up her handbag from the pale green vinyl armchair next to the bed and kissed Ronnie on the head. Ronnie didn't open her eyes.

'We won't be long,' Lewis's mum said.

This had been what he wanted – to speak with Ronnie alone – but now it was happening he longed to follow his mother out of the room.

'Be careful not to touch anything, Lewis.' Ronnie's mum's eyes darted to the bed. 'She's asleep right now. I brought her some stuff to read, if you want to keep yourself busy.' She nodded at a pile of books. A magazine with a bright yellow border stuck out. There was a picture of an old, old woman dressed in blankets on the cover. 'Maybe when she wakes up you can read to her?'

He nodded, although he doubted that's what Ronnie would want, when she heard what he had to say.

The two women left and Lewis sank into the vinyl chair. For a while there was only the sound of the machine next to her bed. He wondered if he should wake her up; he needed to speak to her before their mothers came back.

She shifted, the bed groaning, and he sat up straighter.

'Hi,' Lewis said, as she opened her eyes and turned to look at him.

Before she could say anything, or yell at him, he said, 'I'm sorry. This is all my fault.'

'Lewis.' Her voice sounded weird, a bit strangled.

'I tried to tell them. I went to the police station. I must have been there when' – he looked away – 'when you got hurt. I know you must have been going there because you thought I didn't have the guts to go myself.'

'The police told me,' Ronnie rasped.

'Ronnie,' he began, 'I did talk to them, I swear it. Well, I tried to. I don't know that they believed me, and then my dad came, and he punched one of them, but that was later, when Estie's mum was there, and' – Lewis checked to see if she was following – 'and then I found out that it wasn't Estie I saw.'

Ronnie pulled herself up into a sitting position. Lewis smelled a deep, salty smell that might've been urine.

'But you were so sure yesterday,' she said.

'I thought it was Estie, but I was wrong. Campbell Rutherford got a look at her face and he's sure it wasn't her.' All Campbell's certainty was leaking out of Lewis as he talked.

Ronnie lay back in the bed, frowning. 'What would Campbell know about it?'

Lewis swallowed. 'Campbell was there, okay? We were at the creek together that afternoon. I didn't want to get him into trouble as well, which is why I didn't say anything about him.' Lewis dug his foot into the hospital linoleum. 'Please. You have to believe me.'

Ronnie shook her head.

Someone had put something heavy on Lewis's chest. He tried to breathe.

'I know you've got no reason to believe me, but I swear it's the truth. The girl I saw wasn't even in school uniform. I'm sorry. I'm sorry I didn't listen to you. It was so stupid. I'm so stupid.'

Ronnie didn't say anything.

'The thing is, I don't think I like girls.' Lewis looked at her, to see if she'd intuited his meaning. He could sense the blank shock on his own face at what he'd said out loud. 'That's why I couldn't tell you about Campbell. We were there together, and I was afraid, okay? I didn't want my dad to find out. He'd kill me. And not like when you say it, okay? Not like when your mum is cranky with you. He would actually kill me.'

Ronnie sat up. Her mouth was opening and closing like the mouth of the goldfish. Lewis thought of Estie, of the light in the classroom that afternoon.

After a long pause, Ronnie said, 'Do you know what happened to the dog?'

'What?'

'The dog that bit me. No-one will tell me. Is it okay?'

Before Lewis could muster a response, a nurse bustled in.

Seeing him, she said, 'I'm going to need you to stand outside, young man.'

She ushered him out into the corridor and shut the heavy door, flicking a privacy screen over the small window.



The nurse was still in there when Lewis's mum came back.

In the car on the way home, his mum gripped the steering wheel with both hands and stared straight ahead as she said, 'I'm sorry, Lewis. I'm sorry that I let your father treat us this way. You must think I'm terribly weak.'

He thought of the moment in the car out the front of the IGA, the anger he'd felt. How important it had seemed then.

'I'm sorry if I haven't given you what I should have. I'm sorry if I've relied on you too much.'

'We didn't do anything wrong,' he said. 'Clint just wanted to make us think we did.'

His mum flinched at his father's name, and he could see some part of her wanted to correct him. But it occurred to him that they could live in a new place, now. A world where nobody said, *When your father gets home . . .*

'Things are going to be different now, Lewis. I promise.'

# WE

Later

If you're asking if we knew about Sophie Kennard at the time, then the answer is yes. Or, rather, our parents knew, or should have known, and nobody told us but we knew something was up. After that one Australia Day where the bruise on Sophie Kennard's collarbone glistened, the make-up she'd applied sliding off with her sweat, one of our mothers had pulled us aside and told us to remember that when we grew up we could always come home to her if we needed to. Sophie Kennard had nobody in that town, not like us.

Years later, a year into a marriage with someone our father had begged us not to marry, we would drive to our parents' place in our nightgown and our father would close the door on us. 'You're married now, you figure it out,' he said, as our mother slept. Our uncle used to say, *I believe you, thousands wouldn't*, when we insisted that we hadn't cheated at Balderdash. Those words were on our lips as we climbed back into our car. Our baby screaming, our nipples aching.

Or we became the person that hurt the ones we loved.

We did it again and again and we tried to stop and we couldn't, or we didn't have to stop, could tell they liked it really, and if we had to live in that shitty town then we were taking everyone down with us.

Everyone knew the motel owner's dad hit him. It was why he was no longer in possession of all his teeth. Still, at least he'd got the motel when the bastard shuffled off. Not everyone got that. And he was friends with Clint Kennard, who hit his son. Sometimes it's easier to stick with what you know. Comforting, even.

# CONSTANCE

Tuesday, 4 December 2001

The phone rang and Constance walked into the kitchen. Her number still wasn't on Steve's approved list at the prison, so she didn't expect it to be him. It might be his lawyer, though.

It was Detective Michaels.

'Constance.'

Something about the way the detective said her first name made Constance clutch the phone cord.

'Is it Esther?'

'I just wanted to be sure you were home. I'll be there in a minute.'

'Tell me now.'

'I'll see you soon.'

The detective didn't wait. As soon as they'd both sat down in the small lounge room, she spoke. 'We've found her body, Constance. I'm so sorry.'

'Where? Was it Steve?' Constance asked.

'It's okay to take a moment, Constance. This is bad news. I am so, so sorry.'

Constance did not want to take a moment. She wanted to know what had happened. When the detective saw that, she spoke again.

'She was found on a Durton property, though we don't currently suspect the owner of the land. And we're releasing your husband later today.'

The detective paused, as if letting the implications of the statement wash over Constance, before passing her a slip of paper with the details of Steve's release. Constance placed it in her pocket mechanically.

'But there's no new information about what happened, right?' Constance asked. 'I need you to tell me if Steve had anything to do with it.'

'Listen, we're still in this together, Constance,' Detective Michaels said. 'I'm doing everything I can. We're pursuing all leads at this point.'

Constance laughed, a cold, bitter sound. From where she was sitting, she could see the same yellow curtains in the kitchen, Steve's work number still on a piece of paper stuck to the phone.

'We need to have someone come and confirm it's her. I was thinking a relative of Steven's could –'

'I want to do it. It has to be me.'

'Okay.'

A keening sound rent the air. It was something caught in a trap, low and animal, and Constance was surprised to find the sound was coming from her.

For Constance, seeing her daughter – her body found on Ned Harrison's land – was not the hard part. The hard part was coming home and seeing the collection of things on her daughter's windowsill and wondering what she was supposed to do with them now. Usually, the windowsill was a high-traffic area. Things fell in and out of Esther's favour and were relegated to a box in the wardrobe or stuffed into a bookshelf. The Kinder Surprise toys Esther had kept were mostly pirate-themed: a tiny wench with an eyepatch, a bright green parrot on a stand, a miniature treasure chest.

That this collection would be the definitive one was more confronting than seeing her blue-lipped daughter, eyes closed, laid out on a metal table. They'd warned Constance about the smell, but not about the way her daughter's flesh would make her think of sultanas. Not that. When she looked at the objects crowding the window, she felt unsteady on her feet. The task of clearing them seemed both urgent and impossible.

Constance stripped off the clothes she had worn to see her daughter's lifeless body. She held her breath until her heart and lungs thudded and crumpled the clothes together in a ball. Standing there in her underwear, she imagined someone opening the unlocked front door, stabbing her in the back, between her shoulder blades. Pictured her blood on the dirty clothes. She could hear clicking and popping in her ears. Shel was in the kitchen, but Constance didn't care if she saw.

Constance made it to the laundry at the back of the house. Their washing machine had belonged to Steve's mother. When she died, he'd kept it and given away their machine, which was newer. It was ridiculous, but Steve insisted that it washed better than any other washing machine he'd ever owned. They always did what Steve wanted to do, in the end. A man too stupid to realise that clothes came out of his mother's washing machine cleaner than others because of all the work his mother did before they went in. Rage roared through her. The white knobs on the old machine were yellowed, and the stickers had faded, so you had to guess what the different cycles were. After a while it had become muscle memory, and Constance used the same cycle each time – the knob turned three clicks to the left. Sometimes it would stop on the rinse cycle and sit there full of water until you nudged the dial past the sticking point to get it going again.

She started crying. It was the kind of crying that came in waves, like throwing up. As one sob subsided another one came. Her mouth was hanging open and she tried to close it, but the force of the sob pushed her lips apart again. Shel was moving outside in the hall, now, but didn't come in. She'd said nothing when picking up Constance from the hospital, stayed silent in the car all the way back to Constance's place, just held her hand while Constance sobbed. Constance shoved the clothes in the machine but didn't turn it on. She alternated between closing her eyes and looking at the ceiling. It was completely silent. She pulled a dressing-gown from the hook by the door.

'Shel,' she called. 'You should head home. I'll be right for a while.'

Shel appeared in the doorway. 'That's not happening.'

'Please, Shel.'

The two women embraced. Shel held her for a long time.

'Whatever you need, love. Whatever you need. It's so awful.'

Constance suddenly felt cold and dry and dead. Like there could be no tears left.

Right up to the moment she climbed into his ute to pick Steve up from prison, Constance wasn't sure if she was going to go. What could she say to him? What could they say to each other? But she knew Steve would want to drive himself home, and his keys and the car had been returned to her by the police. When it came to Esther, they'd always done what Steve wanted to do. He'd say, *That's my daughter we're talking about.* Never *our* daughter. Maybe she would leave him to deal with this alone, then. Maybe it would be better if she went to her mother's after all, left the ute in the driveway and the keys in the letterbox and let Steve figure it out. In the end, though, she left the house with Steve's keys in hand, pulling the door closed behind her. She heard the lock catch and knew there was no reason to unlock it.

It was an hour's drive to the prison. She would have to live it all in reverse, with Steve beside her, on the way back.

The prison was surrounded by plants, huge spiky bushes nestled in mounds of sawdust. Constance drove through the main entrance and nudged the car in the direction of the parking bay indicated by a waving guard, his narrow face in shadow beneath the dark green cap he wore. She rolled down the window and felt the cool air in the cabin coming to the same temperature as the air outside. Even parked in the shade, she could feel the sweat under her breasts and at the backs of her knees.

The guard approached from behind the car, startling her. 'You're here for Bianchi?' he asked her side mirror. She nodded, and he said: 'He'll be out in a second.'

Constance could smell the guard's sweat, an unpleasant, funky tang.

A siren blared one long, continuous note. A light at the top of the high fence that surrounded the prison building flashed orange and Steve walked through a gate that was still sliding open. It paused for a second, the metal shuddering, and then started to move back the way it had come. She opened the car door and stepped out into the heat. The stretch of concrete between her and the gate was unbearably bright.

Steve was holding a large clear bag – like a sandwich bag, but the size of an A3 piece of paper.

'You're here,' he said, as he got close enough to the car not to have to shout the words.

The movements of his body, the angle of his head, they were the same. His voice was the same. They could have been having any of the hundreds of thousands of conversations of their marriage.

She looked at the prison instead of into his eyes. 'I don't know what exactly, but I thought they might do something special because you're innocent.' She spoke just to say something. It was the first time she'd said the word 'innocent' to Steve since it mattered.

'Letting me out doesn't count as special enough?' The words were heavy with sarcasm.

And then, as if remembering who they were, who they'd been, Steven began to cry. 'She's dead, Constance,' he said, grabbing her arm and pulling her towards him.

They collapsed into each other, heaving.

So the police had told him. Constance had thought she might have to.

He pulled away, staring off into the middle distance like he couldn't bear to look at her. He placed his hand on the driver's door. Constance walked around the car, going behind the tray of the ute so she wouldn't have to pass in front of him. Steve threw the plastic bag onto the back seat of the cab and slid behind the wheel. For a second, she thought he might reverse, leaving her standing stupidly near where the passenger door used to be, like your friends do when you're a teenager. She let her hand rest on the handle for a second before pulling it open.

Steve started the engine before she'd put on her seatbelt. It kept catching when she tried to pull it down. She had to take a deep breath, breathing out as she pulled the end, angling it down towards the cradle near the gearstick. Steve turned to look through the rear window of the ute. Constance felt the impulse to take his face in her hands, but he faced the front again as the ute reached the end of its turn. He shifted the ute into first gear and they straightened up. The acceleration shifted her back into her seat. She looked at him and for a moment all she could think was that he had such thick, dark hair.

'So, is the phone broken?' he said sarcastically as soon as they'd exited the prison gate, waved out by the man in the cap.

Steve had said before that he thought he sounded bitchy when he got angry. It had been an intimacy, part of a couple's checking in with each other: *Is this noticeable? Do other people see this? You have a shared stake in how people see me, and I trust you not to use this information to hurt me.*

They drove in silence until they reached the highway. Unlike the road to the prison, this was a familiar stretch they'd driven together a lot. All the usual landmarks were there – a particular tree, a particular billboard – all still dissecting the drive home into intervals of familiar time.

What had it been like in prison? Had he been afraid?

'I know this is hard.' Constance was grateful for the hypnotic road, for the opportunity to stare straight ahead as she spoke. 'But you had her shoe, and I couldn't think how on earth it could be there when you said you hadn't seen her. And you punched a cop. Why would you do that? Who does that?'

Constance didn't want them to talk about what had happened to Esther. The unknown was somehow harder. It would sound absurd, but she'd known Steven wouldn't hurt Esther, wouldn't make her suffer. She'd known that much. What kind of pathetic knowledge was that?

As if reading her mind, Steve spoke. 'I'm your *fucking husband.*' It was clear he was spoiling for a fight. 'I'm Esther's father. I love her!' The last words were a hoarse scream.

'Steve, do you remember what happened at one of Toni's parties when you were fifteen?'

Steve was silent, but his expression changed, as if he might be trying to remember.

'Shelly was eighteen,' Constance continued. 'She said a bunch of boys got her blind drunk, so drunk she couldn't stand up, and then they – they took turns . . .' Her voice trailed off.

Steve said nothing, his eyes on the road.

'They took turns raping her,' she finished.

'I heard about that,' he said, still not looking at her.

'Shelly said you were there.' How many times had she kissed this man's face, held his hand? 'She said you were one of the men who did it.'

Steve's right hand flew up from the wheel. 'You think that I'm the kind of bloke who would do *that*?' There was something in his voice, like the sound of a branch coming away from the trunk of a tree.

They were both crying now.

'But I suppose you can believe anything. There's something wrong with you, Con. Do you have any idea what the past few days have been like?'

'I'm not saying there isn't something wrong with me,' said Constance. 'I've never said that. I've never pretended that.'

'I didn't rape *anybody*,' Steve said. 'How could you think I would do that? Or that I would ever, *ever* hurt Esther?' He fell silent, his eyes on the road.

The only sound in the cab was the air conditioning, the rumble of wheels on bitumen.

'Our daughter is dead,' Constance said. 'We're never going to talk about where she'll go to uni. She'll never have another Christmas. She's never going to buy another pair of shoes.'

Steve kept his eyes on the road. Tears streamed down his face and ran into his stubble.

'I wish we'd never moved here,' she said.

# RONNIE

Tuesday, 4 December 2001

There was a phone in the corridor, just outside my hospital room. Mum thought I couldn't hear her through the closed door, but I could. I'd acted surprised when she said Flea had been found by our neighbour, safe and sound, sunning himself in our yard. It was strange, hearing what my mum sounded like when she thought I wasn't around.

I was feeling better. My jaw still hurt, but I wasn't running a fever anymore. My arm ached where they'd given me a shot to stop me getting sick. The doctor told Mum I was recovering well, I'd be able to go home in a few days.

Mum had gone out to make a call. 'Shelly. What are you saying?' I could hear the tiredness in her voice.

My ears pricked. I hoped Aunt Shelly wasn't planning a visit. I wasn't in the mood for her and my cousins.

'Are they sure?'

I'd never heard Mum sound so shocked.

'Oh my god. Where?'

Mum went silent for a long time.

'How's Constance handling it?' Silence, during which I imagined Mum was nodding her head, something she did on the phone all the

287

time, even though the person at the other end couldn't see it. 'Shit. I've got to go, Shelly. I've got no idea how I'm going to tell Ronnie.'

When she came back into the room, I could only see her face in profile, but something in the way she held her neck, like her head was heavy and had to be kept balanced so it didn't fall off, told me something bad was coming.

I thought about feigning sleep, but I was too slow. Mum had seen my open eyes.

'Ronnie,' she said. Her voice broke at the last syllable of my name. She came to a stop near the bed. 'They found Esther.'

The way she said it told me straightaway that they hadn't found all of her. They hadn't found her laugh, her loping gait, or any of the things I loved about her. None of those things would be coming home.

'She's dead?' I needed to hear her say it.

Mum nodded. 'They found her body.'

'What happened?'

'I don't know,' Mum said. Her face was tight and very pale.

This idea that adults didn't know, weren't as in control as I'd imagined, had been taking hold for some time now.

I could feel tears running down the left side of my face.

Mum pulled me into her, and I cried into her shirt for a long time. Eventually, she sat down in the vinyl armchair next to the bed.

I thought of what Lewis had told me the day before. If I'd been able to sit up and lean right over, I could've kissed him – pressed my bandaged face against his smooth one. I'd never kissed anyone, and I'd always been a little bit in love with Lewis. It hurt that he'd never felt the same, and never would. I don't know why I thought of that then; maybe it was an attempt to be in a different moment.

I looked down at the blanket, which had the name of the hospital printed on it in blue. I'd read that when you are approached by some predators, you should stay completely still. They can only see you, and hurt you, if you move. I lay very still and tried not to think of what the words *They found Esther* meant.

Mum took my hand. 'Are you okay, Bup?'

I suddenly felt ashamed that I hadn't reached out for Lewis's hand the day before. I wished I'd let him know that it was alright with me. That I thought he was good and brave, and I was sorry I'd been angry with him. But I had been angry, because he was supposed to love me like I loved him. So I'd asked him about the dog instead. And I could never change that. And now my best friend was dead.

'What do they know?' The words broke out of me, sounding muffled.

'They think she died straightaway, after she went missing. She didn't feel any pain, Bup.'

'And what about her dad?' I asked. I still couldn't believe he'd hurt Esther.

Her mouth fell open. It made her look odd, like someone I didn't know.

'They've released Steven. I suppose that means they no longer think he had something to do with it,' she said.

I thought of Steven, of sitting with him in his car. He loved Esther like I did. I'd known it all along.

'Was it the owner of the motel?'

Even though I knew now I must have been mistaken about Esther being there, at the motel, I had to ask, had to know.

'Oh, Bup.' Mum started crying. 'Sometimes I just want to take you back inside of me. If I could shrink you down, I would squeeze you in and you wouldn't feel pain anymore and I could keep you safe.' Mum gestured with one hand to her slim torso. 'I love you so much, Bup. And the real answer is we don't know. I'm sure the police are looking into it.'

I pictured the police. The police who'd failed to bring my friend home alive.

'I love you too, Mum.'

'How are you feeling? Is there anything I can do?'

'I feel sad, I guess.'

'Yeah. I feel sad too, kiddo.'

'I'm never going to see her again, am I?'

'We'll go to the funeral, if the doctor says you're well enough.'

That was a no. I didn't know what I'd even meant by the question. I wasn't a little kid. I understood what *dead* meant.

Mum hugged me tight, careful not to touch anywhere it might hurt.

'Can I have some chocolate milk, Mum?'

'They're all out, Bup. But I saw some strawberry milk in the ward fridge. Will you be alright here for a minute while I go and get it?'

I nodded and Mum kissed me on the top of my head. She stepped out of the room, pulling the door closed behind her.

I wasn't hooked up to any machines now, but someone in the next room was. I could hear it beeping through the walls. I missed Esther. My body ached with missing her.

Esther is dead.

Beep.

Esther is dead.

Beep.

Footsteps in the hall.

I kept thinking about the first night, at Uncle Peter's, when Mum got into the bed and I thought she said they'd found Esther. The desire for that time rippled through me – when things were still possible, when Esther might still come home.

Beep.

Once, after reading an article in a *National Geographic* Mum had brought home, I'd told Esther I knew who my father was. We were sitting on the white shaggy rug in her bedroom.

'He's a freedom fighter in Africa,' I said.

Esther said, 'But you're white.'

'He's white, but he speaks the language and lives there.'

I'd cut out a picture from the magazine of a white man squinting, his hand raised to shield his eyes from the sun, an African landscape behind him, holding a gun. I showed it to her. Esther didn't point out that the photo had writing on the other side, that it wasn't on photo paper. That I'd told her about half-a-dozen men before this one who were 'definitely my dad'. She'd just listened.

Who would listen now?

# WE

The news that Esther Bianchi's body had been found and that Steven Bianchi had been released rippled through the town, though less quickly than the news he'd been arrested. Innocence travels slower than guilt, we all know that. And people weren't ready to grapple with what his release meant. It had been hard to imagine the girl's father doing anything, but wasn't it usually the father? The husband? The boyfriend? And the girl was dead. How were our parents supposed to tell us that? Look us in the eye and say a girl was dead and nobody knew how or why? Names were muttered. No-one could look Ned Harrison in the eye. The owner of the old motel had been arrested, and greasy Clint Kennard, on the same day Ronnie Thompson had been attacked by a dog at the motel. It sounded like something that should be happening in another town. Somewhere in America, maybe.

Summers in our town consisted of long days that ended in barbecues where the adults would get drunker and drunker and we children would gather in packs and poke at the dying bonfire or congregate behind the water tank and give each other dares. We ran along fences that divided the big backyards of the houses in the middle of town. If the party was held out on someone's farm, we would hurtle past the point where the ute headlights could see us. Reeling and swooping, giddy in all that darkness, we'd return to the fire and use long sticks to hunt through the coals for a foil-wrapped baked potato that might have been missed. We could sit on the other side of the huge bonfire built by the adults and pretend we had made it ourselves, or listen to the adults singing and talking, their eyes shiny with firelight. We threw things we thought would burn into the fire, not for warmth, but for entertainment. There seemed no possibility that we could ever run out of fuel, or that we would ever get old.

The young ones took centre stage, telling long jokes that didn't make any sense but that made the drunk adults laugh. Sometimes our parents would let us camp. We woke in the morning when the tent grew too warm for sleep. We pushed our heads out of the opening, where the smell of kangaroo poo waited for us. Unfurling our bodies into the cool air, squatting or standing to piss, walking down to the creek to stare at its brown waters and returning before anyone else had awoken made us feel like we were the only people in the world who mattered. For some of us, those mornings made us feel whole. For others, they were just another reminder we didn't belong.

After Steven Bianchi was released, people stopped having parties like these. We stayed in small family groups, turning inwards and away. We cried ourselves to sleep thinking about it. We cried more at the loss of our own freedoms than we ever did for Esther Bianchi. People got together in lounge rooms and kitchens. 'Can you imagine if it was one of ours?' our parents said, voices hushed, bent over a plate of Iced VoVos, or with the phone receiver held close to their mouth, their words a whisper. The town buzzed with the question: *If it wasn't Steven Bianchi, then who was it?*

# SARAH

Wednesday, 5 December 2001

Sarah had been at Mack's station since 7 am, trying to get the pathologist on the phone. She wanted to follow up the results from the hairs found on the body, but no-one at the lab was picking up. She'd woken too early. There was still blood on the earth outside their rooms where Veronica Thompson had been attacked. Sarah had walked from the motel to the police station to give her thoughts time to organise themselves, leaving Smithy with the car.

Roland was in the cell at the back where he'd spent the night, and Sarah avoided the kitchen. She'd only just put the reception phone down when it rang. She let it chirrup a couple of times before scooping it up.

'I want to talk to someone about that missing girl,' a woman's voice said. The phone line crackled, like someone else was listening on another receiver. 'Are you the right people?'

'Yes. May I ask your name?' Sarah felt a pang that the girl was not missing, not now. Sarah had failed on that score.

'Anthea. Mrs Anthea Brooks. I'm a widow. And look, I'm not sure if this is something worth telling you. I want you to know that upfront.'

'Any information you have could be useful, Mrs Brooks.' Sarah reached for her notebook.

'That's what I figured – I mean, that's why I'm calling. I was visiting my friend Maude on Friday afternoon. That's the afternoon that girl went missing, isn't it?'

'Yes,' replied Sarah, checking her watch to be able to include the time of the call in her notes.

'I saw Steven Bianchi that afternoon, on my way there. He was on the side of the road as I drove past.'

'Where was this?' Sarah was already writing on a fresh page.

'On the highway out of town, near the *Thanks for visiting Durton* sign, at about quarter past two.'

Sarah knew the spot. It was exactly where Steven had said he'd been, and there was no way he could have made it from there to anywhere near the creek. His foreman was sure Steven's car had sat outside the site office all afternoon.

'What was he doing?'

'Well, that's the only reason I remember seeing him, you see. He was urinating against the town sign! Right there, where anyone could see him. I had a mind to give him a ring, or his aunt. Why is it that men think they can just widdle everywhere? Who died and made this world their toilet?'

'Is there a reason you didn't come forward with this information earlier?' Sarah winced to think again of the days the father of a dead girl had spent in a cell.

'I went away for the weekend,' the woman said archly. 'I just got back and heard you were asking for information.'

'Are you able to come down to the station? We'd like to get that on the record.'

'Of course,' the woman said, sounding flattered. 'And, well, if you like that, I've got more for you.'

'Pardon?'

'Later, when I was rinsing my cup at Maude's sink, I saw an unusual car.'

'Where was this?'

'The house of my friend Maude Sterling,' she said.

Sarah wrote the name down, along with the address – the name of the road placed it near Ned Harrison's property.

'Can I just confirm the date that you saw all this?'

'Friday the thirtieth of November. It's Maude's birthday so I'm one hundred per cent on that.'

'Okay,' Sarah said, keeping her voice neutral.

The woman continued. 'The only reason I was even looking out the window was I was still annoyed about seeing Steven widdling. I was thinking about what I would say to him. You arrested Steven, didn't you? That's what I heard.'

It sounded like the town rumour mill had yet to inform Anthea Brooks that Steven Bianchi had been released the day before.

'Where exactly was this car?'

'It was on the road that goes past Maude's and sweeps out past the creek. It was heading away from the creek, back towards the main road.'

'What did it look like?'

'I'm sorry, but I'm not sure about the make or anything. I just remember thinking I hadn't seen it around before. It didn't look like a country car.'

'In what way?'

'Well, I suppose it wasn't a ute, or a car that I can imagine any of the mothers around here driving. It was black, and too shiny, maybe. There was a rundown old car not far behind it that looked much more like what you'd see around here. It made the black car stand out even more, because the big car behind looked like it belonged there. No point trying to keep anything shiny out this way.'

Sarah scribbled notes – *creek road, shiny car, from city?* – and drew a triangle.

'Can you remember what time it was?'

'Well, I came over about two thirty with some teacake, you know. So it must've been around three. I left around five, I think. I can ask Maude, if it's important?'

'It would be good to know an exact time, yes. What else can you tell me about the car? You said it was black?'

'Yes, black. And just so shiny.'

Sarah examined her notes, a thought suddenly occurring to her. 'And what about the second car you saw?'

'Pardon?'

'The one that came along after the shiny black car?'

'Well, it was this big car. I would call it, oh, what's the bloody word, a *van*.' The woman stifled a cough. 'That's it. I didn't get such a good look at that one. It turned onto one of the tracks that run between the paddocks.'

'What colour was it?'

'Like a dusty ruby,' the woman said declaratively. 'I remember thinking about that, about a jewel in the dry grass. I've written some poetry, you know.' The woman laughed dryly. 'My mother always said I had a poetic mind. If it wasn't for the poetry, I would never have remembered, to be honest.'

Sarah rolled her eyes and wrote the words *red van* in her notes.

'So, do you think this woman is on to something?' Smithy asked.

'I've honestly no idea,' Sarah said, leaning against the counter of the small station reception. Smithy had just come in and she'd updated him on her phone call. 'But we've finally got a sighting of Steven. And I'm curious about the shiny black car *and* the van. I've gone through the vehicle list Mack put together and I can't find anything that fits either description. If the van was where this woman says it was, it's possible it was heading for Ned's place.' Sarah stood upright, stretched her back. 'And I keep thinking, only a local would've known that Ned was away.'

'I'll ask Mack when he gets in if anyone else saw a black car,' said Smithy. 'And I'll see if I can rustle anything up from local registrations on a red van.'

Smithy was already heading for the kitchen.

If Sarah had any lingering doubts about Steven Bianchi, Anthea Brooks's testimony put paid to them. When he got in, Mack said the Bianchis and the Brookses were not friendly (Sarah had to wonder, was Steven Bianchi friendly with anyone?), so Mrs Brooks's testimony carried more weight than it might otherwise have done. Her sighting would not have been enough if they still had the physical evidence. But the fact that Esther's shoes had been on her feet in the back of Ned's ute spoke for itself. Sarah's training sergeant had said that sometimes all it took was lots of little things adding up to tell you everything you needed to know.

It was time to do what she hadn't managed to get to yesterday because of Esther's body being found. It was time to speak to Clint Kennard again.

The same officer as before was on reception at Rhodes HQ. She smiled at Sarah as she opened the partition that separated the business end of the station from the waiting area. The young woman moved only partially out of the way so Sarah had to brush past her. Out of nowhere, the fear of what she'd done to Amira surged through Sarah. Amira could still take out an apprehended violence order – if Sarah didn't lose her job, it would still end any prospect of advancement. She took a deep breath and resisted the urge to look back at the woman.

In the interview room with Clint Kennard, Sarah's body was taut. She fought to keep her movements slow and steady. She'd told Smithy she didn't need him to come, she wanted him looking into the car and the van. Clint was accompanied by his lawyer, this time. The woman's lipstick was the colour of the dirt that Sarah had been knocking out of the grooves in her shoes since she arrived in Durton.

'Well, after looking in your shed we can be confident the speed we found in the dam comes from your lab, Clint.'

Clint slapped the table. 'Bloody unlucky, this business with the Bianchi girl. Brought you lot sniffing around.'

'Bit unluckier for Esther Bianchi than you, Clint, wouldn't you say?'

Clint's lawyer eyed him. 'I've instructed my client not to answer any questions.'

'But I think your client is going to want to speak to me,' Sarah said. 'You see, the thing is, Clint, the plastic we found in your shed matches the plastic we found wrapped around Esther's body. And we found the same plastic wrapped around the speed, which we know for a fact was made on your property. What do you have to say to that?'

Clint looked at Sarah for a moment, as if considering his options.

'I'm not talking about the drugs anymore,' he said. 'You'll have to make your case, and I think my lawyer here would be delighted if I just shut up.'

The woman blew air out of her nose.

'But you should know, Peter Thompson was supposed to meet me and Roland at the pub that afternoon when the girl went missing. He never showed. So if you want to talk dead girls, you should talk to him.'

'Why didn't you tell me that when we spoke on Sunday?' Sarah asked.

Clint raised his shoulders. 'I didn't want you connecting too many dots. If you didn't already have his name, I didn't see the wisdom in giving it to you. But if that's what he's got himself mixed up in, I'm not going down for some dead kid.'

Sarah thought about what Lewis had said – that Peter had come to the house on Sunday and the men had talked about Esther.

'Thing is, Peter has been acting weird since this whole thing with the Bianchi girl. He hasn't been taking my calls. He came over on Sunday morning and I had to talk him out of leaving town altogether. And we didn't even know you'd found a fucking brick.'

'I think my client has said more than enough,' the lawyer said, standing.

She placed a hand on the back of Clint's chair, and the interview was over.

Sarah drove back to Durton to speak to Roland Mathers again. She expected him to stonewall, but as soon as Sarah said Peter Thompson's name, Roland volunteered that Peter Thompson had been supposed to meet him and Clint on Friday at two, and that he'd been acting 'fuckin' weird' the one time Roland had seen him since. If Sarah hadn't asked Smithy to make sure they didn't have time to compare stories, she would have said it was all too neat.

The first thing Sarah did after finishing the interview with Roland Mathers was signal to Mack that they needed to duck outside for a chat. They stood in the field behind the station, away from the building where Roland might hear them.

'I need you to talk me through Peter Thompson's alibi,' Sarah said.

'Peter's alibi is exactly what his wife said it was. His eldest son came in with him and confirmed it,' said Mack. 'I know the boy. He's a good kid.'

'And you believe him?'

'You don't understand this place,' Mack said. 'I've been here ten years, and I'm from the country to start with. I think I know some things you don't.'

Sarah thought she recognised pity in his expression. She was filled with the memory of every time she'd had some version of this conversation. All the male cops in her career who'd told her she didn't understand, that she wouldn't ever *get it*, piled on top of one another.

'It's not my understanding I'm worried about,' she said. 'You should have come to me with this. I don't care how believable Peter's son was, that's not a real alibi.'

'You think only city cops can tell when someone is feeding them bullshit?' The words were surprisingly forceful for the usually amiable Mack. This was the most pissed off she'd seen him since they'd arrived.

'What I think is you were too close, and I've let this go on for too long,' Sarah said.

A moment passed between them. She thought of her original impression, that she'd been relieved to have a good local cop to work with.

Mack spat on the ground. 'It's your case,' he said, before turning and going back inside.

Sarah kicked herself for putting off speaking to Peter for as long as she had. There'd been the body, of course, which brought with it a series of tasks Sarah couldn't simply opt out of. The truth, she had to admit, was that she *wanted* it to be Clint Kennard. His behaviour in their first interview, his reaction in the station when he'd found his son talking to the police, the way he'd tried to take her down on the main street of Durton, these things made it personal. But she couldn't let her feelings get in the way. Clint was undeniably involved in the drugs, but perhaps she'd been distracted by him. The orange hairs she'd seen on the plastic wrapped around Esther's body drew a line to the man she'd only ever seen in a photograph: Shelly Thompson's husband.

The fact was that Peter Thompson had never had a solid alibi – his son could and would have lied for his father, she was sure – and he had access to a vehicle. She should never have let Mack, who had told her himself that Peter was 'a good bloke' (how often did those words mean the opposite?), make the call on the alibi. Peter knew Esther, certainly better than the other two men did. The girl wouldn't have been afraid of him.

The time had come to bring Peter Thompson in. With Clint Kennard and Roland Mathers's testimony, she had enough to arrest him in relation to the speed. She liked the idea of bringing him in already off balance, with a charge to answer. She would use the drugs as leverage to get him talking.

On her second visit to the Thompson house, with Smithy and some uniformed officers from Rhodes in tow, Sarah thought that if there was any money in the drugs it didn't seem to have made its way into Peter Thompson's hands yet. Perhaps the brick of speed they'd found in the dam really was their first output, as Clint Kennard had claimed. Though he would say that, wouldn't he? A beat-up Torana and the green Mitsubishi Delica that Sarah recognised from its almost permanent position out the front of Constance Bianchi's house were in the driveway. Smithy parked them in.

Sarah got her first look at Peter Thompson in the flesh when he came to the door. He was wearing shorts and a footy jersey and seemed sleepy and unthreatening in bare feet. He submitted to cuffs and heard the charge against him with surprisingly little fuss.

'Mr Thompson, will you consent to a search of your property?' Smithy asked.

'Yes,' Peter said, hands held in front of him. 'I will.' His confidence made Sarah think it was unlikely they'd find anything on site.

Sarah left Smithy and the uniforms behind to search.

In the interview room in Rhodes, Peter was adamant he didn't need a lawyer. At least that was something to like about the man, Sarah thought.

'So, Peter.' Sarah crossed her arms. 'What can you tell me about the dam on the abandoned property on the way out of town? The old Caulfield place.'

'No-one's worked that land for years. The soil's crap.' Peter's voice signalled confusion at the question.

'Certainly quite a lot more speed in the landscape than you might otherwise expect,' Sarah said.

Peter pressed his lips together and cocked his head to the side.

'Tell me where you were at two thirty last Friday.'

'Like I told Mack, I was at home. Working on the Torana in the shed.'

'And did any of your children see you there?'

'They know not to disturb me in the shed unless someone's bleeding. They're all big enough now to manage themselves, anyway. But my eldest boy kept bringing me cold water every half an hour or so. He's a good kid. The shed was like an oven.'

'No-one other than your eldest son can confirm you were there?'

'No,' he said.

'Why didn't you meet Roland Mathers and Clint Kennard that Friday like you were supposed to?'

Peter grimaced.

'Okay, look, I lost track of time, alright?' he said.

'Did you ask your son to lie for you?' Sarah asked.

'I would never do that.' There was something odd about his face, Sarah noticed; part of his lip didn't move when he talked.

'Listen, Peter. I know about you, Clint and Roland and the drugs. You need to start getting real with me.'

'Do you have any idea what it's like to be in over your head? To not know how you got there?' Peter asked, sweat on his forehead glistening in the station light. He looked terrified. 'Listen, I'm a good guy. I love my kids. I love my wife.' He was pleading with her now.

Sarah imagined this man sweating on top of her, creating five children. She shuddered internally. Sarah thought of the difference between Steven Bianchi and Peter Thompson. Steven had acted like an arsehole to cover his fear. Peter seemed ready to roll over and show his belly.

Sarah had a vivid memory of being eleven or twelve and sitting at the dining table with her father. She couldn't remember what had brought the conversation on, but she'd been upset about something, someone had wronged her, said or done something she didn't like at school. She'd wanted her father to be angry on her behalf, to come to her defence.

'Let's say this bit of material is trouble.' He indicated the thin lace table runner that ran the length of the table. 'Let's imagine that it's all the things that can go wrong in life, bad marriage, poverty, hunger, doing something unforgiveable, whatever.'

Sarah, who'd received a tongue lashing from her mother for staining the runner more than once, was ready to accept that it was trouble.

'Everyone with the good fortune to be born on this side,' he gestured to the smooth varnished wood of the dining table that sat between them, 'thinks they're there because they wouldn't ever do the sort of thing that gets you into that kind of mess.' Her father reached out and ruffled the runner so that its material bunched slightly along the long edge closest to him, the tucks and whorls of the lace suddenly chaotic.

Sarah nodded to show she accepted his premise.

'All the people on this side confuse *making* good choices with *having* good choices. Do you see the difference?'

Sarah looked across at him.

'Anyone who thinks they're better than the people on the other side needs to take a hard look at themselves. Things happen, and anyone could end up there.'

'Anyone?' Sarah asked, wide-eyed. She remembered swinging her feet in the chair. 'Even Mum?'

'Even your mother,' he said. 'In fact, some days I think I push her pretty close.'


Across the table in the interview room, Peter looked like a fretful child with his light ginger eyebrows, freckled nose and frown.

'No more mucking around, Peter. Tell me: did you kill Esther Bianchi?'

Peter looked a lot more awake all of a sudden.

'I would never hurt Esther. I would never hurt any kid.' The final sentence was almost a whine.

'Did she see something she wasn't supposed to?'

'I told you: I was working in my shed. Oh god. When I said I was in over my head, I was talking about the drugs. Nothing like *that*.'

'Look, Peter . . .' Sarah held his gaze, her own eyes earnest. A friend. 'I'm willing to believe it was an accident. Maybe Esther saw you and then tried to leg it. Maybe you just wanted to talk to her and something went wrong. Maybe it all just went horribly wrong.'

She kept her voice soft and low, like whatever she told him would never have to leave this small room.

'That's not what happened. I didn't see Esther that day!' Peter sounded like he was on the verge of tears.

Sarah knew that tears didn't mean anything. They could be tears of self-pity.

The words exploded out of him. 'Look, I agreed to move drugs for Clint Kennard and Roland Mathers, I did – but I hadn't actually done it yet, and if they say otherwise, they're lying.'

Sarah chose that moment to take a break. She wanted to let Peter stew for a while. Mack had been convinced Peter had nothing to do with it, that he wasn't capable of such a thing, but Sarah knew what it was like to do something you never imagined possible.

In the hallway, she saw she'd missed a call from Smithy and rang him back.

'Found a shovel and what's left of a roll of black plastic in the shed out the back at Peter's place,' Smithy said, skipping the pleasantries. 'It was wedged between a shelf and the wall. The uniformed officer almost missed it. Plastic looks identical to what we found in Clint Kennard's shed and on the girl, and there's blood on the shovel.'

'Well, shit,' she said.

Sarah spoke without preamble when she returned to the interview room, not even sitting down to address Peter. 'The plastic in your shed matches the plastic found on the body, which is the same material we found wrapped around the package of speed we recovered from the dam.'

'What?'

'We also found blood on the shovel hidden in your shed.'

Peter's mouth opened, but no sound escaped.

Sarah looked at the clock on the wall. 'We'll be testing that blood overnight. Let's speak again in the morning.' Peter seemed to consider rising to his feet, but slumped deeper into his chair instead. 'You can have a good, long think, decide if you want to give Esther Bianchi's family some resolution. I'm going to have an officer come and transfer you to a cell.'

Sarah kept her eyes on Peter as she closed the interview room door behind her.

After the interview, Smithy called again and they talked through what would happen next. Sarah knew in her gut it was the girl's blood on the shovel. She allowed herself to think seriously, for the first time since they'd arrived, about heading home. Sarah wondered if Amira had told their friends what she'd done. Fuck it. They were all Amira's friends anyway. Sarah thought about the voicemails she'd left for Amira in the weeks following that night and cringed inwardly. She imagined Amira playing them aloud, laughing at Sarah, laughing at the need in her voice. But Sarah was done with that now.

As Sarah wound up the second call with Smithy, it occurred to her to try the lab again. Now they had Peter in custody, along with the shovel and the plastic, it almost seemed like a foregone conclusion, but it was still worth checking in and making sure they'd at least begun testing.

She found the number for the pathology lab she'd saved in her mobile.

'If you're calling to ask if we've got a match for the hairs we found on the body in our database, the answer is no,' the man said as soon as Sarah gave her name. It was the pathologist who'd been at the autopsy. 'We've only got one hair with enough root attached for DNA comparison, and all I can tell you at this point is that it's definitely human hair.'

'Well, the good news is I'm sending you a sample soon that should be a match. Do you think you can turn it around quickly?'

He paused, as if he were looking around the lab, making a silent assessment before answering. 'I can do that.'

'Fantastic, thanks.'

There was a rustle of papers at the other end of the line. 'Oh, and I should mention, the hair is dyed.'

'What?' Sarah's grip tightened around her phone. Peter Thompson didn't strike her as the kind of man vain enough to dye his hair. 'You're absolutely sure?'

'Yeah, that's easy enough to see when you look at it under a microscope.'

'Right, okay. Thanks.'

The man hung up and Sarah slid the phone into her pocket and flicked through her notebook. She moved quickly through the numbered pages, unsure what she was looking for. She landed on her conversation with Veronica Thompson in the hospital. Something she'd underlined caught her eye. The word *Van*. Sarah thought about what Veronica had said. That she was worried Esther was being held in a van. It would be the perfect way to move her without being seen.

Sarah looked around, like she had something she wanted to share with someone, but the hallway was empty. She wrote something on the page, her pen gouging a deep mark in the paper, before she pulled her phone out again. She punched in Anthea Brooks's number, crosschecking the digits from the notes she'd made during their conversation earlier that day.

The old woman took a while to answer. 'Hello?' she said, finally, just as Sarah was getting ready to hang up.

'Mrs Brooks,' Sarah said. 'Is that you?'

'Yes, who's this?'

'This is Detective Sergeant Sarah Michaels.'

'Oh, hello again, officer. How can I help you?'

'I'm calling because this morning you said you saw a van. The old car behind the shiny black one. I just wondered if you were absolutely sure about the colour?'

'The colour? Ah, yes. I remember telling you about the poetry.' Mrs Brooks sounded pleased with herself. 'It was emerald-coloured, dear.'

'Emerald? As in green?' Sarah checked her notes. 'You said it was ruby-coloured this morning.'

'Did I say ruby?' There was a pause at the other end of the line. 'I meant emerald. It was green. A green jewel. Oh dear. Maude would have a field day if she heard about this. Say my mind's going . . .'

'You're definitely sure it was green?' Sarah tried to keep the impatience from her voice.

'As sure as I can be, dear.'


Smithy answered the phone on the third ring. 'Hello again, boss. Miss me?'

Sarah explained to Smithy that she wanted him to bring both the Torana and the green van from the Thompson house to be checked over.

'No problems, boss.'

'And Smithy?' Sarah flipped to a new page in her notebook and scribbled an additional note to herself. 'I need you to do one last thing for me.'

'What?' Smithy asked.

'Do you have enough kits to get DNA from Peter's wife and all the kids?' she asked.

'I think so, yeah, but they may not go for it,' he said. 'I've got no way of compelling them to do a test, you know that.'

'It's worth a shot,' she argued, and she knew Smithy would do it. She could count on him.

Sarah found the pathology number in her recent calls.

'Calling again, Detective Sergeant?' the man said.

'Listen, do you think you can stay until my colleague gets there?'

'I'll do what I can,' he said. 'I can't stay forever, though. How long will that be?'

'He should be there with some other samples soon. Can you call me once you've had a chance to look at what he's got? I'd like to come and review the evidence from Peter Thompson's house with you, and see Esther Bianchi's body again, too,' said Sarah.

'If he gets here in time, I'll call you with the results,' said the pathologist.

'Great. First, though, can you do me a favour?'

'You mean another favour?' The man sighed, then said, 'What do you need?'

'There're two cars coming in. A Torana and a van. Do you think you can get those results bumped up the queue for me?'

'I'll certainly see what I can do,' the man said.

*Finally*, she thought, *a helpful pathologist*.


Sometimes Sarah wondered why she did this job. No-one became a detective for the money, that was for sure. Sarah's training sergeant had been a pain in the arse, but he'd seen something in her. 'You think you're smarter than everyone else' – she'd opened her mouth to protest, and he'd raised a hand to silence her – 'and you're not wrong. But you want to be smarter than everyone? Go do it where it counts.' That was it. She did it because she knew she was good at it. She'd gone for Child Protection, and then Missing Persons, instead of the more prestigious Homicide, because she wanted to help people who were still alive, like her father had done. Sarah owed something to Esther Bianchi, a girl who'd never get to come home, never get to grow up.

The next morning Sarah met Peter in the interview room. He looked like he hadn't slept at all. He tugged at his red goatee absent-mindedly and stared off into space instead of looking at her.

Sarah undid the chain that fastened the cuffs Peter was wearing to the table and motioned for him to stand up.

'Come with me.'

'Where are you taking me?'

Sarah said nothing. She positioned herself behind him and placed a hand on his shoulder, guiding him through the open door. Peter was silent as she loaded him into the back seat, silent as they drove all the way back to Durton.

Finally, when they were pulling into his street, he spoke. 'What are we doing here?'

Sarah caught his eye in the rear-view mirror.

'We've reviewed the evidence and decided you can come home.'

Peter looked at her in mute shock.

'You don't think I killed Esther?'

Sarah didn't say anything.

Sarah knocked on the front door and Shelly Thompson let them in. She was wearing the same shirt she had in Constance Bianchi's kitchen, when Sarah had met her for the first time. There were dark circles under her eyes.

Shelly brought them into the lounge room. The space was filled with battered brown corduroy couches and the sound of kids playing in the backyard. It smelled like the laundry aisle at Woolworths: a clean, floral smell. Smithy removed Peter's cuffs and Peter slumped down onto one of the couches.

Smithy approached Shelly Thompson with the handcuffs in his hands.

'Shelly Thompson,' he said. 'You are being placed under arrest in connection to the death of Esther Bianchi. You do not have to say or do anything unless you wish to do so. Anything you do or say may be recorded and used as evidence in court.'

Peter jumped to his feet. 'Why are you doing that to my wife? Where are you taking her? She hasn't done anything.'

Sarah eyed Peter before looking at Smithy. Sarah knew he was thinking the same thing. *This could escalate.*

'Please, Pete – the kids will hear,' Shelly said as Smithy closed the cuffs, clicking them home.

Peter's shoulders sank.

Smithy walked Shelly towards the front door.

At the threshold, Shelly turned back towards her husband. 'We'll talk soon, love,' she said, looking at the floor.

Sarah thought of the press conference, Constance Bianchi mobbed by cameras, the way her best friend's dyed red hair had shone orange in the light.

One look at the van and the techs had found a dent in the front bumper, traces of Esther's blood in the small crater of damage. Esther's blood was in the back of the van, and on the shovel. Shelly, by her own admission, had been driving the Delica near the creek on the afternoon Esther had died. And Shelly's hair was on the body.

The tall woman sagged into the back seat of the Commodore, her hands cuffed in front of her. Sarah did not take any special care to make sure they were safely inside before she shut the door.

# WE

Friday, 30 November 2001

One thing Detective Sergeant Sarah Michaels was never able to figure out was the shiny black car. We can start with that small detail. The name of the driver doesn't matter. It is the last day of a hot November and he and his wife and daughter are in the middle of a long journey to see his wife's parents. His wife's mother is dying. His wife likes the idea of finding a quaint little country cafe to stop at for scones and tea and to break up the drive. Like all people who want something, she assumes that the town will have it in abundance.

The shiny car cruises past the chip shop, past the newsagency and the IGA and the butcher. There is no quaint cafe. They drive as far as the creek – past the school where Esther Bianchi is sitting, head in her hands, watching the other girls in her class play netball – before deciding to stop and let their black labrador, unimaginatively named Blacky, out for a wee. The labrador has been farting viciously throughout their long trip.

Sensing freedom, the dog takes off, heedless of his owners' calls, inhaling as much of the landscape as he can. He runs for Durton Creek. We have always called it Dirt Creek. The creek is so low that afternoon that our name for it is fitting.

The man's daughter, let off school for the day, knows that the best way of catching the dog is to approach him slowly, uninterestedly, calling his name as if they don't really care if he comes or not.

The man hates the dog. He wishes he could have left it at a kennel or, better yet, somewhere that would rehome the bloody thing. He hates the dog hair and the shit and the obligatory walks. He hates the randomness of it. Moments like this when the dog runs off and the order of things is disturbed. He hates being beholden to a creature dumber than he is. But his daughter and wife are devoted to the goofy animal.

His daughter walks beside him, her long black hair blowing in the wind as they call the dog.

Not far away, Esther Bianchi is leaving the netball court and walking to get her bag. There is still time. If the family knew what was about to happen, they could hurry to the school, warn her to take the paved path home, to avoid the creek. But they don't know Esther Bianchi. The father and the girl don't notice the two boys observing them from behind a large boulder. The girl finally gets the dog to come with half a ham sandwich – already curling up at the edges from the heat – and they all pile back into the car. These are the things that can change a life. A farting dog, and a girl with a ham sandwich. Two kissing boys.

Across town, a balding Clint Kennard and a defiantly deodorant-free Roland Mathers, in his stained wifebeater singlet, are at the pub, discussing the splitting of profits for the speed they are going to sell. Clint Kennard is eager to tell Roland Mathers about his clever hiding place, the old dam near the highway. They can hide what they don't wish to share with Peter Thompson there, and a friend of Clint's from out of town can collect it without anyone seeing them together. It's a brilliant plan.

*

We can still see what happens next. Esther Bianchi is walking home from school, her back wet with sweat, her backpack heavy. She cuts along the creek from the road, like normal. Head down, she trudges towards home. Looking up, she sees the green flash of Shelly Thompson's van. Up ahead, her path and the road intersect again. She figures that, if she hurries, she can catch Shelly on her way past and ask for a lift. Shelly will have aircon and she'll let Esther sit in the front seat and move the vents so she can feel the cold air on her face.

Esther puts on a burst of speed and makes the road in time. Her bag slips from her shoulders as she throws one arm high, her fingers wide as she waves at the van. She takes a couple of steps forward so Shelly won't have to pull off to the side, where the edge of the road falls away sharply to a deep channel clogged with dead branches and spiky grass and rocks. Esther brings her arm down, confident she has been seen, and her bag slides off her back altogether. She kneels down to snatch it up, brushing off the orange dirt. Any second now, Shelly will stop and throw open the passenger door so Esther can climb inside. All Esther can think about is the air conditioning; she doesn't even notice that Shelly is driving away from town.

And Shelly? Shelly is upset after her argument with Esther's mother. She has had several shots of Bundy to steady her hands enough so she can drive. Shelly is examining a spot on her right wrist with a hyper focus bestowed by the rum and the desire to avoid thinking about what she told Constance. She's driving faster than she should on the dirt road. Why had it come up that day? After being kept down for so long? Constance asked for an explanation, but Shelly should have known better. The act of telling it hasn't made it real again, but she's closer to it than she's been in years. Shelly's been meaning to have the doctor look at that spot on her hand for months now. Every time she does the dishes, she looks at it and wonders if it might be getting bigger. She's even told Constance about it, though Constance is not the type to remember, not the kind of friend who will gently nag Shelly about it until she goes to the doctor. Shelly thinks for a terrible moment about her kids, about her grandson. What would they do without her? The steering wheel pulls a little to the left and Shelly does not make enough of a correction. From our position we can see that it's only the length of a schoolbag that's the difference between where Esther is standing – her head still down, still focused on the dirt-covered bag – and where she needs to be to avoid getting hit by the van. A schoolbag's worth of space is the reason Esther is not left behind, hot and covered in dust on a back road in her home town, whole and scowling as Shelly drives past. But there is no space to spare and so there is a thud. The car shudders. Something is sucked under the front left wheel. Shelly hits the brakes, and the van takes its time coming to a stop on the fine silt of the road. She throws open the driver door, expecting to see a wombat or a kangaroo, thinking it an odd time of day for such a collision and worrying about damage to her car. She's worried, too, about the alcohol she's drunk. Knows she shouldn't have been driving with it in her system.

Shelly sees a school dress, a leg bent at the wrong angle. She is struck by the way it resembles the arm of a doll, its plastic elbow bent, fingers extended jauntily.

Esther is dead before Shelly opens her door – the girl's injuries catastrophic but mainly internal. Sometimes a body simply gives out.

Shelly's first complete, coherent thought is that she can smell the rum on her own breath. Looking down the road, first in the direction she came from, and then in the direction she was driving, Shelly observes a moment's silence for a future in which she might turn around to see her friend's girl alive and well. Then she opens the back of the van. Why? Because she doesn't want to leave Esther on the side of the road while she goes to make the call? There, she sees the large sheet of black plastic that was destined for the bottom of her new garden bed. Just a coincidence it's the same kind used by Clint Kennard to wrap his speed. Less a coincidence, maybe, than the lack of options that come with living in a small country town. There is a new shovel, too, to replace the one consumed by rust. It was supposed to save money on food, the vegetable garden, but the new shovel has likely wiped out any profit.

So many things could change what happens next.

If there was no plastic to hide the body, if there was no shovel, Shelly would have driven to the nearest property and called the police and she would have accepted the consequences. But there is the shovel. The tool being there suggests the possibility of the nearest thing there is, now, to an alternative universe where what has happened will not ruin her life and the lives of her children.

Shelly doesn't know in the higher parts of her brain what Peter is up to, doesn't know it in language, but something inside her tells her that the stakes are high. She does not want to talk to police, she does not want them coming to her home. She has seen in other people a kind of joyful submissiveness to the police that comes from being respectable, from wearing a certain kind of clothes. The police would only see her rundown house and her kids – there are so many – and draw their own conclusions.

The girl is heavier than she would have imagined, Shelly discovers as she lifts her into the back of the van and wraps the parcel closed. Shelly is shocked to see herself do this, but is unable to stop. It isn't anger at Constance that makes her do it. But if they hadn't fought that day, if every nerve hadn't been screaming, things would have gone differently.

Shelly doesn't make a sound – the girl is dead, so thoroughly and obviously dead. She can't see the girl's face now and that makes it easier. She knows, now, why the men who raped her all those years ago kept her facedown.

Shelly is surprised to find that the emotion she is experiencing is closer to irritation than anything else. It will come later, the reality of what she has done. For now, she thinks that she must not be late to pick up Caleb. Her grandson hasn't said his first words yet. He won't guess what is inside the plastic wrapping, so she will pick him up first, from her daughter's place – the place she had been driving towards, the reason she hadn't picked up her own children on that hot day – and then she will take the body and she will bury it. She has a place in mind already. She promises herself that, when this is over, she will make that doctor's appointment.

If her daughter Kylie is surprised that her mother doesn't linger – normally Shelly stays for a cup of tea and a chat – she doesn't show it. Kylie is so exhausted, so relieved to have an afternoon to herself that she stretches out on the couch and nods off before her mother has even left the driveway.

Shelly picks Ned Harrison's property for no other reason than she happens to know he is away and it is on her way home. The dirt track that runs along the fence line is accessible through an unlocked gate. It's difficult, manoeuvring the body through the wire fence. It's even more difficult, carrying it.

Shelly wants to go deeper into the field, away from the fence and the dirt track and the water trough. But she can't carry the girl any further. She needs to get home. And she needs, desperately, not to be seen. Through the open doors of the van she hears Caleb crying in his car seat. There is no shade and the baby must be hot, even with the doors open. Shelly lowers Esther to the dirt as gently as she can and starts digging where she stands.

# CONSTANCE

When the detective, Sarah Michaels, called and asked if they could speak in person, Constance steadied herself, aching with the desire to know.

'Who did it?' she asked, as soon as the female detective let her into the kitchen of the small station.

'You didn't bring your husband,' the detective said. It wasn't a question.

Constance said nothing.

'I was hoping to tell you together.' The detective's eyes found Constance's, as if querying whether Constance was ready for what she had to say.

'Whatever it is, I wanted to hear it alone first.'

'Well, Mrs Bianchi, I can tell you that we've had some new evidence come in, and I'm confident we've found who killed your daughter. We have taken that person into custody.'

'So it wasn't Steven?' She whispered the words. Even now, after everything, the thought festered, a rotten tooth.

'No. We've been looking into Peter Thompson. He, Clint Kennard and Roland Mathers have been manufacturing drugs, and I believed it might have something to do with Esther's disappearance.

The forensic team have been working overtime. We took his car, and the family van. As you may know, it's not registered in his name but in his wife's.'

'My god, Shel must be beside herself,' Constance said, the reality of what the detective was saying hitting home. 'So, *Peter* did it?'

'Constance, you may want to sit down.'

'Do you think sitting down is going to make any fucking difference?'

'At this stage, all evidence suggests that Esther was struck by the Thompsons' van. And we're confident that the person driving was Shelly Thompson.'

Constance let out a strangled cry.

'We found Esther's blood in the back of the van. We took elimination DNA from the whole family, from Shelly Thompson and all her children. There were four hairs found on Esther's body. They're in more than one layer of the plastic, so it's not the case that they just happened to be on her clothing, or that they were in the van and transferred to the plastic. They show conclusively that it was Shelly who wrapped the body. We also know, from her daughter's testimony, that she arrived at the showgrounds in the van before 3 pm. We found Esther's DNA in blood on a shovel recovered from the Thompsons' shed. There was also a dent on the front bumper of the van that is consistent with the kind of collision we believe killed your daughter. We understand that it was an accident, you should know that.'

The words 'Esther's DNA', 'blood' and 'shovel' made Constance feel physically sick. 'That explains why I haven't been able to get her on the phone this morning,' she said stupidly.

Later, Constance will hear the interview transcripts read aloud in court. The police took Shelly Thompson to an interview room in Rhodes – the same place they'd questioned Constance's husband – to confront Shelly with what they'd found. Constance will hear exactly how they laid it out for Shelly: her fingerprints matched prints found on the black plastic, strands of Shelly's hair were found on Esther's body, Esther's blood was in Shelly's van. 'I don't know how that happened,' Shelly will say over and over again in the transcript. Not *it* but *that*.

Constance sat at the table in the Durton police station and was struck by the memory of an afternoon at Shelly's just a few weeks before. Constance had stared out into the wide backyard through the windows over the kitchen sink. Esther was running outside with Shelly's kids, huge peaches clenched in their sticky hands. The small windows segmented the wide, browning expanse of lawn into three squares. Kylie had been bathing baby Caleb in Shelly's laundry and walked him out to the kitchen, still wrapped in his towel. She said, 'You fucking take him. He shat in the bath again.' Shelly had brought one corner of the white towel to Caleb's hair to fluff it. The baby's mouth opened like he was smiling, pink and wet, his head thrown back, his chin in folds at his neck. Esther had run inside. She'd found something and she wanted to show Shelly. A ripple of jealousy that Constance had pushed aside easily. A shaft of light through a window.

Constance grappled with the idea that Shelly Thompson had wrapped Esther in plastic and dug a shallow grave and had let Constance cry about it on her shoulder and said nothing. Her hands and feet went cold. She knew that if she saw Shelly in that moment, she would rip her arms from their sockets. She would pull Shelly's eyes out and squish them in her fingers. She would tear Shelly's nostrils apart with her knuckles.

Having a child had been an optimistic act. It said, *I believe things are going to be okay, that I and the people I love will be happy.* On her bad days, Constance will think of the parents who get to watch their children die and envy them. She will fantasise that Esther got cancer, that she got to see her daughter die in her arms.

Constance will never understand how it happened. Will never settle on an account that makes sense. She will grope around for something to hold on to and go spinning off into space. What she knew then, in that moment, was that her daughter would never again noisily suck the juice from a peach or feel the sun on her face. When Constance died, she would leave no child behind to remember her.

Constance Bianchi betrayed or was betrayed by everyone she ever loved. In the vast, swirling galaxy that is the loss of her daughter, this thought will keep returning to her, like a planet in tight orbit, an intense ball of heat in the firmament that will never fail to bring her undone.

As Constance gets older, she'll feel more protected, an astronaut contained and held apart by the gear she wears. That is what it will feel like: like she is breathing regulated air. She'll find she can observe the planetary movements of her life more dispassionately with each year that passes. She will become fascinated by those trashy reality shows where you can watch as pushy mothers move their daughters towards success in dancing competitions or beauty pageants. It will be somehow both repellent and endearing to see these women who make their daughters' bodies their whole world, dressing them as ambassadors for a future that is imminent yet never seems to arrive. *We'll make it to regionals*, they say, *We're going to win*, they say, as they push and push and push.

Constance will watch these shows mainly because she likes to watch the girls, likes to see how they hold their heads and move their bodies. She likes to watch them eat, picking delicately at French fries or gnawing on carrot sticks while their mothers coach them on what they need to do better next time. It will help her to remember the way Esther would eat, like she had all the time in the world. She'll watch the girls because they are vital and moving and alive. In these shows, the worst thing that can happen is that someone forgets the choreography. Sometimes Constance will think about her daughter's shoulder blades and it will feel like she's been punched in the stomach. In those moments, she'll have to focus on the sound of her own breathing. Other people will say she is childless, but she will know she is a mother, still.

To even consider going on, Constance will have to see her inability to stand by Steve as the result of some deficiency of his. Something in him had made it possible to believe him capable of what they'd accused him of, and therefore he shared some of the blame. Steve had never sent her a letter in his life – even Shelly had got one from stupid, rough Peter Thompson. Anger will be easier, for Constance. The anger will be all she has. Just that, and a photo of her cut from a magazine with the caption: *Constance Bianchi, mother of missing girl Esther Bianchi, and what she never saw coming.*

# SARAH

Friday, 7 December 2001

On her last full day in Durton, Sarah drove to Evelyn Thompson's house. She couldn't have said why. It was just the first place she wanted to go when she was sure her time in the town was up.

'Detective Sergeant,' Evelyn said when she opened the door. The house was still a shabby old cottage, but Sarah was suddenly nostalgic for its cracked concrete and New Age tapestry.

The smaller woman brought Sarah through to the lounge room. Ronnie was resting on the lounge, propped up by pillows.

'We're not long back from the hospital,' Evelyn said.

Sarah nodded. 'I came to tell you that I'm leaving tomorrow.' Her tone made it an apology.

'You won't stay for the funeral?' The words had barely left Evelyn's lips before she followed them with, 'I mean, of course not. This is your job.' A pause. 'We're sorry to see you go.'

Sarah didn't buy it for a minute. Evelyn couldn't be sorry to see the back of the police.

'I've come to say goodbye,' Sarah said. 'And I wanted to see how you were doing, Veronica.'

'What happened to the dog that bit me?' the girl asked. 'My mum says she doesn't know.'

Sarah looked at Evelyn before speaking. 'The dog had to be taken away from its owner.' Sarah didn't have the heart to tell her the dog had already been destroyed.

'Where will you go now?' Evelyn asked, clearly keen to change the subject.

'There's another case.' Sarah leaned on the inevitable truth of the sentence like someone walking along a solid crossbeam running under rotting floorboards. There was always another case.

'Of course,' Evelyn said, crossing her arms. Her eyes were dark in the low light of the room.

For a moment, Sarah imagined what would happen if she stayed. She could get to know Evelyn Thompson. Take her out for a beer. Better yet, a bottle of wine at Evelyn's place one night when Veronica was staying with a friend. Sarah wanted to stay, wanted to watch Evelyn's daughter get better. Sarah was always leaving.

'I'd better get on the road,' she said.

This was the nature of the job. Sarah needed to sort herself out before she could start a relationship with someone like Evelyn, or any woman. Maybe it was time to book in with the counsellor they were always crowing about at debriefings.

'Goodbye,' Evelyn said. It sounded like she was addressing an empty room, like Sarah was already gone.

'Goodbye, Veronica,' Sarah said.

Without speaking, Veronica raised her hand and waved. It was oddly jaunty, a wave more suited to the departure lounge at an airport. The enthusiastic wave must have been simple muscle memory, though. Veronica was already looking away when Sarah turned and left.

Sarah stopped by the station to say goodbye to Mack. He'd been right about Peter Thompson's alibi after all and she wanted to thank him, but he wasn't there. When she called him on the phone he seemed distracted – it sounded like he was at a barbecue. Sarah could hear laughter in the background.

Arriving at Constance Bianchi's house, the sun was setting and Sarah saw that someone had taken down the letterbox. Knocking produced no response, although she thought she heard someone moving around inside. She was ashamed at her sense of relief. She would call Constance when she got back to the city. It would have to do.

Sarah and Smithy spent their last evening in the town talking at the round table between their two motel rooms, drinking beers that were colder in the hand than they were to the taste. From where they sat, she could see the post in the ground and the broken chain where the dog had got loose.

'Well, that was unexpected,' said Smithy.

A moment juddered through Sarah's mind: images of her old station, her old job. The brown jumper with the green and yellow on the sleeves.

Sarah knew better than most that people could lie straight to your face with unshakeable conviction. She also knew what happened when the wrong car drove past a girl, or the wrong shortcut presented itself at the wrong time. She knew what the wrong father, wrong brother, wrong uncle could do – she'd seen it more times than she cared to count. She wonders, now, what stopped her from looking at Shelly Thompson earlier. Smithy told her that the woman hadn't batted an eyelid when they took her van for forensic testing in addition to Peter Thompson's Torana on the day he was arrested. *Just procedure*, she imagined him saying, in that breezy way he pulled off so well. Shelly hadn't even baulked when Smithy had asked to take her DNA and the DNA of her children. Sarah had agreed with

Smithy that it was unlikely she'd consent, but thought that even a refusal might be useful information in itself. Who knew why Shelly had submitted to the voluntary testing? It was more than Sarah could have hoped for.

Shelly's eldest daughter Kylie Thompson would later say in court that she hadn't lied on purpose about the time her mother had spent at her house, but she'd believed what her mother told her. She had a new baby, hadn't even known what day of the week it was, she'd been so sleep deprived. Sarah would never be sure just how much Kylie had known.

It was Sarah's conversation with Veronica that had set the whole thing in motion. Her comment about the motel owner's van being like a small room that had set Sarah looking into Shelly's van in the first place. Just that single word, *Van*, underlined in her notebook, had got her thinking about the other Thompson vehicle. She had no way of knowing what Shelly would have done if her husband had been arrested for killing Esther. Perhaps she would have come forward. Sarah was pleased they had figured it out, hadn't left it to chance.

'Do you think she was lying about the rape?' Smithy asked. 'To try and make Steven look bad?'

Sarah sighed. 'I've got no idea.' She felt bone tired at the thought of the court case to come. 'But tell me, what did you say to Steven, that first night in the interview room?' She'd decided she had to know.

'Oh, you know, just the sort of thing you'd say to any garden-variety kiddie fiddler.' Smithy rubbed an eye. 'Feel pretty shit about that now, to be honest.'

Clint, Roland and Peter had been handed to a local team. Sarah had been wrong about the drugs – they'd had nothing to do with Esther's death after all.

'So, it looks like I can get to my sister's on the train by tomorrow afternoon,' Smithy said, finishing his beer and placing the can on the low table between them. 'I've got some leave saved up, and Kinouac is going to let me take it.'

Sarah tried not to feel betrayed. She'd been looking forward to the drive home. She wanted to be around someone else who'd just done what she'd done. She wanted to feel the last eight days lift off her as she talked with someone who knew something about this hot town.

But that wasn't Smithy's problem.

'How will I even up my tan if I have to drive?' she said, holding up her right arm, now darker than her left, and smiling to show there was no ill feeling. Smithy laughed.

He stood to leave. 'I'll be gone before you're up tomorrow,' he said, sticking out a hand. 'Good work, boss.'

She shook it.

'Oh, I almost forgot,' Smithy said. 'I bought this for the Commodore.'

A bright yellow pine tree nestled inside a slim plastic package: *Vanilla Dream Air Freshener*.


Sarah woke the next morning to the sound of the phone ringing.

'I'm sorry to do this to you, Michaels, but we need you,' said the voice at the other end of the line. Sarah didn't believe for a minute that Kinouac was actually sorry. 'I know you're just finishing up there, but the only other person who could work this is already interstate.'

*The banality of resources* Sarah's old training sergeant had called it, drawing on the phrase *the banality of evil*, which she remembered from history class. Eichmann and his just-following-orders. She was exhausted. Her body was only now settling the account of sleep lost to headaches and dreams of Amira, and of dogs that ran in circles, looking for something. In the dreams, Sarah never knew what it was, but she knew it was very important they didn't find it, and she darted between them, putting her hand into their mouths, forcing her fingers down their soft throats. She thought of Amira. If they were still together, Sarah would have made promises. She would have had to call Amira and explain that she couldn't get time off after all.

Sarah was getting in the car when she was struck by a lucid vision. Another phone call from Kinouac. Her heart would sink when he addressed her by her full title. He would say, *I don't give a shit about your choices, Michaels, till they affect me. And now they do. Do you know what I'm talking about?* There would be cockroaches in her stomach as he spoke. She knew better than to expect a warm phalanx of cop protection. There were plenty of people in the force who'd love to see her go down. *An Amira Hassan is alleging that you assaulted her on the evening of the sixteenth of November. I've seen the photos. You're really in the shit with this one, Michaels.* Imagining it, Sarah felt the same strange feeling of unreality as when she'd first seen Esther Bianchi's body. Everything thin and made of cardboard.

She thought of her father and the lace table runner. And that was it, wasn't it? Was she really any better than Shelly Thompson? Luckier, maybe. That was all. The strangest part was the sense of relief that suffused her body as she got in the car and started the engine. What if she weren't allowed to take on any more cases, at least for a while? What if the worst thing happened and it wasn't so bad? Maybe she could stop chasing after lost girls and start looking at the women in front of her. Maybe she could take a good, hard look at herself. The road back to Sydney stretched in front of her and her hands rested lightly on the wheel. Nothing but silence and the stink of the vanilla air freshener.

# RONNIE

Wednesday, 12 December 2001

The morning of Esther's funeral, Mum kept fussing over my bandage. She sat behind me on my bed, trying not to hurt me as she tugged at it. They'd shaved part of my head and she pulled down on the part of the bandage that ran under my ear, covering as much of my scalp as possible. My head and jaw ached all the time. It felt like there wasn't enough skin, like my skull had got bigger: everything was red and swollen and sore. Flea had poured his body along the length of my lap as soon as I sat down on the bed. He purred. I imagined a tiny factory inside him, a hub of industry and production, peopled by men in tiny hard hats.

Flea thrummed in my lap and Mum kept making small adjustments to the bandage, like if she could just get it into the right position it would be as if it wasn't there at all. The feeling bubbled up of her pulling my hair tight that first Saturday after Esther went missing, like no time had passed between then and now.

'Don't touch it Mum, it hurts,' I said.

'Sorry.' Mum stood, dropping her hands by her sides.

She was wearing a black dress. Her bare legs looked thin and weirdly long. She never wore dresses, and it made me feel uncomfortable, like she was a different person altogether. My own black dress was too tight. It pinched under the arms. I assumed we'd got it in one of the bags of clothes my aunt Shelly had given Mum that year – full of faded pairs of pants, jumpers with stretched collars, shirts that seemed fine until you put them on and saw they sat funny. The room was crowded with things: my old bedcover, the books spilling out of my collapsing bookshelf, the chair with a rip in its seat fabric tucked under my desk. All these things that seemed much more vulnerable to change, to being thrown away or lost. How could they be here when things that were more precious and valued were gone?

Mum said I should make a card for Esther, for the funeral, and left me alone in my room. I found a piece of coloured A4 paper and folded it over. My head hurt. Someone had picked up my backpack after I'd been attacked by the dog and given it to Mum. It sat on my desk. The Peru poster poked out accusingly. Shame washed over me to think how I'd finished it even though my best friend was missing. I took it out of the bag and peeled off the llama drawing. The paper was crinkly from the dried glue and one of the llama's feet tore. The whole thing didn't look quite right when glued to the front of the card, but I wrote the word *Esther* in bubble letters above the llama's head and put a smiley face sticker over the missing foot.

*I love you Esther, and I will always miss you.* There was nothing else to write, so I signed my name, drawing a love heart over the 'i' in Ronnie, but Esther had thought that was silly, so I rubbed it out, pressing a black dot into the paper with my pencil instead.


The funeral was at the same church where Esther and I had split up to walk home the last time I'd seen her alive. Mum parked our car out the front. Cat hair clung to my black dress, and I brushed it off. The sky was an unbounded blue that gave no sense of how big it was, and cars crowded the street. Kids chased each other across the lawn before being hissed at to *come here*. In the heat, flowering shrubs near the front doors of the church gave off a heady scent. It made me think of the inside of the small wooden chest that had belonged to Mum's mother and would one day belong to me, and that made me think of the ice-cream container in the stump, with its Pokémon cards and necklace pendants. I squashed the thought down: more things that had outlived Esther. Mum held my hand as we walked into the church.

Towards the end of the ceremony, I saw Lewis, but he didn't see me. He was sitting with his mother, facing forward. Campbell was there too, further down the same row, and I caught the two boys looking at each other more than once. I closed my eyes through some of the service – I couldn't cry, not even from my good eye. It didn't feel like the right place to be sad for Esther because Esther wasn't there. I saw the white coffin and the picture of her they'd printed big and put on a stand next to it, but neither of those things were my friend.

Esther's parents arrived at the cemetery at the same time, in different cars. I didn't recognise the older woman who trailed behind Constance. She hung back as Constance and Steven walked to the hole, not touching, not looking at each other, two metres of dusty cemetery ground between them at all times. Something happened inside me when I saw that they put the box in the ground. I wanted to yell, *Stop*. Everyone seemed to lean in at once – like they wanted one last look at the box before it was swallowed up by the earth. Mum nudged me forward and I dropped the card into the hole when she said I should. I let it fall from my hand and the llama landed facedown and it made me upset. I wanted to jump down into the hole and turn the card over. I couldn't stand that I had traced it. People who traced things were not pure and good. It was less than she deserved. I was sure that Esther had never traced anything in her life.

I was pulled gently to the side. A line of people that had formed behind me began to throw dirt on the box. Mum asked if I wanted to throw a handful of dirt in and I said no.

From the cemetery, everyone went to the scout hall. The floorboards threw up dust as people walked across them. There were wooden plaques on the wall, some full of names, some with empty bronze plates waiting to be engraved. People kept trying and failing not to look at my bandage. A plate of Mint Slices sat on one of the folding tables where they'd laid out the food. Next to it was the same tired hot-water urn they used at parent–teacher nights. I slipped one of the biscuits from under the net covering, but it hurt to eat. I put the half-eaten biscuit back on the tablecloth. Quietly, her legs like two white flashes below the hem of her black dress, Mum came and steered me towards the car.

# LEWIS

Wednesday, 12 December 2001

On the day of Estie's funeral, Lewis entered the church with his mother. He recognised the man who stood at the front from long-ago Scripture classes, when he and Estie and Ronnie were in kindergarten. The man looked impossibly old. Mrs Cafree was looking after Simon so Lewis and his mum could come to the funeral.

Lewis had worried he would see Clint at the funeral, that he'd just show up like he had at the police station that day. Lewis's mum said it wasn't possible, that Clint was still *on remand* for what had happened, which meant he was still locked up. Police had spent half a day in his father's shed, carrying out things his mother wouldn't let him see.

The two of them were among the last people to arrive. They hurried along the right wall to two empty seats on the end of the row, picked up the pieces of paper on the pew and sat down. Lewis realised with a jolt that Campbell Rutherford was there in the same row, with his mother and father. Campbell's dad nodded at Lewis's mother.

An old woman began playing the organ. The first song was called 'His Eye is on the Sparrow'. The title of the hymn was in bold black at the top of the photocopied piece of paper. The words had a white haze over them. No-one seemed to know how the lyrics were meant to fit in with the music. Estie had always hated Scripture.

Estie's mother got up to say something. She stared at the people in the pews without speaking for a full minute. The priest took her elbow, spoke in her ear. She shook her head, looked away, returned to her seat. Estie's father didn't look at her, didn't comfort her. He stood and thanked everyone for coming. Then his whole face scrunched up, his throat clamped around his words and he rocked backwards and forwards a couple of times. He left the lectern before the priest had a chance to take him by the arm.

The priest spoke again. There was the same singsong quality in his voice he'd had when he read from the Bible in class. The way he said *Jesus* always made it sound like he was saying *gee whiz*, something so good and full of happiness he couldn't contain himself.

The week before, Lewis's mum had asked him to come and sit with her on her bed so she could tell him something.

At first, they were both silent.

Then his mum had said, 'Lewis, darling. They've found Esther Bianchi.'

She'd held his hand and they lay back on the bed and looked at the ceiling. The fan circled slowly above them. Always moving, never getting anywhere.

'I love you, Lewis,' his mum had said.

Lewis could hear Simon moaning gently in the other room.

He folded himself to rest his head on her stomach. She'd stroked his hair like she'd done when he was a little kid, and he heard the gurgling activity of her belly still working away at breakfast.

And then she'd told him what had happened. She wanted him to hear it from her. She said it was a terrible, terrible accident. Ronnie's aunty had hit Estie with her car, had killed her and then moved her body, and lied about it. People in the town had seen Shelly Thompson led away in handcuffs. She was going to be in trouble even though it was an accident because she'd lied about what she'd done and tried to hide Estie's body. She'd buried his friend in the dirt. He felt an odd sensation of pressure, the way you can feel the dentist is doing something in your mouth but there's no actual pain.

Ronnie's voice had still sounded funny on the phone when he called her, afterwards. She said her mum had told her about Esther as well.

'Where is she?' he asked. His own mother was sure to be lurking somewhere in the house, listening.

'She's started smoking again,' said Ronnie, a frown in her voice.

'Are you okay?' Lewis asked.

'Have you seen Campbell?' Ronnie asked in reply.

'No. We haven't gone anywhere since Clint got arrested.' Satisfying, to say his father's name out loud, like the name of a stranger. Lewis couldn't say Campbell's name in case his mum heard.

Luckily, Ronnie let it drop.

'What is your mum going to do now?' she asked.

'I don't know.'

Ronnie sighed. 'I miss Esther.'

'Me too.' He thought of Estie touching the goldfish with her bare hand.

He supposed he and Ronnie were friends again now. Or friends for the first time, maybe.


Two pedestal fans stood on the raised platform either side of the priest, aimed at the people in the pews. They were out of sync as they moved from side to side; one had a longer arc than the other. It struck

Lewis that one day he would be a man and Estie would never be a woman. He could feel his own bones betraying her. Sitting there, on a hardwood pew in the stifling heat, his treacherous toes spreading towards the outer limits of his shoes, his hair tickling the edges of his ears in a way it hadn't on the day Estie went missing.

Lewis doesn't know it yet, but one day he'll get married to a man. A kind man. A man who never raises his voice. They will marry in an old chapel. Lewis will question why they want to do it at all. His parents had been married. What good had that done? And it will be hard to find a chapel where they can marry, even after it becomes legal. How can Lewis forget that? How can it ever be something good and whole? But on the day when Lewis kisses the man who has been pronounced his husband, he won't think about any of that. It will feel pure and shining. A joy one feels on maybe a handful of occasions in a lifetime. A joy that takes you outside of it even as you are deep, deep within it.

Lewis will look into the crowd as he says his vows and see Simon in a sharp suit their mother must've bought him. We rely on little cues to inform the way we treat people. All it takes is pants that are pulled a little high, a polar fleece jumper worn on a warm day, and people will use loud, cheery voices or turn away altogether. With those markers taken away, Lewis's brother will look like a thoughtful businessman, staring off into space. He will have come to Lewis's wedding with their mother and a support worker. It will be strange, when Lewis moves out of home, not to have a lock on the inside of the door. Lewis will realise he's been angry at his brother his whole life: Simon, who least deserved Lewis's anger. Lewis had thought of him as immune from Clint, who wouldn't look at him, wouldn't even say his name if he could help it. Lewis has been angry because it felt like their lives revolved around Simon. When he'd looked at Simon, Lewis had only ever seen the older brother he missed out on. The brother who would've raced him on their bikes, pushing Lewis harder and faster – a brother to stand up to Clint. The truth was Simon is the only brother Lewis ever had or would have. Lewis will want to stop the ceremony, turn to the man he loves and say in front of everyone, *This is my brother Simon.*

Even though Lewis's wedding day will be happy, churches will always make him think of Esther's funeral, the dust illuminated in the air, the off-key singing. Lewis won't be able to see happiness without seeing its opposite. He'll still watch people, frantic that he'll do or say something that will set them off. When the person making his coffee seems pissed off, it will send Lewis into a spin that colours his whole day. But he'll be determined to experience the happiness of life because he'll know that sadness is inevitable. Lewis will see his brother more. Not to make himself a better person or because his brother needs him there but because Simon and he know each other in a way they'll never know someone else.

Lewis will wish he could say that their lives got better straightaway when his mother left Clint. That there was a specific day when she was able to laugh again, let go, forget herself, wear sunglasses. But those years will be blurry, like a dimly remembered video game he played once, a long time ago. Funny, because he will still remember the green pencil tin with the goldfish inside, the feel of Campbell Rutherford's lips on his.

The priest finished his reading, and the organ started up again. There was a sound like a flock of birds taking to the air as the whole congregation simultaneously turned over their piece of paper, moving hot air around the room.

Campbell turned to look at Lewis. Lewis looked steadily back at him. People kept sneaking looks at Ronnie, who was sitting in a row towards the back with her mother. This would be the last time so many people thought about Estie at once. None of it felt big enough. Lewis imagined leaving the town one day, living somewhere else. He would remember those moments in the shade of the creek, the chicken shed, the sound of Estie's laughter, a handball game.

Lewis will wish he could say he was better for all of it, but he will have learned how easily things fall apart and are broken and can never be put back together. Sometimes, no matter how much life he lives, it will feel like he is always that eleven-year-old boy, sitting and watching as they carried Estie's body out of the church.

Estie's father was the tallest man among those carrying the coffin, so the whole thing was on an angle, and the funeral director kept telling the other men to hold it higher and none of it was anything you'd want to hold on to, but Lewis will remember it anyway, and he'll remember the back of Estie's head and Campbell Rutherford's face in profile. They will both be part of a recurring dream in which Lewis is running, white railway-crossing poles clattering to the ground around him as he tries to look them both, Campbell and Estie, in the face. But whichever way Lewis runs they both turn away from him. The most he'll be able to see will be the shaved edges of Campbell's hairline and the faint blue vein near his right ear, the dark slick of Estie's ponytail. His mouth will fill with creek water and dust and he will wake, sweating, in the arms of the man he loves.

# RONNIE

Now

Mum and I left town before school started again.

When we moved to Melbourne, I promised myself I would never ask Mum again who my father was. She'd been through enough. We both had.

I felt bad about leaving Lewis, but there was nothing to do once Mum made up her mind. Later, I heard he didn't go back to our school either; he and his mum and brother went north. If we'd stayed, I suppose I would've had to sit with the Addison twins, or whoever would have me. Mum just wanted to get me away from where it all happened. It's funny, when you think about what didn't keep her away. Still, at least in town everyone knew what had happened to my face, they didn't ask, *Were you born like that?* They didn't need to wonder or whisper to each other. We went to stay with Aunty Kath, in Melbourne, and everyone who saw me for the first time did a double take, until the scar healed. Which was harder, in a way.

The day we left town, all of our stuff packed in a truck, Flea was nowhere to be seen. After the truck left, Mum said we couldn't wait any longer. 'I'll ask Sophie to come and look,' she said. I stared at her. As we drove away, I cried. Much more than I had at Esther's

343

funeral. Mum had bought all my favourite car snacks, but I couldn't eat them.

Mum never spoke about or to Uncle Peter and Aunt Shelly after what happened. It was like they'd been wiped off the face of the earth. My cousins moved to Armidale to live with Aunt Shelly's older brother until Uncle Peter was released. We saw them a few times in the year after Shelly was arrested, with my aunts, but that was it. So I lost my uncle, too. I miss his droopy smile, his hairy knuckles. I know it was because Mum found out he'd got mixed up in selling drugs.

Mum gave me several boxes of photographs when I went to visit her last. There was the thrill of recognition when I could see the parts of who I was now in my baby pictures, the parts of my mum in me, the parts I had always imagined must come from my father. There was a handful of photos of Mum as a kid, though none of them are of her by herself. There she is, standing next to one of her red-haired brothers who's holding a fish up to the camera, his mouth open in a way that makes him look drunk and unruly. Mum is lean with long legs, a sunburned nose and a seventies haircut.

That same visit, she told me, finally, who my father is – or was. Clint Kennard had died by then. And Mum felt like she could finally tell me. 'It wasn't love, Bup,' she said.

'Was it consensual, at least?' I asked.

'Is it rape if you're too out of it to say no?'

'Yeah, Mum. It is.'

She told me that she'd been doing drugs back then. My mum, who I'd never even seen take a Panadol, telling me she'd been a heroin user.

'Did Clint know?' I asked.

'No,' she said. 'I lied, when I came back. I said you were younger than you were.'

'Did Aunty Kath know?'

*Clint Kennard was my father.*

'She was the only other person who did.'

'Wait, is this why my birth certificate is wrong?'

When I'd applied for my learner driver's licence when I was sixteen, I'd discovered that my birth certificate said I was two months older than I was. Mum said it was an administrative error. *Let's just do your birthday early from this year, hey? Easier than worrying about all that bureaucracy.*

She'd been lying the whole time.

'I had to make you younger, Bup. So he wouldn't guess you were his.'

So, Mum was right. My father was no-one. Less than no-one.

'He was a part of you. I didn't ever want you to have to deal with that information, but anything that is a part of you has to be a part of me. Do you understand? None of this is your fault.'

So many things made sense.

Lewis was my half-brother. Which explained the connection I'd always felt. And Lewis had cared about me, in his own way. He'd come to see me in the hospital. And Simon was my brother, too. I've thought about tracking them down, about telling them. I still could. There's still time.

I'm not sure why Mum brought me back to that town as a baby. Maybe she just couldn't conceive of a childhood somewhere else. And I did have a good childhood, before what happened to Esther. I know that.

The photos in the box are organised into stacks not by date, but by activity. Here I am at a swimming carnival; here's one of me at the cross-country, looking away from the camera angrily. There are photos

345

of me in hospital, although in most of them I'm asleep, or leaning into a smiling nurse so you can't see the bandage. The stack of me and Esther is the fattest one. Here we are having a water balloon fight; here's one of us singing into hairbrushes in my bedroom, eyes closed, going for it.

I have a son now. He's two years old. His dad isn't around, so it's just us. I'll tell him who his father is, though. Let him find his dad if he wants. He wasn't a bad guy. I told Mum it was a one-night stand, and it was, but I also think I knew what I was doing. Mum wishes I'd do something with my degree, that I'd go further than her. But I love the smell of my son, love the way he clings to me greedily. It's enough for me. I would like to give him a sister. A little girl. Sometimes I think I'd call her Esther, but I don't know. Esther was the first person who made me feel brave, who made me feel like I could be more than I was. I hope my son finds a friend like her. I hope he becomes a friend like her.

Before Mum and I left town, I went back to the stump to find the ice-cream container still there, covered in leaves. Some kind of insect had ravaged the Tiny Teddies packet. The image on the plastic packaging had come off in places, so it showed white. When I held the bag in my hand, I could tell it was mostly crumbs. I took one half of the *Befri Stends* necklace. I returned the other half to the container and placed it back inside the stump.

We never found Flea, and sometimes I indulge the fantasy he's still there, roaming the town, bottlebrush tail in the air, purring.

Just the other day, on my son's birthday, I found myself thinking of Esther's last birthday party before she died. The party was held at the swimming pool. There were pirate-themed plates from Spotlight and balloons tied to the picnic table – not the kind with helium, but the kind that hung limply down. My little boy loves pirates now, too.

All the children from our class had been invited despite the fact that Esther didn't like some of them, because adults thought we didn't know what we liked, what was good for us. Esther spent most of the party with me in the water. We'd learned about water together, how it behaved, had learned to swim in that very same pool. Our slippery bodies sailing through the water, the smell of chlorine in our hair for hours afterwards. We'd figured out that we could hold our eyes open underwater and mime elaborate messages to each other. Then we'd emerge and try to guess what the other person had said, our eyes stinging while a perfect light played on the surface and we were young and whole and together. I remember thinking she'd picked me. I was her friend. I kicked my feet under the water in pleasure, the water that held us up and gave us something to push back against.

# WE

After

We are the children of a town that has been dying since before we can remember. We wouldn't want you to think that defines us. There will always be children here; there has to be.

We have told you who did what, and why. Now we want to know if you'll tell us where we should put Esther. Should we put her with all the other girls of that town? Should we put her with all the parts of us that are over and gone and far behind us? What do we owe the girl who isn't there?

When we were older, we would tell people about the detectives, about their visits to our school. We would tell them about Esther, her disappearance, in hushed voices in the doorways of loud, elaborate house parties. We would tell them in hotel hot tubs. Or over coffee on the third date – the third date being the time to add a little mystery to ourselves, the perfect time to paint ourselves as the true victims of some now-distant tragedy. We were not in a load-bearing position, it was true, but the people we told need only know that we were *there*, that it *happened* to us.

'Childhood was never the same after that,' we would say, in voices that hinted at our forbearance in the face of quiet devastation. 'We were really close. I never quite got over it.'

We hadn't been close to Esther. We have gripped our memories too tightly, proof of her lasting impact, so that our fist covers what they look like.

Some of us only saw the shadow that Esther's disappearance cast on our own childhoods, like an enormous tree grown overnight on the outskirts of town, its shadowy branches blocking the sun that was rightly ours.

It's true that Esther's life affected the landscape of our own, but some of us wouldn't change any of it. Some of us know it is enough to have lived. That pain and love are not a zero-sum game. Esther made us who we are. She and Lewis Kennard and Ronnie Thompson. We are all who we are because of each other.

Sometimes, even in prison, Shelly Thompson tells herself that she had simply happened across a dead animal that afternoon. To save someone else the job, because she was that kind of woman, the kind who worked hard, who helped other people, she had taken the animal in the back of her van and buried it somewhere out of the way.

And a lifetime of honesty was the perfect cover. She *could* drop a plastic-wrapped package into a hole and move on. Return to her house and her children and never talk about it, not ever, not to anyone, not even to herself. Visit her friend and park her van with the dent from hitting Esther pushed into the bushes. Wait until late at night and shove Esther's backpack deep into someone else's outside rubbish bin. She would grieve for Esther like a friend of the girl's mother. The act of forgetting had begun even before the hole was fully covered over. We can tell you that Shelly would never have told anyone, if things had been different. Shelly is no worse than any of us. We know that: none of us can escape who we are when others aren't looking; we can't guess what we're capable of until it's too late.

Constance Bianchi left town after her daughter's funeral. She didn't go to Melbourne or Sydney. She ended up in Cairns, working at a tourism centre. We see her, in her teal polo shirt, with a fixed smile. No-one there knows about her life before. They assume she is childless. Steven Bianchi remarries. Has another child. Tries to forget.

Steven was there that evening at Toni Bianchi's. He was in the ute when they pulled over with Shelly at Dirt Creek. But he didn't leave the cab. He sat in the front passenger seat, hands clasped over his ears, trying not to hear Shelly's cries in the night. He had known before he got in the car that there was something in the air, something he didn't have the courage to put into words. That is who Steven is when no-one is looking.

It got out, what had happened to Shelly at Dirt Creek. Presumably it was offered in her defence in the court, or perhaps it's simply that people who had heard whispers about it back in the day remembered them. The men knew who they were, of course. But it was uncertain who had been involved, which was worse in a way: a whole generation of the town's men – its fathers, its uncles – were suspect. People moved away (Why? Had they been involved? Moving almost seemed to confirm it), sold up for even less than you'd think and got the hell out of Durton. Dirt town. Dirt and hurt – that's what others would remember about our town. But we remember our friends, our families: the ones who loved us when no-one was looking. We remember standing in assembly, shoulder to shoulder, singing the school song. All the children, singing. It's where we lived, it was our only place. Esther will always be a Dirt Town child, as we are its children, still.

The truth is that being afraid of pain makes it something else, something larger, something worse. You can fill yourself up on fear, like the galahs that congregate around wheat silos, stuffing themselves on spilled grain until they can no longer fly. We forgive ourselves for however we felt, for whatever we did. We forgive the ones who hurt us and the ones we hurt. We accept the pain, we welcome it, we run towards it – school hats flapping in the wind created by our own movement – because we know it means we are alive. We love her, we love her, we love her. We sing her into memory and every Dirt Town child knows her name.

# ACKNOWLEDGEMENTS

I wrote this book on the unceded lands of the Wodi Wodi people, of the Dharawal nation. I pay my respects to elders past and present and thank them for their ongoing custodianship of and care for the country I live and write on.

Special thanks go to the police officer who spoke to me off the record about her experiences. Our time together went on to inform this book in countless ways. I won't name you here, but I so appreciated you speaking with me. Any and all errors are mine alone.

To Dr Shady Cosgrove and all my former colleagues at the University of Wollongong's creative writing programme, thank you for showing me the way. To dear Linda Godfrey (my neighbour, fellow festival runner, and all-round good-time gal) and beloved Jemma Payne (who can always see what I'm trying to say before I can), thank you for being my first readers – I simply wouldn't have a book without you. Helena Fox, for vulnerability-as-strength and for our long conversations. Here's to being alongside each other in our little boats. Julie Keys, for being a kindred spirit, for the jagged and not the smooth. Donna Waters, for being truly kind and for wanting to come away and write with me. To Jackie Bailey for being so wise and for your advice about Detective Sergeant Michaels (even if I was slow on the uptake!). A special mention to Emma Darragh for coming to my rescue when I needed it.

To Jane Finigan, my agent in the UK – I'm so glad I got my woman in the end! And to Alex Saunders at Pan Mac, thank you for your eye for plot and nodding politely while I talked wild-eyed about roller-coasters. With thanks to Grace Heifetz for making it all possible. To everyone who has worked on this book in every capacity. I am blown away by your professionalism and enthusiasm, and I thank you on *Dirt Town*'s behalf.

As I worked on structural edits for this book, my mother was diagnosed with ovarian cancer. I'm so grateful for everyone who helped my mum in what was an unmoored and terrifying time. Systems of caring have never been more important. The people we rely on should not have to be 'heroes'. May we fund them, protect them, help them do their jobs. (For the record, I consider art to be a system of caring, too – it helps us put ourselves back together.) To all my family, but particularly my mum, Danina Scrivenor. Thank you for your sacrifices and for giving me a great start in life. Everything I am and everything I have can be traced back to your unstinting love. I love you, I love you, I love you. To my brother, Chris – here it is! The book I wrote. To my father, Murray, and to Alison, and my sisters, Claire and Lauren: I hope you enjoy it!

Thank you to Dani, for loving me exactly as I am and quietly depositing smoothies on my desk. Like Wile E. Coyote, I'm all the way out here, held up by your belief in me.

# BOOK CLUB QUESTIONS

*These questions contain spoilers.*

1. What do you think about the 'We' chapters that feature throughout the novel? Do you like them? How do they colour and inform the story? What is the overall effect of this omniscient collective voice?

2. The novel begins with the discovery of Esther Bianchi's body, as witnessed by the chorus of the town's children. Why do you think the author chose to open the book with this scene? What is the impact of this?

3. How does the novel's setting influence both the nature of Esther's death and its investigation? How does the hot Australian summer play a role?

4. What are some of the references to the Australian landscape and animal life in the book? How do they colour your perception of Durton and its inhabitants? Do you agree with the author that small towns or communities can be like living, breathing entities?

5. Hayley Scrivenor has chosen to tell this story in several distinct styles, through a mix of points of view. For example, Ronnie's

voice is in the first person while Lewis, Sarah and Constance are in the third person. What is the effect of this? How do the different styles and voices shape the reader's understanding of the different characters, and the crime that has occurred?

6. Violence, both domestic and otherwise, can be found through this book. Were there scenes you found hard to read, or that you felt should have been left out?

7. What is the point Sarah's father is trying to make in his conversation with her on pages 305–6? What are some examples from the story in which characters make misleading or incorrect assumptions about other people and their choices?

8. There are many examples and stories in the book about childhood and the experience of growing up in different circumstances. How can a child's situation, their parents, the parenting styles used to raise them and the experiences – including traumas – of their childhood have long-lasting impacts on their lives? Discuss.

9. At the end of the novel, Sarah realises she is luckier than Shelly, but no better. While she and Shelly are very different people, both have always tried to help others in their own way. However, both women caused harm to another when they did not intend to, although the consequences in their respective situations are vastly different. What do you make of the consequences for each of the various characters in the book? Do these consequences accord with the seriousness of their actions?

10. Why do you think Shelly succumbed so meekly to her fate: allowing her car to be taken for testing and her DNA checked, for example, which led directly to her being arrested? Why do

you think she later allows herself to imagine the accident happened to an animal, rather than to Esther: that she was, in fact, doing the right thing by burying the body and 'getting it out of the way'?

11. The end of the novel jumps ahead in time for many characters. What did this do for your understanding of the novel?

12. Was there a character's perspective that you would have liked to hear more of? What unanswered questions do you have after reading?